Also by Lew Decker

FINGERPRINTS…A Coffeehouse Reader

A memoir

Available from Amazon.com and other retailers.

From the October 2010 issue of *Latitudes & Attitudes* magazine:

"Much more than just a retelling of the author's extensive cruising adventures, this is a reflection on the intricacies of life; choices, decisions, mistakes made for better or worse. The writing is so beautifully descriptive it transports you straight into the moment with Technicolor and four part harmony. It's a great escape book for a rainy day at anchor…"

ALLIGATOR FOOD

THREE
FINGERED
PRESS
SAN DIEGO, CA

ALLIGATOR FOOD

A NOVEL

LEW DECKER

This is a work of fiction. Names, characters, and incidents are the product of the author's imagination. Any resemblance to events or actual people, living or dead, is unintended and purely coincidental.

Published by Three Fingered Press
P. O. Box 503752
San Diego, CA
92150-3752
www.threefingeredpress.com

LIBRARY OF CONGRESS CATALOGING-IN-PUBLICATION DATA
Decker, Lew
Alligator Food /a novel/ Lew Decker
p. cm.

2010940695

ISBN 978-0-9840971-1-1

Printed in the United States of America on recycled paper

2 4 6 8 9 7 5 3 1

FIRST EDITION

Book design by Casey Clemens Decker
Cover photograph by Bruce Koschnik
Back cover based on a photograph by Reesha Gruender
Text set in Palatino Linotype

AUTHOR'S NOTE

When I was still editing the manuscript for this book, I sat in a Starbucks café one afternoon with a coffee, a lead pencil, and a whole bunch of misgivings. I held the stack of pages in front of me and tried to read, but my eyes kept wandering off toward my hands. It isn't often I notice the aging process like that. My hands are lined and wrinkled and laced with the Amazon River drainage of purple veins. Against the stark white of the paper, they looked much older than my sixty-six years. It wouldn't have mattered to me except this book has taken about seven years to complete. My hands didn't look this bad when I started.

A long time ago an old pirate friend offered me some advice. "Son," he said. "Stay between twenty and twenty and avoid them round-eyed women." I didn't follow his advice on either count. Like most people my age, though, I focus on things I can do, not on things I can't. Guys like me can never go back and recapture the years of plundering and pillaging while sailing around the mid-seventies Caribbean. Writing a book can make it all seem real again.

ALLIGATOR FOOD began life as a non-fiction account of the Caribbean lifestyle of some thirty-five years ago. During the writing process, I kept thinking about my pirate buddy and about some of the people I knew. I kept asking myself, "What if?" In the middle of the book I fell in love with a beautiful girl who was a minor character in the story, and this novel was born.

I'd like to thank those people I knew from my Caribbean years who inadvertently lent themselves to the writing process. Though all of the characters and events in this book are fictitious, some of the people down there might recognize that any part of this story could have been true. If they did, I'd take that as a supreme compliment.

Were it not for my wife Kathleen, my son Casey, and my daughter Marielle, I could still be down there hanging around between twenty and twenty with the drunks, transients, and misfits that often frequent the tropics. Because of the love of my family, there has been a lot more direction to my life. Because of them, I can still view the world through a younger man's eyes, no matter what my hands look like.

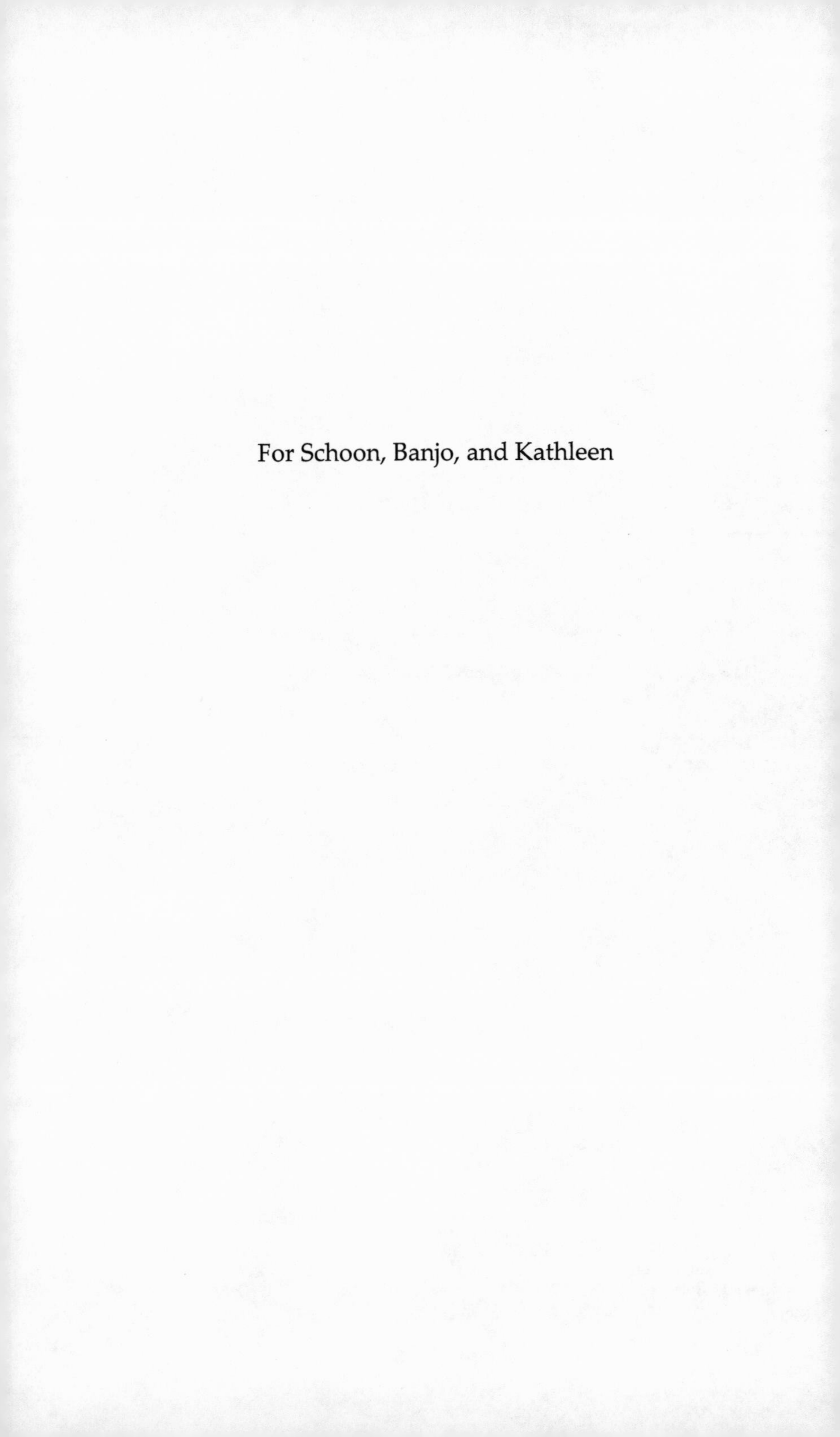

For Schoon, Banjo, and Kathleen

ALLIGATOR FOOD

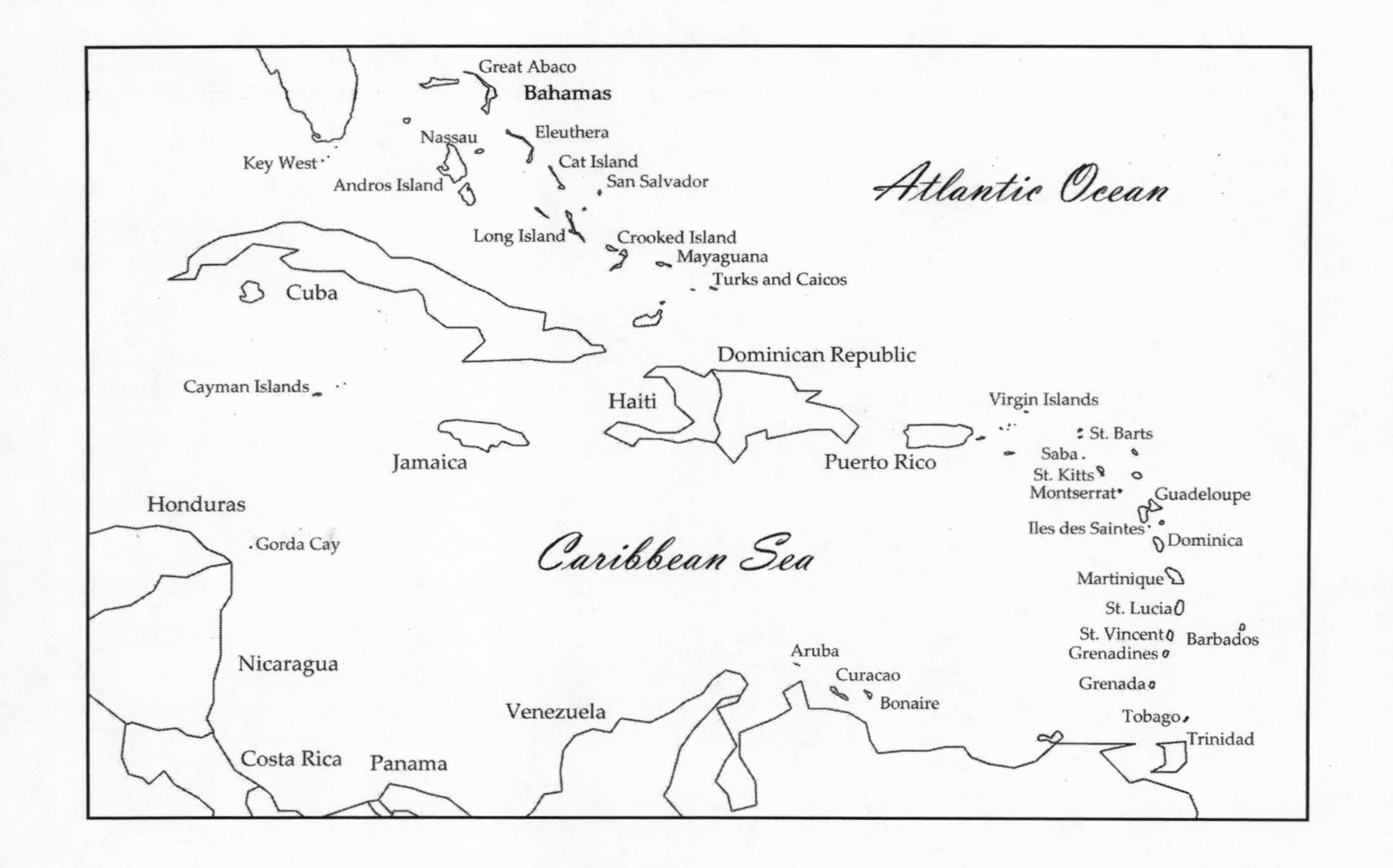
Great Abaco
Bahamas
Nassau
Eleuthera
Key West
Cat Island
Andros Island
San Salvador
Atlantic Ocean
Long Island
Crooked Island
Mayaguana
Turks and Caicos
Cuba
Dominican Republic
Cayman Islands
Haiti
Virgin Islands
St. Barts
Saba
Jamaica
Puerto Rico
St. Kitts
Montserrat
Guadeloupe
Honduras
Iles des Saintes
Dominica
Gorda Cay
Caribbean Sea
Martinique
St. Lucia
St. Vincent
Barbados
Grenadines
Aruba
Nicaragua
Curacao
Grenada
Bonaire
Venezuela
Tobago
Trinidad
Costa Rica
Panama

I waited near the dunes and listened to the sound of the wind.

There were whispers of sunshine and dreams,

and days of heat and shadow,

long past,

and whispers of faraway places,

faraway seas.

There were lonely cries, as well,

of seabirds sweeping through

and the muffled cannons of a booming surf,

marking years too many.

I turned away and walked once more,

down where the sea whispers like the wind,

down where the heart rushes in,

and I knelt in the sand and ached for those dreams again.

- Dana
1979

ONE

Just after dawn a dying front wandered through Key West and left behind a patchwork of puddles that meandered all the way down Angela Street. When the low sun emerged from the clouds, it cast in silver the chain of puddles and the last of the raindrops beading in the thick grass of the cemetery. Nathan Addison stepped off the bus and glanced at the puddles and then at the tombstones streaked from the rain across the way. He yawned out of nervousness and made his way down Angela to the end of the block where the Legal Aid building sagged over the intersection; an aging *Phantom* mask, shiny from the rain and steaming in the rising sun. He ducked through a narrow side entrance and climbed two flights of wooden stairs where he found Frederic standing near an open door at the top of the landing.

"Hi Nate. I'm glad you could make it," he said. "I'm sorry about this."

Frederic stretched himself in the doorway and took a huge breath to try to fill the extra-large shirt he wore. Nate forced a smile and then shook Frederic's outstretched hand. Fred turned and strutted over to a Navy surplus office desk cluttered with papers.

"I really am sorry about this," he said again, "but I think it's a good idea that you clear things up before you leave. Where's Sarah?"

"I didn't want her to be any part of this," Nate said. "I don't want any part of it, either. What have you got?"

"Just some tag ends to complete the proceedings. I think this will wrap it up. We'll have to wait to hear from the court but you can head south to the Caribbean. There won't be anything else, at least not for quite a while."

"I suppose you're right. It makes me feel like a failure, even after all this time."

"I know what you mean. Sign where I've highlighted in yellow. There are four sheets in all. Do you want me to go over the bogus charges?"

"No. Isn't it just mental cruelty or some such nonsense?"

"Basically, but you know how the legal system works. There has to be fault somewhere, and you're it."

"I didn't do anything wrong, Fred."

"Believe me, I know, but if there is no fault, there is no divorce. It doesn't matter that the law defies logic."

Nate took the papers and scrawled a rough signature in each of the yellow slashes. There was an air of finality to it and he felt sick to his stomach. When he finished, Nate stood and looked at Frederic who stared through the windows before turning to face him again.

"You're still hanging around the Green Parrot," Frederic said.

"I should have rented a room up the street and saved the commute time."

"You can kill yourself drinking like that, you know?"

"I know. I feel like shit when I'm sober."

"You look like shit when you're hung over."

"You aren't much help."

"Don't lose sleep over these papers, Nate. It's best for both of you to shut the book. God, I wish I were going with you."

"You can drop everything and go. You've gone with me before."

"Not this time. Gracie would flog me within an inch of my life if I ever came back."

"Well, thanks for the legwork, Fred. I know you're right about the papers. It's hard just the same. I'll look you up when I get back, maybe in June. You're a good friend. Take care of yourself."

They shook hands again but there was nothing more to say. Nate left the tiny office and took the stairs two at a time just to get away. He glanced up from the sidewalk to the second floor window where Frederic stood looking beyond the roof-tops toward the clouds drifting out to sea over the Gulf Stream.

The Green Parrot Bar and Sub Shop didn't open until noon or Nate might have taken a seat in the corner and ordered a few bottles of St. Pauli Girl, probably a lot more. He walked in the opposite direction along Angela Street just to breathe for a while and to escape the tourists littering Duval. The divorce papers reminded him of Dana again and her Carol Burnett smile the day she disappeared through the door of that Air Sunshine DC-3. The empty ladder behind her drooled from the fuselage like the cartoon guy on Bart's T-shirt from the Tongue n' Groove Construction Company. Nate never believed Dana would leave, but the ramp service guy shut the hatch behind her and the pilot started the Pratt & Whitneys. When the sound of the open exhaust slammed against the windows of the terminal, Nate knew, suddenly, that it was over. He couldn't leave the rail until Dana and the DC-3 were lost in the sky far above the Keys that stepped away to the east. He remembered staring at the windsock hanging limp from its tower at the end of the runway, but then he turned and walked away into the heat. Eight months had gone by.

The April winds blew soft out of the south with just enough strength to make the cemetery puddles flicker in the early morning shadows of the magnolias. Nate looked up from the shimmering patchwork in time to see the Green Line bus down on White Street. He waved at the driver who frowned as the bus lurched to a stop. Nate took a seat by the window in one of the middle rows and stared at the front porch of Sarah's old apartment when the bus drove down Caroline. Near the corners of the Conch house there were aloe plants growing stiff and thick-leafed along the flower beds, still wet from the rain at dawn. When the bus made the turn to go up Simonton, Nate shut his eyes and didn't look at anything else until the bus drove past the airport where another Air Sunshine DC-3 warmed itself on the tarmac. He watched the plane run up its engines to roll down the runway and then he turned in anger to look out at the sea until the bus crossed the Cow Key Bridge over to Stock Island. Nate got off in the mud at the next stop and walked through the field of torn shrimp nets toward Tropical Marine Center asleep in the morning sun.

Serendipity and her yellow decks stood out from the rest of the boats tied to the fingers. Nate could see Shanna sitting on the cabin roof. He only reached the end of the dock before she came running up to grab his arm.

"I'm glad you're back," she grinned. "Did it go okay with Fred?"

Shanna was cute and petite and eternally happy, like there were carnivals going on and balloons were floating around over her head. She had those almond eyes that drooped at the corners a little, so bright they always made Nate think of kids watching a magic show.

"I guess," he said. "I didn't much care for signing all those papers. At least it's done. Maybe that will end the nightmare."

"Sarah hasn't said much this morning. I don't blame her, really. I think it will be better now that you're here and we can leave."

"I hope so. I think I'll walk out to the end of the dock to see down the channel toward the reef. I still haven't calmed down."

Serendipity looked light on her feet, like a swan ready for flight. Even after Nate walked beyond her slip he kept turning to look at her. When he reached the end of the dock, though, he shaded his eyes and tried to see the reef and the thin band of cobalt water on the other side. There were residual swells out in the Gulf Stream from the morning front. He watched them running faintly sawtoothed along the horizon until Brady came up from behind looking like an anorexic lumberjack in faded cutoffs and floppy boat shoes. He smiled at Nate and shook his head and then looked away to the reef. Nate squinted again into the glare, but he couldn't tell much they were so far from the open sea. They walked back to *Serendipity* where Sarah and Shanna waited on the foredeck. Nate wasn't sure what to say. Sarah smiled at him and when he stepped aboard, she met him with an embrace.

"Are you okay?" she asked.

Nate didn't want to talk about the morning divorce papers. He winked at her instead. Sarah reminded him of Ursula Andress and he never thought she belonged with the bar crowd in Key West. Her voice was so deep she told Nate once that people mistook her for a man on the telephone. She spoke to him in her sexy register again.

"Do you need time? We don't have to leave today."

"No, I'm ready to go. I wasn't too happy downtown. It just made me want to run off again. Care to join me?"

Sarah smiled and turned away and gave Brady a lighthearted ration about something stupid he had done. She had an infectious laugh and when she shook her head, the blonde streaks in her hair flashed in the sun and made Nate think of Revlon commercials on television.

Nate started the diesel to let it warm up and then watched again while Sarah caught the bow lines. Brady walked along the finger to ease the boat out of the slip and then he pushed the bow in the direction of the channel before hopping aboard. Nate spun the wheel and inched the throttle forward and motored along the line of shrimpers tied to the quay on the other side of the basin. He shaded his eyes from the sun and looked beyond the channel at the reef far across the flats.

Brady stowed the fenders and dock lines and stood near the bow rail watching the stem slice through the water. Sarah stayed off by herself looking first at the sky and then at the water, thin and pale green and sparkling in the light. Nate glanced at her for a moment and then looked at the reef in the distance and at the open sea beyond that deepened to black near the horizon.

They motored out into Hawk Channel and turned to the east toward the cut through the coral and the Bahamas hiding over the horizon. Nate watched one of the Singleton shrimp boats far to the south running just beyond the reef with its outriggers hanging low over the short Gulf Stream swells.

"Want to get the main and jenny up?" Brady asked. "Shanna can take the wheel."

"The jenny is in the port hull in the orange bag," Nate said. "It's heavy."

They walked forward and hanked the big genoa to the forestay and removed the sail cover from the boom. When the sails were set and drawing, Nate shut the diesel down while the boat moved at eight knots through the thin water of the channel. The sensation of flying came back and he felt *Serendipity* come alive with the speed and the quiet motion and by the windward hull lifting free. Her shadow flashed on the white sand of the bottom and then disappeared now and again in the dark patches of coral and sea grass gliding past.

Sarah steadied herself against the lifelines and reached for the starboard shrouds. Her hair streamed in the wind while she looked at the low Keys in the distance. Nate stood next to her and in a moment she had her arms around his waist. They stayed close together with the high sun overhead and the wind blowing warm from off the Gulf Stream. She put a finger to his lips and they leaned against each other and looked to the south and kept their faces in the wind fresh from the sea. Beneath the hulls, those dark coral heads kept sliding by in the soft, green water.

Serendipity sailed through a wide pass in the reef where the bottom sloped away until the coral heads disappeared. In the distance a winding band of sargasso weed drifted along the razor edge of the Gulf Stream where the water turned from just being blue to that incredible eternity you only see in the midnight sky. The south wind stayed light. *Serendipity* tiptoed her way to the east toward the banks of the Bahamas while the SumLog registered a modest seven knots.

Sarah took the helm in the early afternoon and settled into a rhythm with the seas that rolled through from the south. The swells weren't as steep as they had appeared early on and the motion of the boat was more sleigh ride than beam reach.

Nate watched from the bow rail as Sarah broke into a smile each time a swell lifted them from the starboard side and rolled beneath the boat. Sometimes they clipped the tip of a wave and the fine mist fell toward the stern and made the decks glitter yellow in the sunlight. Dana loved this kind of sailing. Nate rubbed his eyes and turned to look to the east and then down into the sea and at the waves that peeled away from the bow.

When the long afternoon run toward the Bahamas eased into twilight, Sarah sat beside Nate in the cockpit while he steered by the faint light of the compass. They watched the stars emerging overhead and the swells to starboard looming out of the darkened sea.

"I'm sorry," Nate said. "I wish I had taken care of the legal problems before this."

"Don't worry. I was nervous about today, but it's okay."

"I could tell it bothered you."

"Were you upset about the end? I never knew Dana. I guess that's a good thing."

"I wasn't sure this morning how I would react. I signed the papers and all I did was get sick to my stomach. I thought I could waltz in and get it over with. I couldn't wait to get out of that office, though. Freddie knew it, too."

"Fred is a little odd, but he's a good guy. I'm glad he handled it for you. I bet Legal Aid did it for free."

"I owe him for that. He wanted to come with us."

"That would have been interesting, a little lawyer running around on deck."

"He was worried about Gracie. For all of his quirks, though, he's a good sailor. We did a couple of deliveries together down to the British Virgin Islands. He'd fit right in, but I'm glad it's just us. Brady and Shanna are the best."

"Well, I bet it was my bad karma this morning that got you upset over Dana."

"I doubt it, but maybe it did rub off on me."

"Shut up, you big jerk," Sarah giggled. "Don't wreck the evening."

TWO

Serendipity slipped easily into the night with a whisper of warm wind on the starboard beam. The low southerly swells lifted her up and then settled her into the troughs and there were no sounds except for the rush of the bow waves trailing astern. An hour before dawn, Nate awoke and stepped out into the cockpit and watched as *Serendipity* rolled gently toward the banks hidden in the distance. He climbed onto the cabin top to try to see the navigation aids on Orange Cay but he couldn't see any light, not even from the rising sun, and he stood near the mast peering into the darkness. The bow waves were nearly iridescent and he turned to watch the white water streaming aft. The night sky seemed darkest astern where he picked up the faint masthead light of a northbound fishing boat. Nate thought they might be closer to the banks, but it took another half-hour before the Orange Cay light came into view. By then he could see the horizon brightening to the east. When Brady steered the boat just south of the islet, they crossed over onto the banks where the water turned silver it was so thin.

The Gulf Stream had been smooth except for the long swells from the south, but the morning gave rise to a freshened breeze. *Serendipity* sailed across the flats at twelve knots like she was skiing through Colorado powder. When the sun climbed higher, the color of the water off the bow changed from the silver-gray of dawn to that blue you only see in Mexican fire opals and for 50,000 square miles in the Bahamas.

Late in the afternoon after they had approached the northern tip of Andros Island, there were miles of shallow water and sand bores that looked from the air like a child's strokes through fingerpaint. They skirted the thin water where it wasn't deep enough to have any color and stayed to the west of the sand bores where the water turned so electric blue it reminded Nate of the arcs from a welding rod.

North of the island, the Andros banks were littered with coral heads that loomed from the bottom like decaying fangs. Nate couldn't tell by the color how shallow the coral heads were, so he gave them all a wide berth and steered into clear, deep water southwest of the Berry Islands. *Serendipity* sailed on a fast beam reach for ten or twelve miles through Northeast Providence Channel and when she ran onto the banks on the west side of Chub Cay, Nate started the diesel while Brady furled the main and genoa.

The entrance to the inner harbor of the island was a narrow pass cut through the ancient coral. Nate motored *Serendipity* into the curving waterway until she reached the tiny yacht basin and the transient dock on the north side where Brady stepped from the deck to tie her off. In a few minutes, a large man in a starched white shirt came aboard to stamp the passports.

"Welcome to the Bahamas," he said. "You on island time, now."

"Is there a limit to our stay?" Nate asked. "We're only passing through."

"No, just go down island. Nobody bother you. You on your own, here."

After a cursory look at the papers, the customs man left with a grin and a wave.

"I love this," Sarah said. "Island time. That customs man was right. We just got here and already I never want to leave."

Nate sat alone in the cockpit after the others had gone below for the night. The air settled in, heavy and silent and thick with the island heat. When he shut his eyes, he could feel the Ferris wheel begin, dizzy spinning up, nausea spinning down. He drank the last of his rum anyway, and stepped below to climb into the berth next to Sarah. He kept thinking about the gold plated fishing fleet lying dormant in the marina and how far away Key West seemed and how good it felt to be on island time. He rolled on his side and looked at Sarah asleep in the dark. Nate felt in the pit of his stomach the ache and the burning that had been missing most of the time since Dana left. He reached with his hand and touched Sarah's face. In a moment they kissed and caressed and he looked in the low light at her breasts and at her legs and at the dark secret between. The burning inside felt to him like a magnesium fire. He was nearly shaking in the heat, but down low where he should have come alive, there was nothing. The burning in his stomach began to ebb even though he couldn't keep his hands and face away from her body. Sarah could tell it was no use and she whispered to him in the dark.

"It's okay, it's okay," she said. "It'll just take time. Please don't worry."

Nate turned away from her and stared through the port at the light standard flickering over the marina office beyond the trees. Sarah held him from behind and in a few minutes she was asleep again. Nate had to wait out the ride on the Ferris wheel.

Right at dawn someone cracked off a pair of diesels in one of the sportfishers next door. Nate pulled the curtain over the portlight and leaned back on the sheets thinking first about those big diesels and then about the night before with Sarah. The pulsing of the engines droned on, keeping time with his headache. He kept thinking about Sarah's body, waiting for the feelings to return, but there was nothing again. He got up and sneaked into the head compartment aboard *Serendipity* and took a cold shower.

Nate toweled off and dressed and stepped into the cockpit. The sportfisher had backed down and motored out of the marina toward the cut, its tuna tower disappearing around the bend in the light filtering through the trees. He watched for another few minutes and then started the Volvo, but the little popping noises from the exhaust made *Serendipity* seem like a bathtub toy. Nate backed the boat from the slip and spun the wheel to port, idling out of the marina into the cut and into the fluorescent glow of the banks in the distance.

Whale Cay hid just beyond the channel to the east. Nate and Brady sailed the boat off the banks into deep water where the color changed from neon to midnight in a matter of feet. After a slow run along the coast, they rounded up into the channel on the north side of a sunken barge where they dropped the anchor. *Serendipity* spent the day drifting about in ten feet of water so clear the blades of sea grass were visible on the bottom.

Just before sundown, Nate and Sarah launched the sabot to go across to the beach on Whale Cay where there was a low hill that overlooked the Berry Islands and Northeast Providence Channel. They pulled the dinghy above the high tide line and walked up a sandy path where they found a place to sit at the top and watch the sunset. Far below in the channel, *Serendipity* sat swinging to the wind and to the current. Sometimes she got confused between the two and sat sideways to both, but she looked beautiful in the low light. Nate was staring out beyond the channel when Sarah leaned close.

"*Serendipity* is lovely down there, Nate. You have to be proud."

"I am proud. I used to wonder while I was building her what it would be like to sail her for the first time. It still feels like that each time I set her free."

"You said she reminded you of a swan. She is one."

"Wait until we get down into the lower Caribbean where the swells roll in from the Atlantic. She can reach twelve knots or better going to windward in the trades. She clips a wave now and then and the spray flies aft and makes rainbows in the wind."

"I wish we could make rainbows. We did once. What's wrong with us, Nate? It isn't working very well."

"I know," Nate said. "It's like we were starting over."

"Maybe it will be better once we've been together for a while."

"Sometimes I think it's having Brady and Shanna so close."

"But they're up in the forepeak. I bet they wouldn't even know."

"Maybe so."

"I guess I need to be patient."

"It's killing me," Nate said. "You know that."

"I know."

"I've never been around anyone like you. It just isn't there sometimes."

"You aren't really over Dana yet. Remember the morning in Key West when we made love for the first time? There were rainbows everywhere. I'll never forget that."

"I won't, either. We'll make rainbows again. You're right, though. Maybe we just need a little time together."

Nate didn't want to talk about it anymore. Eighty yards up current, the dark shape of the barge quivered on the bottom in the channel. He nodded toward the hulk.

"That barge looks like a manta ray from here," he said.

"You're kidding. That big?"

"Not quite, but they can get huge."

"Where did you see one like that?"

"Mouth of the Sea of Cortez. I don't know what a world record manta looks like, but the wings were twenty feet across or more. We sailed right next to it."

"What a thrill that would be."

"It made me nervous for some reason. I could see the shadow from a long way off, like the barge down there. It looked like a reef."

"The barge made me nervous. It isn't very deep. I suppose someone could hit it in the dark."

"What a way to end a trip."

"I don't like thinking of that."

"It'll get better for us," Nate said.

"You think?"

They watched the fading sun that lit the sky in a blaze of rose and red that overwhelmed the horizon and made the white sand of the cays turn pink. Sarah squeezed Nate's hands and looked to the west at the sunset that faded away into a faint glow beyond the casuarina trees of Chub Cay. They sat for a while longer in the dark, but the magic of the evening slipped away too soon in the short twilight. They stood and brushed the sand from their clothes and walked down the hill to the little yellow sabot on the beach.

Rowing out to *Serendipity* took only a few minutes. The water glowed pale blue-white in the light of the moon overhead. The effect made it seem like they were two kids in a wooden shoe floating on a Walt Disney sea, so surreal Nate wanted to see swirls of stars on the water when he dipped the oars. He stopped to let the sabot drift. The current carried them in the moonlight along the channel where they floated in a lazy circle toward the dark sky over the banks in the distance. The lamp aboard *Serendipity* cast its light through the yellow curtains drawn over the ports. They drifted past in the dark where Nate could see the reflections on the water, quiet and still, until he took a stroke with the oars and set the reflections dancing.

They rounded up just astern of *Serendipity*. Brady stepped out from below to help them get aboard and then they lifted the sabot out of the water and walked it up to the foredeck where it rested in its cradle upside down. Nate stood to look at the water again, but the glare from the ports and the open companionway washed the soft moonlight away. He glanced at Sarah who stood near the rail looking southeast toward Nassau. She turned around and looked back at the bluff on Whale Cay and at the dark water of the channel between and then she came over and hugged Nate's shoulders and walked with him back to the cockpit. She kept looking at the water in the channel and at the Whale Cay light in the distance and sometimes up at the moon. Nate wanted very much to be in love with her.

THREE

A cruise ship leaned against the commercial wharf in Nassau disgorging passengers by the hundreds. Nate and Sarah mingled with the crowds and walked the length of Bay Street until they stopped near the straw market and bought baseball-sized conch fritters from a lady who only charged one Bahamian dime apiece. The fritters were light and hot and filled with conch. They ate them in the shade before heading up another block where they heard music from somewhere. The cadence was so slow they waited on the sidewalk just to see. Around the corner in single file came the members of a small brass band dressed in stiff blue and red and white uniforms with their bodies held erect and their feet striding forward in a restrained goose step that reminded Nate of the pomp of pre-war newsreels. Behind the band came a long line of people who were marching to the drums and trumpets and to the trombones sliding sadly up to the melody. Most of the mourners in the procession were well dressed, but toward the end there were common street people, dirty and somber and tear-streaked. The poor were so far from the brass band in the lead they couldn't hear to keep in step.

After the last of the funeral stragglers passed by, Nate and Sarah walked back down the crowded Nassau street all the way to the end of the harbor where *Serendipity* swung at anchor. Nate hailed Brady who was reading on the foredeck. Brady put his book down and jumped into the sabot and rowed over to the beach in front of one of the hotels. There were people sunbathing and swimming in the water and some of them stopped to look as Nate and Sarah waded out in the shallows where they stepped into the sabot. The tourists who were watching went back to their swimming and sunbathing, but Nate caught himself staring at a girl who had untied her top and was lying face down on a towel in the sand. He wouldn't have noticed except her breasts were round and full and he could see a good part of them. She made him think of Sarah in the mornings. Brady pulled the sabot away and the girl disappeared behind the kids splashing in the water.

Shanna made sandwiches with Bimini bread and slices of canned ham and the four of them sat around the deck and watched the lights of Nassau twinkling to life while the sun went down. Twilight turned to darkness and the lights of the town washed away the stars overhead until Nate could barely see the rising Scorpio. Noise from the streets carried all the way out to *Serendipity*. The sounds were vibrant and happy and it made Nassau seem more real than just a tourist stop for cruise ships. They blew out the Aladdin early on and *Serendipity* went to sleep with the companionway open and the night sounds of Nassau drifting through.

Nate awoke sometime during the long night hours, restless and hot and confused by dreams of *Serendipity* lifting off the water in the harbor and flying into the afternoon sky under full main and genoa. The sails crackled fresh and new and the hulls shimmered white in the sun and it felt free to be in the air and not held back by the sea, but there was a funeral snaking through the streets along the waterfront. Nate heard the sad trombones again. He watched the funeral far below, wondering if it was his, but he was desperately afraid of falling. When the boat banked into a steep descent, the fears grew worse and the falling was out of control. Nate tossed and turned and broke into a sweat and he heard the explosion when *Serendipity* hit the street and smashed herself into oblivion. He spun away into the darkness where he saw Dana for an instant and then there was nothing but the sliding of the trombones. He kicked his side of the sheets away and slipped from the berth to go out on deck where he could cool off. Sarah kept up her steady breathing in the dark.

Nate climbed over the coaming and sat on the starboard rail where he let his feet dangle over the side while he watched Nassau asleep on the other side of the anchorage. It was so quiet and still *Serendipity* had drifted over her anchor. The rode hung loose from the bow and disappeared below the surface. The lights in town weren't so bright anymore, but Scorpio and the spring sky still looked washed out. Nate had a hard time finding the array of navigation stars lost in the glow from Nassau.

He leaned against the lifelines and stared toward the deserted beach where the girl with the loose straps had been. The hotel security lights were dull and he couldn't see much of the sand, only the shadows thrown by abandoned castles and by the deck chairs sitting empty. The late night air was cool and he breathed deep and let his legs hang free while the pounding of his heart slowed to a crawl. He looked into the depths and at the reflections of the hotel lights bouncing on the surface and then he stretched and yawned deep into his chest. The shuddering made the nightmare seem real so he slipped below where he heard Sarah again breathing in the dark. Nate climbed into the berth next to her and leaned against the pillow where he kept thinking of Dana and the nightmare and how their world had changed. In the stillness he felt *Serendipity* hunting about the anchor line in a breeze from the east that came up, soft like down. She checked herself and swung away again and the air drifted through the cabin like a circulating fan set on one. Nate could still hear the echoes from the trombones.

During the early morning hours, the wind strengthened and blew with authority across the anchorage and set *Serendipity* tacking back and forth while the rigging moaned into the night. The sound of the wind and the motion of the boat woke Nate out of a fitful sleep. He nudged Sarah and together they went out into the cockpit and moved the anchor line over and tied it off to the big cleat on the bow of the starboard hull and let *Serendipity* ride as if she were on a close reach. She settled down and stopped swinging about. Nate stood for a long time in the darkness to be sure the boat hadn't dragged.

"It's too cold to stay out here," Sarah said.

"I'll be down in a minute. I'd like to watch for a while."

"It's cooler down below, too. Maybe it might help?"

Nate looked at Sarah and smiled. She stepped below where the wind couldn't cut through her anymore. Nate stayed to look around at the empty anchorage and at the dark hotels that lined the channel. There were only a few street lights still burning at that hour and an odd light in a window here and there. The wind still made the rigging moan into the darkness and he leaned against the mast. He could feel it pumping against his back while he looked to the night sky for the stars. There were clouds moving through and he only recognized Antares to the south and then Polaris before the stars disappeared altogether. The darkness that followed made the wind seem colder. He crept below without waking anyone and crawled into the berth and pulled the covers over his shoulders where he shivered a little before Sarah reached for him.

They shared a few moments of quiet where their hearts beat together and there was that feeling of oneness in the cool night air. There were doubts again even though the burning in Nate's stomach felt like an acetylene torch when she pulled him toward her. They embraced and rolled in the bed and kissed and for a time there was some feeling and it got a little stronger, but something happened and the feelings went away no matter how intense the burning got. In the end they rolled apart, hot and sweaty and unfulfilled. Sarah whispered to him in the dark.

"It doesn't matter. I just want you here with me. Please don't be upset."

There were streaks of sweat on Nate's forehead. The burning in his stomach faded away to nothing, but he thought it would have been far better if he had faded all the way into the darkness. Sarah started breathing in her sleep in only a few minutes. Nate kicked the sheets away and stared at the mahogany ceiling. He rolled to the other side of the berth and stared forever at the blackness through the portlight, wondering how it could be that he was so powerless.

Nate fell away into the night, afraid of what might happen in the future if nothing changed, but then the faint light of dawn drifted into the salon. He could hear the patter of rain falling on the cabin roof and on the decks beyond the portlight and the whispering sound of wavelets running up against the hull. He woke up slowly, floating somewhere in a kind of dream state with the rain in the background and the smell of earthy dampness in the morning air. Through the portlight he could see the palms and the hibiscuses and the bougainvillea plants ashore, muted in the diffused light and all of them dripping in the mist. The breeze eddied through to rustle the thin curtains and brush across the berth like sweet baby breath.

Nate yawned and stretched and then turned back to look at Sarah still asleep. Her sheets had fallen away and he couldn't help himself. He stared for a long time at her breasts and at her skin and the burning came back more intense than the night before and there was some feeling where none had been.

He turned on his side and kept looking at her body and there were deep rolls of thunder from somewhere. He took her up in his arms and they kissed a long time and she breathed and opened herself to him and he entered hard and deep and he never wanted it to end. They kept rolling together and Nate went deeper and they were naked and free and flying high and driving deeper and holding it so long it couldn't end, and then with a rush into the light they were sky high together, twisting in the heat of the wind and in the heat of the sun and in the warm, slippery wetness and holding it even longer and then driving slower and slower and they fell from the rainbows, clinging to each other, feeling each other so close, and it was quiet again when a cat's-paw crept through the open companionway. In the cool, wet morning they slept.

When the sun came up bright through the portlights, Nate turned to look at Sarah beside him. The feeling of oneness came back and he wanted to make love to her all over again. There was nothing left of him, though, except the rising sun and the fading wind from the early morning front. He heard someone stirring about in the forepeak and then Brady poked his bearded face into the salon.

"Ready for some coffee?" he asked. "You need to coach me with the stove."

Nate put his arms around Sarah and watched Brady struggle with the kerosene pump. The stove lit without a blow-out, though, and the aroma of Cuban roast drifted through the salon. Sarah reached for her bathing suit. Beneath the covers Nate saw her naked body, smooth and tan against the white of the sheets, and it made the burning return to the pit of his stomach. Sarah was up and out into the cockpit with the coffee. Nate had to lie still for a few minutes before he could do the same.

The wind by eight o'clock that morning had faded to nothing. The still air had a lingering edge to it, but the sun drove the chill away soon enough and Nate set about removing the sail covers and hanking the genoa to the forestay. After Brady lifted the anchor aboard and stowed the gear, they hauled the main and genoa up to the stops. Nate let the boat fall off to ghost down the channel toward the shallows in the distance. Nassau faded away astern while they sailed toward the banks beyond that sparkled like blue topaz in the early morning light. Nate kept thinking of the dawn with Sarah and the rising sun. The trombones and the sad melodies seemed far away.

FOUR

A fading sub-tropical sun lit the silent waters of the anchorage off Highbourne Cay. Nate drank another beer and watched as *Serendipity* tacked over in the slight breeze that eddied over the hill and across the cove. Along the narrow beach there was a line of sea grapes growing above the high water mark. Some of them were so big the branches reached nearly across the sand. The leaves were a different shade than the scrub that climbed the hill behind and it made the island look very much like the water on the banks, only in shades of green. Nate looked over toward Sarah who was sunbathing on the cabin roof.

"I'd like to row ashore," he said. "Want to go along?"

"Sure. Can we walk on the beach up to the point?"

Sarah winked at him and then gathered her towel.

"I had dreams of you all night long," Nate said. "The frustrations are going to do me in, I think."

"Remember how nice it was the other morning in Nassau? We made rainbows again."

"Sometimes I wonder how much patience you have."

"Don't worry. If I didn't think it would work, I wouldn't be here."

The sabot slid to a stop on the coarse sand of the beach. Nate dragged the dinghy up where it was safe while Sarah looked around at the shore break and the scrub up the hill and at the stretch of sand that curled away to the south. They started walking toward the headland, but they only covered a hundred yards before they came to a shaded area beneath some big sea grapes. They flopped on the sand and looked out at *Serendipity* swinging on her anchor line. Sarah yawned and leaned back and closed her eyes for a moment. She glanced over at Nate and he smiled at her, but he caught himself looking at her body again, smooth and nearly bare in the tiny bathing suit. The sun filtered through the leaves of the sea grapes and there were dancing patches of light and shadow. Where the light fell, he wanted to touch because it was scattered low on her stomach and on her thighs and it made him ache to see all of her body. Nate looked back toward the cays in the distance and at the boat floating in mid-air out in the cove. Brady and Shanna were sitting together with books on the port wingdeck. The boat tacked over and the wind fluttered the pages, but when *Serendipity* sat broadside to the beach, all Nate saw were the white hulls and the wide yellow boot stripes and the mast towering tall and straight above the yellow decks.

Sarah sat up and brushed the sand from her back and hugged Nate's neck again before getting to her feet. She stood in the shadowy light and pulled him up by the hands and then she giggled.

"You're still checking me out," she said.

"I didn't think you'd notice. Are you embarrassed?"

"It isn't embarrassing when you look at me. We'll be fine. You proved that the other day."

Sarah laughed and pushed Nate away and ran into the water. He waded over and pulled the sabot off the beach and rowed toward *Serendipity* while Sarah swam for the grotto beneath the wingdecks and the ladder hanging from the stern. When they settled back in the cockpit, the breeze died away again and the water flattened to a mirror finish, so oily and smooth it made Nate think of Saran Wrap stretched tight. *Serendipity* stopped hunting around and settled herself by drifting over the anchor rode. The sun went down over the horizon in a cacophony of orange and in the dark that followed, the first stars brightened to life. The hump of Highbourne Cay loomed like a shadow against the sky just beyond the bow.

Bimini bread and a chowder made from a pair of lobsters caught during the morning dive were enough for dinner.

Afterward, they were all in the cockpit sipping rum and watching the night sky and the still water over the banks. They could have counted a million stars and a million more from the reflections on the black surface. *Serendipity* drifted aimlessly in the calm, nosing first toward the beach and then away to the banks and Nassau beyond and then toward the coral heads hiding like border reivers just below the surface at the edge of the cove.

Serendipity was far enough from Nassau that the only lights visible were on the cay just to the north where there were a few buildings near the water. The spring stars were scattered overhead. Nate kept watching for meteors that left occasional traces across the cosmos and then he looked at the water again that had picked up that eerie glow he first saw near Whale Cay. He stepped below for the flashlight from the galley and leaned over the side to shine the beam into the water. In a moment, there were tiny fish in blues and reds and yellows gathering in the light and darting about near the surface. Sarah came over to see the colors in the water from the fish swimming around in the circle of light. A school of horse-eyed jacks appeared suddenly and charged across the light, flashing their silver sides and carving through the little fish that scattered into the dark. Sarah jumped back as if the jacks were sharks.

"I'm sorry," Nate said. "I didn't know the jacks would show up."

"Those are jacks? The little fish never had a chance."

"I shouldn't have shined the light in the water. It makes me want to get out the elephant gun and blast away. I don't think you can eat the jacks, though. Someone told me you can get ciguatera."

"It doesn't matter, anymore. They scared away all the rainbow fish."

Nate watched the horse-eyes rush by in the beam of the flashlight before switching it off. In the shadows and away from the light from the companionway, the spectral aura of the water returned. Sarah looked in silence at the spot where the rainbow fish had danced in the light a moment before and then she glanced over and shook her head and got to her feet. Nate stayed behind in the dark and stared out over the water and listened as the shore break popped into the night.

The breeze remained light off the sound. They spent a quiet night at anchor with *Serendipity* barely swinging on her rode. In the silence they could hear the hollow sound of the sea on the windward side of the island. When Brady blew out the Aladdin, Nate fell into a confused sleep dreaming of a booming surf line and white water pouring over *Serendipity*. He awoke in the middle of the night, but all he heard was the shore break again, a distant and gentle rush like the sound of the air when he was a kid and his dad held a seashell to his ear. Nate rolled over and touched Sarah on the shoulder. She never stirred. It didn't make much difference. He fell into a sleep so heavy it felt like he disappeared into a mass of dark cotton, deep and dreamless and soft.

There were noises in the night. Nate thought something might be wrong with the mast and boom and he lifted his head and opened his eyes to hear. Sarah was in the galley trying to get the stove to light. Nate flopped back into bed, confused all over again.

"Did you pump the pressure tank enough?" he asked.

"I tried to peg the needle on the gauge. Let's see if I can do this."

Sarah fooled with the pressure tank again and after several more noises, Nate heard the hiss of the burner and some laughter. Sarah came back and climbed into the berth beside him mumbling about the stove. She got out a book and started to read while the aroma of coffee filled the cabin.

Sarah had that fleshy look about the eyes from a long night's sleep. She put the book down and the burning came back to Nate in a rush, she was so close. They were fumbling around again with clothes, but it still felt like Nate was lost in that soft, black cotton and he had to stop and lie there and breathe because nothing happened. Sarah didn't move for a while and the passion went away for her as well. She picked up the book again while Nate turned away and struggled one more time with the confusion and the anger.

Brady and Shanna got up in a few minutes and poured coffee for everyone. Nate was still upset when he slipped out of bed, but he stumbled up the companionway and sat on the cabin roof to look around at the water and at the beach and at the pillowlike clouds that marched in from the east. He looked across the cay to the north where the deep water of Exuma Sound ran up against the reef.

"I'd like to head straight to San Salvador from here," Nate said. "It's an overnight sail but we can do some shopping and refill the water tanks once we get there. Is that okay?"

"I'm ready," Brady said. "I don't think Shanna will mind."

"It's a long run down the sound. If the wind is steady, we'll get there after sunrise tomorrow. I'm ready for some cold beer."

Sarah took the helm while Nate hauled the sails up and let *Serendipity* ease close to the anchor. Brady took in the line and chain. When the anchor lurched free, Sarah turned to starboard to run parallel to the beach. Nate sheeted in the main and genoa and the boat took off down the cay reaching at eleven knots on the smooth water over the banks.

Nate took a spot on the foredeck to watch for coral. There were no shadows anywhere, only the broad expanse of neon blue that seemed to go on forever and the blinding white of the shallows near the beach that slid by in the distance. They headed for a narrow cut in the reef below Highbourne Cay where they could sail out into Exuma Sound, but a three knot current flowed through. When they slipped into the opening, it felt like a patch of black ice on a winter two-lane. The edge of the reef came close where there were brown coral heads rising from the water.

Serendipity burst through the pass into the deep water on a close reach. They fell away again to the southeast and rode up and over the short chop at ten knots in a freshening breeze with spray streaming from the starboard hull. The dark water in the sound made the yellow of the decks stand out and the banks flicker like propane flame in the distance. The low cays in green edged along the bright shallows, close enough for Nate to see the scrub growing on the hills, close enough for him to see the ugly coral heads standing out like rusty Dado blades heaving through the white water that crashed along the beach.

FIVE

Serendipity busied herself at anchor in the small lagoon on the south side of San Salvador while a pair of squabbling gulls flopped about in the clear water astern. Nate crawled from the bunk and found Brady out on deck waiting to get underway and throwing bits of Bimini bread into the wind. They shooed the birds away and loaded the sabot aboard and lashed it down in its spot on the deck just forward of the mast. Nate started the diesel and let it idle *Serendipity* up to the anchor while Brady hauled in the plow and stowed it in the deck locker. Nate spun the wheel to port to avoid a line of coral heads and then steered the boat in a lazy circle back toward the pass in the reef. The coral shimmered below the surface. He watched over the side as they motored slowly into the cut. The lagoon behind them was empty again except for Watling's castle crumbling on the hillside and the gulls still hunting for Bimini bread.

Serendipity made her way through the pass and up the west side of San Salvador just outside the reef. Nate sat in the cockpit watching the hills slide by in the early morning light until Sarah and Shanna came out with coffee to share. He let the boat idle all the way up the coast to the Cockburn Town dock with the Volvo gurgling from the exhaust port.

Brady stood by with the lines and tied them off to the cleats when they coasted up to the pilings. No one came to collect fees or stamp papers and no one yelled at them to leave so Nate shut the diesel down. They left the boat and walked around in the village before finding a little market where they bought rum and cold beer and limes and packets of sterilized milk. Brady lugged it all back to the boat while Nate stayed with

Shanna and Sarah and shopped for canned goods and tinned butter. They found another market where there were little kids running around laughing at Brady who had walked back up the street. He took the box filled with the butter and the cans from the lady inside and when he left the market, there were kids following him down the hill chattering away while they skipped toward the waterfront.

Sarah and Shanna took advantage of the hose on the town dock, washing and rinsing clothes while the local kids watched and jabbered away. Nate and Brady filled the tanks and washed away the crust of salt on the decks. When they were finished, Nate ducked below and sat alone for a moment in the quiet interior. He suddenly felt the sweat and grunge from shopping and cleaning the decks and stepped into the head compartment to shower off. He only meant to take a minute, but Sarah heard the water running and peeked through the curtain.

"Need any help?" she giggled, and then she slid the shower curtain shut.

Nate sagged against the bulkhead thinking about Sarah. She would have joined him, he thought, if it weren't for the kids and the laughter pouring through the open deck hatch. He toweled off and stood in the forepeak and let the cool air from the hatch wash over him. There were waves of desire sweeping through and he shook his head at the timing and reached for his clothes. He was still thinking about Sarah's body when he stepped out into the cockpit.

Nate started the engine while Brady took in the lines. When they headed toward deep water, several of Brady's little friends waved from the dock and then they were laughing and running back up the hill toward Cockburn Town. Brady looked over at Nate and smiled and then turned back to stare at the island again that looked for all the world like an emerald on a chain.

"How far is it from here to the Virgins?" Brady asked.

"Eight or nine hundred miles of open Atlantic, but it's against the wind and current. The actual sailing miles might be a lot more. We could be in for an adventure."

"Maybe the wind won't blow," Sarah said.

"It usually does down here, but you never know. We can aim for Redhook in St. Thomas. I have friends there from the delivery business."

"I'm excited," Sarah said. "Are you nervous?"

"I'd be lying if I said no. We'll do okay."

Serendipity cleared the reef at the southern end of San Salvador and turned to port and headed southeast toward the Atlantic. Nate looked behind at the hills of the island and at the pale blue water of the lagoon still lit like a gas flame in the afternoon light. *Serendipity* began to romp again, sailing into a perfect evening in the open sea. When Nate looked back again, San Salvador was a little purple pillow on the horizon.

There was a soft and gentle motion to the boat. Nate let *Serendipity* go while everyone relaxed in the setting sun that made the decks warm to the touch. Samana Cay hid sixty miles ahead of them over the horizon. There was nothing in between so they sailed at an easy five knots through the quiet Atlantic. When Nate sneaked below to check the charts, he meant to put his head down only for a moment but he snored loud enough to make Brady laugh from the cockpit. Two hours had passed. Nate staggered to his feet and climbed through the companionway where Brady sat at the helm, steering into the darkness and a light wind that still blew from the east. Nate watched as Brady worked the wheel to keep *Serendipity* headed close on the wind. A long swell was rolling through. When they were swept over the crests, the boat wanted to dive to leeward a little. The motion kept Brady busy, but they were clipping along at eight or nine knots again with narrow tracks of white foam channeling off behind them. Samana Cay was still a long reach ahead. Nate wanted to tack away to keep a lot of sea room so he stepped below to see if Sarah was awake.

"We're coming about, now," he said. "I just wanted to warn you."

"Thanks. I was dead asleep for a while."

"How are you doing?"

"I'm more worried about you," she said.

"I guess it could be better. I wish you had joined me in the shower today."

"I know. When I went back out on deck I thought about turning around. I wish I had. It'll work itself out. I'm not giving up."

"When we get down to the Virgin Islands, we'll stay for a while. That's probably all we need."

"I think it will help just having normal sleep hours."

"Well, we're in for a long run at sea," Nate said. "Maybe a week or more if the winds stay light on the nose. Are you okay with that?"

"I think so. I never dreamed of doing this anyway. It's the trip of a lifetime."

"Hang on, then. I need to go help with the jenny."

Brady spun the wheel to port and let *Serendipity* sail into the wind where he backwinded the genoa briefly before falling away on the opposite tack. When he settled onto the new course, Nate cranked the sheets in a little and the boat accelerated up and over the lazy swells. The hulls were spewing foam again. Nate sat in the cockpit and looked to the stern at the trails they left across the water.

The light wind that blew fitfully from the east that first afternoon slowly clocked to the southeast, but the normal trade winds never returned. *Serendipity* eased her way out into the Atlantic. Nate held the starboard tack for several days while he worked eastward toward the sixty-fifth meridian and then turned to the south to put the boat on a close reach with the wind aft of the port bow. *Serendipity* bounced along in the light winds, rolling over the crests of the lazy Atlantic swells and leaving behind her long, thin contrails.

On the morning of the sixth day the breeze died away to nothing. A solid cloud cover moved in and the world took on a gun-metal cast, so uniform that when Nate looked to the horizon there was no end to the sea and no beginning to the sky. *Serendipity* and her yellow decks stood out like she was the center of a huge gray universe. He stood near the mast looking at the silver sea and at the silver sky and at the surface of the water, so oily flat you could see the wake carving an infinite V astern. The diesel lugged its way toward St. Thomas while Nate watched for signs of the trades.

After a full day of diesel fumes, faint patches of wind began to touch the surface of the water once again, like lotus petals falling in a pond. Nate motored into one of the cat's-paws and shut the Volvo down to let *Serendipity* sail again. The genoa slapped in the breeze at first and they drifted along at four knots. By nightfall the trade winds had clocked back to the east and returned to full strength. *Serendipity* streamed her way up and over the swells with the SumLog whining to twelve knots again. The wind blew all night long at eighteen knots or more and at daybreak, they were only a few hours from raising the hills of St. Thomas. All of them were on deck looking and at ten o'clock, Brady shouted about the dull shadow on the horizon. After seven long days, *Serendipity* sailed around the eastern tip of St. Thomas and turned the corner into Red Hook where she ran downwind into the bight and picked up a mooring below the house on the hill where Mac and Alison lived.

SIX

Serendipity hadn't been on the mooring more than twenty minutes when Nate heard a shout. He looked over to see Mac waving from the dock at the bottom of the hill. He rowed ashore alone where Mac greeted him with a handshake and a backslap.

"Nice to see you made it," Mac said. "We've been watching for a couple of weeks."

"Slow trip. Flukey winds right on the nose a lot of the time. It feels good to be here. Where's Alison?"

"Up at the house making brownies. Let's go see."

Mac had a wide frame, thin and athletic. He walked with big strides up the narrow street and to the right where Alison met them at the door of a tiny house with the window covers pulled open to let the trade winds blow through. She hugged Nate and took him inside where a platter of chocolate brownies cooled on the kitchen counter. Nate was so starved for sweets he took two.

"How many more deliveries did you make?" Mac asked.

"Only three after we came down together. Did you get cleared to be a skipper?"

"Yes, I did. I made two deliveries on my own, but then I took the job down here. I manage the charter fleet for St. Tropez, but it has a few more headaches than I planned. Do you need some work? One of the skippers called today and backed out of a charter this Sunday. I'm really shorthanded."

"I was looking forward to just sitting in St. Thomas for a while. I could use the money, though. *Serendipity* will be okay in the anchorage?"

"Sure. We can keep an eye out. Your friends can stay aboard."

"I'd like that. I'll miss them, though."

"The week will go by in a hurry. You'll be back and then you can go on down islands with some extra cash. Want to do it? Brand new boats."

"Thanks for the offer. I didn't expect anything like this."

"Before you get anchored in the harbor, tie up by the office. I'd like to see *Serendipity*."

"We'll run down in the morning to clear customs. I'll see you then."

Nate left the house and walked down the hill toward the dock and the anchorage where *Serendipity* tacked in the wind even though she was tied up short. There were heavy gusts that blew down the channel and across the mooring field. Nate could hear the moans in the rigging and the slapping halyards while the whitecaps rolled through and set some of the boats hobbyhorsing in the chop. The water in the anchorage looked nearly brown, it was so churned. It didn't look much like Paradise. Nate wanted to leave but when he rowed back to *Serendipity*, Sarah and Shanna and Brady were asleep on the wingdeck berths. He sat in the shadows of the cabin thinking about the charter.

Serendipity left Red Hook the next morning. The wind increased to a steady twenty knots and it took some time to slip the mooring and motor out of the narrow bight. Nate steered to the southwest through Current Cut where the water was clear and where fangs of coral slipped by a few feet away. *Serendipity* kept lifting her skirt and trying to surf the short chop running up from behind and at one point she hit fourteen knots. Nate watched the hills and the houses and hotels of St. Thomas sliding by to the north. French Cap Cay loomed ahead in the distance. When he cut inside Capella Island to enter the bay, it was like someone flipped a switch to turn the fans off. *Serendipity* ghosted into the harbor where Nate started the engine to motor up to the ferry dock near the center of Charlotte Amalie to clear customs.

The quay was a nasty stretch of chewed up concrete. Nate put all the fenders on one side of *Serendipity* while Brady and Sarah held the boat off the wall. He left the Volvo running and walked up to the customs office with the papers. There were two uniformed men in the office, one sitting behind a faded mahogany desk and the other standing near the window looking out at *Serendipity*.

"You are the owner of the vessel, Nathan Addison?" the seated officer asked.

"Yes. We've just arrived from the Bahamas."

"Good trip? How long did it take?" the man asked.

"Seven days in all, but we had some light winds."

"You didn't stop anywhere else? Dominican Republic?"

"No, just a straight shot here."

The customs officer made Nate nervous about stopping in Red Hook. The man looked up and smiled.

"How long are you planning to stay? Going down into the lower Caribbean?"

"I think so. We might stay a few weeks. I took a job over at St. Tropez Yacht Charters."

"Good outfit. Mac and Alison are friends of mine."

The customs man stamped the papers from a giant ink pad, clearing *Serendipity* into the U. S. Virgin Islands. Nate was relieved to get back to the boat. He didn't waste any time motoring away from Customs toward the anchorage in front of the Sheraton Hotel where Nate circled around for a bit and then headed into the dock near the St. Tropez office. Brady tied the boat off to the cleats when Mac came out to meet everyone and to look at *Serendipity*.

"Wow," he said. "These decks are huge. This would make a great charter boat."

"I think she would," Nate said. "We were doing twelve knots just in the chop sailing down here from Red Hook. Fourteen knots once."

"Are you serious? We should build a dozen trimarans and put them into the charter fleet. No one else has anything like this."

"I wish I had the money."

"I'll work on it."

Nate kept the boat at the dock long enough to use the charter company hose to top off the water tanks and to wash away a week's worth of salt crust from the decks and from the mast and rigging. He started the Volvo again and backed the boat away and motored along the dock where he got a good view of a ninety-foot schooner registered in France with its hull painted black as obsidian. Beyond it was a white motor yacht owned by the people who came up with the Amway business. It sat flashing in the sun like a hundred-foot disco ball. *Serendipity* popped her way along the cruise ship channel and away from the millionaire yachts at the dock where Nate found a spot to let the plow over the side just forward of a boxy trimaran from San Francisco.

Serendipity settled herself at anchor in the breeze that fell from the hills above the harbor. Mac came out in the St. Tropez skiff and took Nate and his crew back to the dock where he showed them the new C&C Landfall 42's in the charter fleet and then he led them up the stairs to the Quarterdeck Bar and Grill where they ordered hamburgers and pitchers of beer. There was so much laughing and singing it sounded very much like the Green Parrot in Key West, but they left after the sun went down. Mac ran all of them back to *Serendipity* in the skiff before he took off for home.

Shanna lit the Aladdin and put on a tape and sat below to read while Brady and Sarah and Nate stayed in the cockpit watching the lights from the cruise ship and looking up at the well-lit hills of Charlotte Amalie.

"I think I want to go buy some rum," Brady said.

"I hate to tell you this," Nate said, "but rum is duty free here, not even two bucks a bottle. You have to be careful."

"What? Two bucks a bottle? Shanna, let's go."

In a few minutes the sabot was gone. Sarah and Nate sat alone in the cockpit.

"I'm off on that one-week charter tomorrow," Nate said. "I don't want to leave."

"Maybe I can find work," Sarah said. "I don't like the idea of just sitting here. It's beautiful, but I think I'd get cabin fever."

"Mac told me you wouldn't have any trouble if you wanted to go out on charter. Some of the boats here are always looking for lady help."

"I was afraid of that. Maybe I can find a captain who won't expect personal favors."

"I'd like you to stay on *Serendipity*. I can understand why you don't want to."

Nate glanced at Sarah. He suddenly felt close to her, like that rainy morning in Nassau, but he sat quietly looking at the cruise ships and at the reflections prancing on the water. He heard Brady and Shanna laughing while they rowed toward the stern. Brady climbed aboard and broke out the limes and the sugar and opened a bottle of Cruzan. He poured shots for the four of them and brought the drinks out. They sat together in the cockpit and watched the lights of Charlotte Amalie spilling down into the harbor from the hills.

The cruise ship across the channel looked like a floating circus, yet it was quiet in the anchorage except for an occasional dinghy puttering back and forth from the Sheraton dock and the music from the stereo. *Serendipity* rocked from the dinghy wakes and drifted on the anchor line that sagged deep into the dark water of the harbor.

They sat up late bathed in the harbor lights while they drank most of the bottle of rum. Brady wanted to keep drinking. Nate slipped away below and climbed into the wingdeck berth, afraid of the wobbly Ferris wheel that always showed up. He fell asleep, even with the spinning, and never knew when Sarah came to bed.

SEVEN

The Cruzan from the night before made Nate nauseous. He wanted to drink a beer to loosen up but with the charter at eleven coming up, he made coffee instead. He was on his second cup when Sarah stepped out of the companionway and sat down beside him.

"Finished with your coffee?" she asked. "I'm ready to go ashore."

"You don't want any? I made a whole pot."

"Thanks, but I'm a little anxious about this. I'm not even sure I want to go through with it."

"I don't want you to go, either. I wish I weren't going."

"Let's go before I change my mind."

They rowed to the dock and tied the sabot next to a small fleet of dinghies. Sarah went straight to the bulletin board and on the third posting near the top, she found a charter boat looking for crew. Mac walked up behind them.

"Sarah just found a job listed on the board," Nate said. "Do you know the boat *Nomad*?"

"It's that forty-five foot ketch out there with the wide maroon sheer stripe and a giant deckhouse. She's a regular around here, usually with high class charter groups. *Nomad* is hard to miss out in the anchorage. She isn't exactly beautiful."

Sarah and Nate made their way out into the basin where it didn't take them long to find *Nomad*. They knocked on the hull and when the skipper came out, he flashed a lot of teeth and cracked some stupid jokes and then hired Sarah on the spot for an open-ended charter that was to begin that afternoon. Sarah was ecstatic. They rowed slowly back to *Serendipity*, but Nate only watched the oars dipping into the harbor water and sending the swirls astern. Sarah would be gone for a week, maybe more, with a skipper who was already drooling. He wondered how it would be for *Serendipity* when Sarah came back.

Brady met them with coffee when they climbed out of the sabot. Nate joined him in the cockpit while Sarah set about packing for her trip. When she finished, she brought her bag out onto the deck.

"Can I get a lift over to *Nomad*?"

"Are you sure you want to be gone so long?" Nate asked.

"I really don't want to do this. Maybe being apart will help us. The time will go quickly, I think. I need the money, too."

Nate helped her with the bag and together they rowed back to *Nomad* where the skipper waited on the afterdeck. Nate wasn't in much of a hurry. He hoped more than anything Sarah would say something about just going down islands in *Serendipity*. She kissed Nate's cheek instead and scrambled aboard the ugly ketch where the skipper welcomed her aboard with a big, toothy grin. Nate spun the sabot around and watched them chatting on the deck while he drifted away. Shanna took the painter when he finally coasted astern of *Serendipity*.

"Is there anything I can do?" she asked.

"No, I guess not. I wasn't ready for Sarah to be gone already."

"I know. That was too fast."

Nate sat in the cockpit and glanced over at *Nomad* and at the obnoxious deckhouse sticking up. Sarah and the skipper were already below. He turned back to Shanna and looked at her without saying anything.

He took a shower aboard *Serendipity* and then packed for the eleven o'clock charter. His heart wasn't in it. He spent most of the time trying to come up with excuses for not going. At ten he picked up the bag and the shaving kit and Brady rowed him ashore.

Mac was up at the Sheraton helping the charter group with their bags. Nate walked out on the dock to look at the

French schooner where he saw *Dame Foncé* painted in gold script on the transom that was almost dainty for a ninety-foot yacht. A long-haired girl stepped out of the companionway and smiled at him. Etionette introduced herself with an accent so French, Nate couldn't understand her very well. She was cute and shapely and when he told her he was a new charter captain, she skipped over and shook his hand.

"You are new? St. Tropez?"

"Yes. My first charter is today."

"I work here on *Dame Foncé*. I am the hostess, but I help, too. On the deck."

"You're French. What part of the country?"

"Paliseau. Near Paris. I came down here with my boyfriend. He left me for a rich lady from Bermuda. I'm glad, now. I like it here."

Etionette giggled at Nate and squeezed his arm. One of the local deck hands walked by and she broke away and squealed with her French accent tugging at heart strings. She grabbed the guy by the neck and Nate knew straight away she was a flirt and a charmer and all the guys loved her for it. He could see Mac coming down the dock so he excused himself. Etionette came back over and held his hand.

"*J'espère vous revoir,*" she said. "I hope I see you again."

She giggled once more and flashed her long brown hair in the sun. Nate thought every deckhand in St. Thomas must know little Etionette. When Mac walked up behind them, he stayed to talk for a bit. He liked Etionette and stood listening while Etionette smiled and giggled and fractured the English language. When she left to start work in the galley aboard the schooner, Mac turned back to Nate.

"You'll like these charter guys," he said. "They're a real party bunch. I don't think *Nomad* will be back for at least a week, maybe longer. Open-ended charters usually drag on a bit more."

"Maybe Sarah won't be back, but I'm having second thoughts. I feel like I'm missing Paradise."

"I need the help, Nate. I know it's sudden."

"I'll go, but when I come back, I'm heading straight for the Cruzan distillery."

"*Sandpiper* needs to be cleaned. The guys won't be finished for another hour. I can run you back out to your boat if you'd like."

Mac took the St. Tropez skiff out to *Serendipity* and dropped Nate off so he could get a second wind. Nate flopped down in the cockpit and looked out over the anchorage. The full-bodied *Nomad* wallowed at anchor in the distance with no one on deck. He kept looking out toward the hideous ketch. Shanna caught him staring.

"I wish you didn't have to leave so soon," she said. "I bet you're tired."

"I thought I had too much Cruzan last night. Maybe I didn't have enough."

"I know. It was fun having rum after being at sea so long. Maybe a beer will help you feel better."

Shanna handed Nate a can of Heineken. He was happy just to sit in the warmth of the cockpit. The sun and the beer made him sleepy, though, and he nearly excused himself to go below. He shut his eyes instead and leaned back for a moment. He kept thinking about Sarah and how she looked beneath the covers in the morning before she pulled on her shirt and how she had that funny giggle when she caught him staring. The image of Sarah faded away and there was smiling Etionette with her dark complexion and her hair the color of varnished teak spilling across her shoulders and her accent melting the Ross ice shelf, and little Shanna of Key West looking like Miss *Seventeen Magazine* in her black bikini a little too small in the top and her skin so fair all Nate ever thought about was Norma Jeane. There were also fluttering images of that morning in Nassau after so much frustration when he and Sarah rolled together all the way to the rainbows and the blinding light, but there were voices somewhere, too, asking him if he fell asleep. Nate looked up into a shadow. Shanna was there with her droopy eyes, laughing and holding his face and telling him that Mac was on his way out in the St. Tropez skiff.

Nate sat up and blinked in the sun. The sleep made him feel like he had trenchmouth again. He scrambled below to brush his teeth and wash his face, but he could still taste the Heineken. He was sure it was still on his breath and it made him worry about greeting the charter guests. He squeezed a half-inch of toothpaste into his mouth again and swished it about and spit into the sink.

Nate heard the skiff bump along the starboard hull. He grabbed the elephant gun and hugged Shanna and in a moment he was aboard with Mac heading back to the St. Tropez office. Etionette was on the foredeck of the schooner and when she leaned over, the top of her suit barely held her breasts in check. She saw the skiff idling along and she waved with a big smile and a greeting in French, but the image of Etionette's breasts didn't fade away for a long time. Nate was still thinking of her when he climbed onto the dock to meet the charter party waiting aboard *Sandpiper*. He stood the elephant gun in a corner of the St. Tropez office and stepped outside.

"You have two couples," Mac said. "They're from Port Townsend up in Washington. They don't have a lot of sailing experience. They just came down for the warm water and the rum. Mostly the rum, I think."

"I hope they aren't offended by beer breath."

"Don't even think about it. They're already three sheets to the wind."

EIGHT

The moment Nate stepped aboard the charter boat, a paunchy and graying middle-aged man handed him a plastic tumbler filled with rum and Coke and lime twists. He looked like a Key West tourist with an Army-issue tank top stretched tight and a pair of khaki shorts with a belt too thin for the loops. The waist band spilled over like Hemingway's pants.

"Hi," he said. "I'm Steve Harper and this is my wife Rilee. We're down from Washington State ready to do some sailing and some partying. You need to drink that to catch up."

Nate shook Steve's hand and turned to speak to the wife who smiled at him from beneath the bimini cover. She looked like she was only in her late twenties, maybe half Steve's age. Nate didn't quite understand. She had that flawless Irish complexion with eyes that flashed the color of the water near Highbourne Cay, and all of her face was framed in hair so dark it glistened in the shade like the hull of *Dame Foncé*. She stood to say hello and there was a moment where Nate wasn't sure how to react because she was beautiful and he could feel his face begin to flush. She kept looking at Nate and there was some innocence in her eyes that made him smile. Nate held her gaze for a second longer and only managed a breathless hello. The awkward moment ended when Jenson stepped over and shook Nate's hand and then introduced him to red-headed Debra, his ninety-pound wife. She gave Nate a welcoming hug that came straight from her heart. Nate liked them both instantly.

"This might be our second honeymoon," Jenson said. "We get the aft cabin. Steve and Rilee are only the chaperones. They get the forepeak."

Nate glanced over at Rilee. She smiled at Jenson with a lot of affection and then she turned and caught Nate's eye. He had to excuse himself for a moment to stow his bag below in one of the lockers.

The five of them sat in the cockpit drinking Mt. Gay and Coca Cola. By the time the noon hour slipped away, Nate was nearly cross-eyed from the rum. He started the diesel just when Mac showed up with the elephant gun he retrieved from the office. He tossed the spear gun over the transom where Nate caught it one-handed without hitting anything and then stowed it in the cockpit locker.

They motored slowly out from between the pilings with the huge dinghy in tow. Nate steered the boat to starboard and entered the channel along the cruise ship terminal where the anchorage came into view. *Serendipity* was there with a lot of spring in her step while she hunted around on the hook at the edge of the channel. Nate pointed her out to Steve and Jenson who were leaning over the rail. They looked at her and then watched as the stern wake lapped at the rest of the boats in the anchorage. Nate glanced around for *Nomad*. All the hulls he could see were long and lean and graceful. The stubby ketch had disappeared.

Debra took the helm to steer the boat into the Caribbean while Nate hauled the main up to the stops and unfurled the jib and hanked the staysail in place. When the boat emerged from the shelter of the harbor, *Sandpiper* heeled sharply and buried her starboard rail, driving hard to windward. Jenson let out a whoop and slapped his ample flank like he was riding *War Admiral*. With the sails full and drawing the boat rolled rail-down, boiling up and over the short seas with the starboard deck awash. Steve and Jenson held onto the leeward shrouds, bellowing into the trades like they were running down Juarata Street in Pamplona, holding their rum drinks high and yelling at the bulls in the wind.

They tacked over for the approach to Current Cut. After clearing the coral heads north of the channel, they fell away into calmer water with the port rail buried without so much spray.

Rilee sat in the cockpit drying her face with a dishcloth. They were close-reaching across the sound toward the western end of St. John when she threw the dishcloth down onto the galley counter. She saw Nate watching and she smiled.

"It's okay," she said. "It's only sea water."

"I'm sorry. We could have slowed the boat and not done so much bashing."

"I'm glad you didn't. That was glorious."

Nate could feel his face turn red. He smiled and looked off toward the big island in the distance and held the tack all the way through the channel and beyond. When the wind got fluky in the lee of St. John, Nate sailed nearly to Johnson Reef before swinging over toward Trunk Bay where Steve and Jenson wanted to stay for the night. He threaded his way through a couple of charter boats anchored beyond the coral heads and sailed directly for a spot to windward of the others and clear of the foul ground near Trunk Cay. He rounded into the trades and Steve lowered the CQR into the sand. *Sandpiper* drifted astern and then swung her bow to the wind when the anchor set. Nate furled the main and snapped the sail covers in place and then flopped into the cockpit while Jenson stumbled down into the galley to make another round of drinks.

"Wow," Steve said. "What a great day of sailing. I'm ready for some more rum."

Rilee giggled and leaned across the cockpit.

"Steve has never sailed in anything bigger than a Lido," she said. "He'll never admit that. Do you live here all year?"

"No, not really," Nate replied. "I'm just passing through on my way to the lower Caribbean."

"You lead quite the life. Do you have crew?"

"Some good friends from Key West. I have a lady friend, as well. Sarah is out on a slug called *Nomad*. It might turn out to be a long charter."

"Maybe it won't be too long."

Nate was so taken by Rilee's looks he didn't hear what she said. He was afraid she wouldn't talk to him anymore. Steve cleared his throat.

"Why don't you leave the captain alone and let him drink in peace?" he said, and he handed Nate another rum and Coke.

Nate reached for the tumbler and took a big gulp. He liked Rilee and winked at her from behind the rum and Coke. She laughed and kicked his shin.

"Ready to eat?" Jenson asked. "I'll go start dinner."

Jenson fried some steaks in garlic butter and served them with French bread and salad and glasses of cold chardonnay. Rilee spread it out on the dinette and the five of them ate together. Steve was good and drunk by then but he wobbled to his feet.

"Here's to Rilee," he said, "And here's to the terrific sailing and to *Sandpiper* and to Sarah on *Nomad*. And here's to the cook and the captain and the Caribbean."

Another bottle of wine disappeared in a hurry while the toasting went on into the night. When the partying finally came to an end, Nate scrounged around in the lockers beneath the V-berth to find a pillow and blanket. He wished everyone a sound sleep and then climbed into the cockpit to stretch out under the bimini. The wind whistled off the ridge and swirled down on *Sandpiper*, but the boat didn't move much other than a little pumping from the mast. Nate's own swirling was out of control and he had to sit up to get it to stop. Out beyond little Trunk Cay, he could see in the ambient light a big chop running down the channel before the wind. He sat in the dark watching from the cockpit, hoping the night would close in before he got sick.

It might have been an hour or more before the dehydration got to him. Nate sneaked below and switched on the red nightlights to rummage around in the ice box for a cold beer. He found a can of Schaefer and then turned to climb back into the cockpit when Rilee slipped out of the darkness of the forepeak. She was wearing a nightshirt with no bra underneath. Nate had to force himself not to stare. She smiled at him and put her fingers to her lips and then she pointed at the can of Schaefer. Nate poked around in the ice box again and found another and handed it to her. She curtsied like Shirley Temple and then opened the beer and took a long gulp before placing the can on the counter.

"Too thirsty to sleep," she whispered. "Too much rum, then all that wine."

She picked up the can again and leaned against the dinette table. Her nightshirt was short and it left exposed a good part of her legs. Nate glanced at them and when a burning sensation seeped into his stomach, he had to take a long swallow from the can of Schaefer to avoid looking at her. Nate set the can down and there was a moment of nervous silence.

"I'm already hung over," Nate said quietly. "How about you?"

"It's hard not to drink around Steve. I really don't feel well, though."

"I'm sorry that happened. I couldn't turn the rum down, either."

Rilee just smiled and sipped the beer again. They stood across from each other like school kids too shy to speak. Nate couldn't help stealing glances at her legs and at her thin nightshirt. He caught her eye and he smiled and tried to look away, but the fuzzy feeling in his stomach made him look back.

"Do you think anyone would care if I didn't finish this?" she asked, and she poured the rest of her beer in the sink. "I guess I have to go back, now. It was nice having your company."

She smiled at Nate and touched his hand and then she turned away to make her way back to the forepeak. Nate watched her go and in those few seconds he couldn't help wishing her touch had lasted longer. Just before she disappeared into the darkness forward, she turned to Nate and caught him staring. He looked away, but then their eyes met again and they stood in the pale, red glow with neither of them moving. It felt to Nate like the clock on the bulkhead had stopped. Rilee opened her mouth to speak but there were no words, only her eyes, and he thought she wanted to look away. She didn't, and then there was a shy smile. She looked down and turned away and slipped back into the darkness.

Nate stood alone in the galley wondering what had just happened. He looked over at the aft cabin, afraid someone else had seen them. The teak door was closed and there were no sounds anywhere. He leaned against the counter in the soft, rosy light. Somehow, nothing seemed the same. He had an incredible desire to see Rilee again and he stood there for a long time before he turned and climbed the companionway ladder.

The cockpit cushion felt cool against his legs. Nate leaned back and took a deep breath and watched the waves running in the channel, shining bright when the moon was free. The clouds drifted past and the waves and the shadows looked like moving reefs. The dark patches on the water made him shudder. He closed his eyes while the slow spinning of the Ferris wheel returned. He wanted to be back in the galley with Rilee standing near. He wanted to see her smile again in the red glow of the nightlights. Nate finally drifted away, but there were voices again in the rigging and some out-of-control spinning and flashes of Dana laughing in the distance and even a vision of Sarah somewhere on a beach. Always at the edge of those dreams there was someone else veiled in the moving shadows of the dying moon. Even in the deep sleep of the night, Nate knew it was Rilee.

NINE

Just after dawn, the rising sun beat hard on the bimini and woke Nate from somewhere dark and far away. He hadn't opened his eyes for more than a minute when Steve thrust a mug of instant cappuccino in his face. Nate took a long swallow and nearly choked because of the brandy.

"Hair of the dog never hurts," Steve said. "This will get you cranked up again."

Nate was nauseous from the constant drinking of the previous day. The brandy made him feel better. When Steve went below to make another, Nate gave him his cup again and by the time the five of them had the boat free of the anchor, Steve and Jenson and Nate had already finished half the bottle of Courvoisier.

They got the main and jib trimmed while Jenson steered them out of the shallow bay. *Sandpiper* took off into the channel and headed toward Jost Van Dyke for a day of sailing in the trades. Rilee got out her camera and snapped pictures of Jenson at the helm and Steve with his beer belly and his clamor of gray hair streaming in the wind while he hung onto the leeward shrouds. Nate sat on the stern rail and tried not to look at her. They rounded the western tip of Jost Van Dyke and headed out into the open sea where a heavy swell rolled through that sent *Sandpiper* back on her heels while she drove to windward. Rilee put the camera away and sat on the rail next to Nate. He was still so puzzled by those few minutes they had together during the night he didn't know what to say. Steve yelled at them from his perch.

"How about a beer right now?"

"No, thanks," Rilee said. "I don't need anything."

"Sure you do."

Steve tumbled below and then reappeared with cans of Schaefer. Rilee laughed and took the cans and handed one to Nate. They watched Steve lurch back to his spot on the deck where he gulped his beer while clinging to the shrouds. Jenson turned around and looked astern.

"How are you two doing?" he yelled. "I'm having the time of my life."

He winked at Rilee and then he looked at Nate with a big grin. They continued on for another mile into the open sea before Steve scrambled aft again.

"You think Debra needs something to drink?" he asked. "She might feel better."

"Make her a rum and Coke with extra lime," Jenson said. "That might do it."

Steve stumbled down the companionway again. Rilee leaned over toward Nate.

"I know you have a girlfriend," she said. "Were you ever married?"

"When I first lived in Key West. My wife left me when she got mixed up with a friend of mine. Ex-friend, I guess, named Bart. She lives in San Francisco, now."

Rilee looked at Nate for a moment and the same warmth returned that he felt the night before when they were below in the cabin.

"San Francisco has a pretty loose singles scene. She won't be alone very long."

"That's probably a good thing," Nate said.

Rilee smiled at Nate and he couldn't help looking in her eyes. He finished the can of beer and then glanced toward Jost Van Dyke and Tortola glowing green in the distance. Steve climbed through the companionway with a couple of twelve-ounce tumblers balanced in his hands. Rilee took them and handed one to Nate while Steve carried the empty beer cans away. Nate took a long drink.

"I don't think alcohol will help much," Rilee giggled.

Nate felt stupid for not saying anything. He caught her eye again and for a moment they held their gaze before she turned her head. Steve made his way back to the rail where he leaned over and kissed Rilee on the cheek.

"Leave the poor captain alone," he said. "How's the rum and Coke?"

Rilee laughed at him and pushed him away and then she squeezed Nate's arm and took Steve by the hand to lead him forward where they sat down on the windward rail. Nate watched them teasing each other. The wind blew Rilee's black hair in her face and she tried to brush it away, laughing all the while, and he could see a good part of her breasts when she turned to look back. The burning sensation came flooding into his stomach and he looked away at the heavy swells rolling through. There were images again of tanned skin and bare breasts and he couldn't stop thinking of what he had just seen. He stood and leaned against the backstay and watched the thick, white foam peeling from the tops of the swells. Once or twice he looked up at the mast that stretched far overhead, straining in the wind that blew across the open Atlantic all the way from Africa. Nate had no idea where Sarah had gone with *Nomad*.

Steve and Jenson wore themselves out trying to keep *Sandpiper* boiling through the rollers on the Atlantic side of the British Virgin Islands. After an hour of the beating, they tacked through the wind and headed back on a broad reach toward the western tip of Tortola. The relative quiet of the off-wind sailing brought everyone back to the shade of the bimini. Rilee stood behind the binnacle and steered for the hills in the distance while the big swells coming through pushed the stern to starboard. She countered with exaggerated turns of the wheel to keep *Sandpiper* tracking. The boat settled into that easy rolling motion that can put people to sleep. When they entered the calmer water of the sound, Debra slid closer to the helm.

"Can I try to steer again?" she asked.

Rilee switched places and then slid to the forward end of the cockpit. Nate helped Debra steer, but she kept sawing at the wheel and nearly broached at one point. It was all in good fun except that he couldn't stop thinking of Rilee who sat leaning against the cabin bulkhead. Nate knew she was watching and it made him worry because of Steve. He was relieved when Debra turned the wheel over so he could round West End and motor up to the ferry dock.

Nate spent a few minutes ashore clearing *Sandpiper* into the British Virgin Islands. After the papers were checked, the five of them made their way around Frenchman's Cay and headed for the anchorage on Norman Island. They were hit by the trades blowing full force down the passage. *Sandpiper* rolled over on her starboard side again and frothed her way across Drake's Channel. They made it to the island in a little more than an hour, tacking once to avoid the eastern tip of St. John, and then sailed into The Bight and dropped the anchor near the end of a sizeable charter fleet already settled in for the night. At the head of the little bay, Nate spotted the maroon sheer stripe on an overweight charter boat at anchor all the way in just off the shore break. He felt oddly detached, as if Sarah weren't really there, but he furled the main and bagged the little staysail and then pulled the dinghy up to the stern rail for a trip around the point to the caves. He got out the dive gear for Rilee and Debra, but Jenson just wanted to float around in the dinghy. Steve didn't want to go at all.

"Man, I'm tired and windblown," he said. "I'll stay here in the cockpit and guard the fort. Besides, I want another rum and Coke."

The four of them hopped into the dinghy and motored around the point where a series of caves yawned from the base of the cliff. Rilee and Debra pulled on the dive gear and then splashed over the side. Nate showed Jenson how to start the motor in case he drifted away and then he jumped into the water and took the painter and towed the dinghy toward the caves. He caught up to Rilee and Debra when they stopped to watch a school of blue runners sweeping over the coral below.

"Jenson, you ought to see these fish," Debra yelled. "They have blue racing stripes."

Nate glanced at the school of fish flashing silver in the light, but he kept staring at Rilee's legs and at her top. He was afraid Jenson would notice. He swam behind Debra, afraid to get any closer to Rilee. He let the dinghy drift up to him and then grabbed the gunwale and pulled himself up high enough to see Jenson.

"What's wrong?" Jenson asked. "Is Debra okay? She's not a strong swimmer."

"I'm sorry, Jenson. I cannot believe that Rilee. All I'm doing is staring at her. I can't help it."

"Everyone stares at her," he said. "She likes you, Nate, but don't worry. No one will ever know about this."

Nate took the dinghy in tow again and set off toward the cliffs where Rilee was just entering the dark waters of the cave. He caught up to Debra first. She pointed to a black grouper watching from beneath a lip in the coral. Nate thought about the elephant gun back on *Sandpiper*, but then Rilee swam back from the cave and motioned for him to follow. He glanced at the dinghy. Jenson grinned and waved toward the cliff. Nate turned and swam with Rilee into the cave but he still couldn't keep from staring at her when his face was under water. In a moment they were inside the shadows where Rilee took off her mask and snorkel.

"Look at this place," she said. "I've never seen anything like it."

She took a deep breath and floated on her back. Nate could see the smooth skin of her stomach and the hint of what was hidden beneath her swim suit and there were such waves of desire washing over him he had to turn away and catch his breath. He kicked the fins slowly, treading water very near Rilee. He looked about at the ceiling and at the sunlight flooding in at the entrance and at the water that was very much like the grotto beneath the wingdecks on *Serendipity*. He peeled away the mask and rubbed his eyes and then glanced at Rilee's face, soft in the shadows of the cave with her hair streaming dark in the water. She turned and caught him looking. Their eyes met and it felt again like that moment in the early morning when they stood in the red glow of the nightlights. She kept looking at Nate and then she blinked a few times and turned away.

"I'm sorry," Nate said. "I don't mean to stare. Sometimes it just happens."

Rilee looked back at him through the dancing light on the water and the soft shadows falling all over.

"I know," she said. "I keep staring, too. Maybe we shouldn't stay here."

They kicked over on their backs and swam together out of the shadows. Debra was on her way over from one of the caves down the line so Nate pointed toward Jenson who was waving from fifty yards away. They swam back to the dinghy that had only drifted a few feet from where they had left it. Along the way Nate kept stealing glances at Rilee.

Jenson started the Mercury again and when he gave the rope a heave, the motor roared to life at full throttle until he figured out how the twist-grip worked. They motored slowly back to *Sandpiper* where they found Steve reading in the cockpit and drinking another rum and Coke. Steve smiled and half-grunted at Rilee when she stepped aboard. She went below for a quick rinse in the shower while Nate sat on the rail with a towel wondering what that would be like. He stood to look toward the head of the little bay where *Nomad* squatted just beyond the shore break. Jenson leaned against the rail next to him.

"Mind if I borrow the dinghy," Nate asked suddenly.

"No problem at all," Jenson said. "Enjoy yourself."

TEN

Nate slipped down into the dinghy and released the painter. He drifted a few feet away before pull-starting the little Mercury and then motored all the way into the shallow end of the bay where he hailed *Nomad*. The skipper emerged from the boxy cabin with his teeth flashing.

"Sarah took the dinghy ashore," he said. "I think she wanted to climb the hill."

Nate spun the dinghy around and motored toward a narrow beach at the end of The Bight where he could drag the boat up on the sand. He jumped ashore and began the climb to the top of the hill. Nate was breathing heavily early on because the trail was steep all the way to the crest, but he couldn't find Sarah until he wandered over to the north side where she sat alone watching the charter yachts far below sailing across the channel in the afternoon winds. When Nate cleared his throat, Sarah turned and jumped to her feet and in a moment they were in an embrace, clinging like lost children. Sarah kissed him and took his hand and led him over to her spot on the ground where they sat and watched the sun go down.

"The charter is going okay," she said, "but I wish I were back on *Serendipity*. That *Nomad* sails in slow motion. I think the guests get bored sometimes."

"Is the captain keeping his hands away?"

"Be serious, Nate."

"Sorry. I think about you being alone with him all the time."

"George isn't so bad. He motors a lot to keep the guests happy. I have to work long hours cooking and cleaning and then helping out on deck. All the people aboard are friends from the Hamptons. They're more interested in drinking than in sailing. They only drink Mt. Gay, though. They won't drink Cruzan. They're a little stuffy."

"Will the charter go much longer than a week? I don't know if I can last."

"I'm sure it will. Maybe a lot longer. What about your group?"

"I have two couples aboard from Washington State. They've been fun but the drinking is unbelievable. Sometimes I wonder whether I should just stay away."

"Maybe you need to keep that in mind when we go back to *Serendipity*."

"Why?"

"You know why. Maybe it would help?"

Nate looked at Sarah's face in the dimming light. She was smiling so he let it go. She had to get back to her guests waiting aboard the bloated ketch so they walked together down the hill, hand in hand when they could, but mostly they stumbled in the twilight. They came out onto the narrow beach where Sarah turned and kissed Nate again. He could hear music and laughter coming from *Nomad* anchored in the thin water nearby. He would have given anything to be back in her apartment in Key West with *Natty Dread* on the turntable and her clothes and sheets kicked away with her sweat and perfume filling the air and the rain falling outside her open window. He would have given anything just then, never to have met Rilee. Sarah turned away and pushed her Zodiac into the water and rowed the short distance out to the carnival aboard *Nomad*. Nate could see her form outlined against the light spilling from the companionway as she pulled herself aboard, and then there was nothing again but the music and the laughter and the quiet lap of the six-inch shore break.

Nate stood for a while on the deserted beach looking out at the charter boats. In the dark, all he could see were the lights pouring from the cabin ports while the music ebbed and flowed with the wind. There were halyards slapping away and people laughing and he sat on the bow of the dinghy to listen. The wind sometimes whistled over the hill and down onto the boats swinging together in The Bight, but in those moments when the wind let up, the heat of the tropics settled in and it made the night air humid and heavy until the wind whistled once more down the hill.

Nate hadn't been gone more than an hour and he could have stayed longer on the beach with the dinghy, but he shoved the stern into the water and let the outboard down. The little boat floated free and he pull-started the Mercury and backed away from the beach. He shifted the motor into forward and idled past the massive side of Sarah's ketch. She was already below drinking Mt. Gay with the Hampton socialites. He slipped past into the darkness beyond the stern of *Nomad*.

Nate threaded his way through the parade of lights that danced the night away on the wind driven chop lapping against the hulls of the charter fleet. The music and laughter made him feel like he was a cab driver gliding by the windows of a West Egg mansion. *Sandpiper* was still a long way out, but he didn't want to hurry along and kick up a wake so the Mercury idled quietly in the dark. He sat in the stern clutching the tiller while the wind blew the exhaust fumes at his back. One by one he passed the charter boats anchored in The Bight, each of them a plastic island of merriment where Nate could hear Nick and Jay and Daisy with their affected voices and exaggerated humor laughing too far into the night. It was a relief to get back to *Sandpiper* where he coasted to a stop near the stern rail. Jenson stood in the galley mixing drinks while the radio station in St. Thomas played Duke Ellington music from his Jungle Band era. Nate sat heavily on the cockpit cushion when Jenson poked his head through the companionway.

"Can we sail across the channel in the morning?" Jenson asked. "We'd like to go into Road Town for some shopping and some lunch."

"Sure. We can tie up in one of the Moorings slips if they aren't full. We can spend the day if you like."

"Thanks," he said. "The ladies will be excited."

Nate scanned the dark anchorage for *Nomad* again. It felt odd to be looking for Sarah when he had a burning desire to see Rilee again. He excused himself and went below to unpack some fresh shorts and a shirt and to get the shaving kit. He ducked into the shower forward where Rilee had been and the smell of her shampoo made him stop for a moment. He tried to keep thinking about Steve and Rilee as husband and wife and the fact that he was still hung up about Dana and had no right to let his emotions run away. Sarah was still out there on *Nomad* and Brady and Shanna sat waiting in Charlotte Amalie and the whole thing was silly because Rilee probably had no real interest in him. He finished showering and thought he could march right out and let life go on, but he opened the curtain and saw her bathing suit hanging on a hook on the bulkhead. The same emotions came flooding back. He shook his head in frustration. Nate toweled off and slipped into the clean clothes and ran a comb through his hair and made his way out into the cockpit. Debra and Jenson and Rilee waited with fresh tumblers of rum and Coke.

Nate hoped the gulps of rum would take effect in a few minutes. He could feel Rilee watching. He turned to see how Steve was doing after the day of sailing and the afternoon of drinking.

"How about some more steaks?" Jenson asked. "They might go bad if we don't eat them up. Can we use the barbeque hanging on the stern rail?"

"There's a bag of charcoal in the cockpit locker," Nate said.

"Any lighter?"

"I don't think so. I can use some gas out of the outboard tank."

"Holy shit, Nate," Jenson said. "Does fiberglass burn?"

Nate climbed down into the dinghy and poured a cup full of gas/oil mix from the fuel tank. The rum made him loose and happy and he dribbled all of the gas over the charcoal. When Jenson lit it off, there was an instant fireball that engulfed the entire grill. There was a moment where Nate thought the flames would leak through to the deck, but the gas burned away and left the coals smoldering. Rilee watched from the cockpit.

"You've done that before," she said with a grin.

"Did it look like that?"

Nate stepped beneath the bimini where Steve handed him another rum and Coke through the companionway. Rilee disappeared below with Steve for a moment. Nate sat across from Debra who hadn't had much to drink.

"Have you talked to Rilee?" she asked softly.

"No," Nate said. "I can't let anything like that happen."

"Rilee and I talk a lot when we're alone, you know, but I can't speak for her. You need to try."

Nate looked over at Debra who still didn't look like she weighed ninety pounds. He wanted to tell her what he thought of Rilee and how he already had dreams of her and how he had to fight to keep from looking at her, especially under the water, and how it felt in his stomach when their eyes met. Nate cleared his throat out of nervousness.

"I'd like to talk to her," he said. "I can't let it happen."

Jenson stepped out of the companionway carrying a platter of sirloins. Nate patted Debra on the hand and then got up to help with the barbecue. After the steaks were grilled, Nate carried them below where Rilee and Debra had set the dinette table. When Jenson asked Nate to join them, the only place left to sit was next to Rilee. He slipped into the seat trying to keep some distance between them.

Steve gulped the wine and proposed a lot of toasts to the Caribbean and to *Sandpiper* and to Road Town the next day. Jenson drank just as much and they were both loaded by the time dinner was over. They got out the bottle of Courvoisier for dessert and the drinking carried on well into the night. Nate didn't care to drink any more brandy and he started to clear the dishes. Rilee caught his hand.

"Captains shouldn't have to do dishes," she said, and she got up to help.

Rilee stood next to Nate in the galley and it made her shy. Neither of them worked very fast. They finished the job and she hugged Nate's neck and there was some tenderness that made Nate turn and look at her. She winked at him and sat again at the dinette. Steve couldn't hold up his head.

Nate opened the locker where he stowed the blanket and pillow and carried them out to the cockpit. When the others called it a night, he stepped back into the galley and pulled a can of Schaefer from the ice box. He turned the salon lights off and switched the red nightlights on hoping Rilee would come out and say good night. He gave up after a few minutes and started up the companionway when he heard her voice. Nate turned around and she was there again, standing near the forepeak in her nightshirt. He leaned against the ladder and she grinned at him and then she walked over and put her arms around him.

"Goodnight, Captain Nate," she whispered, and she turned and disappeared into the forepeak.

Nate stood near the ladder for a minute longer and stared into the red shadows. He took a deep breath and carried the beer outside where he sat alone on the cockpit cushion and watched the faint wind waves racing along the channel. He kept replaying those seconds when they were so close. It seemed like the hug lasted for a fraction longer than innocence and when he glanced at her, there was a look in her eyes that made him think of early sunsets in Key West and flowers on a hill and puppies in a box at the market and then she winked at him and was gone.

Nate watched the dark hills of Norman Island swinging by, black against the stars of the night. *Sandpiper* hunted on her anchor like a slow-motion *Serendipity*. There were some frustrations and he had to get up and walk to the bow and stand in the wind where he put his face to the east and let the warm air whistle past. It didn't do much good. He walked back to the cockpit and ducked under the bimini and plopped onto the cushion one more time. Out on the water the short chop raced by, cold and lifeless, while the wind moaned through the rigging. There was nothing left of the day but the Ferris wheel and the fitful dreams, all night long, of Rilee in the nightlights.

ELEVEN

The trade winds ripped over the hills and down onto The Bight, whistling through the shrouds to set the halyards banging on the other charter boats. The slapping and the moaning sounded too much like those ragged nights at sea when the wind blew hard and the seas spit venom and Nate could never get any sleep. There were dreams and a lot of confusion and so many visions of Rilee he thought they were real. He kept opening his eyes and she wasn't there and had to start all over again trying to sleep.

Steve handed him a mug of cappuccino and brandy through the companionway again. It woke Nate from somewhere far over the horizon. Steve stepped out into the cockpit with his own mug, but he sat on the cushion and sipped the coffee and didn't say anything. Nate thought Steve looked angry and he was a little apprehensive about what he was thinking. Steve finally put the cup down and looked out toward the island.

"This place looks just like Camp Pendleton," he announced.

Nate looked at the scrub climbing the hills and the pale brown color of the granite outcrops.

"You know, it does in a way," Nate said. "It's not that tropical."

"Want another cappuccino? There's plenty of brandy."

"This one was good, but I think I'll pass on another. Thanks for offering."

No one else was awake. Nate didn't want to sit there with Steve and be all knotted up about Rilee. He sneaked below to put away the blanket and pillow and to grab the rocket fins. Steve gave Nate a blank stare when he stepped out of the companionway.

"I'm just off for a morning jog, if that's okay," Nate said.

"Sure you don't want brandy instead?"

"Maybe when I get back."

Nate peeled off his shirt near the stern and stood in the early morning sun for a moment before he climbed over the rail and dived off the transom. There was a momentary shock at the sudden temperature change. He stayed under water for a long time and kicked toward the open channel to the west. Nate surfaced and glanced at *Sandpiper* and then struck out for the deep water beyond the point near the caves, taking long, lazy strokes trying to keep a steady rhythm. It felt good to be alone and free and to be using his body. He cleared the point and flipped over on his back and kicked away and watched an early charter boat anchoring for a day trip near the cliffs. He could see the mouth of the cave where Rilee had been. It made him wish they were still there with the shadows falling and the sunlight playing on the surface of the water, dancing on the ceiling and on the walls. Nate remembered seeing the same light dancing in her eyes when they caught each other staring. He had an incredible urge the day before to hold her close. He couldn't imagine even a simple kiss. Nate thought about that all the way back to *Sandpiper* with the Mercury puttering away and Jenson making jokes and Rilee sitting across from him with those eyes still dancing.

Nate kept kicking away from the cliffs, though, afraid that if he went back in the cave the memory of those dancing eyes would fade and there would be nothing left but the darkness and the dripping and the cold stone walls. He didn't realize how far out he was from the entrance to The Bight when he finally made the turn to swim back. He was thinking of Rilee again, wondering why he had gone so far. She had to be up by now, waiting for *Sandpiper* to get started. Nate kept up the stroke all the way into the anchorage, but his arms felt so heavy there were moments when he thought he would have to stop.

He kept pumping away with his legs and stroking hard and steady and when he reached the swim ladder, he hung onto the bottom rung like it was the fifteenth round. Jenson took the rocket fins and reached for his arm. Suddenly, Nate was sprawled on the cockpit cushion with Jenson laughing at him.

"Did you swim all the way to Road Town?"

"Feels like it. I was in a hurry to get back."

Nate shut his eyes for a bit and leaned back in the cockpit with the water dripping away and the strength easing back. All he thought about was Rilee in the soft, red glow and Rilee under water near the caves and he thought about those moments when her arms were around him in the galley. Something touched his shoulder, though, and he blinked to see Rilee looking at him from across the cockpit. She grinned at him and then turned back to her book to read. Nate was so tired he let himself look at her without worrying about what anyone else thought. She kept reading, but then she caught his eye.

"Feeling better? You slept for a half-hour out here, soaking wet."

"What?"

Nate sat up and looked around. He could tell by the color of the water and the color of the scrub on the hills the sun was higher. He was a little embarrassed because he had no idea other than he remembered dreaming of Rilee. Someone had placed a clean towel over the coaming and he reached for it.

"For me?" he asked.

"I thought you would need it. Jenson made me leave it there and let you sleep. You were twitching."

Nate rubbed the salt crystals off his face and ran the towel down his back that still felt wet. He folded it and draped it over the bulkhead and leaned back again. He looked over at Rilee who had put the book away and then leaned against the bulkhead as well. She turned toward Nate and he could have looked in her face forever. It made him feel sad that it had to be like that. When he glanced up again, she hadn't looked away and there was an instant where he could see again the sunlight in her eyes. He didn't want her to know how she made him feel.

"Twitching? How long have you been sitting there?"

"Oh, maybe half an hour."

She looked back at Nate with a grin. Jenson poked his head out of the companionway.

"You two want some real coffee?" he asked.

"A gallon would be fine," Nate said.

Nate took Jenson's coffee and walked forward and checked the roller furling gear for chafe and then looked at the big shackle attached to the tack of the jib to be sure the pin hadn't worked loose. He leaned against the bow rail and sipped the coffee and looked up The Bight toward the other charter boats and the high hills beyond the little beach. *Nomad* had disappeared again.

After the coffee was finished, Jenson and Rilee removed the sail covers while Nate started the diesel. The racket got Steve out on deck looking puffy and tired. He was singing some Jimmy Buffett off-key while he ran the windlass to lift the anchor. Nate spun the wheel to starboard and motored out into the channel where he turned to port around the point to idle in front of the caves to let Steve see what he missed. Nate stared at the spot where Rilee floated on her back, the spot where she turned to look at him. He shuddered a little inside and turned the wheel away from the caves and ran the throttle up on the diesel. He glanced back at the stern rail where Rilee was sitting. She looked down at him and there was a sudden feeling of sadness, like this was all there ever would be. Nate turned back to boat driving.

Beyond the wind shadow, *Sandpiper* caught the trade winds broadside. Steve and Jenson eased the sheets to get the boat going and then Rilee tapped Nate on the shoulder to let her take the wheel. She brushed his side while they traded seats and he thought maybe she did it on purpose. He couldn't let himself stay with her, though. He fiddled with the sheets to form a better slot between the headsails. There was a subtle change in the attitude of the boat no one else noticed.

On the six-mile track from Norman Island to Road Harbour, they had to pass the western tip of Peter Island where there is a small wind shadow. Rilee let *Sandpiper* flop about in the shifting turbulence while everyone looked at the island and at the protected waters in the lee.

"That's a beautiful beach over there," Debra said. "Can we come back here and anchor for the night?"

"I think so," Nate said. "It's a private island. They won't run us off, though."

They were soon back in the full force of the trades where Rilee giggled and spun the wheel to bring the boat on course. *Sandpiper* leaned on her port side with the rail awash and took off again for Road Town.

When they approached the middle of the harbor, Rilee stayed at the wheel to take the boat into an end tie at the Moorings docks. Nate showed her how to light the diesel off and the Perkins rumbled to life. Jenson went forward to furl the main and stuff the staysail into its bag. He got out the dock lines and fenders while Nate helped Rilee with the throttle and showed her how to slip the transmission into reverse to stop the boat. She took a deep breath and looked wide-eyed at him.

"You need to stay here just in case," she said.

"Just go in slow. If anything goes wrong, you can throttle up and go around again for another try."

Nate wanted to stay in the worst way, but he was afraid Steve would try to jump from the boat to the dock with the lines. Nate needed to be there to jump instead. Rilee idled the engine down when they were still fifty yards out. They crept in, barely making steerage. She reversed the transmission and *Sandpiper* slowed to a stop next to the dock where Steve and Jenson and Nate stepped off the boat. Rilee shut the Perkins down and climbed over to the rail and leaned over and hugged Nate so hard he heard something pop in his neck and then she kissed his cheek.

"Thanks for letting me sail all the way over. Thanks for letting me dock the boat," she said. "What a thrill."

Nate stood on the finger when Rilee disappeared below. He could feel the wetness on his cheek cooling in the wind.

"Captain Nate. Good to see you, mon."

Nate turned to see Johnny strolling up to greet everyone.

"You not been back for a long time," Johnny said. "You need to leave the boat? You welcome to stay, you check?"

Johnny smiled up at Rilee who had stepped out from below. He had a reputation to uphold. He introduced himself to Rilee and to Debra and then walked by and whispered in Nate's ear.

"Save for me the dark haired one, Captain Nate," he said.

They left *Sandpiper* at the end tie and walked around the harbor to the town itself where some of the streets were lined with shops that reminded Nate of parts of Charleston. The buildings in Road Town had a nice blend of old Caribbean in rainbow and modern boutique in beige and some of the locals had money. There was always the perfume of sophistication mixed with the essence of street people and it gave the town a slight cosmopolitan air. Nate enjoyed walking the streets where he was drawn to the local shops painted in living color where he could sometimes find soursop ice cream and black coral jewelry and green coconuts and madras bandanas all behind the same counter. Rilee and Debra spent a good part of the time looking for artwork in a small studio where a lady sold signed prints of Virgin Island flowers. Rilee bought a large color lithograph of a single yellow hibiscus blossom. The lady rolled the print into a mailer and Nate watched while Rilee wrote the address of someone in Steamboat Springs. They walked over to the post office to send the tube away.

Steve and Jenson had been okay with the shopping, but when they got all the way around to where the Moorings used to be, they spotted Drake's Pub.

"I'm ready for some beer," Steve said, and he marched through the front door.

Nate hadn't been in the bar since his delivery crews had come through. It looked like their business might have suffered when the Moorings moved across the bay. Jenson walked right up to the bar and ordered pints of Double Diamond bitters.

Nate waited for everyone to sit at a table before he ordered two baskets of English chips. He sat between Steve and Jenson and lifted a pint when the toasting started again.

"Here's to Rilee," Debra said. "Captain of the channel crossing. Thanks for not bashing *Sandpiper* against the docks."

"Man, the salt and that vinegar stuff makes me thirsty," Steve said. "Let's order another round of beer."

"Can we get another round?" Jenson yelled. "And can you turn the sound system up? We like reggae."

In a few minutes the whole place lit up with the music. Debra took Jenson by the hand to dance. Steve pulled Rilee away while Nate sat by himself and pretended to watch them all, but he couldn't keep his eyes off Rilee who looked like she was born with reggae in her soul. Nate felt his skin prickling from the heat. He had to reach for the pint of bitters. He turned to watch again until he saw Debra looking his way. Nate drained the mug.

Steve came back to the table in a sweat and sat down with a thud and took up his pint and drank it down. Nate glanced at Rilee standing alone on the floor. She smiled at him when *Stay a Little Longer* began on the sound system, and then she walked over and took his hand. Nate looked over at Steve.

"Go on," Steve said. "I'm done. Enjoy yourself."

Rilee squeezed Nate's hands and led him away from the table. He held her near while they danced to the reggae and there were curves and softness and the happy light was back in her eyes. Nate couldn't breathe but there were times when it seemed so natural to have her close. He wondered if he could let her go. She pulled him toward her when the music finally ended and she stopped for a moment and looked in his eyes. She reached up and touched his lips with her fingertips and held them there and then she backed away and walked over to the table where she sat down and stared at her empty basket of chips. Debra came up to Nate and hugged his waist and they walked together back to the table.

Jenson called for a taxi to get them back to the Moorings. In a few minutes, a Triumph Standard 10 pulled up outside where the driver beeped the horn. Debra and Nate sat in the front because she could squeeze in next to the floor shift. It was still a tight fit for all of them. They bumped their way along the streets of Road Town while Debra kept fooling around in the front seat.

"That was some dance," she whispered.

Nate took a deep breath and looked through the window at the Grumman Goose taxiing across the harbor.

"Was it ever," he said.

TWELVE

Sandpiper hit her stride again, reaching across Drake's Channel in the trades that still ticked twenty knots. Nate sat nearby and watched Rilee as she worked the wheel. They were slightly off the wind heading back toward Peter Island and it was a nice point of sail. They stayed clear of the western tip of the island where Rilee steered them up a little. Nate sheeted everything home, hard on the wind, and they tacked over like a racing crew. *Sandpiper* sailed into the protected waters of Peter Island toward the long sandy beach where there were hills blocking the wind and a half-dozen *palapas* shading the sand.

They dropped the anchor near the beach in ten feet of water just as the sky to the west turned the color of a Christmas fire. At twilight, the sunset colors faded away and they were left with the same electric blue you see on the banks of the Bahamas. Nate saw the colors change in Rilee's eyes. When it was over, she stepped down from the rail and sat next to Steve near the helm. Nate moved to the cabin roof so there would be more room in the cockpit.

"Don't sit up there, Nate," Steve said. "Come down here and have some wine."

"Not much room."

"Move over, Rilee. Let Nate have a seat."

Nate ducked underneath the cover while Rilee moved over and patted the seat next to her. In a moment her bare leg was against his. Nate thought Steve would notice, even in the dark, but he was laughing and telling Korean War stories. Jenson primed Steve with a lot of questions and the stories poured out of him. Rilee kept looking over at Nate, but nothing seemed to slow Steve down until he started talking about the human wave attacks and firing his BAR until his hands were numb and having to shoulder the eighteen-pound weapon and fire on the run until the clips were empty while his platoon fell all around him. He suddenly stopped talking about it. Nate could tell Steve hadn't come to grips with his emotions, even after twenty-five years. He kept swallowing wine by the gulp until another bottle was gone and Jenson had to get more from below. Steve looked over at Nate.

"Have you ever been in the military?" he asked.

"Yes," Nate said. "I spent four years in the Navy. 1965 to 1969."

"Well, that's a good thing. At least you served your country during Vietnam. You didn't run off to Canada like those others."

"I'm not proud of it," Nate said quietly. "I never set foot on a boat or a plane the whole time I was in. I worked on Link Trainers."

Steve glanced at Nate for a moment and then shook his head and looked back toward the deserted beach. Jenson found another bottle of chardonnay below and stumbled back up the companionway.

"Anyone want to hear more reggae?" he asked.

"There's a Jimmy Cliff tape already in the machine," Rilee said.

Sitting in Limbo came booming from the companionway until Jenson found the volume control and then he climbed the steps to rejoin the party. He settled himself in the cockpit and looped his arm around Debra and the two of them toasted the Caribbean while Steve lightened up again and soon was singing off key with Jenson who could actually sing.

Debra asked for help with dinner and when Rilee got up, she brushed her breasts against Nate's shoulder. He didn't know whether the touch was intentional but the burning inside was nearly overwhelming. For a long time he could still feel on his shoulder the soft, lingering caress. Jenson stepped below to help and in a few minutes the three of them had another spread on the dinette table. It didn't take very long to finish dinner and at the end, Steve was slurring his speech and his eyes were at half-mast.

"Forepeak," Steve mumbled. "I think I need to go to the forepeak."

"Grab my shoulder," Jenson said. "I'll get you up there."

Steve lurched forward into the head where Nate could hear him working the pump and then stumbling again when he climbed into the V-berth. Rilee pulled off his boat shoes and covered him with a sheet and then she walked back to the galley where Nate was cleaning up. She climbed the companionway ladder without saying anything and sat next to Debra in the cockpit. Nate felt bad for everyone because of Steve. He shuffled around in a locker where he found one of the liter bottles of Schweppes.

"Jenson, mind if I make a Mt. Gay and tonic?" Nate asked.

"Make me one," he said. "I've never tried that."

"I'd like to try one, too, if you have enough," Rilee said.

Nate mixed the three drinks and added slices of lime and then poured a glass of ice water for Debra who couldn't drink right then. He took the tumblers out into the cockpit where Rilee slipped over next to him and lifted the rum slowly. She took a few sips and then set the tumbler down and breathed like she had been crying. Nate kept thinking of Rilee and her quivering breath and how sensual she looked dancing to the reggae in the afternoon.

"After you guys finish your drinks, can we take the dinghy to the beach?" Debra asked. "I think I'd like to go wading."

Rilee sat up and looked out across the water.

"Good idea," she said. "I'd love to do that."

"Nate has to come, too," Jenson said. "I don't want to run the outboard."

Nate didn't know whether it was such a good idea for him to go. He went along thinking he could stay away. They piled into the little boat and motored over to the beach that glowed bright in the starlight. Nate pulled the dinghy out of the shore break and sat against the bow while the others set off on foot along the narrow strip of sand. Rilee stopped to look back at Nate. She waved for him to follow, but he still hadn't recovered from the moments after the dancing. It made him afraid of what would happen if she knew how he felt. Nate shook his head and stayed with the dinghy while Rilee walked away. He watched her until he couldn't see her shape, only her movements, and then she disappeared into the soft shadows of the moonless night.

Nate turned to the south and waded through the quiet shallows. The broken strands of eel grass washing in and out with the shore break tickled his feet so he stepped away into the sand and walked toward the headland. The beach narrowed and came to an end against a line of ancient coral exposed at the base of the cliffs. He turned around and walked toward the dinghy again looking for shells by the light of the stars. He heard a voice in front of him and glanced up to see Rilee coming his way. She turned to walk beside him, edging closer until their arms met.

"I wanted you to come with us," she said. "Why didn't you?"

"I was afraid it wouldn't look right, you know? It's just better that I stay away and let you have your time. I saw how upset you were earlier. I didn't want you to know."

Rilee stared at the sand for a moment and then she looked back at Nate.

"It isn't easy being married to a man like Steve," she said.

They stood in the sand for a minute before Rilee took Nate by the arm and held him close while they walked slowly toward the dinghy. He could feel his heart pounding because he didn't know what Jenson would think if he saw them together. Nate glanced up the beach. He couldn't see anyone and managed to breathe again. They sat on the edge of the dinghy and listened to the little popping sounds that ended in long strings of S's from the wavelets that lapped at the sand. Out beyond *Sandpiper* the wind still blew hard in the channel. In the lee of the hills the air was quiet. When Rilee finally spoke, her voice was soft, like those whispers across the sand.

"I was a journalism major at the University of Colorado," she said. "Steve came from Washington to be a guest lecturer for the summer session. I met him at a reception at the school so I enrolled in his class. When he saw me sitting in the hall, he asked afterward if I were interested in a job for a few weeks. He had two children. He hired me to stay weekends and watch the kids. It turned out to be a lot more than that. I was young and he was older and rich. There was always a party and I couldn't help myself when he got serious. That was eight years ago. I never even got my degree."

Nate glanced her way. When their eyes met, her tears welled up again. He kept looking at her eyes glistening in the dark and there was a moment where the sparks were flying between them and he wanted to hold her near, to feel her warmth and the pounding of her heart, but he only reached with the back of his hand and touched her face. In that brief second when he could feel the softness and the warmth of her skin, the air was so charged he couldn't breathe again. She took Nate's hand and held it there and he couldn't bring himself to pull his arm away.

They sat on the edge of the dinghy bathed in the soft glow of the night sky. Nate looked at her face and at her tears and he ached inside because he felt so close to her, but he was powerless to change anything. Rilee looked up again. Nate could feel her breath mixing with his. She leaned against his chest and he could smell her hair and her skin and the desire was so overwhelming he couldn't comprehend what was happening, but then there were voices and laughter from up the beach. Rilee took a deep breath and gazed up at Nate and then she took his hand away from her face. She didn't let go, even when Jenson came chasing Debra out of the darkness.

They were laughing and splashing water. Nate got a big dollop in the face and that gave Rilee the giggles. Debra belly-flopped into the water and staggered out with her T-shirt plastered to her chest. Nate could see very well she wasn't quite so thin as he thought. Jenson yelled something about skinny-dipping and he ripped his shirt off and fell backwards into the shore break. Rilee reached over and with her other hand she touched Nate's lips again. She looked at him and the emotions came rushing out of nowhere. He was afraid he would do something stupid. He squeezed her hand and then turned and smiled at the half-naked Jenson.

"Ready for another rum and tonic?" Nate asked.

Debra squealed with delight.

"I'm ready to party again," she said.

When Debra splashed out of the water, Nate had to look back at Rilee to keep from staring through the transparent T-shirt. Jenson carried his shirt over his shoulder and climbed into the dinghy before Nate had it pushed into the water. The little Mercury fired on the first pull. They motored away from the starlit beach with Debra and Jenson sitting in the bow and Rilee across from Nate with her legs resting against his.

Sandpiper hadn't moved in the quiet air of the cove. Nate scrambled over the rail just behind the others and stepped below to mix the rum and tonic. Rilee waited in the cockpit. He handed the tray through the companionway and sat next to her. She moved so close he could feel the softness and the curves of her body again. With Steve just in the forepeak, there were feelings of anxiety that mixed with the charged air and he drank the rum much too fast.

"I'll make us another round," Jenson said.

"Not for me," Debra said. "I want to party, but I'll get sick when I go below, I think. I forgot about that."

"I don't want one, either," Rilee said, and she leaned against Nate. "I'm happy right here."

Debra glanced over at Nate and then she turned and smiled at Rilee. It made him think she knew there were sparks in the air and it didn't matter.

When Jenson came back out with the rum, Rilee sat up and took the first sip and then handed the drink to Nate. She slipped closer and leaned her head on his shoulder. He couldn't stand the thought of anyone being hurt, but when she was that close and he could smell her hair again and feel the weight of her body against his, he couldn't stand the thought of being away from her. Debra and Jenson never said a word. The four of them stayed in the cockpit with the glow of the red nightlights spilling from the companionway like the wind that spilled softly down the hills.

A muffled noise came from below. Rilee glanced over at Jenson who shook his head like he didn't want to deal with it. She looked back at Nate and then she leaned over and held his face and kissed him on the lips and then she climbed down the companionway ladder. Before she took the last step, she reached back for Nate's hand and he could see in her eyes all of the sadness again. Rilee turned away again and disappeared into the red gloom of the cabin.

"Rilee told me how she feels," Debra whispered. "I don't have any answers."

"I didn't mean for anything to happen, you know? I can't look at her without melting inside. There are no happy answers."

"I don't think you need to worry. Jenson and I have talked about it. We think you should enjoy your time together without hurting anyone. Steve doesn't know and then Sunday will come. We will all be sad to see the end."

"Rilee is happier here than we've ever seen her," Jenson said. "All you have to do is see the way she looks at you when Steve isn't around. I don't know if you are comfortable with that."

Nate glanced over at Debra who looked so tiny next to her husband. He wanted to tell them about the beach and how the air was so electric and how much he wanted just at that moment to be alone forever with Rilee.

"No," Nate said. "It's killing me about Steve. I have to force myself just to keep from looking at Rilee all the time. I can't believe what happened today. I don't think I'll ever forget it, either."

Debra reached over and took Nate's hand.

"Maybe you won't have to," she said.

THIRTEEN

Debra's towel was still draped over the coaming. Nate reached for it and folded it into a pillow and put his head down to see if he could sleep, but the towel smelled just like Debra and it made him think of her in the wet T-shirt on the beach. He kept rolling over trying to find a spot where the rough towel didn't chafe his skin. He never found it so he draped the towel like a blanket over his body with his legs sticking out the end. He fell asleep thinking over and over how it felt to be kissed. He had such vivid dreams of Rilee that at one point he woke up sweating. He hardly slept after that, there were so many erotic moments, and when the sun came up the sky was crimson. There were squalls in the distance and the air seemed cooler. It didn't matter because someone during the night had spread a blanket over him and he never knew.

Nate slid forward to lean against the bulkhead. He drew the blanket up to his chin and watched the clouds and the whitecaps and a charter boat rail down in the wind out in the channel. The sun inched higher while the red in the sky faded away and the cloud cover grew thick and heavy. The diffused light made the hills look drab and the water turn dark and the muted colors made the islands look much more like Steve's Camp Pendleton. Nate needed to get up and use the head down below, but he curled up in the blanket and thought about all that had happened the day before. The anxiety hit him hard that Sunday was near. The waves of passion from moments before slipped away and there was nothing left but emptiness.

Someone clanked around in the galley. Nate turned to see Debra in a tiny green nightshirt that made her red hair shine while she put coffee on the stove to brew. Nate got up and tried to sneak by her to use the head. She grabbed his waist and gave him a bear hug.

"Rilee kissed you last night," she said. "I missed it. Jenson told me."

"She did and that's all I thought about the whole night through. I can't even sleep, anymore."

"I still don't have any answers. I just know she's never felt this way about anyone, not even Steve when they were married. I was watching her last night. You could tell even in the dark, she was three feet off the ground just looking at you."

"So was I."

Debra rested her face on Nate's chest while they stood alone in the galley. He took a deep breath and she smiled and winked and squeezed him again before she turned to get the cream and sugar. Nate opened the locker where he stowed the shaving kit and bag and sneaked into the head for a shower. The stream of warm water only trickled over his body and he could hear the pump laboring. He thought about Rilee and tried to control his breathing and in the end he leaned against the bulkhead and let the water flow. The shower took so long that when he opened the door, Jenson was sitting there waiting with a towel over his arm. Nate apologized and had to tell him there was precious little hot water left. Jenson just chuckled.

"I can wait," he said. "My wife and I can double up."

Nate glanced over at Debra. She was lifting her eyebrows at him like Groucho Marx. She poured the coffee and then sat next to Nate at the dinette.

"How did the night go?" Jenson asked.

"I thought about Rilee all night long," Nate said. "I don't know if they were dreams or nightmares."

"Come on," Jenson whispered. "You need to enjoy this time. You're all tied in a knot about Sunday. Steve has no idea and sometimes I don't think he even cares. I saw Rilee last night and that was no good-night peck on the cheek."

"I know. When she kissed me, my heart kept pounding. Do either of you know how bad Sunday is going to be?"

Debra watched Nate fiddling with the coffee mug. She put her hand on his.

"When Jenson told me about last night, I felt so good inside. For you and for Rilee. Just run with it and see what happens."

"Thanks," Nate said, "but I don't know if I can without doing something stupid."

Debra giggled and looked over at her husband.

"Ready for the shower?" she asked.

Jenson and Debra squeezed themselves together and shut the door. Nate tried not to think of Rilee with him in that tiny space. There were hot flashes even when he went topside to take the sail ties off the main and run the sheets aft for the staysail. Nate kept looking for her to step out of the companionway, but Steve came out on deck instead. He still looked tired and haggard. He sipped a cup of brandy and cappuccino while he glanced at the big whitecaps out toward Norman Island.

"Yow, what a wind," Steve said. "Let's get everything up and go water skiing."

Nate got the sheets and sails ready for the big bash to windward and then walked back to the cockpit to wait for the others.

"You need a brandy and cappuccino," Steve said.

"Maybe I'd better not," Nate replied. "With all this wind, one of us has to stay sober."

Steve disappeared below to see if Jenson would drink with him. Rilee passed him in the galley on her way out to the cockpit where she sat and brushed her hair. She looked at Nate for a long time and then she smiled and whispered something silly like "alligator food" and her face lit up. There were little puffs beneath her eyes and they made her look sleepy.

"Do you feel okay?" Nate asked.

"I couldn't sleep," she whispered. "I kept thinking about being with you yesterday, the dancing and being on the beach. I never wanted the day to end."

Nate looked at Rilee and couldn't stop thinking about her kiss the night before, but then Steve was there and Jenson who looked recharged after his shower. Nate couldn't say anything and he kept looking at Rilee in front of everyone. She stood up and leaned over and touched his face.

Nate lifted the anchor out of the sand and let the boat drift away from the beach until they left the wind shadow behind and entered the deep channel. *Sandpiper* set out to thrash around in the trades that blew with a vengeance from the east. The water off the bow churned in anger. When they cleared the point and headed northeast, the wind was a steady twenty knots with gusts even higher and the boat was instantly overpowered. Rilee stood laughing behind the wheel and steering down to hold the course. *Sandpiper* had a mind of her own, though, and rounded up in a flash. Rilee steered down again but the gusts kept blasting away and Jenson kept yelling every time they rounded up and it was a grand sail all the way across the channel. After they tacked in the lee of Buck Island, they came storming back close-hauled toward Cooper Island.

Steve and Jenson were out on the deck riding the windward rail and yelling at the bulls again. Nate wanted to reach over and run his hand through Rilee's hair, soft and shiny and thick and blowing in the wind. She took his hand and held it to her face and she looked over and he could see the same thing in her eyes from the night before. The ache was so intense he thought he would break. Debra slid over next to him.

"You two are a mess," she said.

Rilee got the giggles. Debra stood and planted a kiss on Nate's cheek. He didn't want to leave, but he wondered inside how far the teasing would go before someone got hurt. He looked over at Rilee and she blew him a kiss before he hopped out on the deck to ride the rails for a while. Jenson walked aft and stepped beneath the bimini.

"Anyone need a beer?" he yelled.

Jenson skipped down the companionway and came back out with three icy cans and handed one to Nate while he stood near the starboard shrouds. Nate took the beer and watched the foam curl back from the bow of the boat. The spray that broke free on the windward side sometimes drifted back and caught him in the face and on the legs and it felt good to be out in the wind with the salt crystals forming on his skin. The beer was cold and fizzy and he felt better for drinking it. He looked back to the cockpit and watched Rilee when *Sandpiper* tried to head up. She was a natural sailor and she worked the helm and bubbled with the sheer joy of it. Steve went aft to take over, but Rilee made him wait until they tacked through the wind and sheeted the headsails home.

Nate sneaked below and put the Schaefer can in the trash bag and got out the BVI chart and spread it on the dinette table to check the approach to Marina Cay where there was a good restaurant. Debra was sitting with Jenson in the cockpit. Nate yelled to them through the companionway.

"Would you like to stop at Marina Cay for lunch?"

Yes," Jenson said. "I have something I'd like to share. That might be my best chance."

Rilee stepped below to look at the chart. Nate backed away to give her some room to see. They were out of sight from the cockpit and she turned and took his hand and pulled him through the aft cabin door. She took his face in her hands and they kissed, long and slow and hesitant in the beginning, and then the passion took over and they were so close he could feel the fullness of her breasts and the firmness.

Sandpiper rolled in the wind again and Rilee leaned against him and then she started trembling. When Nate looked in her face, he only saw the tears. He didn't know why they were there and he wiped a droplet from her cheek. She whispered in his ear.

"I'm sorry. I've never been so happy. I know I could stay with you forever. I just can't look at you without thinking of Sunday."

Nate held her close and he could feel her body shaking again. She kissed him but it was only a stolen moment for them and she pulled herself away and looked in his eyes. The tears were spilling again.

"Yes, I'll have lunch with you," she said, and then she turned and disappeared into the forward stateroom.

Nate stood alone near the aft cabin. *Sandpiper* rolled in the wind and he leaned against the bulkhead. He could still feel Rilee next to him and the smell of her skin was everywhere and he waited in the dim light trying to sort it all out, afraid that maybe the kiss and the embrace would never happen again. He reached for the chart and folded it slowly, hoping Rilee would come back. The door to the forward cabin never opened. Nate looked through the small portlight at the gray water rushing past and at the flecks of foam streaking the surface and at the bow waves rolling away to the south. He still thought Rilee would come back to the aft cabin door where he hid from the others, but he opened the refrigerator lid and got out a round of beer for everyone.

When Nate poked his head out of the companionway, Debra looked behind him for Rilee. He handed the cans of beer to Jenson who passed them on. Nate sat on the leeward coaming away from the others and looked at the sky and at the water nearly devoid of color from the cloud cover. Beef Island was nearly abeam on their port side so he told Steve to bear away and head for the low cay in the middle of the bay. Jenson and Nate eased the sheets for the broad reach into the anchorage and when they let the jib unfurl, *Sandpiper* settled in on the new point of sail. Debra slipped over and whispered close to Nate's ear.

"Is Rilee okay?" she asked.

"Maybe you can go below to see," Nate said. "She's upset about Sunday. She had tears in her eyes."

Nate looked over at the hills of Beef Island nearly black in the low light of the day. Debra disappeared below and he glanced over at Steve who was draining the Schaefer. He finished the can and asked for another. Nate got three more cans out of the ice box, hoping Rilee and Debra would come out while he was in the galley. He spent several minutes rearranging the food that had jumbled up and then called Marina Cay on the VHF to reserve a table for the *Sandpiper*, party of five. The door to the forepeak remained shut. Nate climbed out to the cockpit with the beer.

"Where are the ladies?" Jenson asked. "I'm hungry."

"They're both in the forepeak," Nate said. "Getting ready to go, I guess."

Nate leaned against the bulkhead and shut his eyes. Debra came out with a big smile on her face and when Jenson saw the pink shorts and the tight pink top and the ribbon in her hair, he grabbed her up.

"Why don't you and I stay aboard and have lunch here?" he said.

Debra giggled and fell limp in his arms. Nate couldn't sit there and wait for Rilee so he set about rolling the jib onto the forestay and getting the anchor ready. Steve rounded the boat into the wind. Nate dropped the plow over the side and then backwinded the staysail to let *Sandpiper* fall off and snug up against the line. Jenson furled the main while Nate stuffed the staysail into the bag. He looked up to see Rilee smiling at Debra in the cockpit. He walked over to the starboard shrouds where he stood for a moment looking at her hair and at the color of her skin and at the way she smiled with her eyes dancing. He turned around in a hurry and repacked the staysail again so the wind wouldn't strip it from the bag. He only did it to stay away.

FOURTEEN

A waiter sat the *Sandpiper* crew near a window in the restaurant on Marina Cay. They ordered from a menu painted on the blade of an oar and when Steve saw grouper near the bottom of the list, he decided they should all have the same thing. He ordered several bottles of wine. The waiter kept the glasses full and there was a lot of talk and laughter and there were so many times Nate caught Rilee's eye he could feel his face heat up when she looked at him. Steve kept gulping the wine and it wasn't very long before his face was red from the alcohol. The grouper finally arrived and they ate quickly they were so hungry. When the dishes were taken away, Jenson stood to make a toast.

"I would like to lift a glass of wine in honor of my beautiful wife because I have a question," he said, and he looked down at tiny and petite Debra. "Would you ever consider marrying me again? Would you ever consider renewing our vows?"

Debra's face went blank. Before she could answer, Jenson took her hand and slipped a two-carat diamond ring next to her wedding band. There were tears spilling from her eyes.

"Yes," she said. "Yes, I would. Is this what you meant when you said this might be our second honeymoon?"

"I wondered if you caught that."

Debra was stunned and very much in love with Jenson. Nate stood to drink in her honor and he clinked with all the glasses. He didn't want to look at Rilee, but there was no choice. Her eyes were soft and shining and she looked back at him through her tears.

"Alligator food," she whispered.

Nate barely heard what she said. Steve paid the bill and gave the waiters a huge tip and then they left the restaurant and walked down the path to the dinghy dock. Jenson and Debra were locked arm in arm while Steve staggered ahead. Rilee slowed behind the others until she was next to Nate and then she hugged his arm and wouldn't let go. It made Nate's heart pound again. Rilee grinned at him and kissed him full on the lips in front of some charter guests standing around on the deck of a Moorings Gulfstar 50. A big cheer went up. Steve never turned to see and when they got to the dinghy, he nearly fell from the dock. He caught himself and looked back at Jenson. Rilee let go of Nate's arm but he didn't think she was fast enough. When they settled in their seats, his heart was still pounding.

Nate steered the dinghy back to *Sandpiper* where they climbed aboard into the cockpit. None of them had much energy after all the wine so he motioned toward the hills across the channel.

"Jenson, this might be a good time to motor over to the marina on Virgin Gorda. We need to fill the water tanks. We can head down to The Baths for the night after that."

Steve had gone below where he yelled through the companionway.

"Anyone want a rum and Coke?"

Rilee sat at the rear of the cockpit near the wheel. She glanced at the diamond on Debra's hand, but when she heard Steve's voice, she looked away at the hills on Virgin Gorda.

The marina was dead to windward. Nate throttled the engine up and motored out of the lee of Marina Cay and headed across the channel into the teeth of the trades. Rilee spun herself around and leaned against the bulkhead out of the wind and watched him steering the boat. Nate looked over at her. The situation they were in suddenly seemed ridiculous to him and he started laughing. Debra stood beneath the bimini and punched his arm.

"You two are such a mess," she said. She plopped down next to Nate near the wheel and flashed her new diamond again. "What were you before you were a charter captain?"

"I don't know," Nate said. "I haven't thought about the past much. You really want to know?"

"Come on, you big goof," Debra said.

"Not much there," he said. "I got a degree in Geography from North Carolina State in '72. Geology was my first love. I didn't care for the guys in the department so I quit the program. I regretted that for a long time. Geography seemed like an old discipline searching for a place in the modern world. Just right for someone like me."

"You graduated, though."

"Yeah, it only took ten years. The service and the Vietnam issue kind of got in the way. After I got out of school, my parents moved to Bodega Bay in California. I spent three years there building *Serendipity* and then I took off sailing. That's how I wound up here."

"Were you always a sailor, though?" Rilee asked. "It doesn't sound like it. How'd you get from North Carolina to sailing in the BVI?"

"My father traveled a lot. We wound up in the little town of Oriental where I went to high school. I spent all my time on Pamlico Sound fishing instead of doing homework. I saw a lot of yachts heading south and I used to wonder where they were going. I sat in my skiff and dreamed, you know, of the South Pacific. The Caribbean. That's all I ever did. I just dreamed of someday sailing away. Here I am."

Rilee didn't move for a second and then she stood and whispered something in Debra's ear and they both laughed. Nate was a little embarrassed about his mundane past, but Rilee turned to him and wrapped her arms around his neck. Debra tried to steer for him while he drew Rilee even closer across the wheel. The kiss lasted for a long time and neither of them cared who saw until Jenson cleared his throat. Rilee came around the wheel to sit next to Nate and she looked at Jenson who was standing on the companionway ladder.

"Not a word," she said to Jenson. "Understand?"

"I'm getting another rum and Coke," he said, and he disappeared down the ladder.

Debra followed him down. Rilee took Nate's hand and leaned on his shoulder.

"Maybe we just made a mistake," Nate said.

Rilee looked up at him and smiled and shook her head and the light danced in her eyes.

"I need you to know some things," she said.

"You don't have to say anything. You told me enough on the beach."

"But I do. It might make a difference."

"Is it about you and Steve?"

"Yes."

"I don't know if I can take it."

"Sunday will be here and I want you to know before I leave."

"Have you thought about that? Really leaving?"

"I've been dreading that moment since you first stepped aboard *Sandpiper*."

Nate had to stop and look at her again. She leaned up and kissed him lightly on the cheek.

"How could I not be attracted to you?" she said. "You were so tongue-tied when we met. I knew you were in trouble already, and then Mac shows up and tosses you that giant spear gun. You caught it with one hand like some kind of Tarzan. What did you expect?"

"I never in my life ever expected anyone like you," Nate said, "and there you were, standing in the cockpit looking right through to my soul. I was helpless."

Rilee put her head on his shoulder and held his hand in hers. Nate kept thinking Steve would pop out of the companionway and he jumped when there was movement from below. Debra stepped out.

"Steve is in the head right now," she said. "He's coming out on deck to see where we're going."

Rilee hugged Nate and held his face again. There was a kiss so soft it shook him when she moved away and then she went below to see about Steve. Debra sat on the coaming next to Nate and put her hand on his shoulder and gave it a shake.

"Hey," she said. "What's the worst thing that can happen? Sunday can come and you go your separate ways and that's the end, right? Would you rather not have met Rilee so that none of this happened? I don't think so. Just remember that, goof."

Debra giggled and stepped below again. Nate looked around at the water, still gray and angry, and at the hills of Virgin Gorda looming dark in the afternoon light. While he was alone those few minutes driving the beautiful *Sandpiper* dead into the wind, reality set in like doom itself, that Rilee was going to walk up the Sheraton dock. Everything beyond that moment seemed like a black eternity.

Nate motored toward the basin from the northwest trying to stay in the deepest part of the cut. *Sandpiper* didn't draw five feet, though, and she slipped through into the inner marina where they tied the boat alongside the dock. Nate got out the deck wrench and opened the filler caps. After *Sandpiper* took on about eighty gallons, Jenson paid the bill. They got away from the marina and motored around the point and headed down toward the anchorage near The Baths. Nate rounded up in the cove where Jenson let the anchor slip over the side when they were close enough to avoid a lot of the wind that was still whistling through. *Sandpiper* sat still while they walked forward and looked at the house-sized boulders strewn about the beach. Rilee stepped over next to Nate.

"The rocks are beautiful," she whispered.

"There's a grotto beneath the biggest ones, like a big cave. We'll go in early tomorrow to beat the crowds."

"I wish we could go now. Just you and me."

Nate looked at Rilee again and saw her smile and then he looked back at the boulders on the beach.

Rilee set out crackers and some cheddar and Monterey Jack and the five of them sat below in the salon to eat. Rilee kept smiling at Nate and it made him wish the evening wouldn't end.

"Excuse me," Jenson said. "Don't we have some reggae to put in the tape machine?"

Debra put the Jimmy Cliff tape in the cassette player and held her hand just so and the night turned out to be a long celebration for Jenson and for Debra who could not keep her eyes off her husband. Jenson finally stood up and staggered a little and then hugged Debra around the waist.

"Well," he said. "We're going to retire for the night. I hope you all can find your way. Thank you for helping us celebrate. I can't think of a more perfect day."

Jenson and Debra closed the aft cabin door behind them. Nate looked at Rilee across the table and she shook her head with a frown. Steve needed help into the forepeak again and she would have to stay. Nate reached for him and with Rilee's help, steered him forward where Steve sat on the little seat by the V-berth and took off his shoes. He tried to climb into the double berth while Rilee helped him, but she didn't wait to cover him with a sheet. Nate reached into the locker for the blanket and pillow. Rilee followed him up the ladder into the cockpit where they sat down on the starboard cushion.

"I know," Nate said. "It's okay. You need to be below."

"I'm so sorry for this. I know it hurts. What else can I do?"

"If you don't go I'm afraid I'll do something that will upset everyone."

Rilee smiled in the dark. Nate held her close and they kissed again. He felt like he could have spent the night holding her lips to his, but she had to go. She stepped down the ladder and turned to face him.

"I don't think I can do Sunday," she said.

Rilee stood on the ladder staring at Nate. She leaned her face forward until her wet cheek was against his. He could feel her shaking again. She pulled away and stared into his eyes and then she touched his cheek.

"I really don't think I can do Sunday," she said again, and she stepped away and disappeared into the forepeak.

Nate leaned over on his back and stared at the underside of the bimini, dark in the feeble glow of the nightlights. He tried to keep the vision of Rilee's face in his eyes, but there was so much spinning and so much frustration he couldn't keep her there. He took the pillow and held it over his face until his eyes hurt from trying.

Nate couldn't sleep. After a long, miserable hour, he tried to get up and make sense of everything. He stood leaning against the stern rail looking to the southwest down Sir Francis Drake Channel at the black water and at the black hills of Tortola and at the black emptiness beyond. He kept thinking that in another time and place he would have been in love with Rilee and there would have been those boxes of puppies at the market and flowers and balloons and love notes on her dashboard, yet now there could be nothing but black Sunday.

Nate didn't notice the first few drops of rain. When the real rain came, quick and hard, he was so slow to react he was drenched when he slid the companionway hatch closed. He sat on the cockpit cushion and listened to the rain thundering on the deck. There were drops that splattered beneath the bimini and got the blanket and pillow wet. He was too exhausted and hung over and so taken with Rilee he didn't care. The squall lasted fifteen minutes before it moved on to the west. He could see stars behind it before another little front moved through. More cloud cover passed by and there were more stars and it made him hope the sun would be out for Rilee in the morning because there aren't many places quite so enchanting as the little beach at The Baths.

The wind and the wet blanket made Nate shiver. He thought about going below, but in that half-asleep state he couldn't make a decision. He stretched out full length and tried to be still. Even with the spinning he finally drifted up and away somewhere. He slept soundly in a place where there were puffy white clouds and yellow butterflies and a field of Ireland green where Rilee whispered "alligator food" again.

FIFTEEN

The sun and the heat and the sound of the sea birds woke Nate from a deep sleep. He felt crusty from the rain and from the mental anguish the night before. He peeled off his shirt and dived into the deep, clear water and swam away from *Sandpiper*. The shock from the water forced him awake and he kept swimming away from the beach toward the channel. A charter boat motored by and all the people yelled to tell him he was swimming the wrong way. Nate flopped over on his back and waved and then turned to head toward *Sandpiper* where he floated for a while looking up at the masthead towering over the water. He kept looking up at the rig and then at an Out Island 41 across the way. He liked the tall main and mizzen even though the boat itself was tubby and he was looking at the masts when he heard a splash. Someone had dived in and he didn't know who until Rilee surfaced nearby with a huge smile on her face. She threw her arms around Nate's neck and laughed and kissed his mouth full of salt water. She was wearing a different bathing suit and even without a mask he could see what she looked like. Her skin was against his and she was so close he had to tread water a long time just to gather his composure. He watched her splashing about and when she dived deep, he could see her legs and her hips and the vision of her was so erotic he couldn't calm down. Nate had to dive deep and stay below until his lungs were screaming just to get his body under control. When he exploded to the surface, Rilee came close again.

"Wow," she said. "You can hold your breath forever."

Nate couldn't tell her he had nearly drowned down there because of her. Someone else splashed behind them and little Debra sputtered to the surface wearing a suit she must have ordered from the Terri Lee doll catalog.

"Let's swim to the beach," she said. "No one's there yet. It's not that far."

"I'll get the dive gear," Nate said. "It'll make the swim easier."

"Isn't that cheating?" Debra asked. "You don't think we can make it."

"The water is so clear it'll be nice to see. I'll go aboard and get it all."

Rilee and Debra hung onto the dinghy while Nate climbed the swim ladder. He stepped into the cockpit where he saw Jenson making coffee by himself in the galley.

"How was your night?" Nate asked.

Jenson gave him a funny look and then grinned and shook his head.

"What a day yesterday was," he said. "What a night."

Nate opened the cockpit locker and collected the dive gear and then looked down at Jenson.

"I didn't hear a thing," he said. "Want to swim to the beach with us?"

"No. I'm moving too slow today. Have fun. Steve and I can motor over in the dinghy if he ever wakes up."

Nate stepped over to the transom where he handed the masks and fins to Debra waiting near the swim ladder. He pulled on his fins and spit into the mask to keep it from fogging and then jumped from the ladder. Nate waited until they were a long way off before he swam up to Rilee. She reached over and took his hand and they kicked for the cove, side by side, with Debra trailing behind.

They reached the deep sand of the beach where they took the dive gear off and splashed around in the shallows before walking up to the big palm trees near the entrance to the grotto. Nate looked at Rilee's bikini again and the colors reminded him of one of Carmen Miranda's hats. The suit was tiny and there were little bandana ties at the hips that made him want to loosen them. He was glad no one else was there to see.

Rilee ducked through the narrow passage and entered the cavern and looked around like she had in the cave over on Norman Island. The sun was shining through an opening on the back side of a huge boulder, up and to the left, and through some smaller tunnels at the end of the little lagoon. The light was soft and indirect and it made the water look like it was glowing fluorescent green and blue in the grotto. Debra and Rilee waded into the shallows and looked at the flashing light and at the shadows and at the clear water lapping at the sand. Nate slipped over to the slanting boulder on the left and sat down to watch. Rilee swished her hands through the water like she was trying to pick up liquid azurite and then she waded out of the water and sat next to Nate. He put his arm over her shoulders and held her close and they sat for a long time in the shadows and in the soft light from above.

"I want to stay here with you," Rilee said. "I can't imagine the life we'd have."

Nate held Rilee for a moment longer and she kissed him again with that softness he had never felt before.

"Hey, you two," Debra said. "Someone is coming."

Nate thought it might be Steve and Jenson. He bolted for the water and stretched into a racing dive but it felt more like a belly flop when he hit. Nate took a long stroke and then another and pulled up at the end of the pool in a few seconds. He stopped to clear his face and turned around just as Steve mashed himself through the entrance.

"Hey, Jenson," he yelled. "Look at this place."

Rilee stood and looked away at the light from behind and then she waded into the water and splashed herself over the shoulders and up around her face. She turned and smiled at Nate. Jenson squeezed through and he looked around and heard the Swiss Alps echo and he cleared his throat.

"I diddled the old lady, too," he shouted.

Steve looked up at the quiet light settling through the openings above.

"Is there a way to climb to the top and get outside? I'd like to check the view."

"Yes," Nate said, "but you might want to wear shoes. I can run out in the dinghy and bring some back."

"Can Nate swim out through the cave with us and go around to the dinghy?" Rilee asked.

"Yeah," Steve said, "but don't take too much time. We'll be here waiting."

Rilee and Debra fell backward into the water and kicked toward the light pouring through the rocks at the end. They slipped through the opening into the sunlight beyond where Nate took a huge breath. Rilee came over and grabbed his waist and made him stop and then she was kissing him full of salt water again. Debra swam over and hugged Rilee from behind.

"God, I thought you two were dead meat," she said.

They swam back to the dinghy but Nate hadn't recovered from the close call. They threw the dive gear aboard and pushed the little boat into the water.

"Are you okay?" Rilee asked.

"I'm sorry," Nate said. "That scared me."

"Me, too."

Nate could see in her eyes that it did and it reminded him of Sunday again. He hugged her and then stepped into the dinghy. There were a lot of charter boats coming in and several more already anchored and it wasn't going to be very long before The Baths would be too crowded. They motored through the fleet and reached *Sandpiper* where Rilee and Debra scrambled aboard to find some books to read beneath the bimini while Steve and Jenson scaled the Alps. Nate went below and pulled on a pair of boat shoes and then stepped up the companionway. Rilee was stretched out on her back on the cockpit cushion but her Carmen Miranda suit was so tiny he could see a good deal of her body. Rilee caught him looking and she sat up and glanced over at Debra and then she took Nate's hand and led him down into the salon where she turned to face him.

"I am so sorry," she said. "You don't know how many times I've wanted to make love to you. Here I am parading around like it didn't matter. I love it when you look at me but, God, it's frustrating for me, too."

"This isn't going to get any easier. I have to leave or Steve will wonder what happened. I wish I weren't so honorable."

Rilee looked at Nate and then reached up and pulled him to her and they stood together for a long time. He was breaking inside from the frustration and when she rested her head on his chest, he knew she could feel his heart pounding. She squeezed him close and then let him go and he turned and stepped up the ladder. Debra smiled and handed him the two pairs of deck shoes. Nate climbed down into the dinghy and started the Mercury and reached to untie the painter. Rilee leaned over the rail.

"Hurry back," she said. "I don't want to worry."

The little outboard only had six horsepower and the dinghy was huge. Nate opened the throttle and it motored like a snow plow toward the beach. There were a lot of small boats pulled up on the sand so he headed for an opening and never shut the outboard down until he lifted the propeller clear of the water. The dinghy hit the beach hard. He jumped from the stern and dragged the boat high and then nearly ran through the opening to the grotto. Steve and Jenson were sitting on a boulder watching all the other charter people when he came into the cave. They slipped on the shoes and started up the slanted granite without saying anything. Nate was a little paranoid for a minute and then Steve turned around to face him.

"You should have brought some of those Schaefers back," he said, and he slapped Nate's back and stepped away up the slope.

"Hey, Steve," Jenson said. "Slow up. I'm out of shape."

Steve picked his way out into the sunlight and searched for a way to climb the highest rocks. Jenson caught up and turned around and yelled back down into the cave.

"I diddled the old lady, too," he shouted again.

Echoes of laughter poured from the grotto all the way out into the sun. Steve and Jenson took off to climb the boulders. Nate sat down on a rock nearly perfect and smooth and looked out on Drake's Channel where there were several dozen charter boats beating against the wind that had dropped to only twelve knots. The hulls were stark white against the blue of the channel. He wished he had asked Rilee to come. He was still reeling from what she told him and he could feel himself burning again just thinking of her so close. He got up to move around and look for another path to the top. He didn't much care to be around Steve, but he retraced his steps and resigned himself to the job. He waited near the roof entrance to the cave and when they both came huffing up nearly out of breath, Steve's face had turned crimson. Nate glanced at Jenson who just shrugged. They set off down into the grotto with Steve complaining about the beer.

Sandpiper was a good distance out and when the dinghy finally coasted to a stop near the stern quarter, Steve went below straight away while Nate stepped into the shade in the cockpit. A can of Schaefer flew through the companionway. Nate caught it and popped it nearly in one motion and then sat down with Jenson who caught another. They drank the beer and looked beyond the stern toward Drake's Channel. Rilee stepped out wearing a pair of tight shorts and a top that were so Caribbean blue they matched the color of her eyes. The dancing was back and her smiles were electric. Nate could feel his heart beating again. Jenson stared at her, too.

"If Debra comes out looking like that," he said, "I don't think we'll stay in the cockpit very long."

Rilee giggled and winked at Nate and that was enough to get the burning started again. He had to leave to get cleaned up. Rilee stopped him with her hand on his bare waist and when he stepped down the ladder, his heartbeat was deafening. He made his way forward to the locker where he stowed his things and looked around for something decent to wear. All he could find was a red golf shirt with a North Carolina State Wolfpack logo stitched on the front where a pocket would be. Nate pulled it out along with a fairly new pair of shorts and a towel and the shaving kit and then went into the head. Rilee was everywhere again. He glanced at the Carmen Miranda bathing suit hanging on a hook and then he swallowed and turned on the cold water.

The golf shirt still fit and the shorts weren't ragged like all the others. Nate hoped Rilee understood he was just a part-time yacht driver. After the shower he stopped in the galley for another beer and then stepped up the ladder to the cock-pit where Debra greeted him with a wolf whistle. Nate could feel his face turn crimson like Steve's at the top of the boulders. Rilee got in the act and hugged Nate's neck. He could tell she meant it and the heat from his face went straight to his stomach.

"Let's go sailing," Steve said. "I'm tired of hanging around all these other boats."

"We can't leave yet," Jenson shouted from below. "I'm serving Vichyssoise and chilled chardonnay for lunch."

Steve stepped back to the stern rail and looked down the channel. Rilee patted the seat next to her and then pulled Nate down where he leaned against the coaming and looked at her face. He wanted to tell her out loud that Sunday would never come, but Steve turned around and slipped behind the wheel.

"Hey, Jenson. Where's the soup?" he yelled.

Rilee took a sip of the Schaefer and handed the can back to Nate. She turned around to face Steve.

"Would you like anything?"

"Maybe one of those rum and tonics you like so much," he said.

Rilee just nodded and stepped down the ladder. Jenson brought out the Vichyssoise and they ate in the cockpit and drank a lot of wine except for Steve who insisted on more rum and tonic. The lunch ended when Steve reached down and lit the Perkins off. Nate walked forward to lift the anchor with the windlass. Rilee followed him up to help and when the plow came loose from the bottom, she stayed near while Steve spun the wheel and idled away from The Baths and from the charter fleet jammed in the cove. Nate kept watching from the bow rail as *Sandpiper* motored to the north past a sandy beach set off by more boulders. Rilee sat on the other side of the rail and put her feet on his and watched the quiet beach slide by in the distance.

"Is it time to get the rags up?" Steve yelled. "I'll swing out into the channel and turn into the wind."

After Nate and Rilee hauled the main in place and unfurled the jib, *Sandpiper* heeled gently to the breeze. Nate watched Virgin Gorda slip by while they sailed to the north toward the little islets everyone called The Dogs. Rilee leaned on the cockpit coaming next to Nate on the leeward side and looked forward through the slots at the cays ahead. Nate was staring at Rilee, watching her hair blowing in the wind, but a towel came whistling over and hit him. Debra leaned toward Nate and whispered.

"Steve is right behind, you big goof," she said. "You two are a bigger mess than I thought."

Debra gave Nate a push and then turned to Steve.

"Are you ready for a beer?" she asked.

"I'd like one, too," Rilee said.

Debra fished four cold cans from the refrigerator and set them out on the cockpit. Nate handed one to Rilee, but Jenson was sitting out on the cabin roof near the starboard shrouds. Nate carried the beer out to him and sat down to look out at the hills of Virgin Gorda and to try to avoid staring at Rilee. Jenson leaned over and there was an awkward moment before he finally cleared his throat.

"Has Rilee talked to you yet?" he asked. "About her situation with Steve?"

There was more to the story than two couples chartering a boat in the Caribbean, but Nate was uncomfortable asking her. He was deathly afraid of her answers.

"No, I haven't. Sometimes I think it might be better if I just let it go. Sunday will be here, anyway, and it's going to be..."

"Be what?" Jenson interrupted. "The end? I still think you should talk to her. No one knows what will happen. I can see from a mile away you two have the magic going. Sunday may not be what you think. You just need to talk to her. You might not like what she has to say. At least you will know how complicated things can be. You also have to know this, that she is absolutely nuts over you. Sunday is going to be a train wreck for all of us."

"I don't know how this happened," Nate said. "The moment I saw Rilee in the cockpit last Sunday, I was nearly speechless there was so much electricity in the air. I didn't know her from Adam's housecat, but the magic was there already. I can sit here with you now and tell you straight away, I have never felt anything like this in my life. When she walks up that dock on Sunday, I'll never be the same again."

"Just talk to her, okay? There are things she can't change. I never dreamed I had a chance with Debra, either. Here we are married ten years and the honeymoon has never ended."

Nate smiled and looked back at the cockpit where Debra was sitting. She laughed and blew him a kiss. Jenson carried the empty cans back to the cockpit where Debra met him with a hug and a giggle and they both went below. Nate watched Steve at the helm working the wheel. Rilee came out of the companionway with a tumbler and she handed it to him and then sat on the windward coaming where Debra had been. Nate would have given anything to go back to the cockpit and sit with her again and feel her touch and to look into her eyes, but he had to look away because Steve was there. Nate pulled himself up by the shrouds and turned and walked forward to the bow rail where he leaned against the forestay and watched George Dog slide by to the west.

SIXTEEN

Nate stayed out on the bow rail watching the foam peel away from the stem. The water looked deep and blue, like the headers on a Harley-Davidson twin, and it felt like he was staring into a separate universe. He stared into the water a moment longer and then walked back to the cockpit to help tack through the wind. Rilee had fallen asleep on one of the cushions. Nate sat on the coaming trying to steal glances when he could at her face, so calm and at peace he couldn't bring himself to wake her. Steve reached for his empty tumbler and held it out.

"Do you mind?" he asked.

Nate took the glass and stepped below to mix another rum and tonic. Jenson and Debra were sitting together at the dinette looking at the BVI chart. After Nate made the rum for Steve, Debra came over and stood close.

"Jenson is so very right," she said. "I don't know how you can manage it, but I think you need to talk to Rilee before Sunday happens. It really might be the end if you don't and it won't be just you and Rilee who will be hurting. We think the world of you. When we go back home, it's painful to think you won't be part of our lives anymore."

Nate tried to smile. He kept fumbling around with the lid to the tonic. She took the bottle away and pulled his face down to hers and kissed his cheek.

"When I see you looking at Rilee, and I see the look on her face when you're near, I get goose bumps myself," she whispered. "Don't let it go."

"I haven't asked Rilee why she's still with Steve," Nate said. "I don't know that I will ever understand. There are some complications for me, as well. I just want you to know I've never had a week like this one. If Rilee walks away, I'll never get over it and I will never forget you two. I'm surviving this with only one tiny hope, that somehow Sunday cannot happen." Nate stood in the galley trying to find his breath. "I have dreams of Rilee," he said. "When I lie there alone at night in the dark thinking about her, I know you are right. If she only knew."

"She does know, you big goofball," Debra said. "She loves you and as the days go by, she just gets more helpless. She doesn't want you to know how bad it is. All you have to do is look at her and you can tell. Here. You better take this out to Steve."

She handed him the rum and then she slapped him in the rear when he turned to go up the companionway. Nate handed the drink to Steve and then sat on the cushion and glanced at Rilee again. He was thinking about how beautiful she was and then her eyes opened and she looked at him and smiled. Their eyes met and he felt like he was staring into that separate blue universe again and he knew straight away Debra was right. Nate could have leaned over and told her there was going to be no Sunday. In his heart there were only pins and needles and barking puppies and the rush of a stream in a field of green somewhere beyond the sea. He glanced at Steve and then looked over at Virgin Gorda.

"Steve," he said, "it might be a good time to tack and head for the pass in the reef over near Prickly Pear Island."

Steve took a big slug of his rum and tonic and put the tumbler in the holder on the binnacle.

"Here we go," he yelled.

Nate scrambled to cut the jib loose while Steve spun the wheel. Rilee sat up and grabbed the line and took a wrap or two around the primary and hauled the jib in on the starboard side. When they sheeted the sails home, they were headed well east of the pass. *Sandpiper* settled in again on the new course. Steve looked over at Rilee.

"Would you like to steer, now?" he asked. "I've had my time."

Rilee stood on the cockpit cushion and climbed behind the wheel. Steve drained his rum and got to his feet.

"I'm opening the bar again if anyone is interested in afternoon cocktails," he announced, and he disappeared below with the empty plastic tumbler.

Nate slid closer to Rilee and pointed out the spot near the island where there was a pass through the reef to give her an idea where to steer.

"I had another dream about you while I was asleep," she whispered.

Rilee started blushing. Nate touched her face with his hand and he wanted to tell her about his dreams of her in that field of green, but he took his hand away and looked off to the reef in the distance. Jenson brought a rum and Coke for each of them. Rilee took one while Nate set the other in the cup holder. He slid down on the seat and leaned against the coaming and watched Rilee at the helm while she approached the pass through the coral.

"Can you take the wheel?" she asked. "I'm afraid I might brush the bottom."

"I'll watch from here," Nate said. "You can do this."

They entered the pass where *Sandpiper* straightened up briefly when she hit the wind shadow of Prickly Pear. The motion made Rilee take a deep breath, but the boat heeled to the wind again and sailed through the lee of the island and slipped into the calm water of the sound. Rilee steered the boat to port and they managed a couple of short tacks that carried them up to the Bitter End Yacht Club where they let *Sandpiper* round into the wind. Jenson dropped the plow over the side seventy yards short of the dock. Nate snapped the sail covers in place and then stood on the deck and looked at the yacht club and at the cottages stepping up the hill.

"Good place for a honeymoon," he said to Jenson.

Rilee looked at him sideways and then she giggled and pushed him away. Jenson glanced over and smiled.

"You're right," he said. "I'd like to take Debra ashore so we can go into the yacht club bar for drinks. Care to join us?"

"I'd like that," Rilee said. "Debra and I need to go below to freshen up. Do we have time?"

In a few minutes Debra came out pretending a Betty Boop pose and then she flashed her diamond in Nate's face.

"A lady needs an escort," she said.

Nate laughed and took her hand.

"No, goof," she whispered. "Not me…Rilee."

Nate looked away toward the sun fading in the west and then he turned back.

"I'm running out of time, aren't I?" he said.

"Yes, you are," Debra said quietly. "I wish Steve had finished that bottle of rum by himself this afternoon. He didn't, and now Rilee will have to be with him tonight because he'll be worthless by nine o'clock and she has to be there."

"I know. Maybe I should stay aboard and not be the odd man out again. This is your vacation and I'm not supposed to interfere."

"Baloney. Rilee will rake me over the coals if I let you stay behind."

Nate stepped through the companionway into the gloom of the cabin and made his way to the forward head where he leaned over the sink and let the water run cool against his skin. He dried his face and added a little after shave and checked the Wolfpack shirt in the mirror. He left the head compartment and took a deep breath and tried to calm himself. Jenson opened the door of the aft cabin and laughed.

"Yow, I'm ready for this," he said. "Yacht clubs are so civilized."

Nate shut the companionway hatch behind them while Jenson pulled the painter up short to hold the dinghy in place. Rilee came first and put her hands on Nate's shoulders to steady herself. She looked him square in the eyes and the air between them crackled like that moment after a lightning flash. Debra came down the ladder and did the same. She leaned even closer.

"I saw that," she whispered. "You two are hopeless."

She giggled and then stepped into the dinghy. Nate let Steve and Jenson fend for themselves and when the Mercury raced to life, they motored off to the yacht club. They walked into the Clubhouse Bar just as the sun turned the sky crimson over the hills to the west. The soft, pink light made Rilee's face look the same as it did that evening on *Sandpiper* when she stopped to look at Nate in the glow of the nightlights. He tried not to watch and kept his distance, but in a moment she turned to look at him and there was nothing else in the world that mattered. Jenson walked over and spoke quietly.

"I've been staring, too," he said. "She's beautiful, anyway, but she is simply radiant when you are around. I have no idea what to do. Let's go get a single malt and think about it."

The Clubhouse Bar fluttered with the burgees of yacht clubs from all over the world. Jenson pretended to look at them, waiting to see where Rilee would sit to be sure there was an empty place next to her. Nate was embarrassed it should have to be that way and it made him feel like a sneak. When the waiter came over, Jenson ordered three rum drinks and a pair of snifters half-full of Glenfiddich. He handed one to Nate not knowing he didn't care for Scotch. Jenson stood and presented a toast.

"Here's to the finest captain in the entire Caribbean," he announced. "Thank you for agreeing to come along on such short notice, my friend. You are the best."

Nate wanted to slip beneath the table because everyone in the place watched while Debra and Steve and Rilee stood in his honor. He could feel his face flush and his rear end itch and he sipped the Scotch out of nervousness. It went down like velvet gasoline.

Steve ordered another round. Nate settled for a pint of John Courage. Rilee only ordered a glass of white wine when Debra ordered her's, but Steve and Jenson were out to party. The waiter kept the rum coming and got them loaded in no time. Steve wanted dinner and when he got up to look at the menu in the grill, Rilee grabbed Nate's arm and held it close.

"I am so sorry," she said. "I don't want to be here. I was hoping we could be alone somehow. Now, I don't know. Anyway, you are the finest captain."

Rilee leaned close and kissed Nate's ear just before Steve walked back into the bar.

"I took the liberty of ordering steak and lobster for everyone," Steve said. "I hope that's okay."

"Relax," Debra whispered to Nate. "Steve can afford it. There's a lot of money at the table."

Nate looked up at the waiter who had come back.

"I'd like another Courage," he said.

Jenson ordered bottles of red and white wine while Steve gulped it down like Kool-Aid. When dinner was over at nine thirty, Jenson paid the bill with a credit card and with Nate's help, they both got Steve to his feet and walked with him back to the dock where the dinghy waited. They motored slowly back to *Sandpiper* and when they coasted up to the ladder, Steve rallied himself and climbed aboard. Nate followed but he was worn out from the tension. He sat down in the cockpit alone while the others went below to sort out the night. He was looking up at the cottages on the side of the hill when he heard Debra whisper from the companionway.

"Want some company?" she asked. "Jenson is snoring already and I'm still wound up. You look worried sitting out here by yourself."

Debra looked around at the lights and at the still, dark water and she yawned and shook her hair and ran her fingers over her eyes.

"I think this has been one of the best weeks of my life," she said. "Jenson is such a peach for giving me my ring. I can't get over Rilee, either. She loves you. You have to know that."

"Well, when I saw her looking at the glow of the sunset, I could have walked over and picked her up and carried her off to one of the cottages and locked the door behind us. If I had done that, I'd be a lot happier. I just wish right now she'd come back out and say good night."

"You know how Steve can be possessive when he's been drinking. I don't know if she can sneak away. Want me to see?"

"I guess not," Nate said. "I'm just insecure enough to want her to come out on her own. That's just me, but I'll never sleep if she doesn't. I won't sleep, anyway. Who am I trying to kid?"

"I'm sorry you didn't have time to talk tonight. Sunday is so close."

"I know. There hasn't been the time or the place. It isn't like I'm trying to avoid anything. I was hoping after we got back tonight we'd have the chance to be alone for a bit. It just didn't happen."

"You know I can't tell you anything. It has to come from her. I can tell you she's been unhappy for a long time, partly because of Steve who is obviously an alcoholic and needs help, but there are other things in her life that have put her in a very different situation. Promise me you will ask. She's crazy about you and that's all she talks about when we are alone. This has been a week for all of us. I've never seen Rilee in love before and I've known her for years. Jenson and I would give anything to see her stay that way."

Nate looked over at the yacht club still lit for business and at the other charter boats swinging in the quiet night wind and at the lights from the little cottages that snuggled silently up the hill. Rilee never came out from the forepeak. Debra hugged him and went below, but he followed her down to find the blanket and pillow. The nightlights were on and the glow turned the cabin the soft red of the evening sunset. He kept thinking how beautiful Rilee was in that light and how he felt inside when she turned to look at him. Nate waited as long as he could, hoping Rilee would open the door to the forepeak and step out. It didn't happen and he had to climb the ladder to the cockpit alone. A hollow feeling settled in and he leaned against the bulkhead and closed his eyes. He missed seeing Rilee and he missed saying good night, as fleeting as it might have been. He tried to see her face again in the sunset but her image kept fading away.

The wind from the east swirled through the anchorage while *Sandpiper* nestled in the lee of the hills. Nate could feel the mast pumping slightly and he kept thinking it must be Steve. He rolled over and buried his head in the pillow to keep from going crazy. He finally couldn't take it anymore and went below where there was an open liter of Mt. Gay on the counter. He poured the rum and emptied the bottle and wondered why he had bothered with the glass. He carried the rum back into the cockpit and drank it down and waited for the spinning to start.

Nate sat alone in the dark trying to see Rilee's face again, thinking how the color of her eyes looked so much like the sea and the way her hair flowed so loose and free in the wind. He thought of the way she giggled when he mentioned the cottages on the hill and how she danced that afternoon in Drake's Pub and what he would do if he never had her alone again before she had to leave. He knew he wouldn't be able to handle the cold silence that would take over on Sunday afternoon. The mast kept pumping and a loose halyard kept banging away somewhere and the cockpit cushion was thin and hard and when the spinning took over at last, Nate buried his face again and only thought about screaming.

/) SEVENTEEN /)

Nate woke at dawn with a mouth full of dried molasses and a gut full of anger and nausea. He leaned against the bulkhead with his eyes shut while he tried to clear his head. The breeze had picked up during the night and the fresh wind sent *Sandpiper* hunting about on her anchor line. Even that slight motion made Nate dizzy. He could feel the mast pumping again and it made him think of Steve and Rilee in the forepeak. He sat alone in the cockpit feeling rotten. He didn't think anyone would be awake for another hour but he couldn't stay there wallowing in self pity. He sneaked below and changed into a pair of dirty cutoffs.

Nate grabbed the rocket fins and mask and climbed the companionway ladder and stood near the rail to look around the anchorage. The water in Gorda Sound was cloudy and it made him wonder how many of the charter boats used holding tanks. He felt like he was drowning in excrement anyway, so he jumped in and put the mask and fins on and started swimming toward Prickly Pear Island.

On the south side of the island there was a small point of land that had a strip of white sand. Nate swam for a long time in that direction until he could stand and walk onto the beach. He turned and looked back at *Sandpiper*, just one of a dozen little dots a half-mile away, and then he flopped on the sand and stretched out full length and let the morning sun dry his skin. He could feel the waves of exhaustion in his arms and legs. The molasses taste was still there and the nausea faded in and out like bad WWV reception. All he thought about was the pumping away during the night.

After a few minutes of the solitude and the quiet and the blue of the sky reaching overhead for an eternity, Nate shut his eyes and nearly fell asleep. The sand dried and stuck to his back and his head and he finally stood to wade in the water and wash away the tickling. Nate thought he should start swimming again but when he looked toward the anchorage, he could see Jenson coming down the sound in the dinghy. He sat on the sand and waited a few minutes while the boat ran up on the beach. Jenson hopped over the side and slapped Nate's shoulder.

"I'm sorry," Jenson said. "Debra got worried when she went out on deck and you were gone. So was I, to tell you the truth."

"I didn't mean to scare anyone. I just needed to exorcise some demons. Anyone else awake?"

"Rilee was in the shower when I left or I would have brought her along. I think Steve is still down for the count. My wife was just anxious about you so here I am. I wanted to wait for Rilee."

"I wish you had, but don't worry about it. I'm about ready to throw Steve to the sharks, anyway. I came over here to calm down."

Jenson sat on the sand a few feet away and looked out over the sound.

"You have an amazing life here. We're paying thousands just to sail around for a week and you do this for a living. How do you stand it?"

"I don't know. I'm supposed to quit after this week and go down islands with *Serendipity*. I didn't expect a charter like this. I'm not sure of anything after Sunday. Maybe I'll just go back to Key West and stay drunk for the rest of my life."

Jenson looked at Nate for a second. He stood and held out his hand to help Nate to his feet.

"You know, I can't interfere with Rilee's life. I won't lie to you, though. You are the best thing that ever happened to her. I have to repeat what my wife said. Don't give it up. Let's go back and get some coffee."

They pushed the dinghy into the water and motored back up the sound. When they were still a hundred yards out, Nate could see Rilee standing near the stern rail brushing her hair. They drifted up to the transom where she caught the painter and tied it off to a cleat. Nate handed her the rocket fins. She took his hand and pulled him up and kissed him full on the mouth and it didn't matter that he tasted like stale molasses because she didn't let him go until Jenson started complaining about cold coffee. Rilee took the rocket fins and the mask and laid them out on the cabin roof and then she came back and stood near Nate.

"I hated last night," she said. "I didn't see you again after we came back. A dozen times I wanted to get up and go out to the cockpit. I was just too afraid. I couldn't do it. I missed you all night long."

"I couldn't sleep, either, even after I drank a huge shot of Mt. Gay. I had all these nightmares about you and Steve together. I woke up and they were still there. I couldn't stand it. I jumped in the water and swam to the beach down there. It's a good thing Jenson showed up or I'd still be trying to swim back."

Rilee took Nate by the arm and they stepped below for coffee. He sneaked into the head for a few minutes and changed into dry clothes and then brushed the molasses taste away. When he opened the door again, Jenson handed him two mugs of coffee. Nate carried them outside where Rilee sat on the cabin roof. It seemed so natural to be with her he forgot about Steve for a few minutes. They laughed about Jenson's thin coffee and when the quiet took over, they looked about at the yacht club and all the other charter boats crowded around. Rilee glanced at Nate for a second and she started laughing again and trying to kiss him at the same time. Their teeth were clacking and they had to stop it got so silly, but when Jenson came out and whispered something about Steve, the anger came flooding back. Rilee shook her head and frowned and stood to leave. She held Nate's hand for a moment and then she took the empty cups and walked away.

"Hey, Nate," Jenson said. "Steve wants you to look at the BVI chart. He wants to find a place where no one else goes, just to have a real island experience. What do you think?"

Nate stepped below where it looked like a team meeting with all five of them huddled around the dinette. He squeezed in next to Rilee, this time on purpose, and looked at the chart. It was hard not to be serious because it was already Friday. Nate scanned the islands and pointed to the back side of Tortola.

"We can sail around into Cane Garden Bay," he said. "There are a lot of beach bars and a famous tire swing. We can leave from there and go on down to St. John to clear customs."

Steve looked at the chart through some bloodshot eyes. He shook his head.

"No, that's not it," he said. "Isn't there a place where we can go where there aren't any other tourists? I'm tired of being surrounded by all these other boats."

"Well, Brewer's Bay on Tortola might work. It's off-limits to charter boats. We can sneak in there if you want to run the risk of being yelled at by the locals. More than likely we'll be the only ones there."

"You know, all they can do is tell us to leave," Jenson said. "Let's try it out. How soon can we be ready to go?"

"Soon as we stow everything," Nate said. "It's a good sail down there. Lots of wind if we go offshore."

Steve climbed out into the cockpit to start the engine. Nate stayed behind for a minute to fold the chart, but he only wanted to be with Rilee. She edged over to him and put her head on his chest and he felt the chill of Sunday all over again. He buried his face in her hair and breathed. She looked up at him and her eyes were watering again and the ache inside came back along with the tension and the fear. When Nate heard Steve talking to Jenson about the anchor, he had to let Rilee go. She hugged him and then they both stepped up into the cockpit to get *Sandpiper* ready for the long downwind run on the Atlantic side of Tortola.

They sailed out of Gorda Sound through the pass below Prickly Pear Island and bore away on a broad starboard reach where the apparent wind dropped to nothing and the heat on the deck climbed into three digits. *Sandpiper* ticked off the miles until they were well off from Virgin Gorda and into deep water blue enough to match the Gulf Stream. Rilee brought a beer for Nate and they sat on the stern rail and watched the foam and the long swells roll up from behind. It was a nice time for them. Nate didn't want it to stop, but they had to jibe over onto a broad reach again with the wind on the port side. He fiddled with the sheets to get the sails drawing on the new course while Steve aimed for the point of land just east of the bay. *Sandpiper* wanted to roll a little more and flog the jib once in a while. Nate was sorry he hadn't held the starboard reach longer. He walked back to his spot near the stern rail. Steve gave the wheel to Jenson and then sat in the cockpit with Rilee while he sailed toward Tortola with the boat rolling heavily at times.

Around three in the afternoon, they closed on the entrance to Brewer's Bay. Jenson looked beyond the mouth of the cove where he could see the thick line of coral heads in the center.

"Nate, come take the wheel," he said. "I don't want to steer through all of that."

Steve and Jenson furled the sails while Nate took the helm and started the engine. *Sandpiper* slowed to a crawl. On the west side of the bay there was a narrow swath of sand in a canyon between two reefs. He followed it all the way into the head of the anchorage where they dropped the plow over the side in twelve feet of water so clear you could count the links in the anchor chain on the bottom. Nate shut the diesel down and the quiet swept down from the hills. They stood on the deck looking around at the water and at the thin, palm lined beach and at the green hills that towered above the bay. All they could hear was the shore break that lapped and hissed on the sand. On the wall of the reef to the west, the healthy color of the coral stood out even in the deep water. Nate looked to the other side at the reef that clogged the center of the bay just to be sure *Sandpiper* had room to swing. They were the only charter boat around. Steve turned to Nate and waved his hands.

"I've only dreamed of places like this," he said. "I didn't think there were any left."

"There aren't very many," Nate said. "I don't think this one will last long before a beach bar shows up."

Debra and Jenson held hands near the bow and stared at the hills all around and at the deserted beach that lined the head of the bay. Steve was looking over the side at the wall of coral when Rilee sneaked over and planted a kiss on Nate's lips.

"Let's get in the water," she whispered.

Nate waited while Rilee and Debra changed below. They both came out wearing the same Virgin Gorda postage stamps from the day before. Nate took one look at Rilee and his stomach felt like he just swallowed another fifth of Glenfiddich. He had to look away to keep Steve from noticing, but he didn't see how anyone could blame him for staring. Rilee looked up from the cockpit seat and saw how hopeless it was for Nate. She stood and whispered in his ear.

"I wore this on purpose," she said, and then she pinched his side before diving off the transom.

Nate reached into the locker for the elephant gun and stood near the stern rail to watch Rilee tread water for a moment. When she swam away to join Debra, he jumped into the water and rolled over on his back and kicked alone toward the coral wall. There were sergeant-majors and angelfish and a school of blue runners sweeping through and the cold, gaping mouth of a five-foot moray hiding in a hole. Nate watched the eel pumping its jaws and swaying in the slight current and at one point it slithered fully from its cave. Nate backpedaled toward deeper water just to give it some room. Rilee surprised him with a giggle and he turned to watch her swim toward him. He pointed into the shadows. She jumped and grabbed his arm, but the moray never stopped its pumping and swaying. Rilee smiled at Nate around her mouthpiece and then kicked toward a parrotfish grazing along the wall. Nate followed behind but it was torture for him not to stare at her body. They swam slowly along the coral looking at the colors and at the fish and at the white sand on the bottom. When the sun sank low on the other side of the hills, they turned back along the wall and kicked toward *Sandpiper* with Debra just behind.

Nate helped the two of them with the dive gear when they scrambled aboard. He handed Rilee the elephant gun and she cradled it while he climbed up the swim ladder. He stood on the transom again, but Rilee hesitated before going below. She kept looking in Nate's eyes and all the Monarchs and Painted Ladies rushed through again.

"I'll be right back," she whispered.

Jenson handed a rum and Coke to Nate. He drank from the tumbler and sat on the cockpit cushion with his eyes shut. He started to nod off but then Rilee kissed him on the forehead. Her wet hair fell across his face and he opened his eyes and looked at her in the evening shadows. She stayed close for a long time until Steve stepped up through the companionway carrying a pair of fresh drinks. He handed another to Nate.

"You look tired, Nate," he said. "I think you need this to get recharged."

"Can I give it to Rilee? I need to go below for a shower."

"Sure. We might drink all the rum if you don't hurry."

The shower trickled in a pair of warm streams down Nate's back. He leaned against the bulkhead and let the water run. Rilee would be gone soon and he couldn't stop the clock. Sunday would come without any resolution and that would be the beginning of a trail into the shadows that led to where, Nate didn't know. When the water ran cold, the sound of the pump labored away until he closed the valve. He toweled off and dressed quickly and when he opened the door, Steve was standing there with more rum and Coke. Nate took a long swallow and could feel the rum burning its way down. He stepped out into the cockpit where Rilee grinned at him.

"I loved diving on the reef," she said. "That moray was scary, but I'm glad I got to see it."

"Big one," Nate said. "Probably here because there aren't any charter boat people to torture the poor thing."

Rilee took his hand and pulled him down. He leaned against the coaming just as Steve came out.

"Does Jenson have anything planned for dinner?" Steve asked. "I'm starved. No one has said anything about eating."

"I'll cook," Debra said. "I'm not getting sick down there, anymore."

Rilee smiled at Nate and then disappeared down the companionway. Nate excused himself and walked up to the bow in the fading light and looked out over the deserted waters of the bay. A sliver of moon wouldn't make an appearance for several hours and when the sky faded around the boat, the water turned nearly black. They were well inside the wind shadow of the hills and so the anchor line hung straight down. *Sandpiper* floated rock still on the water that looked more like Caro syrup. Nate leaned against the bow rail and looked back at Steve still drinking and at Jenson still laughing and he sagged down until he was sitting on the deck in the dark wondering how he could get through the next two days. He could hear the slap and the hiss of the shore break behind and had an idea to take the dinghy in and go for a walk on the beach. He stayed in the bow by himself looking around at the water and at the stars and at the lights glowing dim at the top of the hills. Jenson yelled in his direction.

"Hey, Nate," he said. "Come on back. It's time to eat."

The five of them sat at the dinette with plates of spaghetti and glasses of wine for everyone and in a few minutes, Steve began toasting again.

"Here's to Brewer's Bay, the finest anchorage in the BVI," he said, "and here's to following winds and following seas. Here's to the two most gorgeous cooks I've ever seen."

Jenson held a bottle up and when the glasses were on the table again, he went around and refilled them all. Nate jumped up early on to do the dishes but Jenson kicked him out and made him sit with Rilee while he and Steve tried to clean up. They were both still drinking wine and when a bottle was finished, they uncorked another. Debra nudged Nate in the ribs.

"There's another case of chardonnay in the aft cabin," she said. "Steve and Jenson made sure the charter was well stocked."

"Maybe I can have a refill then," and Nate held his glass in the air.

"Me, too," Rilee said. "I don't really need it but I don't want to be left behind."

"I need to go out into the cockpit," Debra said. "I'm getting queasy again. Couldn't possibly be the wine."

They climbed the companionway ladder into the cockpit where Rilee took Nate's hand. They sat back near the wheel, partially hidden in the dark, and held hands so close Nate could feel her body pressing against his. The smell of her hair was everywhere and there were times when Nate thought he would come apart, the feelings were so intense. Rilee reached for Nate and they kissed and she put her head on his shoulder and stayed there without moving until Jenson came up the companionway with beads of sweat on his face. Rilee squeezed Nate's hand and then slid over to the other side of the cockpit.

"If I don't sit over here now," she whispered, "I'm going to tear your clothes off," and she kissed his cheek and sat back against the coaming.

Nate took a big slug of wine and looked at Jenson who had too much to drink.

"What do you think we should do with Steve?" Jenson asked. "He took a break to sit at the dinette. Now he's snoring."

Rilee and Debra stepped below and tried to wake Steve. He only mumbled a bit and started snoring again. Debra gave up and made her way back into the cockpit.

"Steve is out of it," she said. "We could try to get him up in the forepeak. Rilee said not to, just to leave him for now. She's going to come back out to sit with you for a while. Promise me you will talk."

"I promise," Nate said. "Does Rilee have any kind of curfew?"

"Not from me. Keep an eye on poor Steve, though. He can do odd things when he drinks wine like that. Give me a hug goodnight."

Nate wrapped his arms around her and she kissed him lightly on the cheek.

"Jenson loves you, and so do I," she said. "I'm going to steer my poor husband into the aft cabin and leave you and Rilee alone. Good luck."

Nate leaned against the cushion and thought about going below for the pillow and blanket. He didn't want to risk waking Steve so he sat looking out at the water, flat and dark and shiny. He could see the lights from high on the hill reflecting on the surface. They were low-watt incandescents and the glow looked more like the light from a dozen waning moons. Nate rubbed his eyes and looked out toward the reef hidden beneath the dancing moons, out where the moray pumped its jaws and waited.

A minute later Rilee stepped out of the companionway and stuffed a pillow behind Nate. She leaned next to him on the cockpit cushion where they sat for a long time looking around at the soft water in Brewer's Bay.

"Sunday is almost here," Rilee said finally. "When I have to leave, I'm going to cry in front of everyone. I don't know what will happen after that."

"When Sunday comes and you have to leave, I don't know if I can let you go."

Rilee lifted her head and looked at Nate again. There were tears welling up and it broke his heart to see them. She kissed his lips and took a deep breath. Nate could feel her breath quivering.

"I have a little girl," she said.

Nate didn't say anything just then, but inside he could feel some relief that she had to leave because of a little girl, not because of Steve or anyone else.

"Does that mean you can't make room in your life for me?"

"This week has made it seem like you are my life. It's all so complicated."

"Why? Because you have a little girl?"

"No. It's because there is so much more you don't know. Andrea doesn't belong to Steve. He married me to help care for my baby. I love him for that."

Nate could feel the chill again and there was a moment where he didn't want to hear anything more. He felt like he was on the outside looking in and there was nothing he could do about Sunday.

"I'm sorry," Nate said. "Now you're telling me you have a little girl, as if that would stop me in my tracks. It won't. If you can walk away from me on Sunday, I will understand, but you have to know. I can't even think about life after Sunday if you go."

The tears were real all of a sudden and they ran down Rilee's cheeks. She looked up at him again.

"I've stayed with Steve these past eight years only because of Andy. She is the happiest little girl you can imagine. She loves everyone and there is so much compassion and so much laughter. Because of her, I never thought I would have to worry about falling in love. She already had all of mine. Then you came along with your face turning beet red and that stupid elephant gun. You shook me to the core. I don't know if anything in my life will ever be the same."

Nate tried to breathe the pounding away. He wasn't sure what Rilee meant and he was afraid she wouldn't leave her marriage for a guy with nothing but a forty-dollar-a-day job, even if it was in Paradise. He couldn't think of what to say and he leaned his head back in the dark and watched the lights dancing on the water in the bay. Nate looked back at Rilee.

"What does Andy call Steve?"

"She just calls him by his first name. She knows her real daddy went away. You also need to know, Steve isn't a big part of her life."

"I don't understand. Why has your marriage lasted so long?"

"I can't tell you because I don't know. I married Steve before Andy was born and everything seemed so fine. He loved me in his own way. I thought we were good for each other. Then my beautiful baby was born and as time went on and she began to grow, Steve drank way too much and became more withdrawn. Suddenly, all he did was provide for her and send her to the best doctors, the best private schools. There was never any father-daughter closeness. She just calls him Steve."

"Steve doesn't seem like he would do that. Except for the drinking..."

"But you don't know the whole story." Rilee looked up again and spoke barely above a whisper. "My beautiful Andrea is a Down's baby," she said. "I was so young no one suspected anything was wrong. After she was born, the doctors told me it was the translocation type. If I get pregnant again, I run the risk of having another Down's baby. Steve couldn't handle that and now there is hardly a marriage left, except that he pays for everything to make Andy's life better."

Rilee put her face next to Nate's and she looked in his eyes for a long time and then she whispered to him again.

"Steve has been impotent."

Nate remembered nearly losing his mind in the night wind because he could feel the mast pumping and he thought it was Steve working in the forepeak and all those times with Sarah when the same thing happened to him and yet, with Rilee, he only had to look at her to be aroused. Nate felt so close to her just then it scared him to think of Sunday. He wanted to make love to her and he thought for a time it might happen they got so involved, but they had to stop when Steve moaned from below. It took a long time to regain control and they stayed in each other's arms while the waves of passion washed over them. Nate couldn't believe she had to go so soon. He wanted her to know the truth.

"Would it make any difference if I told you I could love Andy with all my heart and soul because she's part of you?"

Rilee sat up and looked at Nate. There were heavy tears streaming down her face.

"I have to go. If I don't tear myself away now, I won't be able to on Sunday."

She stopped herself and she reached over and touched Nate's face.

"Could you really love my little girl?"

"I already do, you know?"

EIGHTEEN

From the shadows of the cockpit Nate could hear Rilee talking to Steve who had managed to sit up. He leaned over into the companionway.

"Do you need any help? I can carry him if he can't walk."

"Thanks. I'm used to this. He'll get up in a minute."

Steve struggled to his feet. Rilee walked with him up to the head where he stepped in and shut the door while she stood waiting. There were still tears in her eyes. She looked at Nate and tried to smile, but then Steve came out and they disappeared together into the forepeak.

Nate gathered up the empty wineglasses in the cockpit and carried them below to put in the sink. He switched the lights off, but he thought Steve or Jenson might need to get up again and he reached over to turn on the nightlights. The cabin blushed instantly in the red glow that made Nate think of Rilee and the sunsets. He climbed into the cockpit where he curled up on the cushions and looked out at the silent water of the bay. There were images of Rilee when he shut his eyes and he kept thinking of her and how intense the night had been. He let himself slip full length on the cushion and then drifted away to sleep out of nothing more than exhaustion.

Nate slept all night, even with a dozen vivid dreams of being with Rilee. When the sun came over the hills east of the anchorage, he opened his eyes and fluffed the pillow and leaned against the bulkhead to look around. He couldn't shake the idea that in twenty-eight hours he was going to stand alone on a dock with his life upside down. Some panic set in and he had to keep busy or go crazy. Nate gathered up the rocket fins and the mask from the cabin roof and took his shirt off and was close to diving in when he thought about taking the elephant gun along. He grabbed it out of the cockpit locker and stepped over the side and splashed into the water. There were echoes from the hills and he listened until the sounds died away and then he kicked for the wall of coral flashing orange and brown and white in the distance.

A school of baitfish swam along the coral toward the mouth of the bay. Nate dived to the bottom and hid near the sand and looked up through the school backlit by the bright sky above. He let himself rise through them and they parted and formed a silver tunnel and he drifted without moving into the million tiny fish. They closed around him and it felt like being in a bubble aquarium, but the fish scattered when he reached the surface. In an instant they were gone.

He found the moray hiding in its little world of darkness, staring out to the bay and working its jaw like an angry Buster Keaton. Nate turned away and swam parallel to the reef and watched the rainbow fish and then made his way toward the deep water at the mouth of the bay. He missed seeing the grouper at first, nearly swimming by it when the fish flicked its tail and moved along the coral. Nate hung motionless on the surface and then kicked backward fifty or sixty feet so he wouldn't spook the grouper. He loaded the gun with three of the four bands and swam toward the reef where he spotted the grouper near the bottom beneath a ledge. Nate dived deep for a closer look and then lifted the elephant gun and in a flash, the grouper was hit in the thick area just behind the eyes. It bolted once and arched its backbone and hung still at the end of the spear. Nate towed the grouper to the surface where he spooled the line again and then kicked for *Sandpiper* a hundred yards away.

There were sharks around, Nate was sure, and he kept looking behind for the big shadows to appear while he swam all the way to the boat. Rilee and Debra were watching him from the cockpit. They didn't see the grouper until he got to the swim ladder. Debra started yelling at the size of it and the noise brought Jenson out on deck. He reached down and took the elephant gun and pulled the spear up on deck with the grouper on the end and let it flop into the cockpit where it lay still. Nate reached for the swim ladder and pulled himself up. Rilee wrapped her arms around him and kissed his ear and he felt stupid until she kissed him, trenchmouth and all, right on the lips. It made Nate laugh through the clacking teeth again.

"Stand on the cabin roof," Jenson said. "I want to get a picture. Let my bride hold the fish. It'll look even bigger that way."

After Jenson got his picture, Nate grabbed a fillet knife and put the fish in the bottom of the dinghy to keep the mess off of *Sandpiper*. Rilee sat near the outboard while he cut the fillets away from the bone and left a slimy pile of fish remains in the bottom of the dinghy. He handed the fillets up to Jenson and then took the painter off the cleat and told Rilee to start the Mercury. She reached for the starter rope and yanked the motor to life.

"Where to?" she asked.

Nate pointed to the mouth of the bay. Rilee turned the tiller of the motor and twisted the throttle to full bore. She was laughing at him.

"I grew up with outboards in Colorado," she shouted.

Rilee steered east around the point several hundred yards where the cliffs came right down to the water. They found a spot where the old coral heads were exposed and covered with fiddler crabs. Nate threw the remains ashore. They lodged in a crevice where the birds and the crabs would make short work of the entrails. Rilee turned the dinghy around while Nate splashed water into the bottom to keep the blood from drying. They motored all the way inside the bay to the beach where they hopped out to clean the last of the mess away. Nate was slopping water over the side when he looked up at Rilee who was watching.

"So, Andy is about eight." he said. "Where is she now?"

"Yes, she's eight years old, now...Going on four. She's with my mom in Steamboat. She loves it there. My mom adores

Andy. You should see them together." When Rilee said that, she looked away and there was an awkward moment. "I'm sorry," she said. "I wish more than anything you could see them together."

Nate glanced out at *Sandpiper*. When he didn't see anyone in the cockpit, he reached over and took Rilee's hand and drew her close.

"I meant what I said last night," he said. "Is there any chance I would ever get to see your mom and Andy?"

"I can't answer that right now, but I dreamed of you last night. We were all there and the sky was blue and everything was green. Andy was never happier in her whole life. Neither was I. Maybe it was just a dream."

They stood close together and the air was charged again like it was that night on the beach on Peter Island. Nate put his face in her hair and their hearts were beating together, but he thought about Sunday. There was a ringing in his ears that wouldn't stop.

Jenson shouted from *Sandpiper*. Nate looked toward the boat where Jenson stood waving in the cockpit. Rilee reached up and kissed his lips again and then helped to slosh the rest of the water out of the dinghy. They motored back to the boat where Jenson waited.

"Debra and I want to walk on the beach," he said. "Can you give us a lift? Steve is still asleep."

"Hop in," Rilee said. "We'd like to go, too."

They landed the dinghy in the same spot and the four of them walked together on the hard packed sand toward the eastern end of the beach. Debra turned and grabbed Nate's arm.

"I was going to ask if you had a chance to talk last night. After watching you two this morning, I decided you did and everything is good. What do you think about our Goddaughter?"

Nate looked over at Jenson who was smiling. He took Rilee's hand without one thought of Steve.

"I've had dreams, too, you know? Now there are three of us."

Rilee stopped and looked at Jenson and Debra. She squeezed Nate's hand, but then she turned and walked back toward the dinghy. When Debra ran after her, Nate thought he must have hurt Rilee somehow and he sat on the sand with his arms on his knees and waited, not knowing what else to do. Jenson sat down next to him.

"You know, Rilee is sensitive about Andy. She is really confused, right now," he said. "She's sensitive about you, too, and about what will happen after our trip is over. You need to be patient."

"I'm trying to be. What did I say that was so wrong?"

"Nothing. Nothing at all. Did Rilee tell you anything about Andy?"

"Not really, just that she is the happiest kid on earth."

"She is, but there is so much more you need to know. Andy is quite intelligent for a Down's child. She has an I. Q. of about eighty. When she gets older, she can lead a productive life. That's the rub, here. Andy may not live to be twenty. There are health concerns, especially with her heart. You have to understand that for all of Steve's problems, money isn't one of them. He's in a position to take care of Andy and he has given generously already. I told you it was complicated. Rilee is madly in love with you and I can tell you if Andy weren't such a concern, she would have thrown Steve off the boat the first day."

"That isn't much consolation, is it? I guess it might not matter that I've never loved anyone so much as Rilee. I told her last night I could love Andy just the same. But you're right. I'm just a boat bum, a broke one at that. I have to face the fact that Rilee will leave with you tomorrow. She has to think of Andy first and that will leave me standing on the dock with nothing but a cold wind blowing through my heart. It doesn't matter, I guess, that I could give Andy the one honest thing she's missing in all this."

"What's that?"

Nate looked down at the sand for a moment and then picked up a tiny cockle and turned it over slowly in his hand.

He glanced toward *Sandpiper* where Steve was hidden some-where below.

"A daddy," he said.

Nate stood and looked down at Jenson and tried to smile, but there was a little problem with his eyes. He turned and walked up the sand. When he was thirty yards away, he waded into the water and flopped on his belly and swam away from the beach, away from Jenson and his logic, away from cute little pragmatic Debra who looked so good in wet T-shirts, away from the mother of a happy little girl in Steamboat Springs and away from what he already knew in his soul was the one great love of his life.

Nate kept swimming until his arms and legs ached. He rolled over on his back and glanced at the beach, already so far away he couldn't see Rilee anymore. He kept looking for her and there was some panic while he tried to catch his breath. He was over part of the inner reef and could see the dead coral beneath him. He rolled over again to swim out into clear water where he looked again for Rilee. Nate felt stupid for running away when there was so little time to share and he started swimming back to the beach. He had only gone about half-way when he heard the dinghy approaching. Rilee was alone in the boat. Nate felt little daggers of fear at what she might say. She cut the motor and coasted up and he saw the tears on her face, but Rilee didn't wait for the dinghy to stop. She stepped on the gunwale and dived into the water. When she surfaced, she took a couple of strokes and in an instant she was sobbing in his arms. Nate reached for the dinghy to hold them up while she kissed his face and held onto his neck. Nate couldn't believe Rilee would ever leave on Sunday.

"I can't bear to think of you being upset," she said finally. "I didn't go away angry or hurt. I was overwhelmed by what you said about Andy. I didn't know anyone else could care that much."

"I'm sorry," Nate said. "I didn't understand. I talked to Jenson after you walked away and I got upset at his logic. I know he's right and I have no way to fight back and so I did what I usually do. I ran away. We only have hours left and when I was out here swimming off like a fool, I turned around to find you. That's when I started back. I don't want to waste another minute."

"But you know I can't promise you anything after Sunday."

"I know you can't, but can you promise me hope? That there might be a chance?"

"I don't know. I want to more than you'll ever know. Can we wait for Sunday?"

"Yes, but how will I know?"

Rilee didn't answer. She smiled through her tears and pressed her lips to his. They were so close in the water it was a good thing he was hanging onto the dinghy with one hand because he didn't think they could stop. The little boat drifted around and *Sandpiper* came into view across the reef. They both looked at the same time to see if Steve saw them and then Rilee smiled and pushed away and started swimming for the beach. Nate had to pull himself into the dinghy to start the outboard and follow along at a distance.

Jenson and Debra were still sitting on the beach holding hands when Rilee stumbled ashore out of breath. They met her with hugs. Nate coasted to a stop in the sand and the three of them stood watching him from the line of sea grapes. He stepped out into the water and pulled the dinghy up and walked toward them, but he stopped and looked at Rilee and shrugged his shoulders. She didn't even look toward *Sandpiper*. She walked over and took his arm and stayed by his side until Jenson and Debra came over and hugged them both. No one said a word. They motored slowly back to *Sandpiper* and climbed up the swim ladder and stepped beneath the bimini. Steve yelled at them from the cabin.

"How come you guys left me behind?" he said. "I had to sit here and drink brandy and cappuccino by myself."

Jenson got out more Vichyssoise to heat and more crackers and cheese and two bottles of chardonnay and lunch was served in the cockpit. The morning had been an emotional tilta-whirl and Nate spent a lot of time watching Rilee. He didn't want to drink too much, but the wine relaxed everyone and they had to get two more bottles out of the ice box. It was nearly one o'clock when they finally lifted the anchor out of the sand.

Steve motored *Sandpiper* out from between the coral canyons of Brewer's Bay. Nate stood on the cabin roof looking at the high green hills and at the brown shadows of the reef and at the pale ribbon of sand where *Sandpiper* sat anchored at the head of the bay. He never saw a soul on the beach or on the hills. Except for the grouper carcass around the corner and some footprints in the sand, no one could tell *Sandpiper* had ever been there.

Nate hauled up the main and unrolled the jib. With the downwind run to St. John coming up, he didn't fool with the little staysail. The boat slipped along in the wind shadow where the puffs that swept down from above carried her along the cliffs of Tortola toward the entrance to Cane Garden Bay. Dozens of charter boats anchored close in and a line of beach bars hid at the edge of the sand. Steve took one look at the mess and shook his head.

They sailed on toward Thatch Island Cut and out of the shadows of the cliffs. The winds were good and steady and Nate thought everyone would enjoy the sailing more if they stayed in the clear air. He watched the cut slide by in the distance and then Rilee and Debra joined him near the bow rail and looked at Jost Van Dyke to the north.

"We could have gone over to Foxy's for the night and cleared customs in the morning," Nate said. "We still could. Foxy has a scratch band that plays some real reggae. You'd get a kick out of it."

"Well, it's our last night on *Sandpiper*," Debra said. "I was hoping we'd all have dinner aboard and listen to our own reggae and just be together. This might not ever happen again."

Rilee was still wearing the Carmen Miranda bathing suit from the morning swim and it made Nate ache for her that much more. Foxy enjoyed the women who came into his bar. Nate didn't want to share Rilee with anyone.

"I don't feel much like partying, anyway," Rilee said

They skirted the western end of Great Thatch Island and headed over on a broad reach with the wind on the port side. It got fluky at times and the jib slapped around while the crackling noises floated over the water. They were all back in the cockpit watching St. John drift by along with a half-dozen little cays that dotted the passage. In the late afternoon, they steered the boat into Cruz Bay and let *Sandpiper* idle into the tiny anchorage southwest of Government House. Nate steered clear of the other charter boats and anchored well out in a patch of sand near the entrance. The breeze that swirled over the island sometimes reached down and got *Sandpiper* swinging about.

Rilee and Debra changed into their walking clothes and came out smelling of perfume. They looked so fresh and clean Nate had to sneak into the head with the shaving kit and fresh cutoffs just so he wouldn't offend anyone. He rinsed off in cold water in the shower and shaved and dressed in a hurry. He stepped into the cockpit, but the four of them were already in the dinghy. Nate grabbed the pouch with the ship's papers and climbed down into the bow next to Jenson. Rilee was driving and he smiled at her.

"Hang on," she said.

Rilee twisted the throttle wide open and the loaded dinghy plowed toward the ferry landing.

Clearing customs was a simple matter of checking the ownership papers and the crew documents. *Sandpiper* was cleared into the U. S. Virgin Islands in only a few minutes. They left the customs office and walked around the Government House grounds. In the low afternoon light, the colors were so saturated Jenson took pictures of all of them in front of several thousand hibiscus blossoms flaming red in the sun.

They walked up the hill along a road that wasn't very steep and when they reached the end, they turned to look back over Cruz Bay and the channel and the hills of St. Thomas. The sun was low and the sky turned the color of the hibiscus blossoms. Rilee kept watching the sky and the water change colors. Nate could see the red and the pink and the orange sparkles in her eyes. When they got back to the dinghy, the anxiety settled in one more time. There would never be another sunset. Nate motored slowly toward *Sandpiper* and coasted to a stop just as the night settled over the anchorage.

They stepped aboard and turned the lights on below. Jenson got out the grouper fillets and dusted them in flour and fried the pieces in butter until all of it was on a big platter. There was a sheet of French baked potatoes in the oven and canned green beans in a pot. Steve brought out the bottles of chardonnay. Jenson poured the wine and there were a lot of toasts before anyone could eat. When it was Steve's turn, he started in on the Great White Hunter routine.

"Thank you, Captain Nate," he said. "We'd be eating leftover junk tonight without your help."

Rilee kept watching Nate from the other side of the table and rubbing her feet against his. It got to the point where Nate was sure Steve knew, but he kept gulping wine and opening more bottles and toasting anything that moved and when all the grouper was gone, Steve sat back and smiled.

"That was as fine a meal as I've ever had. The company was even better," he said.

Steve was slurring his words and lifting his wine glass again. Rilee slid from behind the dinette and started to fill the sink with water to wash the dishes. Nate stood to help and she handed him a dish towel.

"Isn't this romantic?" she whispered.

The first of the plates came wet from the rinse and she turned and smiled at Nate and there was so much feeling in her eyes he felt the butterflies racing through again. She kept looking at him and brushing her shoulder against his.

"I couldn't believe the sunset today," she whispered. "It was the same color as the flowers. What a great dinner tonight. Jenson is such a good cook."

"He is. He acts like he's had some training."

"I don't think he has. He loves to entertain, though. You should see what he does at his house."

Rilee stopped for a moment and looked up at Nate.

"I'm sorry. I wish you could see for yourself. I hope we can talk later. I'd like to tell you all about Steamboat, too."

Rilee turned back to the sink, but not before she brushed a kiss in his ear. Nate's heart started to pound because Steve was right behind them. After they finished the dishes, Rilee poured two glasses of wine and handed one to Nate and they sat again at the dinette where Jenson was talking about skiing in Vermont and about all the wet snow. Steve was barely able to keep his eyes open. Rilee slipped her hand down on Nate's thigh and he nearly choked on the wine. She laughed and took her hand away. Debra knew somehow and she looked under the table.

"Feeling good, are we?" she asked.

Rilee giggled and put her hand back on Nate's thigh and his face turned red and there were other problems and he had to reach and take her hand in his to keep everything under control. Rilee kept giggling and flashing her eyes at him. Debra finally got up and came around the dinette and whispered in Nate's ear.

"You two are a huge mess." She kissed him on the other ear and pulled his hand and walked him up the companionway to sit in the cockpit.

"Maybe Rilee will follow you out here, you big goof-brain," she said. "This is your last chance. Steve is just about under the table."

In a few minutes Rilee came out and sat next to Nate.

"I don't know how long I can stay," she said. "Steve told me he wanted help to get into the head and if I do that, he'll ask me to help him into the forepeak. He'll want me to stay. I can't tell him no."

"Maybe I'll go below and run some interference," Debra said. "You might get a little more time."

Debra hopped down the ladder and slid into the dinette seat where she waved back at Nate without looking. Rilee pulled his hand and slid closer to the wheel out of the light from below.

"I thought you were going to tell me about Steamboat," Nate said.

"I'd love to. I was raised there. It's still my home. Do you ski?"

"Well, I could lie, but I've had skis on my feet once. I don't know why I wasn't killed. I liked it, though."

"I was born on skis. I miss it when we don't get away. Steve doesn't much care for it. You'd love Steamboat. There isn't a lot there, but you have the whole outdoors to keep you busy. Someday I'd like to go back."

"To live?"

"Yes, maybe not all the time, though. I love the heat and the tropics, too. It would be nice just to know I had a place there."

"I feel that way about Key West."

"Didn't you lose your wife there?"

"I did, but there was a lot of support for me from my friends. It gave me an odd sense of community, like I belonged there and my wife didn't. It feels a lot more like home than Bodega Bay."

"I know this sounds stupid," she said, "but I feel like I've known you all my life. Tomorrow seems like a funeral. Will we get through it?"

"I don't know. That might depend on you."

When Nate said that, Rilee sat up and looked in his eyes and there were tears welling up in hers. Nate felt sick for opening his mouth.

"I don't know about tomorrow," she whispered, "and I don't know about next week or next month, either. I just have to wait and sort it out. Right now I want only to be with you and I'm afraid Steve will ask for me any second. If he does, I'm going to be crushed because that will be the end of us for now."

She kissed Nate once and then again with passion and they held each other close and waited for someone to call. It didn't take very long. Debra looked out from the companionway.

"Steve just said he doesn't want to fall asleep at the dinette again," she said. "He's really loaded. He's asking for Rilee."

Nate held onto Rilee. He could feel her trembling.

"I'll be back out soon," she whispered, "even if it's only for a minute."

She stood and touched his face and took took a big breath and a big slug of wine and then followed Debra down into the salon. Nate didn't want to look below and see Rilee with her husband. He glanced around the anchorage and in frustration, he stood and walked back to the stern rail. The glow from the lights of Charlotte Amalie spilled over the hills of St. Thomas in the distance. Nate gripped the rail with both hands and stood staring into the darkness. He heard Debra call and he turned to see her step over the coaming.

"Rilee is a wreck," she said, "and so am I. Jenson is already passed out and Steve wants Rilee to stay with him. She won't be back. I know what that means to you."

"You have to go, too," Nate said. "Jenson needs you. All I can do is stand here and be numb."

Nate looked back toward Charlotte Amalie and the hills of St. Thomas.

"You know, tomorrow I go back to my world over there. I don't want it anymore. When Rilee walks away, it will be the end of us. I don't know what I'll do."

Debra stood close to Nate and when she put her arms around his waist, he looked to the west where the darkness hung low over the hills. There were faint flashes of a headlight somewhere near Redhook and he watched it moving along a roadcut until it brightened once, then twice, and then disappeared altogether. There was nothing left over there but a dull glow in the late night sky.

NINETEEN

Debra slipped below to find Nate's blanket and pillow. When she climbed back into the cockpit, she nodded toward the hills on St. John.

"I'd like to come back here again," she said. "I never enjoyed sailing before, but this has been special. Are you going to be okay?"

"I guess. Thanks for asking. I'm just waiting for the hammer to fall."

"It might not, you know?"

Debra blew Nate a glassy-eyed kiss and then she ducked below for the night. Nate stepped down into the cockpit and leaned against the starboard coaming. He could hear music drifting over the water from a party still in progress on a Moorings Gulfstar closer to the beach. He watched the reflections of the lights from the salon windows dancing in the bay. A glass of rum would help him sleep, but he stayed in the cockpit feeling numb and trying not to listen to the ringing in his ears. He sat with his head against the bulkhead until all the boats were dark in the anchorage, even the big Gulfstar.

Nate sneaked below to turn the nightlights on for Steve and Jenson and then climbed the ladder and sat on the cockpit cushions with the blanket pulled over his legs. The breeze had died away to nothing and the air settled in, hot and still. Nate pulled his shirt off and fluffed the pillow and put his head down and stared at the bimini cover glowing dim from the nightlights. His eyes burned so much he shut them tight and slipped away to the kind of sleep where he felt like he was falling in an empty well, spinning down in a dark vacuum where there was only silence and the thick, heavy heat. Nate never knew when he hit.

There were dreams of running free in a field when he was a kid and dreams of hiding from someone, he didn't know who. Nate kept trying to see, but there was a hand over his eyes, soft and caressing, and it moved slowly to his lips and in his dreams it seemed like everything was lost in a pink haze and in the blur he could see someone close. The hand and the fingers were so soft they felt real. Nate came spinning back from the bottom of the well. He opened his eyes. Rilee stood next to him bathed in the red glow again. She leaned over and kissed his ear.

"I told you I'd be back," she whispered.

Nate's heart started pounding. He meant to sit up, but Rilee placed her hand on his chest. He put his head back on the pillow and she reached down and began to unbutton his cutoffs. Nate was suddenly and unbelievably aroused. He caught her hand and held it still and she looked at him for a moment and then she stood and unbuttoned her nightshirt and let it fall to the cockpit sole. She wore nothing underneath. Nate was burning at the sight of her perfect body. She took his face in her hands and drew him to her breasts and he buried himself in her. He still couldn't believe she was real. Rilee held him there and he kept caressing her with his face and his lips and he could feel her breathing and the smell of her skin was all over him. She pushed Nate back on the pillow and reached for the button and zipper again. He didn't want to stop her. She slipped the cutoffs free and she looked at him for a long time and she took him in her hands and caressed him and he was nearly out of control. Nate held it back and it drifted away where it hid, waiting to surge forward again. She turned to him and kissed him without breathing and she fondled him at the same time and he could feel it rushing to the surface. Nate strained to keep it away and she kept caressing him and he could have let it all free, but she was too beautiful and he couldn't let it end, and again it was close before he made it back away. They kissed and touched each other and caressed and her breathing got heavier. Nate didn't know if he could stand it. Rilee kept her hand down low, soft and gentle, and it kept trying to peak. It took everything Nate had to stop it this time but the little pumping sensation was an orgasm in itself. She stood again and he moved to let her down on the cushion. She shook her head and he leaned back while she put her leg over him and slowly eased herself down. Nate could feel himself entering her and he knew it was going to happen again. She kept sliding down and he worked hard to hold it back. She came down and then lifted her legs beside him and they held each other with their mouths together and not moving a muscle, it was that perfect. Rilee was trembling and her breathing came deep and heavy and they both knew it could have lasted all night. There were moments when they looked in each other's eyes and the separate universe was there and then the orgasms came rushing out of nowhere and Nate could feel the great throbbing of her body. They moved like the ocean itself, peeling far away at first and then peaking and hurtling forward and then thundering into the blinding white like the storm surf in Josiah's Bay. They held onto each other and swirled about and rushed in and out, again and again a hundred times over, and when the tempo slowed and the waves rode them up on a distant shore, Nate could feel the ebb and the flow and they came to rest in the heat and in the sweat and in the quiet of the night.

They didn't move again, afraid it would end too soon. They kissed long after it was over. Her body felt more sensual than Nate ever imagined and he never relaxed all the way. He could feel the blood pumping and all of it coming on again and they held each other close.

"I dreamed about this. I knew it would be this good," Rilee whispered.

They rocked together even after it was over. Nate couldn't get enough of her. She slid away from him and he stretched out on the cushion and the pillow and she came down at his side. They stayed in each others arms without sleeping, holding each other, but the idea of dawn on Sunday crept through again and she kissed him.

"I have to go, now," she whispered.

She rolled under Nate and he could feel it coming again. She opened herself and they made love once more, slow and conventional, and the thundering of the surf was deafening. They kissed like it had never happened before and the thought of her leaving made it all that much more intense and again it was over and again they didn't move for a long time, but Rilee had to go. She stood in front of Nate with her incredible body bathed in pale red and he could feel himself burning all over again inside. He caressed her breasts and they kissed and they could have made love right there standing in the cockpit. She reached for her nightshirt and draped it over her shoulders and then she leaned against Nate and looked up in his eyes.

"I love you with all of my heart and all of my soul," she whispered. "I'm going to die inside tomorrow when we have to say good-bye. I don't know what will happen. It might even be that I can't say anything at all and I'll have to walk up the dock without looking back. I will always know you love me. Can you let me go?"

"No. When you walk away, there will be nothing left of me. I may not be able to say anything, either. I know there are no other options right now. I don't know what I'm going to do when I turn around and go back to *Serendipity*."

"You have to get on with your life. So do I."

"I can't imagine a life without you."

Rilee looked into Nate's eyes and there was a moment's hesitation and then she kissed his ear.

"Maybe you won't have to," she said softly, and she turned and stepped down the companionway and walked up to the forepeak and disappeared into the dark.

Nate watched the little door close behind her. There was nothing left but silence. He settled back on the blanket in the early morning blackness with the pale gleam of the night-lights falling across his body, wondering how Rilee could have slipped away. He shut his eyes and saw her again standing in front of him with her nightshirt dropping free and her breasts in the crimson light. The blood started pumping again. He leaned back with his eyes closed and sat there with visions of Rilee and his body exposed and his heart in a million pieces.

At some point Nate fell asleep. When he awoke, he reached for his cutoffs and pulled them on and slipped his shirt over his head. He stretched out on the cushion and was asleep once more in minutes. There were bright lights suddenly and some heat that wasn't there before and he opened his eyes to see the sun streaming down from above the crest of the hill. He could hear Jenson below making his circus-water coffee. Nate leaned against the bulkhead thinking about the night before. He had to sit up to keep the hot flashes away.

"Jenson, is there enough coffee for me?" Nate asked.

"Yes...There's cappuccino and brandy here, too. I'll put some water on to boil."

Nate stepped below and sneaked into the head to wake up. Rilee was just on the other side of the thin door and he fantasized about her joining him in the shower. He turned the water on and let the warm water flow and he washed down and dried off and didn't relax until he had his face full of shaving cream.

When he opened the door to the head, Jenson handed him a cappuccino with a lot of brandy in it. Nate sat at the dinette and sipped it slowly. He thought Rilee would come out and he waited, but Debra stepped from the aft cabin and slid next to him. She looked over at Jenson in the galley.

"Can I have some coffee, honey? Is it ready?"

She leaned close to Nate and put her head on his shoulder and then whispered so Jenson wouldn't hear.

"You smell good. Are you going to get through this?"

"You know I can't."

"I don't think any of us will ever get over it. Before anything happens, you need to give me a permanent mailing address. You just never know. We might need another captain."

"I think I might retire after this. There's a great place in Key West, the Green Parrot Bar and Sub Shop on the corner of Southard and Whitehead. You can't miss it. I'll be sitting at a stool in the corner drinking myself stupid."

Jenson came over and sat with them. He winked at his wife who was holding her diamond high in the light. He looked over at Nate.

"Well, I wish we were just starting out," he said. "You've been terrific. I can't tell you how much the trip has meant to us. If you ever get to Port Townsend, you have a place to stay and everything to eat and drink for as long as you like."

Nate was embarrassed he had nothing to offer in return.

"Thanks, Jenson," he said. "That means a lot to me."

"Here. Take one of my cards and keep it in your wallet. I'm serious. You will probably hear from us again."

Jenson handed him a business card with *JENSON COLORGRAPHICS* across the top and addresses and phone numbers beneath. Nate was sorry he didn't have one to give in exchange. He shook Jenson's hand then and he knew this was his good-bye to avoid the emotional parting on the St. Tropez dock. Nate reached over and gave Debra a big hug and she was lost in his arms for a second and it made him laugh.

"I'll never forget your wet T-shirt," Nate said.

Debra giggled and turned crimson and she whispered in his ear.

"I will never ever forget what I saw in the cockpit after Rilee went to bed."

Nate's heart stopped and his face heated up and his breath turned shallow. Debra pushed him away laughing. Jenson looked at them both with a blank stare.

Rilee came out while Nate was still sitting at the dinette with the stunned look. She sat down next to him and asked Jenson for some coffee and then she turned to look at Nate and she kissed his lips and hugged his neck. Jenson brought the coffee over, but he picked up his own cup and went with Debra out into the cockpit.

"Last night...Well, that was a night for the ages," Rilee said. "I'm going to spend the rest of my life thinking about it," and she giggled and hugged Nate's neck again.

He had to laugh, but there was a heart breaking inside and when they heard noises from the forepeak, Rilee kissed him and took her coffee over to the galley. Steve opened the door and looked at her.

"Any hot water for cappuccino left?" he asked.

"I'll turn the burner back on. Would you like brandy, too?"

Steve grunted and then went into the head. The sound of the fresh-water pump filled the salon. Nate stood and stretched, but Rilee tickled him from behind. He turned around and they held each other. He had to shut his eyes and bury his face just to try to memorize again the smell of her hair and the smell of her skin and how her body felt when it was so close. Neither of them could speak. Nate felt some slight trembling and couldn't tell whether it was him. They held each other until the water pump shut off and Steve was fumbling with the door.

Rilee made a cappuccino and brandy for Steve while Nate sat in the cockpit where Jenson and Debra were cuddling like newlyweds. Debra blushed again and Nate could feel the warmth rising to his face. He didn't ask when it was that she saw him. He shook his head and the heat built in his face until he thought it was a good time to start the Perkins and get *Sandpiper* ready for the last sail of the week. Steve came out with his brandy.

"Want to take the helm?" Nate asked.

"Do you mind? I've had the time of my life. I don't want to give it up just yet."

Steve stepped behind the wheel after Nate walked forward to run the windlass. When the anchor broke free, he secured it in the roller with the clevis pin while *Sandpiper* fell away with the wind swirling around from over the hills of St. John. They motored slowly from Cruz Bay toward the open water of the sound where Steve turned the boat into the wind. Rilee and Nate got the main up and then unfurled the jib for the downwind run to Steven Cay. *Sandpiper* cleared the northern end of the islet and then changed course for Current Cut and went off on a broad reach with the wind on the port side again. The silence and the heat of off-wind sailing in the tropics crept in and Nate sat beneath the bimini and watched the rocks and the islets and the hills sliding by in the distance. Rilee sat next to him. Even after their incredible night together, he couldn't keep his eyes off of her.

The narrow cut approached in the distance. There was sick feeling growing inside and Nate knew it was going to get much worse. The ringing in his ears came back like someone had hit the tourist bell behind the bar in the Green Parrot. Jenson asked if he wanted a beer but Nate only shook his head and watched the cut coming up.

Nate went below to check his bag and to stuff the dive gear in along with his shaving kit. He walked back toward the companionway where he could see Jenson's bags strewn about the aft cabin berth. The sick feeling returned to the pit of his stomach again and he hurried up the ladder. Rilee greeted him with a big smile. He sat down on the cushion next to her and shut his eyes. She reached over and touched his shoulder.

"Tired?"

Nate nodded and smiled. Rilee grinned in return.

"Me, too."

Sandpiper entered the cut on a fast beam reach. Steve was laughing as the boat roared into the shallows and entered the wind shadow of Great St. James Island. The jib flopped about and lost its shape. *Sandpiper* carried her way through and when the jib refilled with a crack, she was off on a broad reach again toward Capella Island and Charlotte Amalie just beyond the point. Nate couldn't get rid of that sick feeling in the pit of his stomach. He stood to go lean against the stern rail for a few minutes when Rilee came aft to join him. They spent the rest of the morning together while Steve steered them toward the harbor in St. Thomas. There was nothing either of them could say.

They had to jibe over just as they had Packet Rock on their starboard beam. Rilee and Nate stepped back to the cockpit where she handled the jib and Nate sheeted the main in flat while Steve steered across the wind. When he came up on the new course, Nate let the main go and in a minute they were romping on a broad reach right for the harbor entrance. Rilee kissed Nate's lips on their way back to the stern rail and her eyes were a little glassy. Nate thought already it had started. He held her hand and looked down.

"We only have thirty minutes or so before we get in," he said. "I can't believe it has come down to this. If I give you my permanent address and phone number will you keep it? Just in case?"

"I'll keep it forever. You know that."

"My parents still live in Bodega Bay. It's my real home, I guess. I'd like to take you there, but I don't want to talk about that right now. It's too painful not knowing if I'll ever see you again."

Rilee had more tears well up in her eyes. Nate brushed a trace from her cheek with his hand. She looked at him with her shining eyes and he had to leave her there and go below where he tore off a corner of the BVI chart and scribbled his father's name and phone number and address. He looked up to see Rilee stepping down the ladder. In a second, they moved near the aft cabin door out of sight and they kissed and held each other. It was over in a flash.

"Hey, Rilee," Steve yelled from behind the wheel. "Can you grab me a brew?"

Nate pushed the corner of the chart into her hand and told her to put it in a safe place while he got the beer.

"Get one for me, too," Jenson yelled.

Nate took three cans from the ice box and climbed into the cockpit where he handed them out. He leaned against the stern rail and watched the mast up high where it bounced around against the blue of the sky. Rilee came back to join him. She tickled him again and brushed her lips against his face and he could have collapsed, his knees were so weak. He drank from the can of beer and then Rilee did the same and by the time the Schaefer was empty, *Sandpiper* had turned the corner into the harbor, into the wind shadows of the hills and into the dark shadows of the afternoon.

Steve started the diesel while Rilee and Nate furled the main again. They touched hands a hundred times trying to get the sail ties in place.

"Why don't you come and take the wheel, Nate," Steve said. "I think the captain should take us into the inner harbor."

Nate stepped behind the binnacle and took the wheel while Rilee came to sit nearby. They steered *Sandpiper* together toward the Sheraton and the St. Tropez docks where *Serendipity* came into view. She looked beautiful in the high sun.

"Can we motor in for a closer look?" Rilee asked.

Nate idled the boat down and crept into the anchorage. The sabot was gone and the companionway door was shut, but *Serendipity* looked light on her feet and ready to go. *Sandpiper* drifted by in the channel. Rilee stared at *Serendipity* and she turned to Nate.

"I hardly remember seeing her on the way out," Rilee said. "She's so pretty, like the yellow hibiscus I sent to my mom."

Rilee looked back as they idled away. Nate would have given his soul and *Serendipity* both, just to have Rilee. He could see Mac waiting on the dock and Etionette watching from the deck of *Dame Foncé*. Nate waved and smiled and his heart ached inside when they waved back. He spun the wheel and shifted into reverse and asked Steve to hold the dinghy up short. Nate got lucky when *Sandpiper* backed dead center between the pilings. Jenson tied the bow lines off and Steve handled the stern. Nate shut the Perkins down for good and sat in the silence and looked at beautiful Rilee and her Caribbean eyes.

Steve was joking about something Mac had said. Nate wasn't ready to face anyone. He followed Rilee and Debra and Jenson below and tried to help. He carried some of the bags to the stern where the maintenance guys set them on the dock. He went below for his own, but he was sweating from the heat and from the stress. He took off his shirt and wiped his face and neck and threw the shirt into the bag and carried the bag outside where he tossed it onto the transom. Nate leaned against the rail and looked toward the dock to watch Rilee while Steve disappeared into the office to sign some papers and get receipts. She stood away from the others and she kept looking at Nate and he thought it might be the only way they could part, just to turn and walk away. He also knew it would kill him. Steve came out of the office and took Jenson by the arm and stepped aboard *Sandpiper* to shake Nate's hand.

"Nate, I have to tell you that was the greatest charter ever," Steve said. "You are the best, and I mean that. Here is a little gift for you. Don't open it until we are out of sight."

Steve handed Nate an envelope. He only glanced at it before he stuffed it in his pocket.

"Thanks a lot, Steve...Jenson. Thanks for including me in your adventures. I'll miss all of you. Take care of yourselves."

Steve and Jenson hopped from the transom onto the dock and walked together toward the Sheraton. Nate stepped off onto the dock when little Debra came running up crying. She grabbed his neck and wouldn't let go until he promised to keep in touch.

"I promise. I guess after last night there are no more secrets between us."

Debra pulled away from Nate and looked in his face and giggled.

"Wow, not anymore," she said, and she lifted her eyebrows at him like Groucho again and then she laughed through the tears. In an instant, she was gone chasing Jenson up the dock.

Rilee stood waiting in the shade of the Quarterdeck. She looked at Nate with tears streaming from her eyes and then she turned and took Steve's arm and walked away. Nate wanted to yell her name but his throat was choked shut. He turned and climbed aboard *Sandpiper* and threw open the cockpit locker to grab the elephant gun. He put the gun over his shoulder and picked up his bag and stood on the dock again, gritting his teeth. He kept staring after Rilee and there were so many tears in his eyes he couldn't keep them from spilling, but he saw when she turned around to look at him again. She said something to Steve and then she ran back down the dock where she rushed up to Nate and took his face in her hands and she kissed him with such tender passion he couldn't think. Nate dropped the bag and held her close one-handed with the elephant gun still on his shoulder and they kissed open and hard and she had her arms around him, holding him like there never would be another tomorrow. She had to let go, but the tears were everywhere on her face. She stuffed a wisp of paper in Nate's pocket and then she backed away and stood looking at him through all those tears.

"Alligator food, Captain Nate." she whispered. "Alligator food."

Rilee's voice was soft and Nate couldn't hear, but he watched her lips and he suddenly knew she said "I love you".

Rilee turned away from Nate and walked with her head down and her shoulders shaking all the way up the dock. When she reached the others, she took her husband by the arm and made him walk away, but not before he turned around again to stare. Nate watched while the four of them made their way up the ramp toward the Sheraton. They disappeared beyond the gate and he stood frozen in his tracks. He kept thinking about Rilee and thinking about the two of them together and he knew then she didn't just walk up the dock for home. She walked up the dock and out of his life.

TWENTY

Nate stared up the dock toward the Sheraton. The swinging gate was shut across the walkway and he couldn't see beyond it to the hotel. He kept thinking what an incredible idiot he was for not running to catch Rilee, but then there was Andy. Maybe there was no other way and it had to end like that. Mac and Etionette were behind him. They stayed away until Nate turned toward the St. Tropez office.

"Holy crap, Nate," Mac said. "What the hell kind of charter was that?"

Mac took the bag away. They walked into the office where Nate threw the elephant gun in the corner and then collapsed into a chair near the desk. He sat there with his face in his hands. Mac left Nate alone until he could gather himself.

"I don't know," Nate said. "I might have just made the biggest mistake of my life."

"I didn't think she was leaving, the way she held on to you. It's a wonder Steve didn't come back and blast you with that spear gun."

"I probably would have let him, you know?"

Mac stepped behind the desk and took another envelope out of the file cabinet and handed it to Nate.

"I wish I could pay you more. There's a little extra for bailing me out. Steve and Jenson had nothing but praise for you. They wanted to know if you'd be back this way after you went down islands. I told them you were a boat bum just passing through. Steve would have booked another charter today if you were the skipper."

"Well, I don't think he wants me, anymore."

Nate pulled the other envelope out of his pocket and slit it open with a ballpoint pen. There were five one-hundreds inside, crisp and new. Nate threw them on the desk.

"I'll bet he wants these back, too."

"Hey, you did a great job. Take it and use it. I know you're leaving soon. The money might be enough to get all the way to Grenada and back. Don't feel guilty."

"The funny thing is, I don't. This week changed my life, Mac. Someday I'll tell you about it."

Nate looked through the window at *Sandpiper* tied stern to the wall. The guys on the dock had started cleaning and she already looked sparkling and fresh and wet. Nate couldn't look at her without thinking of Rilee. He stood and reached in his pocket for the little paper she had given him. He unfolded it slowly.

Britton - Steamboat - (209) 554-2271

I just need time.

Down on the bottom in a scrawl you could barely read, Nate saw she had written *alligator food* and there was a happy face with X's where the eyes should have been. He kept staring at the paper. His hands were shaking and he was afraid if he put the note away, he would lose what little he had left of Rilee. Nate stood in the office holding the slip of paper with his eyes misting over and not saying a word. He kept staring at the handwriting and at the name. Nate held his head back and blinked and then reached for his wallet in the bag and folded the paper again, but he couldn't put it away. He unfolded it and kept reading *I just need time,* over and over. Nate looked up at Mac.

"I'm sorry," Nate said. "I need to go out to *Serendipity*. Can I get a lift?"

"Are you okay? I can run you out in the skiff if you're sure about being alone. Brady and Shanna went to town a while ago."

"I think I'd like to be alone, right now. I just need to go."

Mac took the bag while Nate picked up the envelopes full of money and the elephant gun. He followed Mac out to the dock where the skiff was tied. Etionette came up and reached for his hand but then she hugged him instead.

"Do you need help?"

She looked at Nate with such sad eyes it made him think the whole dock knew already.

"No. Thanks for offering," Nate said. "I can handle it. I had a tough charter."

"I saw when you came back. Did you fall in love?"

Etionette made Nate smile and she still got the flames burning inside, even after Rilee. He looked at her and nodded.

"Yes," he said. "I really did."

"You should fall in love with me," she giggled. "I'm not leaving."

"Everybody falls in love with you."

"I know."

Etionette said something else in French and giggled again and when Mac untied the skiff, Nate threw the bag in the bottom and stepped in behind it. Etionette hopped aboard and wiggled over next to him while Mac idled the skiff out to *Serendipity*.

"Nate, can you do me a big favor?"

Nate looked at her and only nodded.

"Can you help me? The owner will have guests aboard for three days. Sometimes I am afraid, you know, of the men. They like to drink and then they like to get friendly. Can you come with me Monday night? I have to go alone."

"Where is the rest of your crew?"

"They are not here until Tuesday."

Nate didn't want to go, but he nodded his head again.

"Just knock on the hull to remind me okay? I'll be your bodyguard."

Etionette didn't know what a bodyguard was. They reached *Serendipity* before Nate could explain it. Etionette followed him aboard and poked around in the cockpit and then she walked out on the bow.

"She is so thin. Fast, no?"

"Fast, yes," Nate said.

"And the yellow, just like a sunflower."

Nate stowed the elephant gun in the port hull and slid the companionway door open and stepped below with his bag. Etionette skipped down the ladder and looked around in the cabin.

"So different from the schooner," she said. "The big beds. I love those."

She grinned and then climbed out of the cockpit and hopped over the rail and into the skiff. Mac shifted the outboard into reverse and waved and backed away with Etionette sitting in the bow as they motored toward the dock. Nate made his way below and pulled his floppers off and stretched out on the bunk. All he heard was the ringing in his ears again. He reached with his hands to cover his eyes because they were burning out of control. He wanted to see Rilee, to see her face and her eyes again and when Nate concentrated, she was there laughing and walking on the beach in her Carmen Miranda bathing suit. In his vision, she ran to him and threw her arms around his neck and he felt her skin against his and it was so smooth and sensual it was like she was dancing in Drake's Pub again. Nate picked her up and swung her around and she laughed like a little girl in Steamboat. There were waves slapping at the beach and sea grapes waving in the wind near the edge of the sand and all of it was warm and soft in the sun, but the vision faded in and out and he worked hard to keep Rilee in his view. It kept getting darker and his breathing was deeper and he thought it was because of Rilee. Nate slipped away to another universe. He only remembered her eyes and the color of the water in the shallows of Brewer's Bay.

The afternoon sun baked the decks and woke Nate from his troubled sleep. He opened the forward hatch to get some air circulating and then checked the bilge for a beer and found an empty locker instead. He sat on the dinette seat and looked around at the interior, not quite knowing what to do with himself. He stared at the yellow curtains, wondering where Rilee might be. He rubbed his eyes again and leaned back against the cushions and tried to picture her face. There were so many tears on the dock and so many things left unsaid, Nate felt the frustration coming back and the anger at not going after her. He didn't want to think of any of that. He only wanted to remember her smiles and her hair and her eyes, deep as the sea.

Nate heard laughing from somewhere outside and then the sabot bumping alongside. He climbed through the companionway when Brady and Shanna stepped aboard. After some welcome hugs, they opened three cans of Heineken and handed him one.

"How was your charter?" Shanna asked. "You look exhausted."

"I need this beer," Nate said. "You have no idea how different that charter was. I am tired."

"Why?" Shanna asked. "Were the guests rude?"

"No, not at all. They were special. We hit all the good spots and did a lot of heavy sailing. It was just a little too long."

Nate didn't want to talk about the charter. Rilee was gone and there was that sick feeling in his stomach.

"You're not going to go out on anymore charters?" Brady asked. "That means we can be ready to leave for the lower Caribbean when Sarah comes back."

"I guess."

"You don't sound very excited."

"I'll feel better about it when Sarah gets here."

"We could leave tonight. Maybe Sarah will come back today."

"I hope so. I'd really like to put this past week behind me."

Nate didn't want to go anywhere because of Rilee but he cleaned himself up and rowed ashore in the sabot, headed for the French wines at the Galleon House with Brady and Shanna. No one was on the dock and he kept lagging behind, nearly afraid Rilee might still be at the Sheraton. Shanna came back to walk with him.

"What's wrong? You don't look so good. Are you missing someone?"

"Look, if I told you the truth it wouldn't change anything. I have to deal with it. You're right. I don't feel too hot. I think I need about a gallon of wine."

"Are you upset about Sarah being gone? We haven't seen her since you both left."

"No, but that's part of it. I'm not sure things will be the same when she comes back. I'm a little bit in shock, I think, after the charter."

Shanna didn't ask Nate why. They wandered together up the hill to the Galleon House where the two Great Danes slept in the corner. The dogs only lifted their heads when Nate walked through the door. Brady and Shanna took seats at the bar and looked around and placed their orders. Nate thought the rosé tasted like the good Paris street wine that came in liter bottles with crimped caps for lids. He kept ordering more wine and trying not to think of Rilee, but the wine made it worse and when Shanna said she was getting drunk, Nate was happy to get out of there. He thought about Rilee still being at the Sheraton again. Each time he passed someone on the street, he looked for her. All the wine he drank made it seem like she was just a dream in some distant night long past. He didn't walk very fast back to the Sheraton. Shanna kept waiting until she hooked his arm to pull him along. They passed the hotel lobby and in a moment of weakness, Nate walked through to the front desk and asked if there were a Harper or a Jenson or a Britton in the registry. The concierge looked at him and then he said under his breath that no one was registered at the hotel under those names.

"Are you sure?"

"Quite, but our guests don't want to be bothered."

Nate stared at him for a minute and nodded.

"Thanks," Nate said, and he turned away.

They left the lobby of the hotel and walked through the gate toward the marina where *Sandpiper* waited in the night for her next charter. Nate stopped for a moment just to look.

"Are you sure there's nothing wrong, Nate?" Brady asked.

"I was hoping my charter people were still here. I'm having a hard time letting it all go. Don't ask me why. It really was a terrific week. I even got a huge tip we need to spend on some rum."

"We got some Cruzan yesterday and some limes," Brady said. "I'm ready to go back to the boat after that cheap wine."

Brady rowed them out to *Serendipity* in the sabot while Nate looked around in the anchorage. One of the cruise ships across the way was lit like a city block in Manhattan and sounded like a floating carnival. Each stroke Brady took with the oars moved them away from the party in a series of soft surges that carried them further into the darkness. *Serendipity* loomed unlit in the anchorage. She looked very much like she did the day Dana left. Nate stared at her lines and at her black mast reaching into the night sky. He felt like a stranger in his own home. He climbed onto the wingdeck and took the painter while Shanna stepped aboard and went below to light the Aladdin. Nate sat on a cockpit seat and stared across the harbor. Brady made three rums with lime juice and then cranked up the stereo with a Kris Kristofferson tape. He came out with the rum and handed one to Nate and then sat down and put his drink on the deck.

"When we leave, can we sail through the BVI?" Brady asked. "We haven't been anywhere but downtown since you left."

"I'd like to do that. I'd like to see the islands myself without a charter group around."

Nate wasn't exactly being honest, but sitting there in the dark with the lights of Charlotte Amalie all around and the rum warming its way down, maybe a trip through the BVI with Brady and Shanna would be good. He wasn't so sure about Sarah.

Shanna made sandwiches out of some tinned meat that looked like Spam. Nate could eat it if it had enough mustard. He kept looking over toward the Sheraton while they ate together in the cockpit, wondering if the concierge had told him the truth.

"Nate, you're about as happy as a mortician," Brady said. "What's up?"

"I'm tired, Brady. It's good to be back, but I'm worn out."

Brady made more rum and lime juice while Nate sat listening to the Kris Kristofferson tape. He felt every minute of the coming down. He glanced over at the windows in the Sheraton. The lamps were dim, mostly hidden behind curtains, and he kept thinking Rilee was in one of the rooms. He would have given anything to know. The lights might just as well have been fires from a wrecker out on the reef.

Nate stumbled below and made up the double berth on the port wingdeck and stretched out to try to sleep. He couldn't shut his eyes without feeling sick, but it felt good to have a real bed after a week of sleeping in a cockpit. Brady and Shanna blew out the lamp and made their way forward while he stared into the darkness waiting for sleep. Nate didn't understand a lot of things and he was too drunk to concentrate. The little piece of paper in his wallet had a phone number in Steamboat, probably for her mom. *I just need time* the note said. When Nate read the words, they made it seem like there was no end. He rolled over and tried to think of life without Rilee.

Nate kept riding the nausea up and down with the Ferris wheel until he had to get up to use the head and take some aspirin with a can of 7-Up he found in the ice box. He climbed back into the berth and started thinking of Rilee when she let her nightshirt fall and her body throbbed in the red glow from the nightlights. The vision was so erotic he broke into a sweat. He couldn't believe he had let her walk away. He might have had tears in his eyes if he hadn't been so angry, but the vision of her grew less intense and he cooled off a little. The nausea hung around and it made Nate sick to close his eyes. Rilee seemed so close that when sleep finally settled in, the darkness felt like warm wool and he slipped away with the images again of her body caressed in pink.

Beyond the anchorage to the south, there were swells running through before the trades that blew from the east. In the lee of the hills that loomed over the harbor, *Serendipity* drifted aimlessly about her anchor line that drooped in the water, black and still.

TWENTY-ONE

In the light of the morning the cruise ship didn't look much like a carnival anymore, just a Manhattan city block in the heat. Nate watched people no bigger than ants walking along the decks and along the quay below where the ladies' hats stood out like baskets of tropical fruit. Even the Sheraton had lost its luster, looking more like a business than a destination. When the cloud shadows rolled through, it looked more like a hospital than a business.

"Are you hung over?" Brady asked.

"I've been hung over for a week," Nate said. "One of the charter guys told me we went through fifteen bottles of rum and four cases of wine. Who knows how much beer?"

"I could do that. I keep buying Cruzan. It doesn't last long when you don't have much to do."

"No word from Sarah at all?"

"No... *Nomad* sailed out of here and never showed up again. Some guy on the dock told me he thought they might have gone over to St. Martin."

"I only saw them once, over on Norman Island last week. It seems more like a year ago."

Nate glanced toward the Sheraton again while Brady poured more coffee. The hotel looked somber in the passing cloud shadows and it gave him the feeling Rilee was never there at all. At the end of the dock where the big Amway yacht was tied, Nate could see a pair of uniformed deck hands wrestling with a big hawser. He watched them work and tried not to think of her. By the time Brady handed him another coffee, he was only thinking of the moment in the nightlights again when her shirt fell away to the cockpit sole. Brady leaned against the cabin bulkhead and looked out toward the Sheraton.

"We've had a good time here," he said. "It won't bother us to wait for Sarah. She should be back by the weekend. What do you think?"

"Probably. That skipper with the piano teeth was pretty vague about what they were up to. I suppose they'll be back by Saturday."

Nate stared in the direction of the Sheraton and drank the coffee in silence. Shanna came out from below rubbing her eyes. She sat down next to him and squeezed his arm.

"I think there's something wrong," Shanna said. "You don't look the same."

"I don't feel the same. Maybe after a week of wandering the streets, I'll snap out of this. We need to get away and let *Serendipity* run loose in those big swells south of here."

Shanna smiled at Nate from behind her coffee mug while they sat together looking at the other boats in the anchorage. Every now and then a gust of wind swirled over the hills and down onto the anchorage and set *Serendipity* swinging on her anchor. None of the other boats moved. Nate saw a good part of the harbor in the soft, intermittent breeze and there were times when the motion nearly put him to sleep. He sat with the coffee cooling in the mug and the wind rushing through, wondering if he could take the next step.

Brady and Shanna decided to row the sabot into the dock and walk over to the free zone to look around. Nate tagged along only because he didn't need to stay alone on the boat. They climbed out of the dinghy at the dock where Etionette came rushing up to remind Nate about being her escort.

"You will go tonight?" she asked. "You remember?"

"Yes, I'll go. I didn't forget."

Etionette hugged Nate around the waist and skipped back to *Dame Foncé* still shining like black coral in the morning light.

The free zone was in a big warehouse across the way from the deep water terminal. It was always packed with cruise ship tourists buying their legal limit of Mt. Gay and Tanqueray and a dozen other call brands to take home. Nate didn't like the atmosphere much. He left Brady and Shanna behind and walked over to the Sheraton, alone and numb with no place to go. He kept looking for Rilee in every pretty face. She was never there and he couldn't stand the hollow feeling inside. He wandered down by the pool and found a lounge chair over by a small stage that had a guitar and an amp and a microphone. He sat down and ordered a double Mt. Gay and Coke when the blonde waitress walked over from the little outside bar. Nate gave her a five and told her to keep the change if she could come back a few times.

He leaned against the back of the chair and held the icy glass in his hand and shut his eyes. In a few minutes he heard the guitar player setting up his sound system. Nate was embarrassed to be the only one in the audience. The guy didn't seem to mind. He strummed his guitar and told Nate he tuned it to the key of D because he learned to play in Hawaii. He adjusted the volume on the amplifier and started with a lot of Gabby Pahinui stuff.

When the waitress showed up again, Nate ordered another double. She knew the guitar player and they teased each other a little and then she left. He stared after her for a moment and then he looked at Nate and began to play the melody line from Steven Sondheim's *Send in the Clowns*. Nate listened with his eyes shut again while the guitar player sang the lyrics. The waitress came back with the rum and Coke just as the song ended. Nate sat up and took a big gulp and the rum went down like lava. He gave her another five.

"The next one will be on me. Doubles are only a buck," she said, and she smiled and walked away.

Nate took another long sip. The rum made him dizzy and he tried to focus by looking away toward the shadows on the hills and the red tile roofs. Rilee was out of his life. He slugged the rest of the rum down and waited for the spinning to start, hoping the other double would show up. The guitar player watched Nate finish the drink and he waved at the waitress who nodded in return. She came back with her tray and another rum for Nate and a pint for him. He held the beer to toast lost loves. The waitress just rolled her eyes and walked away.

By the time Nate finished the third rum, there was some real spinning when he shut his eyes. Brady and Shanna found him collapsed in the lounge chair.

"I thought you had a date tonight, silly?" Shanna said.

"I didn't forget. I just had a little alcohol problem."

"Big problem if you don't sober up."

They rowed back to *Serendipity* and opened the hatches to let the breeze through. Nate fell into the double bunk to sleep away the rum. He couldn't keep his eyes shut for very long but he kept trying because when they were closed, Rilee was there with her incredible eyes and her smile that made you think she was always a little embarrassed. Nate could see her body in the pale red light that flooded the cockpit. He wanted to hold her again and bury his face in her hair. The frustration built up inside and he rolled over and held the pillow to his face and waited for sleep. All he got was the quick spinning and the waves of nausea and the molasses mouth from all that rum. Nate slept in the end, but there were violent images of accidents with power tools and collisions of trains and images of falling into an abyss so dark there never was a floor until he hit and he could feel himself jerk and recoil in his sleep when the bottom rushed up out of nowhere. Brady was sitting at the dinette reading when Nate opened his eyes. He looked over and put the book down.

"What the hell were you dreaming about?" he asked. "You were trying to talk in your sleep."

"Nightmares, I think. I don't remember."

Nate's mouth was so dry he had to lick his lips and swallow to get the saliva to flow.

"Need a beer? You're dehydrated after all that rum."

"No. I don't want to start over again so soon."

Nate didn't want to drink, but he saw when Brady took a can from the ice box.

"On second thought," he said, "I might feel better if I have a beer. Give me one, too."

Nate sat up in bed and sipped the beer in silence and stared through the portlight thinking about Rilee again. The beer disappeared in a hurry and in disgust, he slid from the bunk and went forward into the head to shower off. He pulled the curtain closed and stood in the weak stream just long enough to soap down and rinse. He shaved and put on some clean clothes from the hanging locker just forward of the head and then stepped into the main salon. Brady was there with another beer. Nate opened the can and climbed into the cockpit to look around. Shanna was outside on the wingdeck lying on a towel in the afternoon sun and wearing her black two-piece, not much bigger than Debra's. She walked aft to sit on the other side of the cockpit.

"Feel like telling me what happened on that charter?" she asked. "I know something did."

"Nothing happened. Nothing I can talk about, anyway. You'll probably know the story soon enough."

Shanna looked at Nate sideways. There was a grin on her face like she knew.

"Well, if you need to talk just say so, okay," she said. "I don't mean to pry."

There was a moment when Nate wanted to talk and he nearly did, but Brady came out drinking another can of beer. Shanna grabbed him around the waist and made him sit next to her. Nate leaned back and smiled at the two of them. He couldn't help feeling a little jealous, they were so free and happy.

It was almost six when Etionette motored out in a big Zodiac. By that time, Nate was ready to hit the rum again. He ducked into the head to brush his teeth and change into a collared shirt and when he stepped out from below, Etionette was sitting in the cockpit flirting with Brady. She giggled at Nate and grabbed his hand and pulled him along to the Zodiac tied off on the starboard hull. Nate climbed aboard while Etionette waved to Shanna and Brady and then she spun the boat around. They roared off toward the St. Tropez dock. Nate caught a glimpse of Shanna in the fading light standing on the transom in her little suit.

Etionette pulled up just aft of the big schooner where Nate tied the boat off to a cleat while she shut the outboard off. There were people standing around on the dock looking starched and anxious and when Nate stepped from the Zodiac, he felt out of place. Etionette reached for his arm and introduced him to her guests as her special friend. Nate knew straight away why she wanted him along. The men couldn't keep their eyes off of her. The three wives greeted Nate with big smiles. One of them spoke under her breath.

"Boy, we're glad you could come along," she said. "All these old guys can do is drool."

Etionette wore a black, spaghetti-strap dress that hung close to her body. Every curve was there to see. Nate wondered himself how incredible it would be just to slip the straps away. They made their way around the harbor and up the hill to the Galleon House where Etionette ordered two bottles of Châteauneuf du Pape. The waiter poured the wine and they sat at a table and ate baguettes and cheese and had to order two more bottles.

They left the Galleon House behind and wandered over to a brick building in the old part of town where there was a bar upstairs that had no windows and a loud and brassy reggae band inside. Mt. Gay was the house rum so the charter guests took to drinking and dancing and laughing with each other.

Nate ordered a rum and sat in a dark corner and watched as Etionette danced with one of the husbands. She kept looking over and smiling. Nate thought he would be able to leave soon, but a nice looking girl came over and asked if he'd like to dance. After they got out on the floor, Nate could tell right away she couldn't move like Rilee. It was unfair for him to think that and he tried to be interested, but his heart just wasn't there. She was an elementary school teacher from Ohio who had come down to St. Thomas with a lady friend to enjoy the Caribbean. She was pretty in the light and there were dimples when she smiled and a hint of freckles like stardust. Nate liked her, but he couldn't deal with the emptiness that dragged him down.

The music stopped and he excused himself and went

back to his corner seat. He saw that the school teacher was looking at him from across the way. When the band started again, Etionette swirled over and grabbed Nate's arm. All the men in the bar watched Etionette swinging about and laughing with her head thrown back. When the band finished and Nate walked back to his seat, the cute little teacher with the splash of freckles was gone. He sat there with the rum wondering if he should order another. One of the other husbands came over and ordered a double for him. The man leaned bleary-eyed over the table.

"Jesus Christ, what a life you have," he said. "You just danced with the two best looking girls in the house and I'm stuck with my wife."

He pounded Nate's back and shook his head and went back toward his poor wife who looked redfaced and bored. Etionette grabbed the man's hand, though, and made him dance. The husband shot Nate a glance and smiled and waved and when Etionette looked over, she winked at him.

"It's okay to go," she said. "I know you don't like it here."

Nate stood and drank the rum down.

"I'm sorry," Nate said. "I did have fun. I just have other things on my mind. Thanks for having me."

Nate turned away and slipped out the door and down the stairs to the alley below. The streets are narrow in Charlotte Amalie. He made his way through the canyons, stepping along the cobblestones still glistening from a twilight rain. He was thinking about the guests and wondering if the owner of the schooner kept Etionette around to be his personal treat, but Nate could feel the rum taking hold. It made him dizzy and when he thought of Etionette and her mahogany skin and her brown hair swirling, she only reminded him of Rilee. He wished he had ordered another double for the road.

Nate turned the corner onto the boulevard that sweeps along the harbor toward the Sheraton. An island girl sat alone on a wall. He thought she might be working the streets, but he got closer and could see she was no more than nine or ten. She smiled at him.

"You like some genips?" she asked.

"Yes," Nate said. "That would be nice."

The little girl handed him a branch from a tree with several dozen genips, green and plump, clustered here and there among the leaves. Nate gave her a one-dollar bill and thanked her and walked alone along the quay toward the marina. There were no lights over the walkway so the water of the harbor was black like the night. The air seemed cool to him and he hunched his shoulders against the chill and the dark. The rum didn't help much and the shadows only made him lonely. He stopped and leaned against the sea wall to eat some of the genips, but he didn't want to spit the seeds onto the street. There were no trash cans around so he carried the branch and the seeds with him. He tried to think about Etionette and those tiny straps and the schoolteacher from Ohio with the hint of freckles. There were only visions of Rilee in the soft red glow that spilled from the companionway and visions of her nightshirt floating down like satin petals. Nate threw the genip branch and the seeds into the muck of the harbor.

At the Sheraton he headed down the dock toward the St. Tropez office. The walk along the quay wall had been dark in the shadows, but the cruise ship across the channel looked again like Manhattan. Nate could hear the hum of the diesels driving the generators, and the sound was deep in the gut somewhere. There were streams of water pouring from thru-hulls just above the water line and wisps of steam and smoke from the stacks high over the ship. People strolled along the promenade deck and in a moment of fantasy, Nate thought about being up there with Rilee and how far removed that would be from reality. He hunched his shoulders again and walked with his head down toward *Dame Foncé* sitting dark and quiet near the end of the dock.

Nate hadn't thought about getting a ride back to *Serendipity*. He climbed the steps into the Quarterdeck to get a pint of Double Diamond. There were some charter people around and a number of deckhands from the cruising boats in the anchorage. Nate took a seat at an empty table and drank alone. Rilee would be home by now, maybe in Steamboat with Andy, and he thought they would be singing and laughing and probably not even thinking of the Caribbean. Nate looked out the window toward the lights of Charlotte Amalie and drank the bitters. He ordered another pint just when Brady walked through the door. Nate ordered a beer for him and he sat down and took a big swallow from the pint and looked around at the bar.

"I've been drinking since you left," Brady said. "Shanna is mad at me."

"She'll be mad at both of us, now."

"Where'd you go? That French girl is a knockout."

"We went to a reggae bar in town. You should have seen all the guys panting over her. I guess that's why she wanted me along. It was safe enough there. The older guys were harmless. I should have stayed, really, but Etionette didn't mind. I left to come back here. I haven't felt much like partying, anyway."

"Shanna is worried. She thinks you want to turn around and go back to Key West."

"I could, I guess. All my life I've dreamed of doing this, though. I can't imagine giving up already, but I've thought about going back. I think after some years go by, I'd realize what a mistake I made. We won't be turning around anytime soon. Maybe when we get to Grenada."

"Well, it's been great so far. If you need to go back, don't worry about us."

They finished the Double Diamond and headed outside and down the stairs where Nate could hear again the low sound of the generators on the cruise ship. There were a lot of people still out on the decks leaning on the rails and looking out toward the city lights. Brady stepped down into the sabot. Nate waited on the dock looking to see if Etionette was on her way back from the reggae bar. The dock was dark and quiet and there was only a dim glow from the portlights aboard the schooner.

Nate stepped carefully into the dinghy while Brady pulled on the oars. They drifted into the channel while Nate glanced again toward the dock looking for Etionette. He didn't know why he looked other than she reminded him of Rilee with her flawless skin and eyes so clear they looked like Yellowstone hot springs. When he didn't see anyone coming, he turned to look out over the anchorage and at *Serendipity* floating in her dreamtime.

Shanna had the Aladdin going and the glow through the yellow curtains reflected off the dark water. The dancing light looked like the night near Whale Cay when the moon lit the water from within and he felt so close to Sarah. Nate didn't know if those feelings would return and there was nothing he could do. Brady pulled at the oars. The sabot pulsed toward the yellow glow where the lights splashed softly on the water.

TWENTY-TWO

Nate woke early on Saturday and propped his head against the pillow to stare through the portlight at the saturated blue over the hills to the east. The winter sky in Bodega Bay had the same color. It seemed out of place for late spring in St. Thomas. Nate slipped from the bunk and stepped into the cockpit and looked to the south where the winter blue stretched clear to the horizon beyond the point that hid the mouth of the harbor. Some deep pulsing of the generators on the cruise ship behind him carried all the way into the anchorage. The pulsing mixed with the pop-pop-pop of a workboat idling along in the channel, its exhaust echoing off the huge steel hull like the *African Queen.*

Nate stood on the transom and watched the workboat make its way toward the harbor entrance. Its bow waves peeled away on either side like a wedge of swimming geese. The trade winds had died away to nothing and he could still hear the little diesel popping away when it was a long way off. Even *Serendipity* sat rock still in the calm. Nate waited for the first breaths of air to drift down from the hills but they never came. The heat and the humidity settled over the anchorage, laying flat the Caribbean. He sat alone in the cockpit and waited for Brady and Shanna. Nate was nodding off when he smelled the coffee brewing in the galley.

"Hot down below," Brady said.

"Not much cooler out here."

"Want a splash of bourbon to go in your coffee?"

"We have bourbon?"

"Buck seventy-five in the free zone. Seagram's Seven."

Nate thought of his dad who drank bourbon in his coffee at Christmas. The sky looked like it could have been Christmas at home, but it was early May in Charlotte Amalie. Nate drank the bourbon and coffee too fast. Brady was there with more, though, and he could feel the numbing take hold in his stomach. The second bourbon disappeared and he slouched in the cockpit and wondered when the spinning would start. Shanna went below and made up some pancake batter for breakfast and relit the stove.

"Can you make another pot of coffee?" Nate asked. "I'm finished with the bourbon, though."

When the pancakes were done and the fresh coffee was poured, they ate in the cockpit while the heat blanketed the harbor like summer out on Pamlico Sound.

"I could fall asleep right now," Nate said.

"I'd like to go ashore to call my mother in Maryland," Shanna said. "Brady can take me in. You can sleep while we're gone. Will that work?"

Brady and Shanna rowed away while Nate stretched out on the settee in the heat of the cabin. The spinning had nearly disappeared, but when he shut his eyes, the coffee made them bounce around like popcorn until he fell asleep. There were dreams then, mixed up dreams of Rilee in the caves and Rilee swimming with dolphins and Rilee laughing in that long dark tunnel and he couldn't keep her in focus. The laughing grew fainter and Nate grew more desperate until he was tossing in sweat and had to open his eyes. He looked around at the empty *Serendipity* and listened to the silence and then rolled on his side and slipped away again, this time to a deep and very black sleep.

Nate slept for nearly two hours. When he opened his eyes, Brady and Shanna hadn't come back. Neither had the trade winds. He yawned and stepped into the cockpit again. The surface of the water was mirror bright in the high sun and he had to shade his eyes to look down the channel. There was no sign of *Nomad*. He ducked below and stripped down for a shower. The water was soft and cold and soothing, but he got out and then shaved and dressed and ran the towel through his hair. He heard Brady bumping the sabot alongside.

Nate helped with a bag of groceries out in the cockpit and then Shanna pointed down the channel. A beamy ketch made its way around the corner from the mouth of the harbor. Nate stared to be sure when the boat changed course and saw the wide maroon sheer stripe as *Nomad* headed into the anchorage. There were some needles and pins in his stomach and he wasn't quite sure what to do. He wanted it to be Rilee, but Sarah was home from her charter. The reality crept in once more there would never be a Rilee.

They watched *Nomad* labor into a slot fifty yards to the west where Sarah's blonde hair fell forward as she let the windlass go. A big CQR slipped out of the roller and down into the murky water of the harbor. Nate could hear the diesel running up, but it took a long time for the ketch to react. It began to move in reverse and yaw away from its track until the anchor line tightened and drew the bow back. The guy behind the wheel let *Nomad* run in reverse to see if the CQR would drag and then the diesel idled down and stopped. Sarah waved from the bow. Nate waved back and smiled, hiding the ache inside. Brady came over and stood for a moment watching *Nomad* wallow around.

"There are cold Heinekens below, if you want one," he said.

Nate nodded without looking. He stared at the heavy *Nomad* and at the Zodiac being lowered from the stern davits and at the Hampton socialites waiting on deck for their ride into the dock. The people had a lot of bags and they were strewn about like stuffed pillows at a bazaar. Nate watched as they handed them, one by one, to the smiling skipper who stood in the center of the Zodiac. When the guests were ready to leave, they turned and gave Sarah and the deck hand a hug before climbing down into the dinghy. There wasn't a lot of room and when they motored by, all you saw were tanned faces and bags of green and red and blue and a lot of teeth from the guy running the outboard. The charter guests waved and smiled, but they were only being polite. They slipped by leaving *Serendipity* rocking in the wake. Nate looked back at *Nomad*. Sarah was there with the deckhand waiting near the stern rail for the skipper to return. She waved again while her hair flashed in the sun. There was no burning inside for Nate, just some nervous churning.

The Zodiac roared back from the dock and left a good wake that rolled all the way through the anchorage and set a lot of halyards banging. The skipper motored straight ahead for *Nomad* where he shut the outboard down and rode the stern wake into the hull where he bounced hard. Sarah and the deckhand climbed down into the Zodiac with her bags and the outboard coughed to life again. It didn't take very long for them to cover the fifty yards between them. When the Zodiac slewed to a stop, the stern wake got *Serendipity* stomping around like a nervous racehorse. Brady took the painter while Sarah waited a bit for the prancing to stop. She looked at Nate and there was a moment where he could feel the doubts return and he wondered what the night would bring. Sarah stepped up onto the deck and rushed over. It felt odd for Nate to hold her again. She turned away and hugged Brady and Shanna and then she turned to the *Nomad* crew.

"Come on aboard," she said. "Have you ever been on a trimaran?"

Sarah was beaming. She turned back to Nate while the skipper stepped onto the port wingdeck.

"Nate, this is George Kensington," she said. "He's the captain on *Nomad*."

Nate was still overwhelmed by all of the teeth flashing behind the smiles. George turned out to be a harmless salesman type and after he introduced Todd, his foredeck crew, Brady brought out a round of Heinekens. They sat in the cockpit and talked for a long time about the charter business. Sarah sat close to Nate and there were times when he thought the feelings would return, but when she looked at him, he was almost embarrassed to return her gaze. She kept pushing him and it made Nate laugh and it was fun to sit there with her and flirt even though he was afraid of the night when they had to turn the Aladdin down.

"Let's all go ashore and get hamburgers at the Quarter-deck," Sarah said. "You don't know how I've been starving for one of those."

"We've been living on hamburgers," Shanna said. "But that's okay. I'm hungry, too."

Brady and Shanna rowed the sabot to the dock while Nate rode with Sarah and Captain George and Todd in the big Zodiac. George was civilized this time, barely running the outboard above idle. They passed Etionette on the big schooner. She smiled at Nate and waved and jumped onto the dock to catch the lines. When Nate climbed out of the Zodiac, Etionette leaped into his arms.

"I wish you could stay the other night," she said.

"Looks like you made it home okay. Did the owner's friends behave themselves?"

"Oh, yes. They had fun."

"What have you been doing while I was gone?" Sarah asked.

Nate turned and looked at her. His heart was beating and it was hard for him to say anything.

"I helped Etionette with some of the guests on *Dame Foncé*," he said. "They turned out to be pretty mellow."

"Is that all?" Sarah asked.

Sarah was giggling while they walked up the steps to the grill. They found an empty table near the back where they sat down and ordered pints of bitters to go around and hamburgers for each of them. Sarah wolfed her's down first. Nate was more interested in the Double Diamond and when the pints were nearly empty, he ordered another round so there wouldn't be any lag time. They were well into the second when Captain George ordered more. Sarah was enjoying herself and there was a lot of laughter from the table. Nate kept looking away toward the door, worrying about the night. When George excused himself from the party, he gave Sarah an envelope with the money she earned along with a modest tip from the charter guests. They hugged and then he was out the door and down the steps. Sarah leaned over and whispered in Nate's ear.

"I think George and the little deckhand are gay, but they're good guys," she said. "The charter was a lot of fun. It lasted forever, though."

"How did it work with three couples being in such close quarters for so long?"

"The husbands kept trying to hustle me in bed when the wives weren't looking. When they did look, those three guys were as nice as they could be."

"Were any of them successful?"

Sarah smiled and winked at Nate. He let the subject drop. Brady wanted more Double Diamond and when the waitress came back, they ordered more chips and sat around the table talking about the trip down islands and where to go. They drank one more round of bitters and then left the Quarterdeck just as the sun was going down. Brady rowed Shanna and Sarah out to *Serendipity* first while Nate sat on the edge of the dock and let his feet dangle over the side like a kid with a cane pole again. Etionette came over and sat down next to him.

"Is Sarah your lady?" she asked.

"Yes, she is."

"But what about the other? The lady on the charter?"

"I don't know about her."

"She was a lovely girl. Secret? I think so."

Etionette giggled and planted a kiss on Nate's cheek.

"*Vous suivrez votre coeur*. You will follow your heart," she said, and she kissed his cheek again and left him sitting alone in the fading light with his feet dangling over the edge.

Sarah rowed back in the sabot, looking over her shoulder the whole time trying to see the dock. Nate stepped into the center of the dinghy and sat down while she moved them away into the channel.

"It feels good to be rowing again after using that Zodiac for so long," she said.

Sarah pulled away from *Dame Foncé*. Nate could see Etionette standing alone on the lazarette hatch and it made him think of her again in the thin, black dress with the tiny straps. Nate turned away and looked for *Serendipity* dancing in the reflections on the water. When they rowed up, Brady took the painter. Nate stepped onto the deck and Shanna handed him a rum and lime juice.

"I'm so excited about leaving," she said. "I could go right now."

"I'm ready, too," Sarah said. "I can't even think straight, I'm so glad to be back."

They sat and drank the Cruzan and it seemed like a natural thing just to start the Volvo and lift the plow out of the muck and head for the BVI.

There hadn't been any wind all day, but Nate felt the first soft puffs rolling off the hills and down across the anchorage. The breeze set *Serendipity* tacking like she was ready to leave. The wind brought with it the damp, earthy smells of the island. When it was calm, the salt air returned laced with the faint smell of diesel and creosote and the quiet sounds of the harbor. *Serendipity* settled down in the silent moments only to drift about again when the puffs and the earthy smells rolled through.

"I forgot how this was," Sarah said. "*Nomad* sat anchored to the water and never moved. *Serendipity* dances like there is music in the wind." Sarah held her face in the direction of the breeze, soft and warm just then. "There is music for her in the wind."

Sarah touched Nate's arm and smiled in the dark and there was a second where he felt that little burn come back.

"I still think I need more to drink," Brady announced. "How about another rum?"

He stepped below and in a few minutes, there were fresh cups all around. Nate thought he could let the rum sit without drinking it, but he kept sipping until there was none left and the spinning was there even when he had his eyes open. Sarah was nearly asleep next to him in the cockpit. Nate helped her down below where she crawled into the double berth on the portside wingdeck.

Shanna put one of the John Prine tapes into the machine and turned the volume low. Nate reached for one of the cruising guides to the lower Caribbean. After Brady and Shanna slipped into the forepeak, he sat alone at the dinette in the soft glow of the Aladdin and opened the guide. There were quiet moments in the music and it was hard not to think of Rilee. He kept turning the pages and looking cross-eyed at the pictures of the Pitons in St. Lucia and the clear blue neon of the Grenadines.

Nate splashed water on his face and tried to sober up a little by drinking the water from the tap in the galley. The faint chlorine taste made him wrinkle his nose, but he drank it anyway and then turned the lamp off and climbed into the berth beside Sarah who was asleep. He leaned against the pillow and looked at the stars outside through the portlight. When John Prine finally clicked off, Nate rolled over on his side and let the spinning begin.

There were dreams again where Rilee kept trying to tell him something. They were in a noisy crowd and she was being pushed away and he couldn't hear. Everyone left and he didn't know what to make of what she said because all he heard were bits and snatches and too much noise. He kept twisting to hear, but when he was left behind, Nate didn't even know where she had gone. He shouted Rilee's name and all he heard were echoes and footsteps and slowly dripping water. He could feel the anxiety set in and he ran down a long hall that had waxed concrete floors, finally stopping when there were no other sounds except for his breathing. He shouted for Rilee. He could have been shouting across a canyon because the echo came back loud and pure and when it died away, he was alone again, breathing hard in the gray concrete hallway. There were windows looking out toward some rolling green hills nearly black in a heavy mist that hung over the countryside like lace curtains. The hills were desolate. They gave Nate an overwhelming sense of loneliness and he couldn't look at them without feeling panic again. He stepped away from the windows and yelled again for Rilee, but there was the echo, taunting him by shouting Rilee's name. Nate turned to walk back along the hallway when something brushed his shoulder from behind. He opened his eyes hoping to find her there.

Someone was there touching Nate in the dark. It made him wish for the cockpit on *Sandpiper* and the red glow of the nightlights falling over Rilee and her breasts so perfect in the shadows, but it was Sarah who touched him. In a moment they were together fumbling with clothes and when they were free, they held each other. Nate could feel the pressure of her breasts and the softness of her thighs and he held her so close they could have been one, but he was aching again for Rilee. They were close for a long time and Nate thought if they stayed, maybe the feelings would return. He felt her breasts and the soft inner mystery between her legs and wanted to make love over and over like he had with Rilee.

"I guess we're back where we started," Sarah whispered. "Maybe it's never going to work for us?"

"I want it to work, though," Nate said. "I don't know what's wrong."

Nate tried to think of how it was before *Sandpiper* and how the sight of Sarah in the morning made his stomach burn for her. It didn't work again, just like the early days in Key West.

"I don't want you to give up yet," Nate said. "We have a lot of time."

"I know. I'm glad we're leaving tomorrow. When we're out sailing I'm going to make it work."

They fell asleep so close it seemed to Nate that Sarah could have been right.

TWENTY-THREE

Nate woke at dawn with that evaporated rum taste back in his mouth and Sarah sound asleep next to him. He leaned back and barely breathed, frustrated with the things in the night that didn't happen and overwhelmed with guilt for feeling that way. Sarah had pushed the covers away and in the gray light that crept in from the open companionway, he could see her breasts, thick and full and smooth to the touch. Nate didn't want to stare, but they were close and it made him want to bury his face in them. He kept waiting for the burning to come back like it had before. There was nothing even though he wanted to touch Sarah and feel her softness and follow her curves with his lips. Nate finally closed his eyes and rolled away.

The sun burned bright and hot through the portlights when he opened his eyes again. He looked over toward the stove where someone had made coffee. Shanna stepped below from the cockpit.

"The pot is empty now, sleepyhead," she said. "I'll make some more."

Shanna pumped the kerosene tank and lit the burner. Nate watched her moving around and he was suddenly embarrassed about his nudity. He reached under the covers for his cutoffs to pull them on and she kept watching him struggle beneath the sheets.

"Big night, huh?" she said, and she giggled and scooped the grounds into the filter.

Brady was sitting on the cabin roof watching the boat traffic when Nate sneaked out into the cockpit. Sarah and the sabot were gone. There were charter boats coming toward the

St. Tropez docks and he thought *Sandpiper* might be one of them. He didn't look to see. There was a sudden urge to get the anchor up and head out and get away from anything that reminded him of Rilee.

"Sarah rowed ashore to make a phone call," Brady said. "She won't be gone long."

Shanna brought the coffee out. Nate took a cup and sat in the cockpit thinking Sarah might not come back at all. Gusts of wind rolled down from the hills while *Serendipity* hunted back and forth in an endless series of tacks. Nate watched the scenery change around him. *Nomad* was still across the way, but the Zodiac was gone and the fat ketch looked deserted. He watched it swing by as they fell away in the wind. Nate set the coffee down and leaned back and shut his eyes and could have fallen asleep except for the cramping in his wrists. He sat up again when he saw Sarah rowing along the edge of the channel. She wore only a thin, white tanktop with her shorts. Nate knew the guys in the Sheraton probably slobbered all over themselves trying to help her make the phone call. She came alongside and he took the painter while she scrambled aboard. She hugged his waist and he saw again how tight her top was and there was some churning inside. He couldn't believe the timing. Sarah was laughing and hopping about like a lady Ben Gunn all excited to leave. Nate slugged the rest of the coffee down and helped lift the sabot clear of the water to set it down in its nesting place.

Brady hauled on the anchor line and chain, cleaning it as it came up, and after he stowed the ground tackle in the deck locker, they motored over toward the St. Tropez docks to wave good-bye to anyone who might be there. Mac came out smiling.

"Have a great trip, guys," he yelled. "Any room left?"

Nate smiled and waved back. He felt bad for Mac standing alone on the dock. Etionette stepped out of the cabin aboard the schooner wearing another tiny yellow bikini.

"*Au revoir, au revoir*...Please come back, Captain Nate," she shouted.

Nate steered *Serendipity* alongside the black hull of *Dame Foncé*. Etionette skipped over to the rail and blew him a kiss. When they motored out beyond the shining Amway yacht, he could still see Etionette standing in the bow of the beautiful French schooner watching *Serendipity* disappear down the channel. She waved again from a long way off. Nate thought of her flawless shoulders and the little black dress and the fragile straps that held it in place. He wondered again how incredible it would have been just to have touched her.

The gusts of wind blew stronger down the hills. *Serendipity* accelerated through the flat water of the harbor entrance, ticking ten knots in an instant only to enter another wind shadow. The boat slowed until they reached the cruising speed of the engine. When the wind picked up again and held steady from the east, Nate shut the diesel down and let the sails take over. *Serendipity* left Charlotte Amalie behind and raced through the short chop at ten knots again, prancing along on a close reach, steering herself toward the open Caribbean. The heat and the wind and the iridescent blue made Nate feel like he was flying again and not dragging several tons of lead through the water. Sarah walked up to stand near the bow rail and watch as the water rushed past the hulls. Sometimes the bow would bury itself in a swell and then rise again like a carnival ride. A lot of spray flew aft from clipping the tops of the waves. Brady and Shanna sat on the deck near the cockpit coaming just to get drenched in the warm water. Nate could feel in the air the tension was gone again. He wanted to go straight for St. Barts and not head up for the BVI, but when he made enough easting to carry Current Cut on one tack, he steered over for the little channel barely visible in the distance. Sarah walked back from the bow rail and stepped down into the cockpit.

"Can I drive?" she asked. "This is like riding a wild horse compared to *Nomad*. That thing was a tank."

Sarah sat at the wheel with a big grin. You could hear the SumLog ticking ten and eleven knots in short bursts.

"*Nomad* couldn't hit seven knots going over a waterfall," Sarah said.

She kept looking over at the white water from the bow waves streaming astern. Nate climbed up and stood for a while near the mast and looked about at the yellow decks and at the white hulls racing along and it was such a glorious sail it made him wish Rilee were there to see. He watched Sarah at the helm steering the boat up and over the swells and laughing now and then when she corkscrewed a little and the spray flew aft and got Brady yelling. Nate leaned against the mast thinking about Rilee again and about St. Barts and how far away everything seemed just then. He was finished with St. Thomas, but it felt like he was running away one more time.

Serendipity clipped another swell. A good amount of spray carried aft in the wind and caught Sarah at the helm when she couldn't duck. Her tanktop got wet and she caught Nate staring. She winked at him and took a big breath and faked a Marilyn Monroe pose. She wasn't wearing anything underneath and she looked like Debra, only much bigger. Nate kept looking back at Sarah who was laughing in the wind and after a moment, he hopped down from the cabin roof and sat next to her by the wheel. She hugged his neck and held him there and waited for *Serendipity* to clip another wave. The whine of the SumLog held steady at eleven knots, even when the boat rolled up and over the larger swells that sent the spray flying aft. Sarah held onto Nate until they were both wet and soggy.

Current Cut was only a mile off when they entered the wind shadow of the islands again. The sea flattened out into the short chop that got *Serendipity* hobby-horsing. She never slowed, though, roaring into the narrow channel and throwing spray into the air.

"Can we sail all the way through?" Sarah asked. "They always started the engine on *Nomad*."

"Sure," Nate said. "Blast right through."

Nate leaned against the coaming and watched Sarah at the wheel. The shadow of Great St. James stole the life from the sails, but Sarah held the course and they ghosted into the cut well clear of the coral heads. She steered down to gain some boat speed and they accelerated again and charged through at nine knots, squirting into Pillsbury Sound where she steered back up, close-hauled for Tortola in the distance.

"You made it look easy," Nate said.

"*Serendipity* acts more like a Ferrari than a boat. That was fun."

The trades blowing across the sound drove the short chop to the west. Sarah steered just off the wind and *Serendipity* tracked through the water like she was on skis. Nate caught himself thinking about Rilee and about the first night below on *Sandpiper* when he knew and about all those places they went in the BVI, falling in love the whole time, and then to be going back again without her made the crushing weight unbearable. He stepped from the cockpit and walked up to the bow to lean against the rail. He looked back at Sarah and her wet tanktop and at her salt blonde hair streaming in the wind. Nate had to turn and look beyond the sound toward the hills glowing green in the midday sun.

In the gusts that cascaded from the hills of St. John, *Serendipity* accelerated and touched twelve knots only to slow when the wind swirled away and left her in the shadows. Shanna wanted to go all the way up to Road Town and have dinner ashore. Sarah hunted about, heading away from the bulk of St. John to avoid the calms. They sailed well past Lovango Cay before turning in toward the Narrows where the wind strength made the water and the hills look more like a river canyon. Sarah steered the boat close-hauled to port and then to starboard while Brady and Nate worked on the perfect tacks. Once they sailed through, Sarah steered off a little and the SumLog whined an octave higher while they made for Norman Island in the distance.

Nate didn't much care to get any closer to the caves than The Indians. They passed close by the rocks and pulled off another racing tack and bore away for the big island of Tortola. *Serendipity* could have steered herself all the way into Road Harbour, but Sarah was in a zone and wanted to stay at the wheel even though she had been there all afternoon. They were hitting eleven and twelve knots sailing across the windblown Drake's Channel and made the harbor entrance without having to pinch into the wind. *Serendipity* fell away and accelerated even faster into the anchorage and passed a lot of the Moorings charter boats. The people watched as they roared through. Nate sat down again near Sarah.

"I'd like to keep going," Nate said, "just to show off."

"Why don't we? Some of those charter boats look like they're in reverse."

"I would, but we need to clear customs."

"It's getting late, I know. I wish we could blow by those boats again."

Sarah steered into the wind to kill the boat speed while Nate let the jib go and then started the Volvo. They furled the sails and motored through the cruising fleet and found an empty slot close to the old Mooring's docks where it wasn't far to row ashore. When the CQR set itself on the harbor bottom, Sarah pressed the stop button for the diesel. The four of them squeezed into the sabot for the short trip to the vacant dock. Brady spied Drake's Pub straight away.

"Drake's Pub?" he said. "You know where to find me."

"Well, we need to get over to customs before they close," Nate said.

"Just kidding. Maybe on the way back?"

They cleared customs at the ferry landing and then climbed the hill to a little restaurant where Nate knew the owner from the delivery trips he had made the year before. Francis was a happy islander who wore a huge madras shift. When they walked through the door, she rushed up with a flourish and the color floated all around in the light and made Nate think of a calliope. She greeted them with a big smile and made everyone sit at the big table by the window where there was a view down the hill to the harbor. Brady ordered Heinekens and when she brought the cold bottles over, she leaned next to Nate.

"Fresh grouper tonight," she said. "Rice and plantains, too. You hungry, Captain Nate?"

"Starved is more like it. I told my friends you were the best cook in the islands."

"No pop story," she giggled. "I have plenty, though. I keep bringing the cold beer, too"

Francis whirled away toward the kitchen and turned up the volume on the sound system. Reggae filled the little room. Sarah kept squeezing Nate's legs under the table like Rilee under the dinette. Nate drank the beer in a hurry.

Francis wasn't in much of a hurry to serve dinner. They went through yet another round of Heinekens before the grouper arrived. She brought in two plates and when she leaned across the table, her huge and pendulous breasts fell away nearly brushing the tablecloth. She straightened herself and rearranged her shift to cover more of the masses of flesh and she laughed at herself and went off into the kitchen for the other two plates.

"I'm in love," Brady said, and he stared after Francis and her giant bosom.

The grouper fillets covered most of the plate and it took a long time before they were finished and ready to leave. Nate left Francis a big tip for her troubles and they strolled out of the restaurant to walk back to the harbor. She stopped them at the door.

"You want to hear reggae, Captain Nate? They playing up the hill."

"Where up the hill? Close by?"

"Yes. Just go up until you see the road to the right. Friends of mine playing. No charge tonight to get in, if you buy beer."

They walked a quarter mile higher on the hill and turned down a narrow street where a lot of red and yellow hibiscuses were in bloom. Sarah picked a red one and put it over her left ear. Nate kept looking at her and at the red flower, dark against her hair, wondering if he would ever see Rilee again.

They got to the end of the road and found a brown stucco building with a dozen local men hanging around the front, some of them Rastafarians. All of them stopped to stare at Shanna and at Sarah when they walked up. Shanna was nervous, but the four of them waded through the door to see what was inside. The reggae was deafening and there were black lights and strobes and dozens of bodies dancing in sweat out on the floor.

Brady went to the bar and bought four bottles of Beck's beer. When he came back, Sarah had already been asked to dance by one of the locals. She looked at Nate first and he winked at her. After the beer showed up, he couldn't see Sarah anywhere in the dark. Shanna was more timid and waited close to Brady, dancing alone to the reggae. Another local asked for a dance and she went off like Sarah and disappeared in the strobe-lit blackness. Nate kept watching for them. The bodies were everywhere and the sweat was wet and shiny. When the band started playing *No Woman, No Cry*, Nate wanted to dance with Sarah, but Shanna came back alone. Nate finished one of the beers and looked into the crowd for some blonde hair. There were too many people and the strobe made it hard to focus. He drank Sarah's warming beer in the corner while he waited.

Nate caught sight of Sarah just once and then she was swallowed up again in the swirl of dancers. Brady came back and handed him another beer and he leaned against the wall and watched without trying to get nervous. There were too many people in the way and he couldn't see until there was a pause in the music. He saw where Sarah stood on the other side with two of the men, laughing and tossing her hair. Nate drank the beer and looked at the people on the dance floor. He wasn't aware that some of them were staring back until Brady mentioned it. Nate kept busy watching for Sarah and trying to avoid eye contact with the dancers for too long. When she finally came back, she was drenched in sweat and very much out of breath. She took Nate's arm and held it close before taking the bottle of beer and nearly draining it.

"I was having a good time out there," she said, "but some other guy asked me to dance. When we brushed against each other, he had the most incredible erection. It scared me. I just left him there."

Nate looked at her face beaded in sweat. There was an awkward silence and he looked over at the bar.

"Can I get you another beer?" he asked.

"Sure. I think I could drink a six-pack. That was fun until that last guy."

Nate walked alone back to the counter and bought beer for everyone. Brady took Shanna by the hand.

"We're ready to go," he said. "Shanna doesn't like it here."

Sarah glanced back toward the dance floor at all of the writhing, sweat-soaked bodies.

"I'm ready to go, too," she said.

They stood around for a few minutes longer drinking the Beck's, but so many of the guys kept coming over and trying to chat the girls up that Brady just turned and walked with Shanna out the door. Nate took Sarah by the arm and followed them. They got outside and walked up the street and suddenly Shanna and Sarah burst out laughing about all the oversexed guys in the bar. Nate kept walking toward the corner where they had to make the turn to get back down to the harbor. In the twilight he could see the leaflets on the coconut palms outlined against the sky, hanging limp from the fronds like rows of stringy wet sausage.

TWENTY-FOUR

Sarah came up to Nate and took his hand when they passed the little restaurant on the way down the hill. They could see Francis inside entertaining her dinner guests. Nate only glanced through the window. Brady was straining to see when Francis leaned over a table and when she did, it took his breath away.

"If you keep that up," Shanna said, "I'm going back to that reggae bar where there were some real men."

Nate looked away at the lights across the harbor. Sarah held his hand and they walked close together all the way down to the corner where the shops were closed and the streets were quiet. The road took them along the harbor toward Drake's Pub. Brady kept looking over at the sign, but when they got to the dock where the sabot was tied, he offered to make everyone rum after they got back to the boat.

Brady rowed again and they inched their way across the anchorage and came upon *Serendipity* soon enough. They stepped aboard and Shanna lit the lamp and started the stereo while Brady got out a fresh bottle of Cruzan and the lime juice. Sarah and Nate stayed out in the cockpit in the light spilling from the companionway. Nate could feel in his face and on his shoulders the short bursts of warm wind followed by moments of quiet when the breeze died away. Across the harbor, the water was clear and glassy and thick, like a sea of baby oil, and it felt good to sit still and look at the harbor and at the lights climbing the hills all around. The heat and the quiet and the soft gusts of wind gave Road Town the feel of a tropical outpost. Sarah leaned over and put her head on Nate's shoulder.

"I love it here, don't you?" she said. "I didn't enjoy it much being out on charter. I was always on call for something. Now, I can just sit and feel like I belong. Are you okay?"

"I guess so. The charters were a long stretch. I just want to watch the lights and take some deep breaths."

Brady came out into the cockpit carrying the yellow cups filled with Cruzan and lime juice.

"There's a lot more left down there," he said.

Sarah took a big sip and then blew some air like she had just scalded herself. Nate wanted more rum than juice, anyway, and the drink was good. Shanna turned up the volume on her Neil Young tape and came outside to sit. She was angry at Brady and so she didn't say much. Sarah kicked her in the shin, but Shanna only faked a smile and then looked away at the flickering lights on Salt Island across the channel. Nate didn't know what to say so he sat there sipping rum.

"I'm sorry for being such a pig back there," Brady said. "I was only fooling around."

Shanna kept staring off toward the horizon, but there was a bit of a smile and she took his hand and pulled him down next to her. They spent the next hour talking about St. Barts and Saba and Montserrat and all those islands to the southeast that step away like garden stones on the edge of the Caribbean. They had several rounds of rum and Nate thought there might be problems later, but the harbor and the town and the hills with their pinpoints of light were nearly hypnotic. *Serendipity* hunted slowly about while Road Harbour slid by in the dark. The other cruising boats in the anchorage came into view looking so much like ducks asleep on a pond and then the lights of the town crept by and then they were back to the sleeping ducks and then again to the black water of the harbor and the tiny lights like fireflies sweeping up the hills. There were the ducks again, quiet and still, and then the lights of Road Town going out, one by one, as the night came down with *Serendipity* drifting through on her anchor line.

Sarah leaned over and put her head on Nate's shoulder again. He liked being outside with her on a night straight from

Rudyard Kipling, but there was some nagging guilt inside. He kept thinking about Rilee and it made him want to drown the images with rum. Sarah didn't care for anything more to drink. She was happy just to watch the lights and sit close. Brady made another for Nate and by the time Sarah excused herself and went off to bed, he could hardly think. Shanna didn't stay up, either, and when she went below, she switched the stereo off and turned the Aladdin down and blew the mantle out.

Nate stayed outside even after Brady left and when he was alone, he couldn't focus his eyes. All the lights were moving around and turning up and to the right and he couldn't make them stay in one place. There were Ferris wheels again and too much cotton candy and he kept turning his head to straighten it all out. His mouth started watering and a wave of nausea rolled up from deep in his gut. He stood and fell toward the stern where he hung his head over the edge of the wingdeck while his stomach convulsed again and again. The vomiting wouldn't stop, even when his body was empty.

Nate heaved into the water for a long time. When the convulsions finally began to weaken and go away, he sprawled on the deck and drooled over the side, not moving until a school of horse-eyed jacks swept through feeding on the little fish attracted by the food particles floating near the surface. Nate sat up with a start when the school ripped through the fingerlings. He watched the jacks slash through, over and over, until the tiny fish were gone. The water calmed once more and he sat on the aft wingdeck alone, feeling nauseous again.

"Are you okay? Are you sick?"

Nate turned around and stared at Sarah who had stepped out of the companionway. He couldn't see her very well. She only wore a nightshirt, looking so much like Rilee he shut his eyes for a moment.

"I'm fine, I guess," Nate said. "I drank too much rum. This time it didn't stay down. I need some paper towels."

Sarah disappeared below and popped back out with a whole roll. She handed it to Nate and sat on the cockpit seat while he tried to clean himself up. She kept looking at him.

"Is there something wrong?" she asked. "It hasn't been the same since I came back off charter. Did I do anything? I didn't mean to."

Nate was self-conscious, even in the dark, about his breath and about the smell on his face. He didn't want to go near Sarah just then.

"I don't know what's wrong. It isn't anything you did. I wish I could hit rewind and start the last two weeks over again."

"But what happened? Suddenly, it's like we're strangers again. I couldn't wait to get back from *Nomad*. As soon as I came over, I could tell something was different. Can I do anything?"

Nate looked at her face in the dark. He could see her blonde hair and how it fell loose over her shoulders and how her nightshirt didn't hide much. He wanted to hold her but he smelled like vomit.

"I don't know. We haven't given it any time. I keep thinking that's all we need, unless I drink myself stupid every night."

"I would rather you didn't, you know? That might be a place to start."

"I know. I'm fine, now. I fed all the rum to the fish."

"I heard. Why don't you wash your face and come to bed. We don't have to do anything. I just want you near me."

Nate watched her stand up. The shirt she wore barely reached her thighs and he stared after her while she disappeared below. He wanted to go with her just then, but he was afraid again of what might not happen and he waited for a few minutes before he went below to wash up. He used the hand pump in the galley and the water poured forth. He could smell the chlorine again. He let the water drip down his face several times before he toweled off and then he stood in the dark of the cabin wondering what to do. In the end Nate stripped away his clothes and put them at the foot of the bed and slipped beneath the covers next to Sarah who had done the same. In a moment they were in an embrace and he could tell it was no use. Sarah didn't seem to mind. She held him close beneath the thin sheets. He kept waiting for the rum to make him sick again, or help make things work, but nothing happened. Nate nodded off thinking about the lights in the night and the soft breeze that felt so warm and about Sarah's body next to his, soft and warm again, and then there were no lights at all.

After an hour of sleep, something made Nate open his eyes. He watched the stars through the portlight from his pillow as *Serendipity* turned about and fell away on another tack. There was a faint drop in temperature and the wind had come up and he kept watching the stars disappear behind the clouds. Nate eased his way from beneath the covers and slipped down onto the settee to go outside to check on the anchor. When he heard the patter of rain on the deck, he hurried through the companionway and closed the hatches in the hulls and shut the forepeak hatch.

The rain went away for a short time. Nate stood near the port shrouds and looked at the other boats in the anchorage, all of them dark and ghostlike. The breeze was cool on his naked body and he wanted to stand there and let the wind blow through, but the rain pelted the decks again. He left the shrouds and stepped below and pulled the companionway hatch nearly shut. There was still some air drifting in through the opening and he sat on the settee by the dinette and waited for sleep to return. The downpour got even heavier and in the dark of the cabin, he listened to the drumming. There were gusts of wind that got *Serendipity* moving fast on her anchor line and for a moment Nate thought he might have to go out again to check, but the gusts weakened as the squall moved on and the rain lightened until he couldn't hear it on the decks anymore.

Nate slid the big hatch open again and stepped outside to breathe the clean air and to feel the wind again on his body. He could see the decks glistening in the faint light of the new moon coming out from behind the clouds in the squall line. He walked up to the bow rail and leaned against the forestay. The wind and a few stray droplets of rain made the air brisk and fresh and he took some deep breaths and looked across the harbor at the tiny lights splattered on the dark hills in the distance. Nate stood alone in the cool air and in the fine mist from the lingering squall and watched the lights slide by while *Serendipity* tacked her way through the wind that was then only a whisper.

A moon shadow on the water moved across the harbor like the waving cape of a B-movie Dracula. Nate watched it come down the channel. In a minute *Serendipity* was in the shadow, but the cloud moved on and he could see the wavelets in the harbor dancing again in the light from the flickering moon. He looked away toward the harbor entrance, but there was a shuffling noise behind him. He turned to see Sarah emerging from the cockpit. She hadn't bothered with her shirt and in the soft light from the half-moon, he could see her breasts and her skin and the pale shadow below and it made him self-conscious about his own body. She stepped along the wingdeck and Nate watched her moving closer. He wanted to hide himself, but he didn't move because there was a prickly feeling in his stomach. She came close and put her arms around him and her skin was smooth and warm and he felt her breasts against his chest. She leaned her head against him and she whispered like the wind.

"I couldn't sleep after you left. I wondered if you had rowed away in the sabot. I'm glad you're here."

"The rain came and I got up to close the hatches. I liked being out here in the wind and in the mist just before it quit. There are moon shadows coming through. I stayed to watch."

Sarah reached for Nate's face and she kissed him on the lips and held him there and he felt her hand down low caressing him. The burning came back in a rush. They kissed with passion and there was that morning again in Nassau when the magic came together and they kept kissing near the bow rail like it wouldn't end. Sarah pulled away and took Nate by the hand and led him along the deck and down into the cockpit where they kissed again, long and hard, before stepping through the companionway. By the time they climbed into bed, there was no doubt they would make love. They pressed together and Nate found her body, soft and wet and warm like the night, and there was so much passion he couldn't think of Rilee until it was all over. He had to lie awake for a long time before the waves of guilt slipped away.

Nate kept glancing at Sarah in the night, wondering why he was so deeply taken by Rilee. He never made any sense of it and when he couldn't stay awake any longer, he reached over and touched Sarah's face. Nate wanted very much to be in love with Sarah, instead. He wanted very much to make love to her all night long. There was nothing left of him and when he thought of the time when she had to learn the truth, he turned away and hid.

There was another squall that night. Nate tried to sleep through the calm in between, but when the wind picked up and the rain slammed hard on the deck, he could only lay in the dark and listen.

TWENTY-FIVE

Serendipity occupied herself tacking back and forth in the morning breeze. Nate watched through the portlight as the scenery changed again from the buildings of Road Town to the open harbor and the hills beyond and then back to Road Town and then to some of the ducks from the night before, still asleep in the anchorage. He leaned against his pillow without moving, thinking if he got up to make coffee the noise would wake everyone. He was nearly asleep when Sarah turned on her side. Nate could see her body uncovered in the morning light with her smooth skin dark against the sheets. He kept staring at Sarah, trying to remember the night before and all of the passion and how it felt like he could go on forever. He leaned back and stared at the morning sky in pastel and at the silken clouds wandering through.

Nate fell asleep again and might have slept for a long time, but he felt Sarah's hand tickling down his stomach. He turned to look in her eyes and saw the smirk on her face. Her hand felt good and he didn't want her to stop. When there was nothing, she hugged his neck and reached for her nightshirt and he watched as she slipped it over her head and down. Nate was sorry the morning had ended that way. The anger and resentment came back in a rush. He rolled over so Sarah wouldn't see and didn't climb from the wingdeck berth until he could smell coffee brewing. Brady came out from the forepeak whistling another John Prine song. Sarah poured the mugs full and then stepped out into the cockpit. Nate dressed quickly and took his coffee out into the sunlight so blinding he had to shut his eyes for a moment.

"You look like you need to sleep for a week," Sarah said. "Maybe you should. We can handle *Serendipity*, you know? We're only going up to Bitter End."

"I know. I may fall asleep on the way."

They set about getting *Serendipity* ready for the beat to windward. Shanna stepped up on the cabin roof and looked at Nate.

"I heard when you were sick last night," she said. "I wanted to come out to help. I didn't when I heard Sarah get up. Do you feel okay?"

"I was sick from all the rum. Don't let me do that again."

"You and Brady need to cool it. He moaned all night long."

Shanna hugged Nate and then helped to remove the last of the sail ties from the main. When Brady started the Volvo, Nate went forward to haul the plow off the bottom. He leaned against the bow rail thinking about the night before when Sarah stepped out from below. He could see the image of her body in the light of the moon and he could feel again the warmth in his stomach. Nate turned to watch the Goose taking flight out on the harbor but Sarah walked forward and leaned her body against his. Waves of desire suddenly washed over him and he wondered why nothing had happened in the early morning when she reached for him. The feeling ebbed away and she slipped from his arms to help raise the main.

The wind blew heavy across the bay. Even with just the main up and drawing, *Serendipity* began to make tracks toward the harbor entrance. She cleared the boats in the anchorage and then Brady turned her to the east. Sarah and Nate hauled the jib in place and when Brady steered down again, the sails filled with a snap and they were away, headed once more for Drake's Channel with *Serendipity* ticking twelve knots. Nate sat on the cabin roof, still frustrated by the morning. Road Town already looked small in the distance. He kept looking back trying to find some relief at leaving behind another part of Rilee.

They sailed through the harbor entrance where Nate saw to the south a cluster of tubby charter boats tacking up the channel. He wished they were closer so they could see *Serendipity* streaking away. Brady held the course for Salt Island and they charged through the short chop like they were on skis again. Sarah and Shanna rode the windward hull flying three feet out of the water, laughing when the spray flew aft. Nate stayed on the cabin roof and watched while the charter boats to the south grew smaller. Up ahead lay Dead Chest Cay and the hills of Peter Island hiding the beach where he walked with Rilee in the starlight. When the boat roared up to Salt Island, they tacked away to the northeast. Nate kept looking back, thinking about the beach while Dead Chest Cay disappeared astern.

Serendipity bobbed and weaved across the channel. Brady steered up to clear the southeast point of Beef Island, boiling to windward all the way to Scrub Island before tacking over toward Virgin Gorda. They took advantage of the narrow Mosquito Island Passage into Virgin Gorda Sound where a light wind down the channel made the water surface dance in the sun. They furled the sails and started the diesel to idle their way through the quiet waters up to Bitter End where they dropped the hook one hundred yards off the yacht club dock.

Nate stood on the cabin roof in the quiet and looked over at the restaurant and at the bungalows beyond it stepping up the hill. The hotel and the grounds were saturated with color in the low light and there was a moment where he wished he were alone. Brady rowed to the dock with Sarah and Shanna while he sneaked below to clean up. He wasn't in much of a hurry. He could hear Brady bumping the dinghy along the hull long before he was finished. He pulled on a clean shirt and stepped outside to find Brady standing in the sabot.

"I took a look in the Clubhouse Bar," Brady said. "Let's get back. They serve John Courage in those big pints."

They rowed over to the dock where Sarah and Shanna were waiting with full mugs at a table near the back of the yacht club. Sarah handed Nate a pint of Courage and pulled his chair close to hers. She had a way of smiling with her eyes and she laughed when she caught him looking. Brady and Nate had two of the pints and then they left to walk along the hotel front where they stopped near the flowers that grew along the wall. Nate could smell the perfume from the blossoms drifting through like those moments when Rilee stood there in the evening light. They walked toward the beach with the flowers and the wind all around and after Sarah took his arm, it seemed for a moment like she belonged there. Nate wanted to tell her about the little cabins up the hill. He thought about Rilee again and didn't say anything at all.

They had dinner aboard and when Brady made everyone rum and lime juice, they sat around the cockpit watching the stars that ducked in and out of the clouds.

"Will it be rough tomorrow," Shanna asked. "I heard it could be."

"Maybe," Nate said. "The Anegada Passage has a bad reputation when the wind blows. I don't think it will."

"We should get a weather report," Brady said.

Nate nodded and stepped below where he switched on the Transoceanic. There were no winds forecast except the usual squall lines and eighteen-knot trades that would get *Serendipity* up on her toes.

"Good weather for the next few days," Nate said. "Just some squalls here and about. We picked a good time to go. We can't leave now, though. Might hit a coral head in the dark on the way through the pass in the reef."

"That's okay," Brady said. "We have more time for rum tonight. You need a refill?"

The four of them sat up late drinking rum in the cockpit. The night settled in, dark and breezy and warm. Nate leaned against Sarah and watched the lights of Biras Creek swinging through while *Serendipity* hunted in the wind. Sarah was about to leave and go below, but a few raindrops splattered heavily on the deck. They scrambled around to shut the hatches and then stumbled below while the rain fell harder. The drumming was so loud Nate couldn't hear anything above the roar.

Brady and Shanna disappeared in the forepeak when Sarah blew out the Aladdin. She stood alone in the dark listening to the wind and rain, and then she stepped over to Nate and put her arms around his neck. He fumbled with her top and her wraparound and they fell away to the floor. She tried to unbutton his cutoffs but they were stuck and so she giggled and climbed into the wingdeck berth and waited. Nate was embarrassed to undress, even in the dark, because he never felt anything below and he didn't want her to see. He picked up their clothes and put them at the end of the bed. When he slipped under the sheets, she could tell straight away. It didn't much matter because the rum made Nate dizzy. He shut his eyes and all he could feel was the spinning. Sarah shivered against him in the dark.

"Maybe it's my turn to be sick," she said, and she bolted upright. She breathed for a few minutes trying to clear her nausea away. "I'm sorry. All of a sudden I really don't feel very well."

In a few minutes, the passion was gone and she was breathing again, only this time in a deep, rum-induced sleep. Nate waited forever in the dark listening to the rain beat on the deck. The roar above was deafening and he couldn't imagine it raining any harder. He kept wondering if there were leaks in the deck somewhere and he kept rolling back and forth trying to find a spot where the spinning wasn't so bad. The rain eased up and soon the drumming gave way and he could hold his eyes shut without being sick. He looked over at Sarah who hadn't moved at all. In the dark he could see her bare breasts again. Nate's eyes closed and he drifted away to a place where he could hear the rain falling again, listless and soft and nearly silent.

TWENTY-SIX

Nate didn't know why he was suddenly so wide awake. Sarah was still asleep beside him. He slipped from the berth and slid onto the dinette settee wondering if his eyes were as red as they felt. He dressed in the shadows of the cabin and stepped out into the morning sun where there were a dozen terns diving into a school of fry astern. He watched them while *Serendipity* tacked in the whispers drifting down through the anchorage from over the hills. The terns drove the baitfish away and the birds followed them down the sound. Nate sat on the wing-deck thinking about Steamboat and the high Colorado sky. He felt like diving into the water again and swimming back to the beach a half-mile back like he had when he was so upset about Rilee. This time there was no Jenson to the rescue. Nate sat in the morning heat waiting for the others.

Beyond the honeymoon cottages he could see the billowing top of a thunderhead, silver above and shading to black beneath. It looked heavy and bloated and sinister. Nate watched it change into odd shapes while it approached and when he stood to stretch, the boat was already in the shadow of the clouds. None of the hatches except for the companionway were open, so he stood on the cabin roof while the thunderhead towered over Virgin Gorda. There were odd puffs of wind swirling from different directions that confused *Serendipity*. She rode up on her anchor line at first and then fell away again. Nate walked up to the bow and let out about seventy more feet of line for a better angle on the anchor, leaving enough room to swing in case of wind shifts. He watched from the rail while another cruising boat skipper did the same.

Nate stayed near the bow and looked around at the boats in the anchorage and at the black clouds moving overhead. The wind that was still swirling never got above fifteen knots. When the rain started, he ducked below and slid the companionway shut. He sat at the dinette and listened to the drumming again when the boat was hit with a sudden blast of wind. *Serendipity* shuddered at first and then accelerated and fell away so fast with the gust that he thought the anchor had come adrift. The boat hit the end of the rode and the bow snapped around and she shook to a stop while the wind whistled all around. Sarah woke up at the noise and glanced around the cabin. She smiled at Nate and shut her eyes again. The door opened to the head and Brady lumbered out.

"What a night," he said. "I don't feel too good. Want some coffee?"

"Sure," Nate said. "Are you up for making it?"

Nate looked through the portlight in the galley to see if *Serendipity* had dragged in the wind. Sarah smelled Brady's coffee and sat up in bed with a sheet wrapped around her shoulders. Nate looked over at her and thought about her naked body underneath, but the moment went by and when the coffee was poured, the three of them sat in the hot cabin and drank from the mugs in silence.

They could hear the rain outside being driven before the wind and it came in rolls, slapping at the hulls like birdshot. There were peals of thunder and flashes of light and sometimes in between the blasts of wind, it felt like the end of the squall was near, but there was always another volley to follow. They waited while the aroma of the coffee filled the quiet air of the cabin and the wind ripped through the anchorage outside the companionway door.

Another violent gust blew down from the hills. *Serendipity* shook like a wet cat, dancing around on her anchor, but the wind died away one more time. It gusted up again and then never came back with any strength. Rain still fell and the noise below was a steady roar and then the squall moved toward the islands to the west. There was nothing left but a heavy mist.

Nate slid the companionway open and stepped out on the wet decks to look around. The air was still and muggy and hot, even under the cloud cover, but there were shouts and laughter coming from the other cruising boats. Nate looked to the east beyond the rooftops on the hill where there were patches of blue in the sky. Sarah stepped out on deck in the same flowered bikini from the night before.

"So much for the weather report," she said. "Are we ready to head out? I see some blue sky."

"I don't want to stay here any longer than we have to. There are some skeletons I need to shake loose."

The wind blew down the length of Gorda Sound. Nate pulled the anchor line while *Serendipity* followed along like a hungry kitten. The plow worked free from the bottom and the boat drifted away from the dock and to the west toward the pass in the reef. Brady and Shanna freed the main and were hauling it up while Sarah took the helm. Nate hanked the jib in place and got it up and drawing and they sailed down the sound and out through the pass below Prickly Pear Island.

They reached the deeper water beyond the coral heads where *Serendipity* picked up the pace and drove to windward across Virgin Sound toward Necker Island. Nate walked up to the bow to be alone and when it came time to tack back toward Virgin Gorda, he stayed where he was and watched Sarah work the wheel. Brady and Shanna handled the sheets and when they came about, Nate turned to see Biras Hill and the end of the island in the distance. He wanted to be at sea again, far away from everything, and he leaned against the rail and watched the port hull flying clear of the water and the incredible blue grotto beneath. There were thunderheads and dark shadows out over Anegada Passage, but the clouds were far apart and not so big as the morning squall. They tacked away from the reefs on the north side of Virgin Gorda while Nate looked toward the open sea ahead.

They held the course for a long time, heading for Horse-shoe Reef until they had a clear track to the southeast. When they tacked over again, Nate went aft to help with the sheets.

He trimmed the main and jib and you could hear the SumLog cable go up in pitch when *Serendipity* reached her twelve-knot stride. Nate didn't want to look back at Virgin Gorda, but when he did he stared for a while at the reefs and at the hills already muted in the distance. He turned back toward the southeast and watched the spray and the streaks of foam racing past.

There were heavy swells rolling down Anegada Passage that caught the boat just forward of the beam. *Serendipity* began to labor. If she had been going off on more of an angle, she would have broken free and started surfing. Nate was okay with the wind off the port bow, but the big boomers rolled through and *Serendipity* heeled down the slope only to roll upright again at the crests. She sailed along being lifted way to the right and ticking twelve knots then settling upright for a moment and slowing to ten knots then being lifted way to the right again and back to twelve before slowing again to ten. The motion made everyone sleepy.

Sarah stayed at the helm for several hours. Nate saw her yawning, though, and when he took the wheel, she was asleep below in a matter of minutes. Brady was already asleep. Nate sat with Shanna in the cockpit watching the clouds in the distance and the swells rolling up. When Shanna looked at him she had a big grin on her face.

"I never got rid of that headache from last night," she said. "I'm going to do what Brady says. Would you like a beer?"

Before Nate could answer, she slipped below and came back with two Heinekens. He took one and drank nearly half of it. She set her can down and slid closer.

"Something happened on that charter, didn't it," she asked.

"Sort of."

"I talked to Etionette. She told me about the kiss on the dock. It was serious, wasn't it?" Shanna reached over and touched Nate's shoulder. "I won't tell Sarah."

"It wasn't as serious as it looked," Nate said. "She walked away with her husband and I'll never see her again. It shook me up. It's had an effect on Sarah. She doesn't know, but she's suspicious. I wish it had never happened. To be honest, Sarah is beautiful."

"So are you, stupid. She's nuts about you. It won't last if you spend too much time moping around."

"Am I moping? When we get down to St. Barts tomorrow, I think the change in scenery will help. It helped just getting out of Dodge."

"I know what you mean. I really loved being in the Virgin Islands, but it was time to go."

Nate looked to the north from the crest of a big swell and he could see forever an endless procession of wind-driven waves marching in from the deep Atlantic. The boat slowed in the trough that followed and Nate glanced back at Shanna sitting next to him. She stood and looked at Nate for a moment.

"I love you, silly," she said.

Shanna turned away for a moment. When she looked back, she was blushing and grinning and it made Nate laugh.

"I love you, too," he said.

Shanna kissed his cheek and turned to go below. Nate watched her for a moment and he couldn't help himself.

"Shanna…?"

She looked back with those soft, magic-show eyes.

"Yes?"

"Do you remember that night in Key West?"

"How could I forget?"

"Could I ask you one thing? You don't have to answer. Why didn't you come back to *Serendipity* with me that night?"

Shanna stood in the companionway looking away at the sea to the south.

"If I had come back with you to *Serendipity,*" she said, "I never would have left. I just met Brady, though. Somehow I knew."

Shanna turned and looked at Nate again and there was a shy grin on her face. She winked at him and disappeared below. Nate sat for a while looking at the empty companionway. There was a funny moment where he felt sad again. He had the same feeling when he slid the companionway door open and fell into the wingdeck berth that dawn in Key West after he left Shanna in town and he sat alone in the cabin, sweating in the heat from the rising sun. Nate looked off to the south in the direction the swells were running and he couldn't stop thinking about that night until the whine of the SumLog hit eighteen knots and woke him with a start. Nate spun the wheel to get the boat back on course for St. Barts, but he was lucky the boat hadn't broached while tearing off downwind. Nate shook his head, mad at himself for falling asleep at the wheel. He brought the wind back on the port bow. *Serendipity* settled into the lift-to-the-right, roll-to-the-left motion. Nate yawned and reached for the half-empty can of Heineken.

There were still some thunderheads early on, but the skies had cleared and left behind those puffy trade wind clouds that looked like Carolina cotton bolls. The sun was low and the colors of the sky and the sea were deep and intense and made Nate think about Colorado again and how the sky stretched forever in the spring with cotton-boll clouds everywhere. He didn't know where Rilee was and he didn't want it to matter, but he could feel the ache coming back in the pit of his stomach. She ran up the dock and took her husband's arm and led him away while he looked back and stared at Nate like he was a common thief. There was some loud ringing in his ears from the frustration and confusion, only it was the whine of the Sumlog cable again when *Serendipity* pegged the needle at twenty knots. The noise snapped Nate awake. He spun the wheel to port just before the boom jibed over. It was loose for a second and it clattered and banged when the main refilled. Nate nosed the boat back on course and then Brady stepped out into the cockpit.

"What the hell is going on?" he said. "You can't believe the racket down below."

"Sorry. I keep falling asleep. We tore off surfing and outran the wind just then."

"Are you okay? I can drive, now. I slept pretty good."

"You know what? I think I'm ready. Do you mind?"

"No, but you have to get some sleep, okay? You might get us all killed."

Nate slid over while Brady took the wheel.

"Don't fall asleep," Nate said.

"You need to go below. There's the companionway."

The yawning started again and Nate's eyes watered in the wind. He gathered up the two beer cans and slipped below where he could hear the rush of the water beneath the hulls. Sarah had fallen asleep on the starboard settee, so Nate climbed into the wingdeck berth and leaned back and listened to the sounds and watched the trade wind clouds marching across the portlight. He didn't know he had fallen asleep until Sarah shook his shoulder.

"Care to join us for dinner?"

Nate opened his eyes to find the Aladdin burning bright and the aroma of beef and gravy and potatoes filling the cabin. Shanna saw him awake and turned up the stereo.

"It's been four hours," Sarah said. "Don't worry, though. Brady is still outside driving. Dinner is ready. We found some bottles of wine hidden away."

Nate sat up and blinked a few times. He stayed in the bunk watching Sarah move in the galley. She caught him staring and she curtsied and handed him a tall glass of chardonnay. He propped the pillow up and sipped the wine and looked out at the stars in the night sky. They were probably half-way to St. Barts by then and he wondered whether to slow the boat to arrive at dawn. Sarah came over and sat at the dinette.

"The wind has died," she said. "We're only doing six or seven knots."

"That's good. We'll get to St. Barts after daylight."

Serendipity spent the next few hours reaching into the night with a much easier motion in the light winds. The waves had flattened until they were long and lazy and smooth. When they blew the Aladdin out to go to bed, Nate turned to check on Shanna who was at the wheel. He could see her face through the companionway, bathed in the soft glow from the light in the compass.

Someone whispered later on and woke him, but it was only Shanna asking for Sarah who had volunteered to drive during the long midnight watch. Sarah got up and in the half-light, Nate could see her slipping on a shirt and some shorts. She stepped through the companionway and there was a lot of giggling and more whispering. Shanna came down in a moment and drank some water using the hand pump and then she disappeared into the forepeak. Nate stayed awake for a while listening to the soft hum from the SumLog cable. It didn't sound like they were moving even at five knots. He looked out at the night sky where there were several million stars in view. He thought about getting up to see, but he heard more whispering. It was Sarah telling him it was four o'clock in the morning.

Nate yawned for a long time and then scrambled from the wingdeck berth and stood in the dark trying to find his clothes. Sarah watched him dress from the cockpit and it made his face warm. He stepped out to take the wheel and she giggled.

"You didn't have to dress, you know?" she said.

Nate's face heated up again. Sarah kissed his cheek.

"The stars are magnificent," she said. "There were dolphins around, too. I heard them blowing at the surface. *Serendipity* is bouncing along through the water without a care. So am I."

Nate looked up at the night sky. The moon was down and a veil of stars spread unbroken all the way to the horizon. He didn't look at Sarah again until his neck began to hurt.

"What a night," Nate said. "You never see this living in a city."

"The air is so balmy. Reminds me of what I used to imagine when I read all the Hawaii ads in the travel section."

Sarah smiled in the dark and kissed Nate's cheek again and then she stepped below to go back to bed. He kept watching like she had done and in a moment, she stripped away her shirt and Nate could see her breasts before she disappeared into the wingdeck berth. He took a deep breath and glanced up at the masthead light dancing high above the deck. There were no other moving objects, no other lights anywhere, and he listened for the dolphins to see if they were as alone as it seemed. He didn't hear them at all. Nate looked toward the horizon to the north and to the south, but there was nothing except the line between the black of the water and the black of the night sky where the stars swept out of the sea. Over the bow, he could see a faint line of artificial glow down low, the lights of St. Martin just beyond the curve of the earth. He watched the band of light get brighter as the boat carved her way to the southeast.

Serendipity approached St. Barts at dawn. The wind continued out of the east so Nate held the port tack until the course carried past the entrance to the harbor of Gustavia. At eight o'clock they were still five or six miles out. Nate released the jib and spun the wheel and tried to let *Serendipity* round into the wind without too much gear shaking. Brady didn't come out until Nate had everything sheeted home.

"I need some coffee," he yawned. "Is that St. Barts?"

"Yes. It won't be long before we get into the harbor."

Brady turned to go below where he started fooling with the stove. In the bright light of the morning, Saba loomed in the distance to the south. Nate was looking back in that direction when Sarah came out all excited about making landfall. She looked at the hills of St. Barts and then behind at Saba.

"This really feels like the Caribbean," she said. "Ready for some coffee?"

Nate fiddled with the sheets and balanced the main and jib to let *Serendipity* steer herself. He left the wheel and worked his way forward to see if there were dolphins, but even in water so clear you could see infinity there was nothing. He leaned against the bow rail and watched the island taking shape.

Sarah brought Nate's coffee forward and stayed to watch as well. The hills of St. Barts turned green and then there were some tiny white dots stepping up the slopes and then a road cut and a cluster of buildings, all with red tile roofs, and then the entrance to the harbor yawned in front of them.

Nate went back to start the diesel and get the sails furled to make the approach to the anchorage in the inner harbor. Brady fished around and found the yellow quarantine flag and the French tricolor and ran them up the little halyard to the spreaders where they snapped in the morning breeze. The boat entered the harbor and tucked into the lee of the hills where the wind died away to nothing. Nate ran the diesel barely above idle. *Serendipity* tiptoed through the quiet water all the way to the end of the harbor. Brady dropped the CQR in a spot where there was room enough to swing and the diesel slowed to a stop. Nate stood on the cabin roof staring at the narrow streets and at the tiny shops so white in the mid-morning light. Sarah took his arm and looked over toward the village.

"I used to play with dolls when I was little," she said. "I think they must have come from here."

TWENTY-SEVEN

There were people walking the streets and tiny cars driving by on the narrow boulevard above the quay and fishermen working in their boats below where the sea wall was dark with slime. Nate watched the fishermen from the deck for a while and then went below to freshen up and wash away the salt and the grime and to change into clean clothes for the street.

Brady had already launched the sabot and rowed up to the quay where there was a small dock and a rusty ladder bolted to the wall. Sarah and Shanna stepped out of the dinghy and climbed to the top. Nate grabbed the satchel with the passports and met Brady just as he rowed back. They made their way ashore to find the customs man.

It was only a short walk up to the government building where the official in charge stamped the passports and asked the length of their stay and then cleared them into St. Barts. They left the stamps and the ink pads and the customs man behind and walked the length of the harbor in Gustavia. Brady found Le Select soon enough where the bartender had Kronenbourg on tap. They sat at a table and ordered glasses of beer and some cheese and a baguette. The bartender leaned over the counter.

"*Monsieur,* you would like to buy wine?"

"Maybe some rum, too," Brady said, "if they have it."

"*Oui,* you can buy these things across the harbor. There is a warehouse. You can buy Mt. Gay in big containers. Four liters. The wine comes in plastic. Ten liters."

The bartender waved them toward the store across the harbor where there were boxes and barrels piled high and a green Mini-Moke parked in front of a building that looked like it came straight from Sweden. The interior was dark and musky but Brady found some of the plastic wine containers stacked in the back and the rum standing in rows of dusty glass jugs along a low shelf. He wasn't sure the wine wouldn't taste like pool toys because of the plastic so he only bought a jug of Mt. Gay for seven dollars from the man who ran the place.

They had to carry the four-liter jug all the way back around the harbor to where the sabot was tied. When they stopped on the quay near the little dock, Sarah and Shanna took off to go shopping while Nate rowed Brady and the rum out to *Serendipity*. Brady opened the jug down below and poured a big shot, standing there like a *sommelier* swishing the rum about and creasing his forehead and smacking his lips.

"It's real," Brady announced. "It's real Mt. Gay. What a lucky day."

Brady poured a shot for Nate who only sipped at the rum and even then he nearly choked. The rum was good, though, and they sat in the cockpit with some Mt. Gay and lime juice in the yellow cups and waited for Sarah and Shanna to come back.

Serendipity planted herself like *Nomad* while the anchor line drooped off the bow and the Tricolor hung limp overhead. Nate kept nodding off, he was so tired, but he broke into a sweat just sitting. He walked up to the bow where it was cooler and leaned against the rail. When Sarah and Shanna yelled from the top of the quay, Brady rowed ashore and brought them back.

"You should see what we bought," Shanna said. "A big round of cheese and a half-dozen baguettes and some French wine in bottles."

"I bought something new," Sarah said to Nate. "I'll go try it on."

Sarah disappeared below and in a few minutes, she stepped back through the companionway wearing a miniature pink bikini that made her look like a bronze centerfold. Brady had to catch his breath. He ducked into the galley before Shanna could hit him.

"You could get arrested wearing that," Nate said.

"Not in St. Barts. The girls on the beach are topless."

"Where?" Brady shouted from below.

"Shut up, nutcase," Shanna said. "Make us some drinks with the Mt. Gay before I bop you one."

After sunset the light breeze from the east swept through the harbor with a little more force. Sarah and Nate sat on the wingdeck watching the lights come on in the town and in the houses scattered up the hill. She was still wearing the pink bikini.

"You haven't stared like this since I sat across from you at the Green Parrot."

"Yes, I have. You haven't noticed?"

"I bought this for you, Nate. I thought maybe...Well, you know what I thought."

Nate looked over toward the shops along the quay, still white in the dim light. When he didn't answer, she put her arms around him.

"I'm sorry," she said. "I'm not trying to make a joke out of it. It isn't funny, is it."

Nate glanced at Sarah and at her eyes and he could see the tears welling up. He leaned his head against hers.

"I'm sorry, too. When we were sitting together in the cockpit before dinner, all I could think about was being in bed with you again. I'm afraid it won't work, even after all the rum."

"It doesn't matter to me. I didn't mean to make light of it. I'm just as content to be next to you. I wanted you to be happy, that's all. If it doesn't happen, don't be upset. Besides, maybe it's my fault?"

"Not a chance."

"Are you sure? Anyway, I like my new suit. Brady likes it, too."

She pushed Nate away with a giggle and then wiped her eyes. She stood and reached for Nate and they walked together back to the cockpit where Shanna waited alone looking across the water toward the lights of Gustavia.

"Brady is passed out in the forepeak," Shanna said.

Sarah sat down and leaned back looking like a centerfold again. Nate stood for a minute before she pointed toward the open companionway and the lamp burning dim. Nate yawned and rubbed his eyes and smiled at her and then stepped down the ladder. He stretched out full length on the cool sheets, but he could hear noises in the rigging and voices from somewhere else along with the steady ringing in his ears. He stared at the mahogany ceiling and at the books in the shelves and when his eyelids drooped shut, he fell so far down into a black abyss he never knew when Sarah slipped into bed.

It took a long time for the initial rush of sleep to wear off. Nate woke in the dark of the early morning and turned on his side and found Sarah asleep beside him. There were no pink straps over her bare shoulders. Nate kept thinking of her body beneath the covers and he watched her sleep for a while before rolling over to face the portlight and the dark sky beyond. *Serendipity* was tacking on her anchor line in the night wind. Nate watched the stars move across, first one way and then the other, but he kept thinking of Sarah and waiting for the slow glow to start in the pit of his stomach. There never was anything. He fell asleep again, tired and upset. When the abyss was all around again, he drifted weightless in a black void of nothingness.

Nate's face suddenly felt hot, though, and he opened his eyes. The sun fell across his pillow and he rolled into the shade and looked over. Sarah was gone. There were voices somewhere that sounded like the night before when he was exhausted. Shanna poked her head through the companionway and saw Nate awake. She turned back to the cockpit.

"Sarah," she said. "Nate finally woke up."

Sarah came down the ladder in her pink bikini. He saw her step into the galley and there was suddenly some feeling again and it made him wish it was still early and they were alone. She came over and sat down at the dinette.

"Feel better?" she asked.

"Yeah. I wish it were still dark, though. I wish you were still here."

"I really didn't want to wake you up after last night when you were so out of it."

"I know. I needed the sleep, I guess."

"I did want to know if my new suit worked, though."

Sarah giggled and looked shy and then she reached up and touched Nate's face. In a moment, she was away in the galley clanging the pots and pans and the coffee pot.

A morning breeze still swirled about inside the little harbor. Beyond the channel entrance, the wind blew hard from the east. Nate decided right then to leave St. Barts and sail off to the southwest toward the island he had seen the morning before rising like a trident from the sea. He wasn't sure if the dock had been built in the lee of Saba, but it didn't matter much since not many yachts visited the island where there were no safe anchorages.

Nate rowed ashore alone with the papers to clear customs and when he came back, everything was stowed and *Serendipity* sat ready to leave. He idled *Serendipity* out of the harbor while Sarah stood watching the whitewashed buildings and the red tile roofs of Gustavia slide by. The doll houses stepping up the hillsides looked tiny and quaint. Sarah kept watching the town in the early morning light.

"Now I'm not sure I want to leave so soon," she said. "It's pretty, looking back."

Sarah stared at the hills of St. Barts while *Serendipity* slipped her way beyond the harbor entrance, but then she looked over the bow toward the clouds that hid Saba some thirty miles away.

Shanna and Brady hauled the sails up and trimmed them for the broad reach that would carry them around the western end of Saba into the lee where a boat could anchor close in if someone stayed aboard to watch. *Serendipity* picked up her skirt and ran off before the low swells, once in a while spinning the SumLog up to eighteen knots. When the dark shape of Saba materialized, Nate stood with Sarah in the cockpit watching the Caribbean peel away and the island turn brown and green as they approached.

A steady procession of trade wind clouds marched across to the west. Some of them caught the top of the ancient volcano at the center of Saba where they shuddered and fell apart and were swept into a vortex and then were torn away again by the trades that never stopped. When she reached the wind shadow of the island, *Serendipity* was cast in some of the cloud shadows. She ghosted along in the quiet of the lee with the clouds rolling over like massive gray comforters. Nate could hear the sea rushing in against the steep shoreline and the sea birds winging along the cliffs.

They dropped the main and jib and lit the Volvo, but Nate only let the engine idle to keep the noise down. *Serendipity* eased her way around the base of the cliffs until a concrete dock came into view. He steered the boat in a lazy circle just outside and then turned the boat toward the landing and coasted to a stop alongside the concrete wall. Two men came over and took the lines and then walked *Serendipity* all the way to the shallows before they tied her off. Nate hit the stop switch for the diesel. The men motioned him ashore where one of them took a cursory look at the papers and handed the bundle back and welcomed them all to Saba.

Nate saw from the dock the extreme pitch of the road cut going up the cliff. One of the men introduced himself and said he had a taxi to take them up to The Bottom if they wanted to go. He waited while everyone changed and when they stuffed into his eighty-eight-inch Land Rover, he drove the narrow road toward The Bottom about four hundred feet up the cliffs.

Colin Hassell was a tiny, fair-skinned islander who had been born and raised on Saba. He took them on a tour of The Bottom and Windwardside and Upper Hell's Gate along the roads that curled around the mountain like tangled gray string. There were houses painted white and red tin roofs and flowers in the yards and so many of the people were blonde and fair it seemed like Holland had been pushed and compressed and folded into a mountain range and someone had turned the heater up to nine.

The Land Rover finally rolled to a stop near the center of The Bottom. Nate helped Sarah climb free from the back seat. Brady hopped out with Shanna and they walked the streets together. The people smiled as they passed. Sarah bought bottles of Heineken in a little restaurant where they sat outside in the wind that was constant and in the intermittent shadows of the clouds that rolled by overhead. There was an old man sitting alone at a table across the way.

"Don't leave Saba until you have climbed the volcano," he said. "You can see St. Kitts and even St. Barts. Sometime St. Martin when the peak is free of the clouds."

"Is there a trail?" Brady asked.

"Yes…Carved into the side of the mountain. There are steps in the places where it's steep. The top of the volcano will be raining a lot of mist when you pass through the cloud forest. You can sit in the shadows where it's very nice."

They finished the beer and left the little man who waved and smiled as they walked away. Sarah took Nate's hand while they spent another half-hour exploring the tiny town and watching the kids run along and hide and peek while they passed. At the end of the lane they found Colin again standing by his Rover. The four of them piled into the taxi for the descent back to the concrete dock far below where *Serendipity* waited in the shallows.

Down the narrow road Nate could see to the west for a long way out to sea. The clouds tore free and the Caribbean looked like an endless palette of blue split by a bolt of yellow from the setting sun. The reflection was so bright it made everyone squint, but the sunset was brief and when they pulled to a stop on the dock, it was nearly twilight. Nate made arrangements for Colin to return the following morning. The taxi driver tooted the horn and his Rover groaned up the road cut in compound low and disappeared around the bend.

They walked back to *Serendipity* and stepped aboard, spoiled already at being tied to a dock. Nate lit the Aladdin and kept it low while Brady made rum drinks. They sat in the cockpit and listened to a Bob Marley tape and ate a baguette and a tin of Danish ham and a small block of cheese. After Shanna and Brady disappeared into the forepeak, Sarah and Nate stayed behind listening to more reggae. Nate could hear the rush of the sea against the cliffs and the bickering of the gulls somewhere in the dark. There were stars in the night sky, but he only saw them when the clouds tore away to the west. The tiny lights of The Bottom flickered high above them. When the clouds stacked against the peak, the island and the sky went dim.

Sarah yawned again and they stood without talking and stepped below into the fading light of the cabin. Nate blew out the lamp and slipped into the wingdeck berth with Sarah. She moved close to him, but she was tired and he could hear her heavy breathing in only a few minutes. Nate stayed awake thinking about her and how she looked in the pink two-piece and how funny it seemed when she curtsied. He couldn't make the burning happen and it felt to him like he was sleeping with a lifelong friend rather than a lover. He started wondering about Rilee then and where she might be. He saw her face again the day she walked away on the dock and he couldn't believe, one more time, it had ended. The ache returned and the searing in the pit of his stomach got so intense he had to roll away from Sarah and wait for it to go away.

The dock where they spent the night was on the west side of the island. When the sun broke from over the cliffs the following morning, it was already late. Sarah opened her eyes when Nate pulled the curtain to cover the portlight. She smiled at him and he watched her yawn and scrunch up beneath the sheets, but there was some beeping outside on the dock. Through the opposite portlight he caught a glimpse of the taxi driver pacing the dock. Brady came shuffling into the salon from the forepeak just then and stepped out through the companionway.

"We haven't made coffee yet," he said to Colin. "Would you like some?"

Colin hadn't waited long so he joined everyone in the cockpit. He drank from his cup and looked up the road cut toward The Bottom.

"I was born in my parents' house, Upper Hell's Gate," Colin said, "but all my friends from the island are gone."

"What happened?" Brady asked.

"Go away to the States, most of them. To make money. They don't come back."

"Why did you stay?"

"I love Saba. I worked for a long time fishing, then I bought the taxi. Now we have the dock here. More yachts stop to visit and they all want a taxi. I make more money than my friends in the States."

Colin chuckled to himself while they finished the coffee and locked *Serendipity*. In a few minutes the Rover was off again for the carnival ride up the road that seemed to drop from the clouds. Colin didn't stop until the volcano stood in front of them rising into the mist.

They set off on a path that was level at first and easy walking. The sun burst from behind the clouds and the heat felt good, but the path got steep in a hurry. They weren't saying much, only trudging up the path that turned to steps cut into the side of the hill. Sarah climbed ahead of Nate and he could see the sweat collecting on her back and soaking her shirt. They entered the lower levels of the cloud forest near the peak where it was cooler in the shade and where the wind came swirling over the top to blow the branches of the trees. The air was softer up there and the sun only filtered through the canopy. It was like being in a grotto where they only saw the green of the trees and the tiny flashes of sunlight. It was a relief to sit for a while and breathe deep and to listen to the sound of the trees shimmering in the wind.

Sarah and Nate sat on a rock just off the path where they could look down through the tree ferns to the red roofs of The Bottom and to the blue Caribbean beyond. They could have stayed just for the view, but Brady and Shanna walked by without stopping. Nate and Sarah joined them and then broke free of the trees into an area of exposed rock, barren and windblown and hot from the sun. They scrambled to the top where they had to lean into the wind that blew fresh from the east. Nate could see the other islands in the chain, stepping away across the sea, and when he stood at the highest point and looked about, he could feel the heat in the rocks and the cool of the air. The wind brought with it an endless run of clouds that crossed the mountain and bathed them in fog and then sun and then fog again and it made Nate feel like he was flying.

They sat on one of the rock faces to breathe the sea air when a big cloud rolled through and lost them in the fog. The air was nearly cold then, but the rocks gave off a lot of heat absorbed from the sun. Sarah and Brady and Shanna leaned back in the warmth and shut their eyes. Nate left them behind and climbed closer to the windward side. He stood staring into a cloud that never ended, but the wind tore the mist from the mountain and he burst into the sun with the Caribbean below and the islands stepping away again and he could have been doing a barrel roll in an old Stearman because another cloud was on the way and then another and it seemed the flying would go on forever. Nate kept looking out to sea to the south and to the east and when the clouds rushed in, he was lost in the cold. Sometimes the clouds were so big they kept him in the fog so long they never seemed to end, but then they tore away again and the sun exploded all around and lit the Caribbean below, so deep and blue Nate only thought of the light dancing from the propane colored banks in the Bahamas.

He kept watching the clouds hurl themselves toward the peak, one after the other, and when they swept through, the sun blazed and the sky erupted in light and he couldn't help thinking of Rilee again and why she wasn't with him. Nate sat on one of the warm outcrops and watched the clouds and the sea and listened to the wind in the trees. When he turned away to find the others, there were moments walking back when he didn't care.

Brady and Shanna and Sarah were still lying on the warm rocks. One of the larger trade wind clouds rolled through and the air stayed cool so long it felt good to be near the heat. The wind made Nate shiver. Sarah opened her eyes and reached and pulled him down where the wind wasn't so sharp. He could see from where they were an old mahogany tree, bent and drooping and covered with moss, and when the fog was thin, the branches stood out against the pale gray cloud. When the fog grew thick, Nate could barely make out the shape of the tree. He kept watching the fog rush through. The tree faded in and out until the sun burst through again and the colors came alive. The heat felt so good he sat up to look how far away the next cloud might be, but another swept over the peak and swallowed the mountain again and the tree disappeared in the fog. In a moment the fog thinned and Nate could see the tree again in the haze, drooping and wet and dark. He leaned back on the warm rocks and shut his eyes next to Sarah. He could feel her body next to his and it made him think of the pink bikini and how he kept staring, but the warm feelings only came from the rocks beneath them. Nate opened his eyes and there was nothing but the wind and the fog and the brooding mahogany tree that faded away on the lee side of the peak.

TWENTY-EIGHT

They left the top of Mt. Scenery and passed through the cloud forest again and stopped in an area where there were a lot of tree ferns waving over the path and some lacy irises below hiding in the shadows. They could look down the mountain to The Bottom where the red roofs of the village stood out against the brown hillsides. It was cool and quiet beneath the ferns, but they left in only a few minutes and hiked the rest of the way back to the village to find a market where they could buy cold beer. The trail began to flatten out and Brady nearly ran toward The Bottom and the beer where he spilled out onto the asphalt, hot and tired and thirsty.

They walked down the street and around the corner to the store where they bought bottles of Heineken from the lady behind the counter who told them it was brewed on the island of St. Lucia. They stepped back into the heat and opened several of them. Another cloud had roared through and shielded the sun and they were cool again and ready to walk through the town and find Colin who could spare them the long hike down the twisting road to the dock.

They hadn't gone far when a few of the local kids came running alongside Brady who kept going after them like a cape-less Bella Lugosi. In between the screaming and laughter, The Bottom was quiet. The tiny white houses and the clean red roofs and the mountain half buried in the clouds that towered over the town made Nate feel like the sound was off and all he could hear was the wind. Sarah squeezed his hand and giggled at Brady and the kids who followed them all the way to Colin and his Land Rover.

They jammed into the seats and then pulled away while a dozen kids ran along the road and waved good-bye to Brady. Colin kept up a running commentary on the engineering of the road and the number of switchbacks they had to make. Nate looked from the open front seat at the houses and at the islands in the distance and at the sea itself, endless and absolute and blue as December birth stones. He could see Statia to the southeast and St. Kitts beyond and it made him wonder if the locals could see on a clear day all the way to Montserrat. Sarah tapped him from behind and he turned to look where she was pointing. In the distance far to the south, he could make out the hull and the sails of a trading schooner running off before the wind. He watched it moving away while they bumped along in the Rover. Nate thought the schooner might be headed for St. Croix, but they were swallowed by a cloud caught on the peak above that spilled down over the road and he lost the schooner and the islands and the sea itself. Colin laughed and said it would clear in a moment. The cloud was a big one, though, and didn't tear itself free until they had bounced through Upper Hell's Gate and were on their way back to Windwardside.

They flashed into the sun again and slowed along the narrow road in the center of the town just to be closer to the tiny white houses. Many of the windows were open. Sarah kept watching the thin curtains swirl in the wind, rolling and unrolling like the waves in a South Dakota prairie, only in delicate white lace. When they reached the edge of town, Sarah turned and stared at the dollhouses behind them. Nate watched her looking back toward the tiny streets and the tiny houses with the rolling lace in the windows.

"I think those might be the Lost Boys back there," Sarah said. "I kept looking for Peter Pan," and then she smiled toward the village and the spotless white houses and the pixies along the road waving good-bye.

They made the 400-foot drop down the cliff to the pier and *Serendipity* below. Colin shook hands with everyone and turned the taxi around. While Nate made his way along the dock, he heard the Rover complaining for a long time after it left. When the engine noise fell away, he stepped aboard *Serendipity* where there was only the sound of the Caribbean rushing in along the rocks.

It didn't take Brady long to break out the jug of Mt. Gay. He brought the filled glasses out into the cockpit where Sarah and Nate sat for a long time drinking the rum. He could tell when she looked over at him, but he watched the heavy surge that broke against the rocks across the way. She leaned over and put her head on his shoulder while they waited for dinner through a long orange sunset and a short blue twilight and then they moved out on the cabin roof to eat. Nate picked through the limp spaghetti and looked away at the cliffs of Saba rising straight from the darkening sea. Sarah glanced toward the road cut angling its way upward to the distant lights of The Bottom and then she looked over at Nate again.

"Sometimes you make me wonder why I'm here," she said.

Nate could tell she was upset, even in the dark.

"I'm sorry. I don't mean to leave you out. Saba is a special place."

"I guess I'm selfish. I want to be special."

"You are special," Nate said. "I don't know what's wrong. Do you remember the night in Road Town when it rained and I was standing near the bow rail? You came out looking for me. When I saw you coming, I couldn't believe how beautiful your body was. We didn't have any trouble then. I've thought about that night ever since. Sometimes those feelings come back but it always happens at the wrong time."

"Maybe we need to try the bow rail again," she said, and then she grinned and leaned her head against Nate and breathed for a moment and then she sat up. "I think I want another glass of rum and lime juice. Is the bar still open?"

Nate watched her step down the ladder. He could hear her flirting with Brady who already had the rum out again. She came back with the drinks and handed one to Nate. She stood in front of him for a second and he suddenly had that vision of her in the mist when she stepped from the cockpit wearing nothing and the warm feelings came back with a rush. She might have known what he was thinking because she giggled and sat close to him. They sipped the rum and watched the lights high up the hill. When the clouds hung themselves on the peak, the lights went dim and they could barely see The Bottom, but the clouds ripped away and the lights went bright and twinkling again and it made the village look like Brigadoon.

Sarah nearly fell asleep so they stepped below into the cabin. She climbed into the double berth while Nate turned the stereo off and blew the lamp out. He could hear her heavy breathing in the dark and he waited only a few minutes before he climbed into bed next to her. Nate leaned against the bulkhead in the dark with the image of Sarah stepping out from the cockpit that night in Road Harbour and he waited for the burning sensation. There was nothing again. The anger came back and he rolled over on his side away from Sarah who wouldn't understand. Nate covered his face with his hands and waited for the rum to take over. There was some slight spinning and he thought he would have to open his eyes to stop it, and then the anger and the spinning slipped away until he was left with an empty feeling and a vague sense of nausea and an eternal wait for sunrise.

Nate must have slept during the night because he awoke from a long way off when Sarah climbed out of bed to make coffee. He watched her from beneath the sheets, wondering if she had run out of patience. She lit the stove and then looked at him with a big smile. Their eyes met and he could feel some sparks flying and it made him wish she hadn't started the coffee. She went outside to look at the sky and then she ducked below and sat on the settee.

"How is it today?" she asked.

"I didn't hear you until you dragged out the coffee pot. Now I wish you were still here."

"I could turn the stove off."

Nate looked at her and started to say something, but Brady stepped out from the forepeak scratching his beard. The sparks went away. Nate glanced at the sky through the portlight and at the cliffs of Saba rising straight away. Sarah gave Brady a push when he went by and he stumbled out into the cockpit. She looked over and shook her head at Nate and then she stood to pour the coffee.

They sat outside with mugs of coffee and watched one of the workboats behind them being loaded with nets and gear. When the men finished, they motored away from the dock and left room to back down. Nate finished the coffee and started the diesel while Brady and Sarah walked *Serendipity* backwards until they could swing around. They eased away from the pier in a lazy circle and then set out into the Caribbean with the fishing boat only a dot on the horizon.

They broke from the lee of Saba where the trades got *Serendipity* up on her toes like a welterweight. The dull shape of Statia loomed in the distance below the clouds. St. Kitts was just beyond and they romped their way toward the islands hard on the wind ticking eleven and twelve knots, sweeping up and down the swells like Sunday sailors. *Serendipity* seemed very much alive just then. When they reached the island of Statia, they sailed into the calm of the lee. All of them were salt stung and suffering from exposure and filled with adrenaline because of the trades and the heavy seas and the hard charge to windward.

They ghosted along the southwest shore of Statia looking at the hills and the little houses and the ruins along the beach. It was early yet and Nate didn't want to stop so they drifted out of the lee of the island and headed for St. Kitts where they could anchor for the night. The wind picked up and they charged across the short channel with *Serendipity* dancing again over the swells. When she entered the lee of St. Kitts, she slowed to a crawl once more. Brady and Shanna and Sarah stood on the deck while the ramparts of Brimstone Hill loomed against the green of the mountains. They could see the ruins of the British fort and the rusting cannons aiming out to sea.

Serendipity kept getting headed by the quiet puffs that swirled from the peaks beyond the fort and the sails went slack and then filled and then collapsed again. Nate started the diesel while Brady and Shanna furled the main and jib. They motored the rest of the way into Basseterre.

They didn't arrive until the sun was nearly down. Even in the low afternoon light they could see the dirty water, and the open roadstead that served as the harbor was rough and crowded and busy. Nate found a spot to drop the anchor and then sat on the cabin roof looking at the boat traffic and the bustle of life ashore.

An island trading schooner floated next to the concrete pier. Nate watched from the deck while Brady rowed ashore with Sarah and Shanna. All the guys working in the hold popped their heads over the rail to watch when Shanna climbed from the dinghy onto the pier. Sarah turned and looked back at *Serendipity* and motioned for Nate to hurry.

Brady rowed up soon enough. When they reached the dock, Sarah and Shanna had walked up to the street and were out of sight. Nate tied the sabot off on the beach just east of the schooner and walked over to the street where Sarah and Shanna waited. There were cars and people and noise and a lot of trash and filth, but they set out toward the center of town hoping to find a market. They only walked a few blocks when Shanna turned around with a look of disgust.

"I'm sorry," she said. "I don't like Basseterre very much."

"Me, neither," Sarah said, and she turned to Nate and wrinkled her nose.

Brady took a deep breath without saying anything and then he stopped and looked around at the scrubby little town.

"I don't like it here, either" he said. "This is nothing like St. Barts or Saba."

They hurried through the twilight back to the pier to untie the sabot. Nate rowed Sarah and Shanna out through the chop in the roadstead where *Serendipity* waited. Before he could row away to get Brady, he could hear the two of them giggling over the jug of rum. Brady was at the end of the pier watching the deckhands on the trading schooner when Nate got back. He climbed down the ladder and sat in the stern.

"You ought to see those guys," Brady said. "They all look like heavyweight boxers."

Brady stared through the fading light toward *Serendipity* bobbing in the waves that rolled through the anchorage. Nate looked beyond Brady toward the schooner while the deckhands ignored them and kept working. The schooner and its stubby masts and blazing spreader lights stood out like a miniature cruise ship in the murk of the darkening roadstead. Nate was well out into the anchorage when he turned toward *Serendipity*. He could see the light from the Aladdin shining dim through the yellow curtains, pouring from the open companionway to light the cockpit. Neil Young's voice carried out into the roadstead from the cabin.

They stayed in the cockpit watching the boat traffic and listening to the noise from the street mixed with the Neil Young lyrics. The soft air swirled through the roadstead like it would if you could step into a travel poster, but there wasn't any of the exotic feeling from being anchored near a tropical island. Brady looked around for a moment at the dark water and at the lights and at the trading schooner tied to the dock across the way.

"I wanted to climb Brimstone Hill when we sailed by today," he said. "I don't want to anymore."

"I don't much care to, either," Nate said. "Maybe we ought to keep moving."

"I don't mind," Sarah said. "There are much prettier places than this, I think."

Even in the dark they could feel the layer of grunge over everything. The little white houses of Saba with the red roofs shining in the sun were a long way off.

Shanna handed out some bowls of stew and joined the three of them in the cockpit. They ate while *Serendipity* poked around her anchor line. There wasn't much wind, only the fitful puffs that drifted down from the hills. There was just enough to move her about and change the view of the dock and the lights and the other boats in the anchorage. Sarah kept watching the schooner tied to the pier because there were so many people moving on the decks.

"That looks like a painting," she said. "The way the deck of the schooner is lit. All you see are dirty white shirts. It makes me ashamed I was so nervous on the dock waiting for you."

"I felt the same way. It made me feel like we didn't belong. Remember the guys at that bar in Road Town and how they glared when we walked up?"

"I only remember the last one I danced with."

Nate stared at the white shirts and the black arms bulging in the light of the afterdeck on the schooner. There were five or six men in dreadlocks hauling on the boom trying to lift a heavy pallet from the dock, up and over the rail. Nate could hear the sheaves squeaking and squealing and groaning under the load. The boom rose stiffly from the dock and the pallet lifted clear of the pier and over the rail where it clumped once against the hatch before disappearing into the hold. Nate kept watching as the men scrambled to free the cargo net and there was some shouting and laughter. He felt Sarah's head on his shoulder. Nate leaned against her and shut his eyes.

"I'm sorry," Sarah said. "I didn't mean it that way."

"Are you ready for more rum and lime juice?" Brady asked.

Nate nodded his head and then looked back at the men working aboard the schooner, their skin shining in the light they were so sweat soaked. The boom was up and free of the deck and swinging out over the dock for another load. It drooped over the next pallet to be lifted. Nate shut his eyes again and waited for the glass of rum.

The schooner went dark around ten o'clock. Brady and Shanna were already asleep in the forepeak when Sarah slipped below and turned the Aladdin down before climbing into the wingdeck berth. Nate saw that she didn't undress. He stayed for a while alone in the cockpit, wondering what to do again.

The anchorage wasn't all that quiet, even at that hour, and there were people on the streets and cars going by and he could hear music and laughter from some of the other boats. He stepped over near the transom and looked out into the black Caribbean. There were no lights anywhere and he couldn't make out the horizon, only the indistinct line where the sea ended and the stars began. Nate leaned against the backstay bridle and stared to the west beyond the roadstead to the open sea, dark and trackless and vast. The emptiness made him afraid that Rilee would fade from his memory like the stars that faded away near the edge of the horizon. He shook his head and he could feel his skin flush, thinking someone might have seen. He stepped back into the cockpit and glanced forward at the dim riding light on the bow before ducking below into the still air of the cabin. Nate blew the Aladdin out and climbed into the berth beside the sleeping Sarah.

TWENTY-NINE

An early heat settled over the open harbor. Nate breathed the dense air of the cabin and propped himself on his elbows to look through the portlight. A cattle egret had landed on the lifelines outside and was struggling to keep its perch. Nate watched while it spread its wings for balance. The egret's feathers were so white in the morning sun it was hard to focus. He looked away to the subtle light of the cabin where the shadows fell across Sarah who was still asleep and then he glanced again at the egret flopping about on the lifelines. Nate eased from the sheets and stepped onto the cushions and down to the sole below and then ducked through the companionway.

The egret was still there slapping its wings. Nate didn't move for a moment, thinking it would see him and fly away. He was curious to see how close he could get, though, and he stepped out on the deck. The egret fluttered once more and then swooped away, gliding and stalling toward the beach like a seventh-grade paper airplane. Nate stooped to pick up a feather it had left behind on the deck. He ran it over the back of his hand and he watched it bend slightly back and forth and it was soft and stiff to the touch and it tickled his hand. Nate tossed it into the water and glanced over at the palms standing tall along the beach. There were no egrets anywhere. The feather floated off before the morning puffs.

Nate turned to look out to sea to the south and to the sky on the horizon nearly the same color as the egret. The boat anchored behind them had moved out early on and there was nothing for *Serendipity* to hit. Nate thought he could get them underway without starting the diesel. All of the lines ran aft to the cockpit so he stepped to the cabin roof and removed the sail ties and freed the main halyard and shackled it to the head of the sail. When he had everything ready, he stepped forward to lift the anchor free. Like the feather from the egret, *Serendipity* fell away drifting before the puffs while Nate stowed the ground tackle. He got back to the cockpit and raised the main without a lot of noise and picked up a little steerage and headed out from the roadstead toward the open Caribbean.

The wind shadow of St. Kitts extended a good distance out to sea. *Serendipity* drifted along in the lee while Nate looked at the green hills and at the blue sea that thinned from cobalt to pastel as it shoaled near the island. He turned for a last time and caught a glimpse of the old schooner still tied to the wharf. In the morning light, he could see how hammered she was and how much she looked again like a painting. The boom was still cocked downward after the loading in the night. Nate only glanced at it before turning again to face the Caribbean and the island of Nevis just across the channel.

Now and again they were headed up by the wind that swirled from over the hills of St. Kitts. There was no strength to the gusts and *Serendipity* only shook a little before Nate steered away and got her moving again. Brady stepped out from the companionway and stood looking at the sea and the sky and at the island just a half-mile away.

"Do you want the jib up?" he asked. "It might help a little."

"Yeah, I just didn't want to wake anyone. Do you want to hank it on and run the sheets aft?"

"I'll try to be quiet. Shanna is still asleep. So is Sarah."

Brady walked up to the bow and brought the sheets aft through the lead blocks and back to the primary winches. He made his way forward again to work the shackle and then the bronze piston hanks. When he finished the last of them, Brady motioned for Nate to haul away on the halyard. When the jib was set and sheeted home, *Serendipity* picked up speed and heeled to leeward as she made her way out beyond the wind shadow.

The trades were only whispers coming down the Narrows so she barely ticked six knots on the SumLog. Brady stayed near the bow rail watching the foam peel away from the hulls. He turned when the forward hatch opened and then smiled and climbed down into the forepeak to join Shanna. Nate was alone at the wheel again. *Serendipity* was rolling as the swells came through. It was a lazy motion and he couldn't help thinking about the forepeak and the gentle rolling.

There were only a few clouds drifting through. The sky had that tropical whitewash that made the glare intense, even through polarized sunglasses. Nate kept squinting beyond the bow toward Nevis and at the odd clouds that clung to the peak like they did on Saba. Nevis looked like an inverted funnel and made Nate think of one of the topless dancers he saw at the Cat's Meow back in Key West. The mountain towered over the sea, but the clouds only lingered for a moment before drifting away. Most of the time, Nate could see the top of the volcano. He watched as they crossed the channel while the hills swept up from the sea toward the peak and the intermittent clouds to the high sky above. Nevis was pretty and clean and when Nate approached the lee, it was nice to slow again and drift along in the flat water and watch the island go by a quarter-mile away. He heard some clanking below and then Sarah stepped out into the cockpit.

"Wow, I really slept," she said. "I heard the main go up. After that, I was dead to the world. What time is it?"

"A little after eleven. I didn't think you'd mind sleeping so I left you alone. I was just in a hurry to leave St. Kitts. We sneaked out of there under sail."

Sarah glanced over at Nevis towering to the clouds.

"Will we stop here? It's beautiful."

"I don't think so, unless you really want to go ashore again. I had hoped we would get down to Montserrat by nightfall. There isn't much wind, though, and we got a late start."

"Want some coffee? Where's Brady?"

"He was up earlier. I think he and Shanna decided to sleep in a little longer. I'd love some coffee. Do you need help?"

"I didn't have any trouble with the stove the last time. Maybe I can sneak up on it again."

Nate watched while Sarah pumped the kerosene tank. She finished priming the burner and lit it off and it burned blue the first time. She glanced at Nate and smiled and then put the coffee on while he looked over at Nevis and the quiet water near the beach. They were still only drifting along but they came upon Charlestown in only a few minutes. Sarah brought out the coffee and they sat behind the wheel and watched in silence as the little town edged by in the distance.

They were heading due south to clear the end of the island. *Serendipity* took on a slight hobbyhorse motion as she intercepted the low swells that curled around the last point of land. She entered the clear water beyond Nevis and picked up speed and rode the swells in a lazy, corkscrew motion that made Nate yawn after only a few minutes. There was so little wind he wasn't sure they could make Redonda and Montserrat before the sun went down. Sarah didn't say much. Nate was happy to ride up and over the swells in the light breeze and let *Serendipity* sail herself.

St. Kitts and Nevis stayed in view and he kept glancing back at the islands receding in the distance. When the cockpit heated up under the midday sun, Sarah ducked below where Brady and Shanna were sitting on the settees and reading in the shade of the cabin. She came back out wearing her pink bikini and carrying a beach towel and then she smiled at Nate before climbing onto the cabin roof to lie in the sun. He watched her moving around to spread the towel on the warm deck. There was so little fabric to her bathing suit he couldn't help staring when she leaned over. Sarah caught him and giggled. In a moment she was sprawled out with her eyes closed. It was hard not to look at her barely concealed breasts and at the hint of the darkness below. Nate turned away and watched the puffs of cloud that marched across the sky.

The islands faded astern. Nate kept glancing over the bow in the direction where Redonda should have been. Brady came out to take the wheel when Nate walked forward to the rail for a better look. There were some clouds clinging to a spot on the horizon and he knew the islet was beneath them, but it was another hour before he could make out the flat-iron shape of the island itself. Sarah came up to join him and they watched while *Serendipity* ticked away the last few miles. Nate could see straight away there was no safe anchorage anywhere, just the sheer cliffs of Redonda rising in vertical, guano-stained walls to a plateau that sloped upward to nearly a thousand feet on the northern end of the island.

There were currents that ran along the foul bottom of the shoreline. Nate saw the confused seas pounding the rocks at the base of the cliffs and heard the booming echoes that followed. He turned to Brady.

"This place gives me the creeps."

"I know," Brady said. "It could have been someplace special, but I guess not."

"Steer away for some clear air. Let's go on down to Montserrat."

When the ragged wind filled the jib, *Serendipity* fell away for the deep water out of the lee where Montserrat stood tall in the distance. Brady picked up the light east wind and pointed the boat toward the middle of the island. They were tracking at about five knots, but with only an hour to go before sunset, they wouldn't let the anchor go until well after dark.

Nate watched the swells rolling in from the open sea south of Antigua. The trades were quiet, barely a few knots, but the swells carried with them the energy picked up from the winds that blew across the Atlantic. They rolled through, rounded and soft and gentle, lifting *Serendipity* up and to the right and down again to the left and they ghosted toward Montserrat, lifting and rolling with the swells and going ever more slowly until by nightfall, the wind had died away to nothing. Brady volunteered to make rum drinks for everyone while Sarah helped Nate furl the main and genoa and get the diesel started. Shanna sat at the helm watching them. She looked up at Nate while he was trying hard not to stare at Sarah and her pink bikini.

"You never looked at me like that," Shanna said.

"Want to talk about that night in Key West again?"

Nate could see she was blushing, even in the red glow of the compass light. The diesel popped to life and Shanna let Nate take the wheel for the night approach to Montserrat. She hugged his neck before she stepped below to get the rum drinks from Brady. Sarah sat down beside him at the helm.

"You two better cool it," she said.

Nate could feel her breath on his face while he steered toward the twinkling lights of Montserrat. Shanna came out with the rum and Nate nearly gulped it down he was so thirsty. Sarah kept leaning against him and watching the lights ahead. Nate wanted to be back in Key West where Bob Marley spilled from the turntable and where Sarah looked like a goddess on the white sheets of her bed.

Nate took another long swallow of rum and lime juice and looked forward into the night trying to pick up the lights of Montserrat down low where there was a shallow bay on the west side of the island. They were moving only a few knots through the water and it was nearly nine o'clock when Brady let the anchor over the side. Nate could only see the dim lights of some buildings near the head of Old Road Bay.

They stood looking toward the beach while *Serendipity* settled in by nosing into the odd puffs that drifted down from the hills. It was quiet in the bay and it made their voices conspicuous so they talked just above a whisper until Shanna started the Chuck Mangione tape and turned the volume up. Nate listened to the trumpet while the lights from the beach reflected off the black water in the bay. Sarah brought him another rum and stayed to look at the water and at the lights bouncing on the surface and at Soufrière, the volcano brooding heavy and dark against the night sky.

The noise from the diesel had made Nate's ears ring. It was nice to stand in the dark to watch the lights that twinkled up the hills beyond the bay. Sarah leaned against him, staring toward the beach and the line of trees backlit by the glow from behind. Nate could see the reflections in her eyes.

"Shanna has put on some chicken and rice for dinner," she said. "She wouldn't let me help. It's so quiet here. You can't even hear the shore break."

"Maybe we can go ashore tomorrow for a long walk. There might be a hotel nearby where we can get a pint of Courage."

"I'd like that. This is nicer than St. Kitts. There aren't even any cars on the road."

Nate glanced toward the lights on the bluff to the north, a pale yellow glow of some shuttered windows and a lone streetlight hanging from a pole behind the trees. He put his arm around Sarah and drew her close and her hair tickled across his arm. She took a big breath without saying anything. They stood in the dark while the mellow sounds of Chuck Mangione drifted out across the silent water. Brady yelled from the galley.

"We just finished the last of the Mt. Gay," he said. "Can you believe it? We have one bottle of Cruzan left in the bilge. That's it."

Nate finished his rum with a last swallow and handed the empty glass down the companionway. Sarah pinched his side.

"Maybe we should save the Cruzan," she said. "I don't want any more."

Nate heard Brady thrashing around in the bilge and in a few minutes, another full tumbler came poking up the companionway along with the bowls of rice and chicken. Nate didn't want to make Sarah mad so he took the glass and set it on the seat. They ate dinner in a hurry it was so late, but Nate picked up the rum again and drank it down. Sarah shook her head and went below to clean the galley. When she stowed everything away, she climbed into the wingdeck berth out of sight.

Nate sat there with the empty glass while Brady and Shanna disappeared into the forepeak. *Serendipity* drifted here and there in the tiny wisps that brushed across the bay. The warmth of the night made Nate drowsy and he wanted to go below and strip away his clothes and hold Sarah next to him. He waited in the silence and then stepped out of the cockpit to stand near the port shrouds and breathe the thick island air that settled over the bay. Rilee was hiding in the darkness somewhere and there was a moment where Nate could feel her near. He shuddered and then turned away and went below where he sat on the settee and watched for a long time while the light of the Aladdin went dim. He blew the mantle out and plunged the cabin into night. He climbed into the berth without waking Sarah and then rolled over with his back to the world and shuddered again while the shadows closed everything down.

THIRTY

When the sabot bumped along the pilings of the dock at the end of Old Road Bay, Nate hopped out first and gave Sarah a pull to help her up onto the wooden planks bleached white in the sun. *Serendipity* stood out like Rilee's yellow hibiscus blossom floating on the water more army-tank green than anything. The drab color of the bay made the hulls look fresh. Sarah turned to walk toward the road, but she glanced back and laughed because Nate hadn't moved yet.

"It's no secret who your first love is," she said.

Sarah turned again and left Nate standing in the sun at the end of the dock. He kept looking at *Serendipity* until Brady and Shanna rowed up and tossed him the painter. They walked on the road up the hill to the north where there were some low buildings at the crest that turned out to be a small hotel. Along the shore a line of trees shaded the beach and above it a low bluff formed the northern side of the bay. The hill beyond was grassy and faded green like the fairways on the old course at St. Andrews. There were storybook houses scattered about and Mini-Mokes puttering along the narrow roads lined with flowers and the Central Hills towered above looking like smoking guns with the clouds, heavy and gray and bloated, tearing away from the highlands. To the southeast they could make out the somber shape of Soufrière.

Nate looked toward the volcano in the distance. There were moments when the upper slopes turned emerald in the sun. The light was brief, though, and the clouds returned again to bathe the hills in shadow and he never saw the top. Ireland is the greenest country in the world, but standing on the little road in Montserrat and looking at the hills above when the sun flooded through, it made Nate wonder if Ireland were only in second place.

Sarah stood nearby watching the clouds, but then she turned and walked along the road with Shanna and Brady. Nate stayed behind for a bit looking at the shadows and the peaks and the bursts of green. When he turned again to join the others, they were well off down the hill.

Brady stopped to wait where the bottom of the hill was sheltered from the wind. When Nate walked up, his shirt was already stained with sweat. They climbed the far side and didn't catch Shanna or Sarah until the road flattened out where they had stopped beneath a breadfruit tree to cool off in the shade. Shanna started to walk away and then she turned around in the center of the road.

"Sarah and I have decided we want some ice cream," she said. "Want to join us?"

"What about beer?" asked Brady. "Can't we get some beer, instead?"

"Not if you want company tonight."

"C'mon. Let's get a beer."

"Nope. Not right now. We're leaving."

Sarah and Shanna took up the march in the middle of the road while Brady and Nate followed like ducklings. Beyond a stand of trees in the distance, there were some buildings and a market with a shining tin roof. They walked through the door and found a small lunch counter in one corner that served ice cream and milkshakes. Sarah and Shanna asked for vanilla swirl cones. A chocolate shake sounded just right to Nate. Brady ordered one for each of them. The little girl who took the order set the shakes on the counter and looked at Brady.

"Shot of rum?" she asked.

"Rum? You put rum in milkshakes?"

"Yes, all the time."

Brady looked at Nate with a grin.

"Yes," he said. "We'll have shots of rum. Maybe we'll have two."

The little girl pulled a bottle of Mt. Gay from behind the counter and free-poured a couple of shots in each of the shakes. She handed one to Nate and he used the straw to stir it up. The first swallow went down like chocolate fire. Sarah didn't want anything to do with rum and ice cream so she walked outside to finish her cone. Nate sat at one of the counter stools and sipped the shake and waited. She didn't come back and in a few minutes he went out to sit with her.

"Why are you drinking so much?" she asked. "You didn't need that."

"I know. It's easy to drink too much around Brady."

"Don't blame him. You could have turned him down. I don't want to sound like an old shrew, but maybe if you didn't drink so much we'd be getting along better. In bed, I mean."

Nate looked at Sarah sitting in the shade with her melting ice cream and her soft brown eyes that seemed to be melting as well.

"Maybe you're right," Nate said. "I'm not giving us much of a chance."

"No chance, I'd say. I don't know. Sometimes it makes me want to leave."

There was a cold shiver inside. Nate sat with the rum shake in his hands and didn't move.

"I don't want you to go," he said.

"I don't want to go, either, Nate. I love *Serendipity* and more than anything I want to love you, but you won't let me. Maybe I won't have a choice."

Brady swallowed the last of his rum shake and threw the cup into a trash bin. He and Shanna walked hand in hand back in the direction of the bay along the road where the breadfruit trees cast their thick morning shadows. Nate threw his empty shake into the same can and held out his hand. Sarah took it in hers and they followed behind. Nate didn't want to say anything.

When they reached the dock, Brady had already rowed out to *Serendipity* with Shanna. Sarah sat down at the edge of the pier and let her feet dangle over the water. Nate sat down next to her and hugged her shoulders and she leaned into his chest.

"This spot reminds me of growing up," Nate said. "You can't count the number of times I sat with a fishing rod at the end of a dock on Pamlico Sound. Looked just like this except the water stretched out forever."

"North Carolina?"

"Yes. I love the Low Country. I'd like to take *Serendipity* up the Intracoastal Waterway just to see the places where I caught all those fish."

"You'll do that someday. I know."

"I lived there in the late fifties. It's probably changed a lot in the last twenty years."

"All places change. So do people, but I bet you'll find it hasn't changed that much. Sometimes the soul of a place stays around even with all the development. Steinhatchee is like that. You'd like it there, too."

"Isn't there a river nearby?"

"Yes. It's great for canoeing. Lots of alligators, and the bird life is amazing. I could show you around, if you like."

"Is there a chance that could happen?"

"I'd love that, Nate, but I can't let myself look that far into the future."

"I don't want you to leave."

"I know. Let's not talk about it."

Brady rowed up and held the sabot steady while Sarah took a seat in the stern. Nate lost his balance pushing them away from the dock. He recovered enough to land on the square seat in the bow.

"No more rum for you," Brady said.

Nate glanced at Sarah sitting in the stern. She was looking off toward the Central Hills and watching the clouds tear free. Beyond her Nate could see *Serendipity* swinging in the breeze that swirled through the trees on the bluff. He wondered if her yellow boot top would get stained by the tannins in the Intracoastal Waterway. He wondered if Rilee had ever seen the Outer Banks.

They stayed another day and night in Montserrat where the mountains east of them sometimes looked like torches with the clouds ripping through like smoke. Brady and Shanna took off to explore the island when Sarah left to walk over to the little market that sold the rum shakes. Nate stayed aboard to take the head apart and rebuild the flapper mechanism and the water pump to get it to flush better, and then he removed most of the plumbing to the holding tank and broke the scale free and reassembled the system. When he finished, Nate washed down in the shower and took a cool Heineken from the bilge and sat out on the cabin roof to wait for Sarah. She left the sabot tied to the little dock, but in a few minutes he saw her carrying some bags and stepping into the dinghy. Her blonde hair gleamed in the light and when she pulled away from the dock, he watched her as she rowed. She turned once in a while to see *Serendipity*. Nate leaned in the shade of the boom and waited until she came swirling up to toss him the painter.

"That was fun," she said. "I bought some canned meat and some peas and corn. The bag is heavy."

"Brady will be upset if you didn't buy more rum. Okay, I will be, too."

"Don't worry, Nate. They had cheap rum there. Who knows what it tastes like? At least it's the same color. I bought four bottles."

"Thanks. I won't get stupid."

"Promise?"

"Yep. Maybe the rum will last through the night."

"You big dope."

They set about stowing the cans and the bottles of rum, but there was a whistle from the beach. Brady and Shanna stood at the end of the dock with more bags.

"I'll row in, okay?" Sarah said. "I love the sabot."

"Sure. Just be back in time for evening cocktails."

Sarah drifted away looking like that centerfold again with her bronzed face beaming and her Revlon hair loose on her shoulders and her skin shiny from the rowing. Nate kept thinking of her when he went below to find another beer. The

Heineken was cool to the touch and he took the can out on deck to wait while the others rowed back from the dock.

Shanna sat in the little bow seat, but she kept turning around to see while Sarah rowed hard toward *Serendipity*. Nate helped with the painter when they coasted up and then with a couple of bags. Brady climbed aboard and disappeared below.

"Holy smokes," he shouted. "Cockspur Gold. Who bought this? Sarah?"

"Oh, no. C'mon Brady," Shanna said. "Can't we save it for later?"

"Nope. It's too good to let it sit. Might go bad. Who wants a rum?"

Nate glanced over at Sarah. She just shrugged.

"Why not?" she said, and she slapped Nate on the arm. "I'm going to put on that pink bathing suit and sit on the deck for a while. Care to join me?"

Brady came out with two of the yellow cups filled with rum and lime juice. Nate sipped his, but it was so strong he didn't know why Brady bothered with the limes. Sarah and Shanna stepped out into the cockpit to spread towels on the deck. Nate stayed in the shade of the boom and watched the hills swinging by. It was hard not to look at Sarah and he shut his eyes to keep from staring. He had visions of Steamboat again and little girls with pie pan faces. He couldn't see Rilee anywhere. Nate gulped the rum away trying to find her.

"You finished that already?"

Sarah stood over Nate, one hand on the mast.

"Maybe you'd better switch to beer," she said. "I'll get you one if you like, but not rum. You'll be sick again."

"Yeah. It's hot sitting here. I'll have a beer if you join me."

"Sure, but don't get carried away. You know what happens."

"I never know. Maybe Cockspur will help."

"I don't think it will turn you into Valentino."

Nate looked up at Sarah and then leaned back against the mast and shut his eyes.

"I'm sorry," she said. "I didn't mean that."

"It's okay. I'll take a beer."

Sarah turned away and climbed down into the cockpit. Nate's face was burning. He opened his eyes again to find Shanna looking over at him from her spot on the foredeck.

"Are you okay?" she asked.

Nate nodded and then shut his eyes again until Sarah brought the beer. He took his away and nearly drained it in one swallow. Sarah watched him and then sat on the foredeck next to Shanna. Nate walked back to the cockpit and stepped below to sit at the dinette. His head was suddenly spiraling down into some kind of dark pit that felt like quicksand on the bottom. Shanna came down the companionway ladder and opened one of the canisters full of pasta. Nate reached into the bilge for a can of Heineken.

"Care for a beer?" Nate asked.

"No, thanks. You don't look like you need one, either. Maybe you can help me with the stove. The sun is going down so I might as well start dinner."

Nate pulled the pressure tank from its locker and began pumping until the needle was pegged on the gauge. Shanna lit the stove and it sputtered twice and then burned blue. She put a pot of water on to boil for the pasta and they both went out into the cockpit where Brady sat with an empty rum glass. Nate sat down next to Sarah and took several big gulps from the can of beer. She seemed angry so he watched the hills and the high bluffs of the bay slide by while *Serendipity* drifted about in the wisps that brushed across the water. Shanna picked up the cruising guide and took it below to read while the water boiled.

"It's thirty miles or so down to Guadeloupe," Brady said. "Are we leaving early?"

"If the trades are blowing at all we'll get down there in only a few hours," Nate said. "We can wait until everyone is ready. Probably just head for Deshaies on the northwest coast, if that's okay. It's supposed to be beautiful there."

"There was a picture of it in the guide. Just a dock and some old buildings. The bay looked just as nice as this one."

"Is there an airport there?" Sarah asked.

"Why?" Brady asked. "You aren't leaving are you?"

"Well, I don't know yet. Sometimes I think about it."

Brady stood and nearly fell on top of Sarah trying to hug her neck.

"You can't leave us. Nothing would be the same. Is it something I did?"

Sarah started giggling at Brady. Shanna yelled out from the galley.

"If you leave, I leave. Period."

Brady dived down the companionway and wrestled Shanna onto the settee where he planted a full mouth kiss on her face.

"No one is leaving," he said. "We're in this together. I'm here to make sure we're all happy. How about some rum?"

"Get off me you big oaf. Maybe I will have some rum, but let's eat first."

Sarah looked at Nate for a long time and a smile sneaked in and he thought the airport question was done. She hugged his shoulders before stepping below to help Shanna. The idea that Sarah might leave made Nate cringe. He slid closer to the companionway just to watch her.

THIRTY-ONE

They finished the first bottle of Cockspur Gold late in the evening. Sarah sat with Nate for a few minutes when Brady and Shanna disappeared into the forepeak. He thought she wanted to talk, but they sat close together watching the odd Mini-Moke bouncing by on the road at the head of the bay and at the branches of the trees blinking in the lone streetlight.

"Without you here," Nate said, "I think we'd all just go back to Key West."

"I get upset, you know? It just doesn't seem to work between us. I know that when I go below, the rum is going to make me dizzy again and I wish I hadn't taken it from Brady, but you're right. He's hard to refuse."

"I know. I'm lit, but at least we ate. Maybe it won't be so bad."

"Well, I'm on my way down. Are you coming or do you want to be alone?"

"I'll be down in a minute. I've had a lot more to drink today than you know. I don't think I can sleep right now."

Sarah kissed Nate on the cheek and he watched as she stepped down the ladder. She reached for the knob on the Aladdin and turned the flame down and then slipped from her pink bikini and disappeared into the portside wingdeck berth. Nate kept staring below for some reason, maybe hoping she would come back. He leaned against the bulkhead and let the spinning begin.

There was a good breeze aloft, but Nate couldn't feel it much down on deck. It set the mast pumping slightly and the pulsing made him think of that horrible night at the Bitter End.

He shut his eyes hard and the pressure made his head swim. There were images again of Rilee dancing in Drake's Pub and of Debra in the wet T-shirt and images of Jenson shouting at the top of his lungs in the Baths. He stepped below and washed his face and arms in the cool water from the galley pump. He thought about a real shower, but he didn't want to bother Brady and Shanna. Nate breathed a few times and climbed into the double berth where Sarah was asleep. He fluffed the pillow and put his head down. He was surprised there was so little spinning and in a moment, the sun came pouring through the portlight.

Nate opened his eyes and realized no one was awake, not even Sarah who had barely moved all night long. He looked at her face in the light and the ache and the sorrow came back in a rush. He wanted to bury himself in her, but there was nothing but a hollow feeling in the pit of his stomach. He didn't want to stare so he slid from the sheets and let himself down on the settee and stepped out into the cockpit.

The trees on the bluff leaned in the trades that blew in from the east. Nate watched as the ripples in the water swept one way then another as the wind swirled and dropped over the edge into the bay. *Serendipity* dodged about on her anchor line. She wasn't frantic, just swinging in the wind as if there were music in the trees and she wanted to dance. Nate yawned and stretched and felt like diving into the water for a swim. The bay had the color of a green algae bloom so he stood alone on the deck in the rising heat of the morning and breathed the salt air.

The clouds clinging to the hills east of the bay were backlit and it was hard to focus in that direction. Nate turned and looked out to sea to the southwest where the green of the bay faded to the blue of the Caribbean. There was an island workboat painted in gray and yellow and red just off the point. Nate watched as it motored through until it disappeared beyond the bluffs on the west side of the bay. The faint whine of its outboard faded into the rush of the trade winds through the trees above. He thought it would be a good time to head out for

Deshaies and the island of Guadeloupe. He tried not to make any noise when he removed the sail cover from the boom. Sarah poked her head out of the companionway.

"Good morning," she said.

"Sleep well?"

"Yes, I did. I hardly remember going to bed. Want some coffee?"

"That would be nice. Want me to pump the tank?"

"No. I'm good at it, now."

"Yell if you have a blowout."

Sarah disappeared below so Nate folded the sail cover and then went forward to shackle the jib to the halyard. Brady climbed out of the forepeak hatch and ran the sheets aft while Nate walked back to the cockpit to stand near the transom. He looked toward the mouth of the little bay and stared for a long time at the horizon to the west.

"Coffee is ready," Sarah said. "I'll put some mugs out."

Brady fairly sprinted down the deck to reach for a cup.

"Are you hung over?" Sarah asked. "I'm making another pot right now. You don't have to wait very long for seconds."

"Hung over? Are you kidding?" Brady asked. "I'm still drunk from all the Cockspur last night."

Serendipity pointed her nose out of Old Road Bay where the wind swirled softly from the bluffs. When they escaped the lee of the hills on Montserrat, the wind filled in from the east. *Serendipity* got up on her toes again and charged to windward at ten or twelve knots, clipping the tops of the swells to send the spray flying. Sarah wanted to steer so Nate sat forward and rode the long blue swells while the spray flew aft and made those tiny rainbows that pranced in the morning sun. The dark shape of Guadeloupe hunkered down on the horizon, but the boat moved so fast the green began to fill in and the volcanoes on the island took shape and there were more clouds tearing away from the peaks. Nate glanced at Sarah to see if she wanted help. She just waved and smiled. He turned back to face the oncoming swells.

After several hours of the hard charging, *Serendipity* rushed into the lee of Guadeloupe where the wind shut down. She ghosted over the flat water barely making steerage. The island drifted by, another emerald in the afternoon sun looking very much like a Gaugin painting. Sarah steered the boat around the little point of Le Gros Morne and tucked her into the bay. Nate and Brady dropped the main and jib and lit the diesel just to motor around a bit to pick a spot to drop the anchor. There were two other cruising boats snugged down. Their crews were ashore so Sarah idled a short distance away where Brady slipped the CQR over the side. *Serendipity* nudged to a stop with the anchor firm on the bottom and then she drifted forward again to settle in a spot just to the south of the dock.

"What a great sail," Sarah said. "We were water skiing. I'm so crusty with salt spray I might take a shower before we go ashore. Do we have time?"

"I don't think anyone is in a hurry," Nate said. "Brady will get into the rum if he can sneak it by Shanna."

Sarah smiled and disappeared below while Nate stayed on the cabin roof looking at the tiny village of Deshaies. He turned to help Brady splash the sabot over the side and then went below to wash up and change shirts. Brady followed him down and opened a fresh bottle of Cockspur Gold. Nate nodded in his direction when Brady started mixing drinks. Nate could hear Sarah in the shower and it would have been easy for him to slip in beside her, but he took the rum and stepped up the companionway ladder with Brady to look again at the little town across the water. They watched a local workboat motor through the anchorage and tie up at the town dock. The wake slapped the sides of the hull and it set *Serendipity* rocking. In a moment the ripples died away and the water in the bay looked like a sheet of silver in the sun. Sarah stepped out into the cockpit and took a big breath.

"That shower felt so good. I'm ready to go light up the town."

"Not much town, I don't think," Nate said. "There might be ice cream somewhere."

"I hope so, and some ice. Shanna and I need some ice for our evening cocktails."

"I can row you two ashore if you like," Brady said. "Shanna isn't ready and I need to clean up, too. Want me to give you a lift?"

Nate stepped below to get the satchel with all the passports in case there was a customs office. Sarah and Brady were waiting in the sabot still tied to the deck cleat when he came back out. He climbed in the bow again and got the line free and they set out for the dock, looking more like tourists than boat people. Brady let them out at the pier where they turned to walk up the narrow streets of Deshaies. There were palms and breadfruit trees and rainbow houses that stepped up the hills and an ancient hotel falling into ruin and when they walked back to the dock, they found a tiny shop that sold ice cream. Nate and Sarah walked out on the pier where they could see the yellow sabot heading toward the beach. There was a lone boardsailor out beyond the anchorage drifting along in the puffs that tickled the bay into ripples. Nate was still watching the boardsailor when Brady and Shanna rowed up. They tied the painter to a rusted cleat on the shallow end and the four of them strolled off to find the ice cream store.

Brady only wanted beer. The lady behind the ice cream counter pointed him next door where they had bottles of Kronenbourg. Nate was used to drinking cool Heinekens from the bilge locker on *Serendipity*. The Kronenbourg froze his brains. The pain eased away and he walked back inside and bought two more bottles. Nate didn't drink the second one so fast. Sarah watched him while the ice cream melted off her cone.

They set out to walk the streets of Deshaies while Sarah and Shanna were still sticky with ice cream. The main road climbed a slight hill to the north. They walked up the street past a small white church and a school playground and a field where they found an old Ferguson tractor nearly buried in the soil. A lot of kids were laughing and playing so Brady went into his Dracula routine again. The kids scattered but they could hear them giggling and sneaking around the corners until Dracula reared from his cape once more. The kids ran laughing back to their field with the buried tractor.

Shanna and Sarah decided to find a market where they might sell potatoes and peppers and carrots. Brady and Nate left them in the village and turned to the right on a country lane just to see where it went. In no time they were alone on a road that swept up the hill to the south. They didn't walk very far because of the heat and the slope of the road, but there were a lot of trees and it was nice to walk through the shadows. The trade winds set the branches and the palm fronds waving. Nate listened to the rush of air as it swept down from the hill above. They took another narrow lane back toward the bay and walked past houses with gardens and hibiscus blossoms and palms in the yards and there were trees laden with green breadfruit that lined the street, but then they were in the village again looking for the little store and the bottles of Kronenbourg.

They stood at the edge of the street and drank the beer and waited to see if Sarah and Shanna would come back. Nate kept looking toward the dock and *Serendipity* beyond. In a minute he heard a shout from up the lane to the north. He turned and saw Sarah walking along the road carrying some bags. Nate walked up to meet her and she thrust a bag of potatoes and onions into his arms.

"Now it's our turn for beer," she said. "This stuff is heavy."

Shanna did the same, but not before Brady drained his beer and put the empty into the bag.

"I know just the place," Brady said.

Nate walked past the Kronenbourg store and down the street to where the dinghy bobbed at the end of its painter. He put the bags in the bottom hoping no one would steal them. He kept the satchel and walked back toward the village center where the Sarah and Shanna and Brady were drinking beer.

A little office across the street had a sign over the door with *Bureau de Douane* printed in red letters. Nate pointed toward the customs office and crossed over to check to see if it was open. The door swung free and he stepped inside where there was a uniformed man sitting behind a desk covered with stamp pads. The officer had a big nose and a Yosemite Sam mustache that hid his lips. When he spoke, Nate couldn't understand his English very well.

"The yellow yacht?" the man asked.

"Yes. *Serendipity,* from Bodega Bay, California."

"I see. How long in Guadeloupe?"

"Only a few days. Here are the papers."

The customs man took the passports and the papers of documentation and stared at them for a few minutes. He glanced Nate's way again before opening a stamp pad.

"Your last port, Gustavia? St. Barthelemy?"

Nate stopped for a moment. He hadn't cleared into St. Kitts or Montserrat and he thought there could be a problem.

"Yes," Nate said. "St. Barts."

There was some nervousness in his voice. The officer looked at him again, but he began stamping the passports and initialing each of them. When he handed the papers back, he just winked.

"California, a lot of the hippies?"

"Used to be. They all had to go to work."

"You can stay one week," the man said. "If you want to stay longer, please come back to see me. *Bienvenue en Guadeloupe.*"

"Thanks," Nate said. "*Merci.*"

The customs man rose from his desk and shook Nate's hand. Even behind the monstrous mustache Nate could see he was smiling. He left the tiny office and walked back to the Kronenbourg store.

"Problems?" Brady asked.

"I think he was suspicious of our last port. Is there any beer left inside?"

"Yes, but we need to find a restroom real quick."

"Is there a restaurant around? We could eat ashore. I don't think it's too early."

"I saw a restaurant sign up around the corner when Brady was scaring all the kids," Sarah said. "Let's go look."

Shanna took Brady by the hand and marched him up the hill and away from the Kronenbourg. They reached the street corner and turned left where they saw the restaurant sign swinging in the wind with the word *poissons* written near the bottom.

"I think that means fish," Sarah said. "Is that okay? I'm hungry."

"I don't care what they serve," Brady said. "The restroom needs to be open."

They walked through the swinging door and took an empty table near the front window that looked across at the field with the sunken tractor and at the tiny white church down the street. The restaurant was clean and airy with a big fan rotating in the corner and a French bar song coming from a stereo in the kitchen. A big maroon and gold Kronenbourg sign hung on the wall over the serving counter. Brady came back from the single restroom and pointed at the sign. The lady waiting tables brought four bottles and four glasses without saying a word.

Shanna was next for the restroom. The waitress smiled and waited near the entry to the kitchen. Sarah kept looking out the window at the church beginning to turn pink in the light from the setting sun and at the steeple capped with a red tin pyramid. She turned to glance at Nate and then she looked away again through the window. The sun sank lower behind them and the church and its high, thick steeple picked up the reflected pink from the clouds and then the shadows of the trees tiptoed across the road to creep slowly up the walls. For a moment the steeple and the red pyramid at the top were bathed in pink and the church below was lost in the shadows and then twilight settled over the steeple and the church and the rest of the village.

"That was pretty," Sarah said, and then she looked down at her lap.

Shanna walked back into the restaurant. Sarah excused herself and headed off to the restroom. Brady was already finished with his beer and wanted the lady to bring another. Shanna didn't want any more.

"Do you have soft drinks?" she asked.

"Yes. We have cola and ginger ale. Ice cold."

"I'd like a ginger ale. Bring two. I think my friend would like one."

"Yes, I bring two, and beer for the man."

"Another beer for me, too," Nate said.

The lady smiled and swished her long skirt in the air from the fan and disappeared just as Sarah returned to the table. Nate got up and walked to the back of the restaurant where the door to the restroom opened onto a rear patio where he could see the bay through the coconut palms. It seemed like the restaurant was turned around and that it should have a view of the Caribbean rather than a pink church steeple. Nate stepped into the tiny restroom and shut the door.

Sarah was laughing when Nate returned. He sat down and the waitress came back to take the orders. She brought two more beers and two ginger ales.

"I'm in heaven," Brady said. "Cold beer again."

"Keep drinking. You'll find out how it is to sleep on a cold deck," Shanna said.

"C'mon, this is fun."

"It is until you get too drunk to walk."

"I won't do that. What did we order to eat? I forgot already."

"Does the deck sound good to you?"

"No, ma'am. I'll be good."

The waitress came back with plates of rice and fried fish and plantains in sweet syrup. Brady looked at his dinner and started eating without another word. All Nate could hear were the forks hitting the plates and the rustle of napkins and then Brady ordering another beer.

When they left the fish restaurant, there weren't many lights in the town so they walked slowly down the hill toward the dock to the sabot tied to a cleat. The bags with the potatoes and onions were still there. While Brady rowed Shanna and Sarah out to the boat, Nate stood at the end of the town dock looking at the quiet water and at the stars sweeping down like tiny candles in the night sky. He couldn't tell when Sarah made it aboard *Serendipity* until the light from the Aladdin came on and lit the yellow curtains. He kept watching and only saw the shadow of the sabot briefly as Brady made his way back. Nate lost him in the darkness again until he was nearly back to the pier. Brady was breathing hard.

"Man. Too much beer," Brady said. "Time for some rum."

"How much is left?"

"Two bottles and a little more. Plenty for tonight."

"How about lime juice? We must be getting low."

"I'm not sure. I know there is a bottle of ReaLemon in the bilge. Almost be the same as lime juice."

They coasted up to *Serendipity* where the light coursing from the open companionway made the rest of the anchorage seem dark. They climbed aboard just as Shanna started another John Prine album. Nate stayed out in the cockpit where it was cool while Brady sang and made rum drinks. He watched the dim lights from the other cruising boats flicker on the water. Behind them there was only the pop of the shore break and the hiss of the trades sweeping over the hills, rustling the fronds on the palms that grew on the beach. Nate put his head down to breathe in the quiet evening air. Rilee was there on Peter Island walking down the sand in the pale light from the Milky Way, asking him why he didn't go with her. Brady handed him a rum.

"The ladies forgot to buy ice today. They don't want anything to drink."

"There's wine down in the bilge locker."

"No, they just want to read. I'm too drunk."

"Me, too. I'm sitting here getting the melancholies. Thanks for the rum."

"It's hot down there. I'll go forward and open the hatch. I might sit up near the bow rail. Cooler up there. Come on up."

"No, maybe I'll just sit here and guard the Cockspur."

In a moment Nate could see Brady opening the hatch and climbing from the forepeak. The hiss of the trades and the slap of the shore break came back and Rilee kept looking in Nate's eyes. He kept his head down and his eyes shut to let the spinning drive away the vision of her face. It didn't work. Nate drank the rum until the glass was empty.

THIRTY-TWO

Nate stayed in the dark with the empty glass until Brady came back from the bow rail. He was stumbling when he made it into the cockpit. Brady wanted more rum and lime juice and when he stepped back up the ladder with two more drinks, Nate took one and leaned back against the coaming.

"Man, this might kill me."

"I doubt it," Brady said. "I didn't make it very strong this time."

"If I spill this, I bet it eats the deck paint."

"You better not spill it."

Nate wasn't so sure he could get through another cup of rum. He sipped the drink and it disappeared in a few minutes.

"One more and I'm finished," Brady said. "I think I might be sleeping on the deck tonight anyway. I don't know what I'm worried about. Maybe I'll have two more."

"I don't know. I'm loaded."

"C'mon. One more? I still think Cockspur goes bad."

Brady didn't wait for a reply. He took Nate's glass and stepped below. Nate couldn't focus on the lights from the other boats in the anchorage but when Brady reappeared, they drank the rum and slipped away into oblivion.

Sometime during the night Nate fell asleep sitting in the cockpit. He awoke with a jolt, drunk and disoriented. He left the empty glass in the cockpit and glanced forward where he could see a human form buried in a blanket on the foredeck. Nate stumbled into the stillness of the cabin. He pumped a little fresh water to rinse his mouth and then climbed fully clothed into the wingdeck berth on the port side. Sarah wasn't there. Nate's eyes adjusted to the light and he could see across the cabin that Sarah had taken a sheet and a pillow and was sound asleep on the starboard wing. He tried to focus, but he couldn't keep his head from spinning and then the saliva began pumping. Beads of sweat popped out all over and he tumbled onto the cabin sole where he dived for the open companionway and the cockpit beyond where he managed to reach the stern just before vomiting over the side. Nate couldn't catch his breath and he was choking and retching all at once and the rum burned on its way up and didn't stop until all of it was gone and the retching was just an empty reflex.

Nate didn't know how long he drooled into the black water. He finally wiped his mouth and sat upright. The wind was cold on his face and arms and he thought the retching would start again, but there were only chills and the sour taste he couldn't wipe away. Nate turned and looked toward the bow again. Brady was still there wrapped in his blanket. The companionway was dark and no one was moving around down below. He sat alone in the stern and shivered in the quiet breeze that drifted across the bay from the hills above the village.

The smell of vomit wouldn't go away. Nate pulled himself up by clinging to the backstay bridle and then wobbled forward where he managed to get down through the companionway without stumbling. When he reached the galley, he pumped enough fresh water to bathe his face and arms. He toweled off with a dish cloth and stripped away his clothes and nearly fell into the portside berth where the violent spinning kept him from falling asleep until nearly dawn.

The heat of the morning finally made Nate open his eyes. He sat upright and looked through the portlight and saw the sabot tied to the dock. He climbed from the bunk and checked the door into the forepeak. Brady and Sarah and Shanna had left him behind.

The drinking and the vomiting from the night before made Nate sick to his stomach. He stepped into the shower and let the water run free over his body, hoping the cold would shock him into feeling better. In the end he toweled off and dressed and stood alone in the cabin wondering what to do. He heard voices outside and climbed into the cockpit just in time to see a dinghy from one of the other boats drifting by with a man and a woman laughing together. The sabot was still tied to the dock.

Nate made his way below and sat on the settee while he tried to clear his head of the ringing sound that had come back. The winds were quiet in the lee of the hills. *Serendipity* ghosted here and there, but there was so little air movement that it soon got too hot to sit in the cabin. Nate propped the forward deck hatch open and saw in the forepeak where Brady had left a pile of dirty clothes, rumpled and limp, lying on the V-berth mattress. Nate turned and walked through the cabin and stepped into the cockpit and looked toward the dock. Brady and Shanna were climbing into the sabot. He didn't see Sarah.

Brady's back was turned but Nate could see Shanna's face while they rowed closer. He could tell she had been crying. Nate took the painter while Brady shrugged his shoulders and helped Shanna climb aboard. She didn't even look at Nate. Brady heaved himself aboard where he stopped to look toward the hills above the bay.

"We just came from the customs guy," Brady said. "Sarah wants to catch the twelve o'clock bus for Pointe á Pitre where the airport is."

"Where is she?"

"She's afraid to come back to *Serendipity*. She thinks she won't have the guts to get on that bus if she does."

"Oh, no. She threatened to leave. I didn't think it would happen."

"She's mad and disgusted, you know? I guess last night was too much for her to take. You need to talk to her. She's having coffee at the little fish restaurant. I'll row you in if you like. If I'm not careful, Shanna will buy a ticket, too. I'm on good behavior from here on out."

Brady wasn't smiling. Nate remembered seeing the lumpy blanket on the foredeck when he stumbled below the night before.

"Any chance Sarah might change her mind?"

"I don't know. She had her passport this morning when she woke me up. I think she's tired of waiting for you to get out of your funk."

"You're probably right. Shit, I feel terrible."

Brady climbed down into the sabot to man the oars. Nate sat in the stern and looked toward the dock where there were piles of green bananas stacked and waiting for an island trader. When they coasted up, Nate stepped free of the dinghy. Brady pulled away from the dock and headed back to *Serendipity* still hunting around her anchor line.

Nate turned to walk up the hill past the little church and beyond where he could see the *Restaurant de Poissons* sign hanging over the street. He was nervous and upset. He stopped for a moment to look at the shops and at the school and at the sunken tractor in the field. The church stood white again against the trade wind sky above and it made Nate sad to think of beautiful Deshaies in the sunset. He kept thinking of clouds and blue skies and about Steamboat Springs that summer day the only time he drove through years before, but he didn't stay long in the streets of Deshaies. He trudged the rest of the way up the hill where Sarah sat with her coffee in the restaurant with the rotating fan and the restroom entrance with the million-dollar view.

Sarah slumped over a table in the back, staring down at her cup. Nate paused again at the door, afraid to go in, but the waitress lady pushed it open and welcomed him in and he had no choice. Sarah glanced up. Her eyes were red and puffy. She looked away while Nate walked over to her table and sat down.

"I don't know what to say, Sarah. I don't want you to leave. You know that."

"I have to go. If I stay, it will only be because of *Serendipity* and the Caribbean and the islands. God knows I want to stay for that, but it isn't fair to you or to me, either. You aren't in love with me. That's what really matters. I'm a big girl. I can take it."

There were tears on her cheeks. Nate reached to wipe them away. She unfolded a napkin to dry her face.

"I wish it had happened for us," Nate said. "I wish more than anything we had never stopped in the Virgin Islands."

"Why, though? I didn't do anything except go out on charter to make money. When I came back, it just wasn't the same. Even when we could make love, it only felt real once and then it was over too soon. I don't know how to make it better for you."

"It isn't you. I was hoping the sparks would come back after being together long enough, you know?"

"Don't tell me things like that. I'm going to walk out of here when Shanna brings my bags. I will be on the twelve o'clock bus for the airport. I can't wait for you. All you do is drink too much. I'm sorry. I just can't wait any longer."

"Don't go. Nothing will be the same."

"I can't stay. You know that, too."

Sarah pushed her chair back and stood at the table looking down at Nate and then she turned and walked out the door. Nate asked the restaurant lady about the bill. She frowned and waved him away. He followed Sarah down the hill toward the dock where all the bananas were still stacked, waiting for the boat that hadn't come. They stood in the shade of a coconut palm that hung low over the dock. Sarah took his hand while she sobbed. She was staring in the distance at *Serendipity* floating like an autumn leaf in the heavy air that settled on the bay.

"I didn't want to see her again, but I couldn't just go. This is breaking my heart."

"You don't have to leave."

"Please don't. You know as well as I do that it's time for me to go. I want to get on with my life. I thought you might be the one. I guess not."

Sarah pulled away from Nate and walked to the end of the pier. He could see her shoulders shaking. Nate stood alone in the shade of the drooping coconut palm and waited for Brady and Shanna. When the sabot pulled up, they climbed out with a backpack and a shoulder bag. They took them over to Sarah who broke down and cried again when she hugged them both. Nate stood there like an idiot not knowing what to do. Sarah and Shanna turned and walked by on the other side of the banana stalks. He watched them for a moment moving up the street before Brady came over.

"You ought to go to the airport," he said. "I think Sarah would appreciate that."

"It might be harder for both of us. I can't even think."

"You better get. I'll wait here for Shanna."

Brady pointed at Sarah who had crossed the street heading for the bus stop on the island highway. She was walking on the edge of the road in the shade of all the breadfruit trees near the old hotel when Nate caught up to her.

"I'd like to go with you to the airport, if that's okay?"

Sarah turned around with a puzzled look, but she nodded and shifted the bag on her shoulder. They walked up to the highway and turned left where there was a bus stop and a small building with a man inside who sold tickets, one way for Sarah and a return trip for Nate. They walked outside to wait in the shade of another breadfruit tree. Shanna glanced his way and he caught her eye. She looked away to the road to the south and pretended to wait for the bus to arrive.

The rapping sound of a diesel engine echoed from up the hill and then an old Bluebird smoked to a stop in front of them. Sarah turned to hug Shanna and then she stepped up through the swinging doors. Shanna was mad, but Nate hugged her anyway and then he followed Sarah into the crowded bus where she found a seat near the middle on the aisle. Nate had to sit three rows behind. The bus lurched forward and he glanced through the window at Shanna who was crying at the side of the road. She looked small and frail and lost standing in the noonday sun.

The noise on the bus wasn't bad except for a two-year-old wailing in the back seat. Nate shut his eyes and folded his arms across his chest and sat rock still while the bus plowed its way over the hill to the north of Deshaies and angled to the east. It was only fifteen miles to the airport, but there were a lot of stops and when they arrived at the end of the bus ride, Sarah rushed into the terminal to buy a ticket for an Air Guadeloupe flight to St. Barts where she could connect for St. Thomas. Nate followed her into the ticket counter. She never said anything until a man asked for her passport and if she wanted a return flight.

"No. I've cleared it with customs in Deshaies. I'm free to leave, as you can see."

The airport man looked at the stamps in the passport. He grunted and cleared his throat and made notes on a clip-board and then issued her a one-way ticket to St. Barts for a flight that was to leave in twenty minutes. Sarah checked her big shoulder bag and kept her backpack. She left the counter and turned to Nate and took his hand again.

"I am so sorry, Nate. I don't know why I'm doing this. I just have to go."

"I can't make you stay. You have to know, though. I do love you."

"You have a funny way of showing it, but it's weird. I know you love me in your own way. God, I wanted it to work."

"What will you do, now?"

"I'm not sure. I need to go up to Steinhatchee to see my dad. There is always *Nomad,* too. They wanted me back, you know? I'd like to keep sailing."

"I don't think we'll go back that way."

"What about you. What about your beautiful *Serendip-ity?"*

"Might just turn around and go back to the Green Par-rot. Without you here, there isn't much point to the trip."

"Don't do that to me. This is your dream. You need to finish what you started."

Sarah looked at the clock and squeezed Nate's hand.

"Do I need to go through the customs gate? That guy didn't say."

"I think so. It's just over there."

Sarah looked over her shoulder at the uniformed officer at the far gate and then she turned and kissed Nate on the lips. There were more tears on her cheeks.

"I'm so sorry it didn't work." she said.

Sarah turned and ran toward the customs man who only thumbed through her passport. Another man in a uniform took her ticket and in a flash, Sarah was gone through the gate and out of Nate's life. He walked out the front of the terminal and turned to the right where a Piper Navajo waited on the ramp and an older couple stood in line to board. Sarah was behind them. She didn't turn to look back. In a moment the three of them stepped up the ladder and into the cabin. The pilot shut the door when they were seated and shook the handle to be sure the door was latched and then he walked around the plane and climbed behind the controls.

Dana turned to wave to Nate in Key West. He never saw Sarah do anything but stare straight ahead. When the portside engine chugged to a start, there wasn't the explosion of an Air Sunshine Pratt & Whitney radial, just the dull and efficient firing of a six cylinder Lycoming that sounded more like a Mercedes than an airplane. The starboard engine coughed to life and the throttles ran up. Nate listened while the exhaust notes beat together, slower and slower, until the two engines were in sync. The pilot released the brakes and the Air Guadeloupe flight taxied down the side runway with the sound nearly fading away. In a few minutes Nate heard the pilot throttling up again. The Navajo gathered speed down the tarmac and lifted off into the wind that blew so hard from the east. He kept watching as the plane climbed away and banked to the left where it came on course for St. Barts. In a moment it was swallowed by a long string of clouds running off before the trades.

THIRTY-THREE

A twenty knot wind swirled down the runway and pressed Nate's shirt against his back. He glanced at the windsock standing straight from the tower and then turned to walk toward the bus stop where a dozen people waited in the gusts with their bags. At the end of the line an old man who had no teeth greeted him with a smile. Nate didn't want to smile at anyone, but he nodded in the old man's direction and then turned to watch the trade wind clouds still marching away to the west.

The bus showed up after a ten minute wait. It was only going back to Deshaies by way of the road that followed the pass between the two volcanoes. Nate settled into a seat and stared through the windows at the mountain peaks buried in the gray clouds sweeping in that stacked up on the windward side and tore away to leeward.

The bus was newer and didn't smoke or creak and it was a pleasant ride over the hills to the west, except for Sarah. There were fewer stops and it didn't take so long to get back to the intersection in Deshaies. Nate stepped from the bus into the afternoon sun and into the shadows of the breadfruit trees. He trudged up the street and around the corner where the bay came into view. He could see *Serendipity* swinging on her anchor line and the deserted pier where the stacks of bananas were gone. Nate reached the foot of the street and glanced at the sabot floating off the stern, following *Serendipity* around like a puppy on a leash. He walked over to the Kronenbourg store where he bought two bottles and opened them to drink on the way to the dock. He stepped out on the pier and sat with his legs dangling over the side like that kid in Pamlico Sound.

When Brady looked out toward the dock from the deck on *Serendipity,* Nate was nearly asleep with his feet still over the side of the pier. Brady rowed up in a few minutes. Nate stood to throw the empty beer bottles into a fifty-five gallon drum at the end of the dock.

"I told Shanna to get out the rum," Brady said. "Thought you'd be needing it when you got back."

"I'm so hung over nothing will help. Already had two beers."

"I guess we have some decisions to make. I think the rum will help me, anyway."

Brady had beads of sweat on his forehead from the rowing. Nate stepped into the center of the dinghy for balance and sat in the stern. Brady spun them around and rowed hard before he circled to a stop near the transom on *Serendipity*. Shanna reached from the deck to grab the painter and when Nate climbed aboard, she slipped her arms around his waist.

"I'm so sorry," she said. "I didn't mean to be such a crab this morning. We were all so upset about Sarah."

"I know. I couldn't make her stay. She didn't want to leave you and Brady. It was just me."

"I thought about leaving, too, you know? I just couldn't. You want a rum? I squeezed some fresh limes. I'll make three. I'm so ready to cry again, I can't stand myself."

"Same here," Brady said.

Nate slipped down into a cockpit seat and stared off to the Caribbean that looked more like a pool of pink mercury in the setting sun. He kept staring at the sea and at the hills above the bay and at the quiet water beneath the wingdecks. One of the other cruising boats had disappeared. Nate glanced at the hole in the anchorage where it used to be. The other boat hung rock still on its anchor line and it made him think of fat *Nomad* again and whether Sarah would be aboard tonight. He didn't think she wanted to go back to Steinhatchee, or to Key West for that matter.

Due west of Deshaies there was a twelve-hundred mile run across the open Caribbean to the Panama Canal Zone and then another thirteen-hundred up to Key West. It seemed like an eternity to Nate even though it was mostly a sleigh ride, running off before the trades. Without Sarah, there wasn't much point in going down the rest of the island chain. He wanted to blink his eyes and plop himself in the corner seat at the Green Parrot Bar and Sub Shop. He looked up at the hills that sheltered the bay from the trades and then at the glossy surface of the water turning black in the twilight.

"Here's your rum and lime juice," Shanna said. "I made it weak so you and Brady don't get sick again. That was disgusting."

"I didn't get sick," Brady said.

"Well, all you did was moan and groan again until I kicked you out of the forepeak. I hope you enjoyed the deck."

Brady shook his head and sat down across from Nate.

"Well, now what?" he said. "It's up to you. Shanna and I have loved being on *Serendipity*. We'd like to keep going, but if you're too wiped out, we'll understand."

"I know. Everything got a little messed up. I can't believe I'm here, finally. I wonder whether I should head back to Key West. I didn't want Sarah to go. I wanted it to work for all of us."

Nate sipped the rum and it was limey and cool. Shanna came out to sit with Brady. She still looked small and frail like she did when the bus left her standing alone in the street.

"I'm so sorry it's turned out like this," she said. "When Sarah told me she was leaving, I couldn't stop the tears. She loves you. It was just too much for her to take, not being loved in return."

"I couldn't help myself. The spark just went away. I couldn't bring it back. There were other problems, too, I guess."

"That's okay," Brady said. "It'll all work itself out. We'll do anything you want."

"You still want to go on down the islands?"

"Is it possible? In the cruising guide there's a picture in it of St. Lucia and those two volcanoes side by side. We were excited about it when we left. We're so close, now."

"I know. I'd like to go myself, but this might be the end of the line. We can decide in the morning. Do you have enough money to get by if we keep going?"

"We're okay," Shanna said. "If we don't get stupid with the rum."

"Big decisions," Brady said. "Let's just do it."

"I need to think about it over some more rum. Shanna has to make it, though. That last one tasted like a real drink instead of kerosene."

Brady stepped below into the cabin. The voice of John Prine began drifting through the open companionway. Nate couldn't sit in the cockpit and listen so he stepped up to the bow rail and looked around at the green hills above the anchorage. Shanna's first rum drink made him mellow. He drank the next one down. Nate set the empty glass on the deck and leaned on the rail and watched as *Serendipity* tip-toed around her anchor line. Sometimes the trade winds gusted up and a soft swirl of air swept down from the hills and pushed the bow away for a bit. In the moments of calm, she crept back toward the line where it hung loose again from the roller.

Nate saw the trees at the top of the bluff bending in the wind. The sun sank below the horizon and the same boardsailer from the day before drifted by in the fluky winds at the mouth of the bay. There was a broad red stripe that bisected the sail like the label on a bottle of Jamaican beer. Nate watched as the sunset colored the sky and there was no difference between the horizon and the stripe on the sail. The boardsailer ghosted along in the lee of the hills and then disappeared toward another boat anchored in the distance. Nate breathed in the cool evening air and there were no sounds except for John Prine. He picked up his glass and walked back to the cockpit and stepped below. He switched off the cassette player and climbed into the empty wingdeck berth. Sarah had gone away and there was a lot of sadness. Nate didn't sleep for a long time thinking of her. He finally rolled on his side and slept the rest of the night through.

A morning wind shifted to the southeast and got *Serendipity* tacking about again. Nate opened his eyes and watched as the green hills swept slowly across the portlight. He yawned and rolled over where Sarah used to be. The sheets were cool on her side and he waited for them to warm up before rolling off the side of the bed. He stepped out into the brightness of the cockpit and looked over toward Deshaies awake in the morning heat. There was an island trading schooner tied to the pier and a truck waiting in the street with another load of bananas. Some of the men from the day before were lifting the stalks from the bed of the truck and carrying them to the dock and the waiting schooner. Other men were using a net and the boom to lift a load up and over and down into the hold through the deck hatch. Nate watched them sweat and work in the heat. When the last of the bananas were loaded and the deck hatch was secured, Nate went below and pumped the kerosene tank to light the stove for coffee. Brady came out a few minutes later and sat on the settee while the coffee brewed.

"Hot today, but there's some wind," Nate said. "Want to check out and head down toward St. Lucia?"

"Man, we were hoping you'd want to go. Shanna will be thrilled."

"They loaded that trading schooner with bananas this morning. You don't get to see that kind of thing in Key West. It made me want to keep on, maybe just to St. Lucia. I wish Sarah hadn't gone away."

"I know. She loved it down here, Nate. I wish I could have done something."

"After St. Lucia I'd like to go back to Florida and head up the Intracoastal Waterway. Since I'll be alone, maybe I'll go back to North Carolina and poke around where I lived when I was a kid."

"Well, it'll be a good trip home, no matter what we do. I'll go wake up Shanna."

Brady got up from the settee and disappeared into the forepeak. Nate heard some sleepy giggling and some laughing and in a moment, they were both in the galley smiling and waiting for the coffee. Nate took his cup out on the deck where he sat on the cabin roof and looked back toward the schooner still tied to the pier. There were bundles of sugar cane ready to be lifted into the hold. The deckhands worked the net and boom and it didn't take long for the cane to be stowed. A plume of black diesel smoke poured from the exhaust riser. The schooner backed from the pier and chugged its way past *Serendipity* and into the waiting Caribbean beyond the mouth of the bay.

Brady volunteered to take the jerry cans ashore so Nate grabbed the satchel with the passports and the three of them rowed up to the pier. Brady pulled the sabot all the way into the sand and tied it off. Nate left them behind with the jerry jugs while he made his way up the street to the customs office. When he walked through the open door, the man with the giant mustache greeted him in French.

"Bonjour, mon ami. Allez-vous sortir?"

Nate stared at the man and shrugged his shoulders.

"I just say 'good morning'," the man said. "Would you like to clear? Where are you going?"

"Good morning," Nate said. "We'd like to leave today and head down the islands, maybe as far as St. Lucia."

"I understand. Your lady friend wasn't happy here?"

"No. She made the flight for St. Barts yesterday. She wasn't happy with me."

"Affaires de coeur ne sont jamais faciles," he said, and he looked through the window toward the street where a black Renault 4CV was parked.

Nate handed him the three passports and he spread them open on the desk and stamped each of them several times. He had to initial where he stamped and then he handed them back with a smile.

"Bonne chance, mon ami. You have a safe trip," he said, and he reached across the desk to shake Nate's hand.

"Thanks. We could have stayed longer, but with my lady friend..."

"I know of these things," he said. "I know of these things."

They shook hands again. Nate turned and walked out the door past the little Renault melting in the heat. He glanced toward the Kronenbourg store and then hurried down the hill where Brady had just finished loading the water jugs.

While Brady rowed them out to *Serendipity,* Nate turned to look back toward the little town and the palms that lined the narrow beach and at the breadfruit trees that cast those thick shadows across the road. He liked Deshaies, but Dana and Sarah and Rilee were gone. He turned back to watch the lovely *Serendipity* dancing in the swirling wind.

Brady poured the water through the deck fitting to top off the tanks and then stowed the empty jugs in the port hull. Nate started the Volvo and after Brady secured all the ground tackle, he eased *Serendipity* toward the open part of the bay and to the Caribbean just beyond the point. Once he cleared the headland and steered due south, he turned to watch the rest of Guadeloupe slide by in the morning sun.

Brady stayed up near the bow rail watching the water for dolphins. Shanna sat with Nate in the cockpit while they motored for several hours, just looking around. When the Iles des Saintes came into view, they headed a little east to pass by for a closer look.

They cleared the southern end of Guadeloupe where the wind picked up. Brady and Shanna set about raising the main and working jib while *Serendipity* heeled in the wind that blew down the passage. She began to romp in the swells rolling in, long and lazy from the east, and Nate heard the whine of the SumLog as she hit twelve knots. Brady left again to ride the bow rail. The extra weight forward nearly got the deck awash as the swells lifted the bow and sent the white water flying. They dodged the spray that flew aft in a fine mist and when the Iles des Saintes loomed close, they dropped the jib to slow the boat and then sailed into the lee. Nate started the diesel again while Brady dropped the main. They watched the islands drift by a quarter-mile away.

More tiny white houses with red roofs dotted the hillsides. Far below, a thick line of coconut palms sagged over the white sand beaches. Nate steered *Serendipity* toward the shoreline just to see. There were coral heads in some of the coves and he carved his way in and out and kept some distance until he motored beyond Bourg des Saintes where he rounded the point and slipped into Baie de Marigot, narrow and protected and deserted. An old fort looked out from the top of the hill. The ramparts were broken down and there were stone blocks scattered around in the brush that grew all the way down to the sand on the beach. A wall of coral grew to within a few feet of the surface. Nate turned and steered parallel to the reef and motored away from the hill and the fort where he came upon an area where the bottom was only sand. On an impulse Nate told Brady to let the CQR over the side.

Serendipity eased to a stop with the plow buried on the bottom. Nate shut the Volvo down while the boat drifted in silence. The coral wall was just behind and he kept watching to see how close the boat came as she swung on the anchor line. Below the old fort on top of the hill, a dozen coconut palms lined a narrow beach. The water at the end of the bay was so transparent and thin it looked like the Bahamas again. Nate stepped out of the cockpit and walked forward where Brady and Shanna were standing. He nodded toward the fort.

"I'd like to go ashore just to walk on the beach. We can stay the night if you like."

"Shanna and I can dive on the wall back there. I bet there are grouper."

"Use the elephant gun."

"No, I'll use the sling. I can't miss with that thing."

They launched the sabot off the stern. Brady and Shanna pulled on the dive gear while Nate rowed alone across the field of coral. When the bow crunched into the sand, he hopped out and pulled the dinghy free of the water and then struck out along the beach toward the headland where the fort tumbled from the hill. The sand was white and fine, not fine enough to squeak beneath his feet like it did in North Carolina, but it was a soft sand that kicked in front of Nate as he walked. He turned to look back at *Serendipity*. There were spouts of water flying from the snorkels as Brady and Shanna hunted for grouper. Nate only glanced their way and then turned back to find a place to sit. He walked again toward the fort where the beach curved around to the base of the cliff. Several cannons lay half buried in the sand. Nate sat on the breech of a big one and looked up the hill where he could see several more cannons strewn about. He turned again and watched as the intermittent spouts from the snorkels shot skyward. Nate knew the note by heart.

Britton – Steamboat – (209)554-2271

I just need time, and at the bottom, *alligator food,* and then the smiley face.

Nate shifted his weight and looked along the length of the cannon. It was made of iron, not bronze, and he wondered if it would last another two hundred years before it rusted completely away. He stood and walked away from the cannons and made his way toward the point in the distance where the beach began to narrow. When the sand disappeared altogether, there was nothing left but coral. Nate turned and started back toward the dinghy sitting dry on the beach. Britton must be her maiden name.

Beyond the sabot there was another long stretch of sand. Nate walked further on the beach and splashed through the shore break that lapped the edge of the bay. Sarah should have been with him and it made Nate feel rotten to think of her. He held his eyes shut until there was only Rilee. He wondered if she had kept his mother's address, or whether she had lost it along the way. A sinking feeling came over Nate and he walked back to the sabot and pushed it into the water just as the sun disappeared behind the fort on the hill.

THIRTY-FOUR

Brady had already filleted a five-pound Nassau grouper and fired up the stove when Nate rowed up in the sabot. He stepped into the cockpit and sat down near the helm. Shanna handed him a sweating tumbler filled with rum and lime juice. Nate winked at her and it made her blush. She threw a dish towel at him through the companionway.

"Stop flirting. Brady is my man, anyway."

"Thanks for the rum. We have much left?"

"No, you guys drank it all. We just have one open bottle left. It's almost full."

"What else is down there?"

"Maybe a case of Heinekens and those bottles of wine from St. Barts. I'll check, though. Might even be more rum buried in the bottom."

"Where did Brady get the grouper?"

"Down the wall maybe fifteen feet. There's a cave down there. Brady got it in the head on the first shot."

Nate looked back over the transom at the edge of the coral and at the deep blue of the drop-off. The line between the two extended all the way out toward the point to the west where the coral fell away. He could see another small reef near the entrance to the bay. Even in the fading light, the water was nearly transparent over the coral heads and the nervous shapes looked like dark clouds in the water. The sky turned yellow and pink and then twilight settled in and the light was soft, like a kindergarten blanket. In a moment, there was nothing left of the day but the lingering splash of light beyond the fort at the top of the hill.

Brady lit the Aladdin and turned the mantle high. The glow spilled from the companionway and made the waning light behind the fort turn dark. Nate leaned against the coaming and took some deep breaths. The rum drink wasn't strong enough. He shut his eyes and tried to see Rilee again and there were flashes of the red nightlights and visions of her legs under the nightshirt and the burning came back in a rush when he thought again of that night in the cockpit. A chill swept over him. Nate opened his eyes and looked away at the lights on the hills of Guadeloupe across the channel.

Serendipity sneaked away from Baie de Marigot and the Iles des Saintes the following morning just as the sun rose above the mountains to the east. Nate steered her clear of the reef at the mouth of the bay and then rounded the point where he followed the shore and passed close by Bourg des Saintes. He saw again the red roofs of the houses and the wrought-iron rails along the balconies and the gingerbread trim above. The town looked clean and fresh in the morning light. Nate skirted the western tip of the island where he steered the boat through the narrow pass under power until the east wind caught her just as she cleared Terre den Haut. Brady scrambled to get the main up and drawing and then he hauled the jib in place. It filled with a crack and the boat tore away at eleven knots. Nate sailed through the pass to the west of the islets on the south side and then raced toward Dominica looming high in the distance. *Serendipity* swept across the passage on a sea that sparkled like sequins in the sun at first and then faded to deep blue in the shadows of the trade wind clouds that scuttled across the sky.

Dominica was solemn and mysterious in the afternoon sun. When *Serendipity* entered the lee of the mountains, she crept into the wind shadow barely making headway. The jib hung from the forestay like tenement laundry, but intermittent breaths of air drifted from the heights to fill the sails as she moved toward Prince Rupert Bay just around the point. Shanna and Brady were watching the hills and the trees ghost by and when the bay eased into view, they could see the little town of

Portsmouth nestled among the palms and the breadfruit trees. Brady looked back. Nate smiled and shrugged and started the diesel.

Nate motored toward the town dock where there were a dozen skiffs pulled onto the sand and a working schooner tied to the little pier, an extension of the street that bisected the village. Brady let the CQR over the side and then *Serendipity* checked herself up about one hundred yards out. Portsmouth was quiet. There were school children in the streets and fishermen mending nets on the beach. Nate felt the gentle pulse of the island just by watching from the deck. Brady untied the sabot and launched it over the stern where it floated to the end of its painter and bobbed back to the transom in the quiet water of the roadstead. Nate picked up the satchel with the ship's papers and the three of them rowed ashore, anxious to see the town that looked nearly asleep in the light that shimmered through the trees.

The customs officer was a Pinky Lee type, so thin the shape of his skull was visible beneath the skin on his face. He was quick with a smile and he welcomed *Serendipity* to his island home.

"We won't be staying long," Nate said. "Maybe a day or two."

"I can stamp you in and out," the man said. "You won't have to come back, unless you change plans."

There was some bluster and some pad stamping and some signatures and when Nate stepped from the tiny office, he could still feel the man watching as he crossed the street to find some cold beer.

Dominica had been an English island. It was apparent soon enough the people were poor and the town was struggling. They walked up the street toward an open market where the school kids sneaked from around the corner. Dracula spread his cape and they all ran away laughing like they did on every other island. Behind the counter in the market stood an ancient lady nearly the color of anthracite who sold bottles of Heineken from the ice box on the porch behind the store.

"Cold," she said, "from the brewery on St. Lucia."

"Not on your life, Brady," Shanna said.

"How much is the beer at the brewery?" he asked.

"Oh, very cheap. They got the beer coming out from the back in the trucks. You go in the front. They serve it up cold, just like these."

They thanked the lady and took the bottles out into the street where they sat in the shade of a coconut palm and only sipped the beer to keep from getting brain freeze. Nate kept looking around at the houses and at the streets and at the palms lining the bay. There were bits of paper and trash strewn along the road and the brightly painted buildings had faded to dirty pastels in the tropical heat. Most of the houses had tin roofs. They were unpainted and he could see streaks of rust on some of them, but there were trees and flowers and shadows from the sun. Portsmouth was still a pretty town.

South of the village, the Indian River passed into the interior of Dominica. They finished the bottles of beer and walked down to the bridge that crossed the mouth and watched a man rowing a skiff into the heavy, thick jungle that swallowed the river after only a few yards.

"We could row up the river," Nate said.

"Why not?" Brady replied. "Might be slow going in the sabot with three of us."

"We can get one of the locals to come along as a guide. Wonder how far in the river goes?"

"I'll go get the dinghy."

Brady took off for the landing where the sabot was tied. Nate walked with Shanna to a spot just north of the river where there were more skiffs dragged onto the beach. One of the local fishermen greeted them.

"Care for the boat ride, mon?"

"Yes. Just me, though. Can you guide us up the river?"

"I can. Quiet and cool and nice in there."

Brady returned in a few minutes. Shanna stepped aboard the sabot while Nate rode in the stern seat of the fisherman's skiff. They left the bright sun of the river mouth and rowed beneath the jungle canopy. Aside from the dipping of the oars in the still water, there were no sounds except for the occasional bird cry. Beyond the first of the bends, a steel trestle nearly overgrown by the vegetation sagged over the river. It hadn't been used in a long time and it was nearly rusted away in the superheated air, clinging to the banks on either side like a mesh of brown spider webs.

They slipped beneath the crumbling bridge and entered a stand of bloodwood trees that were strewn along the banks in a tangle of surface roots. The banks and the roots and the trees drifted by in the dancing light. Nate looked back at Brady and Shanna. They were sitting rock still with the sabot drifting along in the same light that shook through the leaves of the trees. He didn't want to think about Sarah who should have been there.

The river water was dark and cold in spite of the heat trapped in the tunnel. Nate dipped his hand to wet his forehead while the fisherman continued with his easy rowing. They moved deep into the interior where the river banks closed in and the jungle hung lower until they had to stop because the water was too shallow, even for the sabot. They left the boats behind and hiked a short way into the jungle. Nate could hear the rush of the river and the squawking of some parrots somewhere up the hill. Brady and Shanna held hands and stood in the shade of the trees and listened to the sounds of the river and the rustle of the leaves overhead. Nate turned away and slipped back to the river where he stood alone on the banks and watched the leaves floating through the riffles on their way to the sea. The river was the same color as Sarah's eyes. He reached down and cupped his hands and let the water drip on his face. The wind through the trees dried his skin and left streaks like evaporated tears.

After a few minutes of the heat and the quiet, they stepped into the boats and drifted again with the slow current through the bloodwood trees and beneath the rusting trestle into the overwhelming brightness of the setting sun at the mouth of the river. Nate handed the fisherman a five-dollar bill and shook the man's hand and walked alone toward the town dock where Brady and Shanna met him in the sabot.

"That rowing got me thirsty," Brady said. "I'd like to get another beer."

"I didn't have to row and I'm ready for another myself," Nate said. "I wish Sarah had been here. I think the river might have reminded her of Steinhatchee. I kept thinking of the Low Country and the cypress swamps. I think I will head that way after this trip."

"Need some crew?" Shanna asked. "I've never seen the Low Country."

"I could be talked into that. You guys are the best."

Nate walked up to the little store where the same jiggling lady sold him a half-dozen bottles to carry back. He popped one of them open with a rigging knife and drank it while he walked down the hill. It was gone when he reached Brady and the sabot. Shanna sipped hers slowly and watched the short red sunset. Nate sat down on the edge of the dock with Brady where they drank the fizzy beer and talked about the bloodwood trees and the old trestle and about the parrots squawking beyond the end of the river.

Late in the night Nate tossed and turned trying to sleep in the still air of the cabin. He got up several times and looked at the lights of Portsmouth and at the dark shape of another cruising boat that had sneaked into the roadstead just after twilight. It was after midnight when he fell away into some kind of half-sleep state where he kept hearing voices that sounded like parrots and kids and sometimes like squeaks. There were dreams somewhere along the way. The faces were missing again and he couldn't tell who was there. The faceless dreams and the sounds of the parrots faded away and when the morning sun woke him, it was nearly ten.

Brady was already up and out on deck where he had an old *Yachting* magazine spread out on the cockpit seat. Nate poked his head out into the sun and then ducked back below to light the stove for some coffee. He thought Shanna might still be asleep, but he heard her feet stepping along the cabin roof. She looked down into the galley.

"Morning, Nate. You look tired."

"I didn't sleep well. Not enough rum, I guess."

"You don't like the drinks I make? Tough. You and Brady are on rations."

"I know, Mom. Want some coffee?"

"Sure, but we ought to have something to eat. I'll make some pancakes if you leave the stove on."

"We still have syrup somewhere."

They ate quickly and cleaned the galley and set about getting *Serendipity* ready for the slow trip down the coast in the lee of Dominica. Nate looked again at the beach and the town dock and at all the tin roofs, shiny and bright against the thick trees on the hill. He started the Volvo and let *Serendipity* idle her way out of Prince Rupert Bay. They spent the day motoring just off the beach and watching Dominica slip by, lush and quiet and dark.

The mountains in the interior stayed hidden in the cloud cover. Sometimes Nate got a glimpse of the peaks, one of which was over four thousand feet high, but the clouds swept across the sky and the peaks disappeared once more. He was left with the lower slopes of the island and the small beaches and the hills smothered in green that drifted by until he cleared Scotts Head at the southern tip.

The heavy, late spring trades caught *Serendipity* off the port bow while she streaked across the twenty-five mile channel between Dominica and Martinique, ticking twelve and thirteen knots at times. Martinique towered in the distance looking closer than it was, but the boat tore over the swells, clipping the tops and sending spray clear back to the cockpit where it felt warm on Nate's arms for a moment before the wind dried it away. Brady and Shanna stayed out on the windward hull while *Serendipity* stormed across the passage in only a few hours.

They rushed into the lee of Mt. Pelee where the wind staggered and dropped and fell away to a knot or two. *Serendipity* ghosted along on a flat sea so pale it could have been liquid moonlight. Nate didn't want to start the diesel so the boat flopped around a bit with the jib filling and collapsing and then filling again. They crept their way closer to the island where the volcano swept up and away from the beach and the palms hung free in the quiet Caribbean air. *Serendipity* made the only sounds with the jib filling and collapsing and the main shaking the boom. When the whispers drifted through and the rig was drawing and silent, all Nate could hear was the hollow slap and the rush of the shore break.

The village of St. Pierre was close by so Nate started the diesel while Brady and Shanna furled the sails. He idled the boat into the open roadstead where Brady let the plow over the side in ten feet of water just to the north of the town dock. In the fading afternoon light, Nate stared at the ruins left behind from the eruption of Mt. Pelee in 1902. There were a few new buildings and some red tin roofs and more gingerbread and wrought iron, but it seemed as though there was some lingering weariness that the town couldn't shake, like the air over the cemetery on Angela Street in Key West. *Serendipity* hunted on her anchor line in the wind that blew quietly down the mountain.

"Some of the buildings look like they were built right on the old ruins," Brady said.

"Looks like it," Nate said. "Want to go ashore and see?"

"No, not now. I'm beat. That was a terrific sail. I could use a shower and some rum."

"I think I'm ready, too. I don't much want to go ashore if we don't have to. You two should go."

"What about customs?"

"I don't think there's an office here. It doesn't much matter. They'll just clear us in and out anyway."

"I think we'll stay aboard. Shanna might let me make my own rum cocktails."

"Fat chance," she said.

Nate slipped below and sneaked into the shower and let the cold water run for a long time. He changed into some clean clothes and lit the Aladdin when he stepped back into the cabin. Brady disappeared into the head to clean up. Nate sat out in the cockpit to watch the lights of St. Pierre. Shanna sat across from him looking out to sea.

"How are you doing?" she asked.

"I'm okay. I really missed Sarah when we rowed into the jungle. She would have loved it there."

"I know. You blew it, Nate."

"Maybe I did. I have dreams about her. I don't know why."

"I do. She loves you, Nate."

"I needed some time. She didn't have any left to give."

"You never told anyone about the charter. That might have helped."

"I didn't tell anyone because it ended. I thought I could get on with my life with Sarah. I feel sick about it."

Shanna kicked him on the shin and then went below to make evening cocktails before showering off. Nate sat alone for those few minutes thinking about Key West without Sarah. He didn't know whether he could stay there anymore. He thought about Rilee and Steamboat and Sarah again, but Brady stepped up the companionway with the rum drinks. Nate was ready to toss one down.

"Here," Brady said. "Shanna made these with a little more rum. Must mean we're behaving."

Nate took the rum and it made him realize how weak all the others had been. He watched the lights again while *Serendipity* drifted in the puffs that crept along the roadstead.

"I might go back by way of Panama again," Nate said. "It was a nice time in my life with Dana. We left and sailed to Jamaica and Grand Cayman and on around Cuba to Key West. We were okay then." Nate stopped for a moment and looked out into the black Caribbean. "But she met Bart after that."

"I remember the night on the dock when they disappeared the first time."

"So do I," Nate said. "So do I. Want to make two more rums before Shanna gets out of the shower?"

Brady stepped outside with the fresh drinks when Shanna started another John Prine tape. Nate swallowed a good bit of the rum and shut his eyes to keep them from watering. He could see Rilee again with her long dark hair and those eyes so deep there was only eternity. Nate could nearly hear her voice again when Shanna came out with a towel around her head and a drink in her hand.

"Wow," she said. "I'm ready to party after that shower."

Brady grabbed her around the waist and pulled her down in his lap. Shanna giggled and kissed and fussed around with Brady's beard. Nate wanted to see Rilee again and he shut his eyes tight, but Sarah was there and then Dana once more and the moment was gone. He stared out beyond the dark water of the roadstead to the tiny lights shuddering through the palms of St. Pierre.

THIRTY-FIVE

Nate climbed from the wingdeck berth and stepped outside where the air was cool and the lights were going out in the village. *Serendipity* had ridden up on her anchor line and she sat still for a change with the rode falling away from the bow. Nate yawned and swallowed and tried to get rid of the sour cotton in his mouth. Martinique looked nearly black in the pale light, but the sky slowly brightened and there were patches of green, even where the clouds still hung at the top of Mt. Pelee. Brady stepped out and looked up at the slopes.

"Be a long time before the sun shines here," Brady said. "Want to go?"

"I'm ready. Is Shanna awake?"

"She's awake. She's all excited to see the Pitons on St. Lucia today."

"Me, too. Want to get the anchor?"

Nate leaned over and turned the key to start the diesel while Brady dealt with the ground tackle. They motored away from the ghosts of St. Pierre and the shadows of the ruins and turned to the south where the coast of Martinique was still dark in the distance. Nate hugged the shoreline for two hours or more before following the curve of the bay into Fort de France. He wasn't prepared for the bustle and the crowds and the water traffic. Shanna and Brady stood on the cabin top looking up at the shops and the markets and the restaurants that marched up the hill beyond the waterfront and at the whitewashed churches that stood stark over the city. The solitude of St. Pierre and the quiet of Portsmouth and the villages of the Iles de Saintes made Fort de France look like Miami.

"You two want to go ashore?" Nate asked.

"No," Shanna said. "It's too big. We can save it for another trip."

"I don't much care to, either," Brady said. "Unless we need to buy more rum. We have enough for tonight?"

Shanna nodded and looked over at Brady.

"Yes," she said, "but I'm still the bartender."

Nate throttled the diesel up again and motored away from Fort de France and headed south again to clear the tip of Martinique. The winds in the lee were light and flukey and they didn't raise the sails until they were well past Cap Salomon and they could see Diamond Rock and then St. Lucia, dark in the distance. The trades kicked up to nearly twenty knots. *Serendipity* went flying over the swells and the wind waves. Nate fell off the wind a little more and he could hear the pitch of the SumLog cable go up as the boat accelerated. She was clipping waves again and the spray was sometimes so fine the rainbows shined again in the sunlight. The mist settled out and the rainbows went away until she clipped another swell and the colors would dance once more in the midday sun.

In the late afternoon light, the little town of Soufriére nestled against the hills just north of Petit Piton. Nate steered in for a closer look and got caught in the wind shadow and had to motor all the way around into the anchorage between the volcanoes. *Serendipity* crept her way close to the beach where Nate turned the bow to the open Caribbean. Brady slipped the CQR over the side. They launched the sabot and rowed ashore with a stern line where Brady carried it across the narrow beach and tied the tag end around a coconut palm. *Serendipity* was snugged down for the night just as the sun dipped below the horizon and flashed the color of the miniature rainbows that had shimmered in the afternoon spray.

When Brady and Nate climbed aboard, Shanna handed them two very strong rum drinks and then turned the stereo up to listen to Bob Marley. Nate settled down in the cockpit and stared up at the two lava cores on either side of the bay, black as coal in the pale light of the twilight.

They ate in the cockpit with the dark, mammary shapes of the Pitons towering over *Serendipity*. After the last tape stopped playing, they sat in the night and listened to the shore break and then Brady and Shanna disappeared into the forepeak. Nate stayed alone outside watching the stars and the light reflecting off the quiet water. When he started yawning, he stumbled below and blew out the Aladdin and slipped off to bed.

There were soft red lights somewhere in his sleep and then Rilee was there with her nightshirt falling away and he could see her breasts and her flawless skin bathed pink in the light. The dream was so intense Nate opened his eyes to the blackness in the cabin and it took a moment for him to focus in the dim light. He pushed the curtain aside and looked out at the night sky. He could make out the silhouette of Gros Piton reaching high into the stars over the anchorage. He stared at the peak through the portlight. *Serendipity* hung suspended between the anchor and the stern line and she didn't move. Nate leaned back on his pillow and shut his eyes. He wanted to see Rilee's face again and he wanted to see her body glowing soft and pink in the nightlights and he wanted to hold her close and feel her warmth and her softness and her wetness, but there was nothing but the stillness of the air and the blackness of the night. Nate rolled over and buried his face in the pillow and held his eyes shut until there were flashes of light. Sleep finally came and he drifted away into a canyon where there were dark caves on either side and he had to walk without seeing anything. The anxiety stayed with him all night long.

Brady got up early and clanked around in the galley. He lit the burner on the stove and it hissed blue in the cool cabin air. Nate yawned beneath the covers. The dream from the night before was so real he looked away at the light streaming through the port. He could smell the coffee brewing and he turned back just in time to see Shanna bounce through the companionway.

"I can't believe this place, Nathan," she said. "This has to be the most beautiful spot in the whole Caribbean. Maybe in the whole world."

"I'll be there. I need a minute to wake up."

"Coffee's ready," Brady said. "Want yours there?"

"No. I'll get up."

Nate eased from the sheets and stepped onto the cabin floor. Brady handed him the coffee with cream and he took a slow sip and then carried it up the ladder and out into the bright morning where the two volcanic cores soared over the water. Nate looked up at the peaks and nearly got dizzy they were so high and close.

"Isn't this something?" Shanna said. "I'm glad we came this far. I never imagined ever being in a place so beautiful."

"Must be quite a view from up there," Nate said. "I wonder if you can climb those things?"

"I don't know. We'd like to hike over the hill in between. I think you can walk to where the steam is still coming out of the ground."

"You don't have to wait for me," Nate said. "I'm not in any hurry today."

"Are you sure"

"Yes. I need to clean up a bit first. I'll take you two ashore after we finish the coffee."

Nate rowed Brady and Shanna to the beach. He watched while they hiked up the trail and disappeared into the palms. *Serendipity* floated a few yards away with her bow pointed toward the open sea to the south. She seemed trapped suddenly, like the stern line had her tied down. Nate rowed up to her starboard wing deck and climbed aboard while she sat motionless in the still air.

Nate stripped down and stood in the shower for several minutes, still trying to recover from the incredible dream. The water made him shiver and he buried his face in the stream and waited while the cold soaked away the visions from the night before. He shaved in the quiet of the cabin and dressed and went topside to check the anchor. *Serendipity* hadn't budged from her spot. Nate leaned over the bow rail and followed the anchor line down through the clear water where he could just make out the beginning of the chain before it disappeared into the gloom. He stood there for a few minutes thinking of the color of Rilee's eyes and then the long downwind run through the Caribbean. Nate turned away and walked back to the stern and the waiting sabot.

A coconut plantation clung to the hills above the anchorage. Nate left the sabot on the beach and walked through the trees toward the crest of the ridge that formed a saddle between Petit and Gros Piton. He followed a narrow path that curved through the palms and passed near a small copra house where there were two ladies inside wearing long madras shifts and matching bandanas. They were laughing and cracking coconuts when Nate walked past the open door. The path wound a half-mile up the ridge through the plantation and he could hear the ladies all the way to the crest where there was a small hotel that overlooked the sea to the west. Nate walked up the steps and through the lobby to the patio where he sat alone outside at the bar. He asked the waiter for a rum. After the bartender poured a shot in a coconut shell for him to drink, he sat with the rum and stared out to sea.

A little girl came walking up with a pearly smile and skin so dark it glistened in the morning sun. She curtsied and then she handed him a red hibiscus to wear. She helped Nate pin the flower to his shirt and he gave her a one-dollar bill. She giggled and skipped away into the hotel. Beyond the patio wall, the white and yellow dot that was *Serendipity* nestled close to the beach. There were no other boats in sight, not even at sea. Nate looked out through the canyon between the Pitons to the Caribbean that shimmered clear to the empty horizon. He could hear the trade winds blowing through the branches of the trees, but in moments of calm he could hear the ladies again, cracking and laughing, faraway down the hill.

Nate didn't want to sit alone any longer so he stood and gave the barman a tip as he left. The man nodded and smiled while Nate walked down the steps to the road below. He turned away from the hotel and headed toward the interior where Brady and Shanna went searching for the steam. He hadn't walked far when he met them trudging back from the vents.

"Man," Brady said. "That steam smelled like rotten eggs. I couldn't stay very long. Look what it did to Shanna's silver chain."

Shanna giggled and held her blackened necklace for Nate to see.

"Brady told me he would buy me a gold one in Key West. Gold won't tarnish like this."

"How close did you get?"

"Not very. Maybe twenty yards. When the wind gusted, look out. Brady tried to get closer but the smell kept him away."

"That's it for me," Brady said. "No more volcanoes. Is that bar open in the hotel?"

"I just had some rum in a coconut shell. They have other drinks. Maybe some beer on ice."

They walked back to the hotel where they sat outside at the same table and when the barman came over, they ordered beer and some chicken roti from the kitchen. Nate kept glancing out toward *Serendipity*. Shanna looked over the rail to the west and then she sat down again.

"The Caribbean looks huge from here." she said. "It's almost frightening to think about sailing all the way back to Key West."

"It's a long way, I know, but it really is mostly downwind. I bet we average more than two hundred miles a day."

"We could go back through the Panama Canal if you'd rather do that."

"We'd all go broke, I think. There's no more beautiful place than this and I'm happy we came, but I'm looking forward to seeing the Outer Banks and Pamlico Sound again."

"Don't worry about us," Brady said. "We'll do whatever it takes."

"It's been great with you two. It doesn't seem right to go back without Sarah."

"Maybe if you were alone with Sarah on the boat, things would work out?"

Nate glanced over at Shanna and then looked out to sea again and didn't say anything.

The roti burned with curry. They ordered more beer to cool things off when the little flower girl came to clear their table. Brady smiled at her, but she was so shy she stood to the side and waited for everyone to leave. Nate left a good tip and the little girl ran back into the hotel kitchen with her fist tight around the dollars.

The walk back to *Serendipity* didn't take long. They were by the copra house in only a few minutes. The madras ladies were gone but there were piles of coconuts in a corner and shells strewn about and more coconuts stacked outside. Nate wondered if the ladies were off to lunch. He never heard them cracking and laughing again, even from the quiet anchorage.

Brady and Nate shoved the sabot into the water and then settled into the seats and rowed the short distance to *Serendipity*. Shanna disappeared through the companionway to change in the shadows of the cabin while Brady got another beer from the bilge locker.

Nate fished about for the rocket fins and the mask and snorkel. He lifted the elephant gun from its spot in the port hull and then dived deep into the water where he could see the dark sand on the bottom sloping away to the west. He struck out swimming to the north where he stopped in about fifteen feet of water over one of those coral heads that look like spilled chocolate syrup. Nate hung motionless for a long time watching to see the fish after they got used to his shadow. He dived to the bottom and peered into the tunnel below the shelf where there were squirrelfish and some gobies and a lone parrotfish backpedaling away. He rolled over on his back and looked up toward the diamonds on the surface. He didn't move and it felt good to be alone in the cool, deep water where it was quiet except for the cleaner shrimp clicking away.

The parrotfish swam from beneath the ledge. Nate watched while it poked its way across the sand and disappeared underneath another coral head in the distance. He stared for a moment longer into the gloom, but his lungs were ready to burst and he kicked hard toward the sun flashing above him. Nate crashed through the surface and breathed the air in gulps and rolled over on his back again to see. Rilee wasn't anywhere around.

Nate swam toward a big coral head in the distance, still thinking about Rilee when a six-foot barracuda, thick and pulsing about the gills, slipped out of the gloom. There was some flashing of the silver chain and tiny schooner Nate wore around his neck. The barracuda watched the flickers of light and hung motionless with its jaws working like the moray in Brewer's Bay. Nate kicked backwards toward *Serendipity* bobbing in the distance. The barracuda followed close behind and he rushed at it and tried to drive it away. It came right back and hung motionless again, staring at Nate through its eyes, cold and still. Nate thought about blasting it with the elephant gun but he left it alone. It followed a few feet behind until Nate reached for the swim ladder. The barracuda turned sideways and flashed like chrome in the light and then flicked once and disappeared toward deep water.

"Get anything?"

Brady was still drinking beer in the cockpit.

"No. Lots of little fish down there, except for the barracuda. Made me nervous."

"Big one?"

"Yeah. Long and toothy. I was just hoping for a little grouper. Man, I'm tired. Any rum left?"

"No. We finished it off last night. Shanna has the wine, though. Might be good for a change."

"Did she open a bottle?"

"It put her to sleep, I think. Want some?"

"Yes, but you have to pour it in a big glass. I think I'm going to sit in the cockpit for a while and just look around. This place is Paradise."

Brady stepped below while Nate stowed the elephant gun along with the dive gear. He stretched out in the cockpit when Brady handed him a glass of wine and then wandered off exploring in the sabot. Nate watched him until he disappeared around the bend to the north toward Soufriére. Nate was nodding off to sleep near the wheel, but he opened his eyes when there was the flash of a white towel. He glanced below and in the shadows he could see Shanna drying her hair after a shower. She didn't know Nate could see and he didn't mean to stare. Her breasts were small and firm and there was another dark shadow below and Nate wanted to turn away, but their eyes met and she stood looking back at him. It seemed like a long time before she wrapped herself in the towel and then she looked away. Nate couldn't tell whether she was embarrassed. He watched while she disappeared in the forepeak and there was a moment where he wondered what it would be like to be there with her. He drained the wine in his glass and looked toward the ridge between the Pitons high above the anchorage. In a few minutes, Shanna came out wearing her tiny black bikini and carrying the wine bottle.

"Want another splash?"

"It might put me to sleep if I have more, but that's okay. I'm sorry. I didn't mean to stare at you."

Shanna looked at Nate and didn't say anything. She finished pouring the wine.

"You don't have to be sorry," she said quietly. "I didn't mind when you stared. Don't tell Brady."

Nate looked at Shanna and her brown eyes that were always so bright. She leaned over and kissed his forehead and giggled.

"Thanks for bringing the wine out," Nate said. "Makes me think of Dana, though"

"Wonder where she is. Still in California?"

"I think so. She hooked up with an art school in San Francisco. It's funny."

"What's funny?"

"I never dreamed she would be published. She's teaching poetry, now."

"She showed me some of her work. I liked it, too. I'm glad she's found a good spot. Here comes Brady again."

The sabot poked around the base of Petit Piton with Brady pulling hard on the oars. Nate sat up and watched while Brady made his way toward *Serendipity* with the sweat shining on his back. He slowed to a stop while Nate took the painter and tied it to a stern cleat.

"I wanted to row far enough to see Soufriére. It's a long way, though. I need some beer."

"Dive in the water and cool off," Shanna said.

"I'd rather have a beer. That water gets deep in a hurry over there. I couldn't see the bottom. I bet there are grouper all over the place."

"I didn't go far enough," Nate said. "Now, I'm too tired."

Brady pushed Shanna into the water while she complained about her clean hair. They stayed around and swam in the grotto beneath the wingdecks while Nate sat in the cockpit listening to the laughing and the splashing. They climbed aboard and dried off and disappeared below to find another bottle of chardonnay and a beer for Brady. Nate waited for Shanna to refill his glass and then he walked forward to the bow rail and looked out over the Caribbean. The bow was aimed to the west and it would have been easy enough to slip from the coconut palm and lift the anchor and head off to the horizon, but he needed to get up to Castries for water and diesel and food for the trip. Nate looked to see the wind waves. The lee of the island extended too far and the horizon appeared as flat as the water in the anchorage. Brady walked up with his beer and motioned toward the sea.

"Getting ready to go?" he asked. "Like Noel Coward once said, we're in for a long run."

"I don't know. No weather to speak of, just a Caribbean full of twenty-knot trade winds. I think I'm ready. How about you two? Nervous?"

"A little. What a place to take off from, though. We'll never forget it."

"We could stay longer, you know. It isn't likely we'll ever get back here."

"Speak for yourself. Shanna and I would like to get our own boat. We'd love to come back."

"Let's get *Serendipity* going."

Brady and Nate rowed ashore to untie the stern line from the coconut palm. *Serendipity* came alive again and began slow dancing in the puffs of wind drifting down from the hills. Nate motored the boat out from between Petit and Gros Pitons and turned to the north toward the village of Soufriére asleep in the trees flowing down from the hills. *Serendipity* slipped by at only five knots. Nate wanted to get a good look at the town so he never throttled up again. St. Lucia unfolded like a slow-motion travel film. He turned to the west to clear the coral reef that runs out deep from the point and the dark sands of Anse Chastanet came into view. There were palms lining the beach again and cottages sprinkling up the hill and beyond the the last of them, the high mountains clouding at the peaks again.

Nate motored through the afternoon and watched the beaches and the coral reefs and the mountains in the interior all the way to Castries where he anchored at the head of the bay near the town where the customs house was close. The three of them freshened up and gathered the diesel and water jugs and off-loaded the sabot into the dull water of the harbor. Brady rowed Nate ashore first and then stashed the jerry jugs at the base of the town dock before rowing back to get Shanna. Nate walked over to the customs building with the passports and the very polite officer behind the desk stamped him in and out at the same time. Nate walked out of the office where he could see *Serendipity* riding at anchor in the dirty water. She looked closed in by the narrow confines of the harbor.

Nate left the sabot at the dock and walked up the street to find a market that sold rum and limes and sugar and beer. He piled the supplies into the dinghy, but it took two more trips to load the water jugs and diesel. When all of the stores were put away below, Nate thought it might be a good idea to get out of the foul harbor and run back down the coast to the quiet anchorage between the Pitons where it was cool in the wind from over the hills. Brady was on his hands and knees trying to sort through all the canned goods.

"Why don't we leave right now?" Brady asked. "We've still got some daylight."

"We could, I guess. Would that make Shanna nervous?"

"No, she might enjoy it. Night sailing didn't bother her before."

"Let me check the weather on the radio. If there's nothing going on, there's no reason to stay unless you want to go back to the Pitons for the night."

"I'm not sure I'd want to spoil my memory of that place if there are other boats anchored where we were," Brady said. "I think we're ready to go."

Nate turned the Zenith on and listened for the weather from the high frequency broadcast from Trinidad and then dialed over to WWV where he could hear the general forecast for the Western Atlantic and Caribbean. The weather recording trailed in and out with the changing conditions. Nate concentrated on the faint voice that reported a disturbance in the Caribbean to the east of Jamaica, but to the south and west there were only the normal trades. He stepped out into the cockpit and looked around at the town of Castries and then leaned over and hit the key switch to start the Volvo.

Shanna and Brady pulled the anchor free of the harbor bottom and stowed the gear in the deck locker. Nate turned the wheel to follow the channel out to the northwest, but off to port he could see a reef lurking just below the surface. Nate gave it a wide berth and steered away toward the middle of the Caribbean and the Yucatan Channel.

They were caught in the wind shadow of St. Lucia so Nate motored into the setting sun until the normal breeze filled in from behind. Brady raised the main and jib and sheeted them home while Nate steered the boat to the west. The sails shook and popped while Brady hauled away on the halyards, but *Serendipity* soon ran off before the trades, surfing from twelve to fifteen knots at times. The sun sank below the horizon off the bow and they celebrated in the cockpit with rum and lime juice and fresh mango slices. Nate looked back in the pale light of the sunset. He could make out Petit and Gros Piton looming in silence on the southwest coast of St. Lucia. By the time the short twilight ended, he couldn't even see the lights of Castries.

THIRTY-SIX

Serendipity spent her time surfing to twelve or fourteen knots and then slowing to eight and then back to fourteen while she pulsed her way across the Caribbean under a shower of stars above and the shadows of the cumulus that ran off to the west before the trades. There were endless days of downwind silence where the trackless Caribbean stretched beyond the bow all the way to a blue infinity. North of her there was some unsettled weather. Nate steered down to try to stay below it, but there were evenings where he could only shoot two stars instead of three because of the cloud cover. He plotted the progress on a general chart of the Caribbean and the track was a lazy curve that bent to the south. *Serendipity* kept reeling off two-hundred-mile days to the west toward the Yucatan Channel.

On her sixth night out from St. Lucia, one of the shadows that hid the stars came with some soft rain that pattered on the deck. Nate could hear it whispering through the companionway. The rain and then Brady's voice woke him from a slot canyon that was so narrow there was no sunlight on the bed of the stream. He blinked his eyes in confusion. The whispering got louder. Nate slipped from the wingdeck berth to take over behind the wheel.

"Wow. You woke me up and I was somewhere in Utah."

"I've never been out there," Brady said. "I'm headed for bed. I'm really tired. It's hard to steer sometimes."

"Big following sea?"

"Not too big. *Serendipity* wants to let her stern fall away. Catches you by surprise. There was some rain, too, but it's about gone."

Nate slipped behind the wheel when Brady made his way below. He looked up at the black sky and then at the black seas rolling through and at the red glow of the compass. He had to shake his head to concentrate on the steering while *Serendipity* took the swells on her starboard quarter. She could be pushed to leeward and Nate kept trying to correct the course before she fell away. It was fun for thirty minutes or so, but it became tiring. He steered with the swells and tried to keep *Serendipity* dancing. Beyond the night black as the hull on *Dame Foncé*, there was the breaking surf along a string of reefs across the western Caribbean. Nate kept looking forward into the darkness. The star sight from the evening before showed they would pass north of Serrana Bank by thirty miles. There was always some doubt so the midnight watch dragged on forever. Nate watched the stars emerge through the cloud cover and a momentary moon that sent shafts through the overcast to light a patch of the sea, and he listened for dolphins surfing on the bow waves. Nate peered ahead into the blackness and wondered about the reefs. At four in the morning, Shanna poked her head out of the companionway.

"Did I oversleep?"

"No, you're fine. You might want to bring a foul weather jacket. We had some rain earlier. There might be another squall line."

"Seen anything in the water?"

"No, but that's good. I would rather not see any of the reefs."

"You worry too much, silly."

Shanna disappeared again and then stepped back out wearing a long-sleeved shirt and some old cutoffs. She sat beside Nate and took the wheel. He watched her working the helm, but he was too tired to stay long. He stumbled below where he could hear again those noises in the rigging that weren't really there. The chart was still out on the dinette. Nate stared at it to check the track again just to be sure. He stretched out on the bunk and listened to the rush of the water and the odd moaning that sounded so much like kids in the night and then he fell into a coma-like state that carried him away for another hour before he awoke just before dawn.

There were voices somewhere. It turned out to be Shanna at the helm singing a Neil Young song. Nate climbed out into the cockpit where she smiled at him from beneath her big straw hat. The wind and sea state hadn't changed and the skies were laced with high clouds that hid the stars more often than not. *Serendipity* rushed away before the oncoming swells with the SumLog whining to thirteen knots and then winding down to nine while she streaked to the west with the white water boiling astern. When the horizon line finally became visible, Nate slipped below and switched on the WWV time ticks. Shanna stopped singing while he climbed on the cabin roof and listened for the ticks and rocked the sextant to bring the stars down to the horizon. It didn't take long to shoot Polaris again and he found Antares in the cloud breaks. Nate went below to plot the position.

Serrana Bank was twenty-eight miles due south, but the weather window was closing in from the north. Nate looked at the chart and the reefs still out there waiting. He plotted a course that would keep them away from the depression and still allow room to skirt the reefs off Honduras. He returned to the cockpit where he drew the jib and main in slightly. In a few minutes, *Serendipity* went waltzing again on a broad reach, surfing to twelve or thirteen knots. Nate watched the sunrise to the east and scanned the horizon for ship traffic. When Brady came out with coffee and some toast with grape jam, Nate ate in silence and sipped the coffee and tried to figure how long a sail it might be up to the Yucatan Channel. *Serendipity* continued with her lazy surfing. It was such an easy point of sail and fast enough that Nate thought they would be near the western tip of Cuba in less than three days.

Brady took the cups away and washed them in the sink and then disappeared into the forepeak. Nate walked forward to check the chafe on the jib where it fell against the bow rail. He stayed up there for ten minutes watching the swells rise up from astern to send *Serendipity* off surfing again.

Shanna was good at the helm on a broad reach. Nate left her at the wheel and fell into the wingdeck berth and shut his eyes, thinking about dolphins again for some reason and the chuffing noise they made breathing at the surface. There were voices in the rigging again and they got mixed up with the chuffing and made it sound like a party somewhere until there was nothing but the churning in the dark.

Nate awoke just before noon after his restless sleep and stretched and leaned back on his pillow. He thought he might try to get a quick noon sight to advance the line of position. When he opened the curtain to see, the cloud cover had moved in and the sun was well hidden in the gloom. Nate stared at the dull sky beyond the portlight and then crawled out of bed to check what the sea was like. Brady was at the helm when he stepped out into the cockpit. Nate nodded at him and then stared at the sky again and watched the wake boiling off behind them. They were still averaging around ten knots through the water, but Nate was disappointed at the overcast. More reefs were ahead and he kept looking for breaks in the sky. There was only an endless spread of clouds and an ominous squall line looming up astern. He stepped below to check the charts one more time before he took the wheel.

Brady had the yellow foul weather jacket in the cockpit. When Nate came out to steer, he handed it over.

"Look behind us," Brady said. "You might need this."

Nate looked astern at the front that was approaching.

"It rained again this morning?"

"Actually, it rained pretty hard. There wasn't much wind in the squall. I ducked below to get the jacket. I didn't wake anybody."

"Man, I never heard a thing."

"I need to get some sleep. Good luck with the weather."

Brady made his way forward while Nate sat alone with the jacket unzipped until the squall caught up. There were a few gusts of wind at first, but the rain began and the breeze dropped back down so he shut the companionway door about two-thirds of the way. Nate zipped the jacket up to his neck and sat still while the rain pelted the decks and ran in rivulets down the the cabin sides. The wind picked up and then fell off again. *Serendipity* accelerated in the gusts and there were times when she was at fifteen knots. The squall passed through and she slowed to twelve and then ten knots and then the swells rolled through and there wasn't enough force in the wind to get her surfing. When the rain stopped altogether, Nate slid the companionway open to let the air circulate down below. In a few minutes, he saw Shanna step from the forepeak into the galley. Nate looked at her dark hair that fell loose over her shoulders and there were long comb marks where she had brushed the length of it. Shanna turned and grinned.

"I caught you staring again, didn't I?"

"Your hair reminded me of someone for a second."

"Someone on that charter? Etionette told me she was beautiful."

Nate looked at Shanna in the soft light that made her eyes sparkle, even in the shadows of the galley.

"Yes," Nate said. "She was."

Shanna looked out at Nate and smiled and then she shook her hair again before she stepped out into the cockpit.

"Poor Sarah. She never knew, did she?"

"No. I didn't want to tell her."

"Why? She loved you, Nate. I bet it would have helped."

"I'll never see the girl from the charter again. She's married. I just wanted it to work with Sarah without her knowing. I guess that was selfish."

"It wasn't selfish. Stupid, maybe, but I guess it's over, now. What was her name?"

Nate looked at Shanna and her black hair streaming in the wind and he shook his head.

"Sometimes I wonder what might have been for Sarah and me, but then there was Rilee and the charter. She's all I think about, anymore. She's gone, though."

"Everyone is gone, now," Shanna said softly. "You could have had me, too, but then Brady came along. Everyone is gone for you except *Serendipity*."

Shanna leaned against Nate and kissed his cheek and then she slapped his rear end.

"Brady didn't wake me up," she said. "Am I late?"

"No. You just missed the rain."

"I'll keep the jacket out here just in case. It's really overcast."

Shanna slipped behind the helm when Nate ducked below into the galley.

"I'm ready to rock all the way back to the Green Parrot," she said. "Are you okay?"

"I was feeling bad about Sarah. Like you said, everyone is gone. I guess I'm starting over again. Sometimes I wonder if I can do that."

Nate looked over at the chart on the dinette. He felt like there was a cold wind somewhere and he didn't have a jacket anymore. He scaled off the distance with the dividers to the Yucatan Channel and then to the run of reefs along Nicaragua and Honduras and then he leaned against the sink and looked through the companionway at the white water trailing behind in the sea of gray. It made the ten knots seem like twenty. Nate felt sick about Sarah again. He stepped back into the cockpit to look at the sky. There were patches where the cloud cover was thin, but there was no blue sky anywhere. He left Shanna behind the wheel and sneaked below to climb into the port wingdeck to try again to sleep.

Nate kept thinking about the Intracoastal Waterway and the quiet cypress swamps and about fishing for catfish beneath the drawbridges where the water was always so dark and still. He wanted to go back, maybe because he was alone, but he imagined Rilee would be there except that in his dreams, she never had a face anymore. There were noises out on the Waterway and they seemed out of place. Nate shook his head to clear his ears. Somehow it sounded like Shanna and he didn't know why she was on the river. Nate opened his eyes to see her face grinning at him in the dark through the open companionway.

"Hey, are you awake? Can you get Brady? I think he overslept."

Nate rolled out of the bunk and stood in the cabin trying to rub his eyes into focus. He was still mixed up about the river. He rinsed his mouth with water from the galley pump and lit the Aladdin and turned it low and then stepped outside into the night.

"Did you get some sleep?" Shanna asked.

"I guess I did. I had some screwed up dreams."

"Silly. You really look tired, though. We'll all be glad to get back to Key West."

"I think we're ready for a St. Pauli Girl. Any changes in the weather?"

"Wind isn't much right now, but we're still moving. Stars come out once in a while."

Nate looked at the night sky where there were pinpoints of light here and there and a hazy glimpse of the moon. There was no horizon. He yawned and winked at Shanna.

"I'll go get Brady. Are you ready?"

"I'm tired, too. I hope he's awake for this."

Brady shuffled about in the forepeak and then stepped through the doorway scratching his beard again.

"Yow. I was out of it. Is Shanna mad?"

"You owe her a case of St. Pauli Girl."

"I'm fine with that. It won't be long now."

Brady climbed out into the cockpit while Nate sat near the dinette and stared at the chart again. Shanna stepped below and started rolling things around in the bilge locker.

"How would you like a rum before dinner?"

"What? I'm not on probation?"

"You're not. You have time to sleep it off. Brady can't have his until midnight when he gets off watch."

"I'd like one. Make it a double."

Shanna handed Nate the glass. He sat back against the settee while she opened up some tins of beef to cook with pasta. Nate watched her moving about in the galley and it made him think of her in the shadows of the cabin when she stepped from the shower to dry her hair. Nate blinked his eyes and Shanna smiled at him.

"If I didn't know any better, I would have bet money you were staring again."

"I was thinking about last week in St. Lucia."

"I hope you didn't tell Brady about that."

"No, but watching you in the galley makes me miss Sarah."

"You should. I hope she stays in Key West. It won't be the same without her."

"I know. *Serendipity* isn't the same."

The three of them ate in the cockpit while the swells from the east lifted *Serendipity* from the starboard quarter. The soft whining of the SumLog cable slowly went up in pitch to where she was running off on the reach at thirteen knots again. They finished with dinner and Nate washed the dishes. He wanted another rum, but he needed to take over the helm from Brady at midnight. He opened a Heineken and sat at the dinette looking at the chart again. Nate used a pencil and straightedge to advance the track along the compass course and it still looked like they would clear the reefs by eighteen or twenty miles. He advanced the track all the way to the Yucatan Channel just to see. Nate could have fallen asleep if he had put his head down.

"You okay?" Shanna asked. "You're tired. I can drive again if you like."

"No, you don't have to do that," Nate said. "I'm fine. I was getting bleary from staring at the chart."

"You sure? It's turning out to be a nice night out there. The moon is breaking through."

"Thanks. I'll be fine. You need to get some sleep. You have to drive at four in the morning."

"I'll wait for Brady. Sometimes I wonder if he isn't falling asleep out there now."

"I'll wander up in a few minutes. He doesn't have to keep steering until midnight comes around."

"Are you sure you're okay for that?"

"I'd like to drive," Nate said. "It'll wake me up."

Nate fumbled around with the foul weather jacket just in case and then stepped out into the cockpit where Brady was humming again. The moon shadows were all around and where the pale light shined through, it gave the water that blue-white aura he saw in the Bahamas. Nate glanced up at the sky. There were only scattered stars visible in the cloud breaks and he still couldn't see the horizon. He sat behind the wheel next to Brady.

"You can go below if you want," Nate said. "I can steer."

"Are you sure? It's only eleven-thirty."

"If I don't take the wheel, I'll fall asleep and feel all gooey-mouthed if I have to wake up in thirty minutes."

"Okay. I'm out of it. If you need some help after midnight, just yell."

"Go get some sleep."

Brady bounced below into the cabin. Nate watched while he blew out the mantle in the Aladdin and then he and Shanna disappeared forward. The darkness below made the moonlight seem even brighter. There was still no horizon. Nate leaned back and tried not to worry about the evening star sight. They had sailed 170 miles since dawn, but there was no choice in the weather. Nate steered the compass course and watched the shafts of moonlight make the water glow.

The cloud shadows came rushing up while *Serendipity* sailed in darkness for miles. A break would let the moonbeams through and the water beneath took on that Whale Cay aura for a short time and then the boat was plunged into shadows again, so dark Nate's eyes had to adjust. He kept watching the sky trying to identify the stars that drifted between the clouds. Sometimes they only twinkled for a second in the night sky. Sometimes they hung on for a few minutes before the clouds whisked them from sight. Antares was there, low in the sky, but the horizon was so indistinct Nate didn't think a sight would be accurate, and then even Antares disappeared. There were some heavy swells rolling in from somewhere and *Serendipity* surfed up to fourteen knots when the big ones came through. Most of the time, she slid forward on the low swells and then eased back in the troughs and inched her way toward the Yucatan Channel in an endless series of rhythmic surges that ate up the miles.

Nate spent the next several hours scanning the skies for navigational stars and watching the moon duck in and out of the cloud cover. The slow surging and the quiet of the troughs made him drowsy and he had to stand on his feet to keep from falling asleep. He looked astern at the swells and at the dark sky behind. The sea was as trackless to the east as it was to the west. Nate got tired of standing and sat again and stared at the red light of the compass and steered the course into a sea of nothing. The moon burst through and he was bathed in the blue-white light again with the dark patches racing ahead.

There were cloud shadows all around him once and it was like *Serendipity* was being spotlighted on a stage. She sailed through the moonbeams and into the shadows again where the red glow of the compass stood out once more against the dark of the night. Nate liked sailing in the moonbeams. They streamed from between the clouds and he had to turn to watch because they were so fleeting, and then the shadows beneath the clouds closed in to shut the moon away. The moonbeams reappeared in a few minutes, sometimes ahead where the shadows seemed even darker, and then the moon was wiped away again and Nate was left alone with the rhythmic surging and the stern wakes roiling away and the red light of the compass shining like those nightlights.

He stood once more to clear his eyes. He glanced around at the sky and at the sea behind and at the dark moon shadows directly ahead. Nate rubbed his eyes and sat down and caught a glimpse of Antares again, faint and a little lower in the sky. He watched to see if it would shine brighter, wondering if there was time for a star sight. He turned back to check the cloud shadows in front, but there were no shadows off the bow, only a hideous mass of coral, black in the moonlight, jagged, cold, and as sharp as those Dado blades in the Bahamas. *They were dead ahead.*

Nate spun the wheel to starboard to bring *Serendipity* harder into the wind to give her a chance to claw her way off the murderous reef. He grabbed the jib sheet and hauled it in to get her on a close reach. He could feel her begin to accelerate.

An instant later, she grounded on a coral head. Nate heard a loud crack as the skeg and rudder snapped off at the waterline. He kept grinding in on the jib because *Serendipity* could power her way off the reef even without the rudder. There was another gut-wrenching crack as she grounded on another coral head. Nate grabbed the sheet to trim the main and he could feel *Serendipity* shudder and heel once more and Nate thought she was free, but she was in the surf zone then and being lifted and set down hard on the coral, lifted again and set down hard, and then Brady and Shanna were in the cockpit with Nate while *Serendipity* was lifted again and set down, this time so hard there was nothing but mush left of her keel and bottom. Nate stood by the helm, still holding the mainsheet in his hands. *Serendipity* was lifted again, but when she slammed down, the coral tore away at her bottom until Nate couldn't tell anymore when *Serendipity* hit, like she was being set down in wet sponges. The breaking surf washed her over the coral. The port and starboard hulls kept her afloat in the thin water until the port side grounded hard and the skin tore away from the keelson and the hull flooded out. *Serendipity* stopped in her tracks. Nate sat in the cockpit with his head in his hands. He felt every wave that lifted her, every coral head that tore at her belly, every sideways lurch as *Serendipity* was shoved to her death over the teeth of the reef.

THIRTY-SEVEN

There were so few clouds left in the night sky, the moon illuminated all of Gorda Cay. Nate could see the horseshoe shape of the reef and water the color of the moonbeams stretching unbroken clear to the horizon. *Serendipity* was hung up solid on the reef with her belly torn away, listing drunkenly to port with her starboard hull flying high over the jagged coral beneath. Nate knew it was over the minute the rudder cracked away and he couldn't get the jib sheeted in fast enough. He remembered thinking at the time that if he had steered fifty yards to the east, *Serendipity* would still be romping her way to the Yucatan Channel and to the Green Parrot Bar and Sub Shop at the corner of Southard and Whitehead in Key West.

Nate tried to sleep in the tilted wingdeck berth. The ringing in his ears was relentless and there were high-pitched voices in the rigging. He kept trying to scream. There were empty faces again, staring back, and he knew someone close to him was around somewhere. He just couldn't see. He tossed the sheets away and rolled in sweat while *Serendipity* mushed her way deeper into the reef. When dawn came streaming through the portlights, Nate opened his eyes to a different world.

He rolled off the bunk onto the settee below and looked around at the slanted interior. Everything seemed the same. Even the cabin sole was intact. Nate lifted one of the hatches to peer into the bilge locker where he kept the canned goods and the bottles of rum. There was no bilge locker, only the saw-toothed coral and some smashed anemones and the salt water surging in and out. The coral was brown and lifeless and cold to the touch.

Nate stepped up the companionway ladder and climbed from the cockpit onto the coral below to see the damage to the hulls. The starboard side was whole and complete and untouched, but the port hull was torn away along the keelson for twenty feet or more. The main hull had no bottom left at all. He couldn't look anymore.

Nate turned away from the wreck toward the sand and the remains of a concrete base where a navigation light used to be. There were a thousand or more boobies resting on the cay. Nate walked out into the rookery to see the crude nests the birds had scratched out of the sand. The females sat on the eggs and looked at him, not knowing enough to be afraid. Nate sank to the ground and watched the birds shuffling about in the sand while several of them took flight and spread their wings to glide next to him. He stood again to watch as one of the boobies edged closer in the wind where it hung suspended in the trades that blew steadily across the cay. The booby kept gliding closer until it was no more than three feet from Nate's face where it stayed with its wings spread wide, riding the wind like *Serendipity* and staring into his eyes.

Brady and Shanna walked over from the wreck. The three of them stood in the sand with all the boobies looking at them. There were no words to say. Shanna put her arms around Nate and there were some aching sobs and those deep breaths where she couldn't get enough air and it made her body shake in his arms. He held her close and put his face in her long hair that twisted in the wind. He kept thinking maybe it was all another nightmare. Nate looked over at Brady who kept staring at the wreck and at the reef and then back at the wreck. All Nate could see then were the tears and the bloodshot eyes and the lines of agony and sorrow in his best friend's face.

They walked back to *Serendipity* where they climbed aboard and made morning coffee and toast with the stove that lit right off. The coffee was hot and strong and steamy, but all of them knew then, in the light of the rising sun and in the endless trades that swept across the deserted cay, that *Serendipity* was dead.

The three of them set about stripping the hulls of anything that had value. They unbolted the winches and the cleats and removed all the running rigging and all of the blocks. They let the turnbuckles go to bring the mast down and then removed the fittings, even the masthead itself, and left the extrusion lying in the coral. They couldn't deal with the Volvo because of the weight. Nate disliked the stove and the head so much he left them to waste away on the reef.

There were a million bits to collect it seemed. They worked for two days until Shanna spotted a boat on the horizon. They scrambled around and lit a bonfire on the reef using a spare jerry can of diesel and pieces of the rudder and keel and bottom that had washed up on the coral. The boat crew saw the smoke and turned around and approached in the lee of the reef.

The *Joven G* was a Nicaraguan fishing boat cruising the Gorda Banks. The captain and crew waded ashore, but they were only interested in climbing all over the wreck to steal pots and pans and anything else that wasn't bolted down.

"You can't do this," Nate said. "You are required by law to help us off the reef or take us into Honduras."

"No, we are only passing through. You have food and water."

"You can't steal from us."

The captain looked blankly at Nate and then said something in Spanish that made his crew laugh. The men turned and walked back across the reef taking with them some of the pots and pans from the galley.

The Honduran gunboat arrived at ten o'clock the next morning. The captain was an Annapolis graduate and spoke perfect English.

"I can give you until two o'clock to salvage what you can," the captain said. "We'll load it into the Whaler and run it out to the cutter."

"I don't know if that's enough time," Nate asked. "Why two o'clock?"

"We overheard a radio contact between the *Joven G* and another Nicaraguan boat. The crews are plotting to come back and take everything. We can't afford an international incident over some piracy out here. You have until two o'clock."

"I don't think we can make it."

"It doesn't matter. We are leaving with you at two o'clock."

The gunboat captain wouldn't back down. In anger Nate worked with Brady and Shanna to remove the last of the fittings and to collect personal things and get them across the reef and into the Whaler. At two in the afternoon they weren't close to being finished. There was nothing they could do. Nate walked over to the gunboat captain.

"I need to make one more trip across the reef," Nate said.

Before the captain could refuse, Nate turned and walked away toward *Serendipity*. He scattered a few boobies on the way, but he didn't much care at that point. Nate climbed into the cockpit and lurched below where he opened the valve on the fuel tank and let the diesel spill into what was left of the bilge. There were spare diesel jugs and one of kerosene in the stern locker. He spilled the fuel over the mattresses and cushions and countertops and then grabbed the flare gun from its holder in the galley. Nate stepped back into the cockpit where he turned and fired flares into the belly of *Serendipity,* one after another, until the pack of twelve was gone. There was a lot of smoke at first, but the flames burned red and then orange. Nate stood on the transom and watched his boat burn away. The heat got so intense he climbed from the transom and stood in ankle deep water while the black smoke billowed skyward. Some of it blew back in the wind and he was caught up in it. The choking didn't bother him and he stood on the reef and didn't move until the fire burned to the water and put itself out in the surge that rolled in from the sea. Nate turned away and walked across the reef to the waiting Boston Whaler and the Honduran gunboat swinging on its anchor in the lee of Gorda Cay.

◊ EPILOGUE ◊

Nathan Addison walked across the reef with a few dollars left over from the charter and a business card from Jenson Colorgraphics and a wisp of paper from Rilee Britton in his wallet. When he reached the lee of the cay, the Honduran crew was busy helping Brady and Shanna with some of the salvaged gear. The enraged captain stared at Nate, his face sweaty and shiny and bulging in red.

"Why did you burn the boat?" the man shouted. "You are under arrest. All of you are under arrest."

"I don't care," Nate said.

The Hondurans kept them confined to the quarters on the gunboat at the navy base in Puerto Cortes. Nate kept trying to get in to see *el comandante* but he was refused an audience until after the tenth day. At the appointed hour, Nate opened the door into the office where a cigar-smoking, three-hundred pound colonel sat perspiring behind the desk with a pair of overworked oscillating fans set on ten to keep him cool.

"Why are we being kept under arrest?" Nate asked. "Why aren't we free to go?"

The man grunted a few times and exhaled his cigar smoke and sat upright in his groaning chair.

"You cannot leave because you have entered the country illegally," he droned. "You will remain confined to the base until it is convenient for us to let you go."

Nate looked at the mass of papers scattered on the desk and at the rippled screens over the open window and at the fly carcasses lying still on the sill. He shook his head and walked out of the office.

They were allowed to leave on the fourteenth day. He and Brady and Shanna rented a pensión in town and then set about building a crate to ship all of the salvaged gear from *Serendipity*. Nate found the Western Union office and contacted his family in Bodega Bay. Nate's father wired enough money to ship the wooden crate to Miami and to buy plane tickets home for the three of them. They rode the bus to the airport in San Pedro Sula and boarded an aging DC-6. When the Pratt & Whitneys fired up, one by one, the open exhaust didn't remind Nate much of Dana, anymore. The exhaust sounded more like death knells.

Nate might have set some kind of record for miniatures consumed during a flight. He kept looking through the window at the cays and the reefs and at the islands below that appeared to be floating in eddies of sand and blue that looked again like a little boy's swirls in fingerpaint. He ached inside to be down there, surfing toward the Yucatan Channel on *Serendipity*, but the flight took him over western Cuba and across the Florida Straits beyond and then there were the high-rise hotels of Miami Beach and a final approach and a couple of thumps and a roar on the runway.

Brady and Shanna went back to Key West where they settled into the life they had left behind. Shanna got involved with amateur photography until the local paper published some of her work. She was hired by *Florida Keys Life* as a staff photographer. She got pregnant soon after and gave birth to a beautiful little boy who looked very much like his father without the beard. Brady went back to Florida Keys Community College where he learned to be a travel consultant and then started his own agency. He and Shanna bought a thirty-foot Cheoy Lee and spent some time restoring it. When they finished, you could see the reflections of the new yellow boot top in the quiet waters of the marina. Over the years they sailed her through the Bahamas all the way down to the Turks and Caicos. They never made it back to St. Lucia. They both frequented the Green Parrot Bar and Sub Shop down on Whitehead and played softball in the summers when the air was hot and still. Key West for them slipped back into the thirties mode where they ignored the tourists and lived a quiet life on the back streets of Paradise where the areca palms grow so thick they hang like lace over the sidewalks.

Beautiful Sarah, who could have been Nate's love in another place and time, stopped briefly in Key West and left town before Nate arrived. She still had sailing fever and before long she was up in Maine crewing on tall ship charters. She became a captain in her own right, but then she left it behind again and went down to Nashville to work in the country music industry. She owned motorcycles and horses at times and there was a lot of drinking and sometimes aimless wandering with boyfriends, but she never returned to Key West. Nate never knew what became of her.

Brady thought Bart, who was Dana's lover, had gone off with a lady friend to start a catering business in Mobile but that it went under after a year. The lady friend stayed with her family in Alabama. Bart left town with most of the money and dropped off the charts. No one in Key West seemed to care where he went.

Nate saw Dana only once more. There were some legal questions concerning the divorce that could only be handled in person and he had to go. She looked good, very much the girl he had married years before. They shared some laughs and some tears and some regrets, but the court proceedings ended and they parted as friends. Nate drove away and didn't look back. Dana was hired as an editor at *Golden Gate Soul*, the very fine literary magazine in San Francisco, and has had success publishing her own work. She loves her new life, but she told Nate before he left that she couldn't write about *Serendipity*.

After the plane landed in Miami, Nate wound up in Coconut Grove where he stayed aboard another trimaran owned by a good friend of his from Tampa. He picked up the crate filled with the blocks and line and winches and the sails from the customs warehouse and spread the gear out on a parking lot in front of a bar and sold everything, right down to the last bits of line. *Serendipity* was then only a memory.

He took some of the money and bought a '72 Ford Pinto Runabout from a used car salesman who assured him they had just taken the car in trade and if he bought it just then he could get him a deal. Nate didn't much care. He threw his bag into the back and drove from the dealership all the way down the Keys and parked just up the street from the Green Parrot Bar and Sub Shop.

Nate stayed for a long time in Key West, long enough to play softball and drink beer and listen to the music on Duval Street. There were more parties and picnics and diving trips to the reef, but there was a constant emptiness he couldn't shake. The cold northers blew down and the rain swept through and shotpeened the island. Nate watched from the corner seat in the Parrot while the tourists stomped in and out through the big double doors in front.

He beat himself up trying to analyze what had gone wrong, why the reef suddenly appeared that night, twenty miles from where he thought *Serendipity* should have been. In the end, there were no excuses. Alcohol abuse and emotional exhaustion had clouded Nate's judgement. *Serendipity* had sailed too fast and too far to continue without another star sight. The general chart of the Caribbean showed a following current of from one to three knots, but the chart was a static display of a living set of currents that swing many miles in either direction. *Serendipity* was steadily set to the west by the meandering stream. Nate had no way of knowing without a star sight, and he hit the reef at thirteen knots. He couldn't drink enough beer in the Green Parrot to drown the terrible sound of *Serendipity* grinding to death on the coral.

He must have dialed the number in Steamboat Springs a dozen times. On the two occasions when he had guts enough to let the phone ring more than once, there was no answer. He used to take Jenson's business card out of his wallet just to look at it. He couldn't get over the feeling he was no better than Bart if he called the number.

One night at the Green Parrot, Kellog flashed the lights on at closing time. Nate looked up from his bottle of St. Pauli

Girl and told Brady and Shanna that was the end of it. He was going back to Bodega Bay to see his mom and dad. He thought maybe graduate school might be an option. Nate had no other ideas except that he needed to go. Their good-byes were filled with hugs and tears and promises of letters and apologies for how it all ended on a reef in Honduras. Nate left the next day and drove up Duval Street and turned left on Truman Avenue and headed out on A1A, bound for Miami and the freeways beyond. He could only get to Sugarloaf Key before he had to pull over to the side of the road.

Nate drove non-stop after that, heading west on Interstate 10 for a thousand miles before he took a cheap motel room in Beaumont, Texas. He bought a steak in a sleazy restaurant about a block away and on his way out he looked at the road map they had taped on the wall in the entrance. He tried to figure out how long it would take him to drive non-stop again to Bodega Bay. He looked at Colorado and at Steamboat Springs and at the highways in between and then went back to the little motel room to call his mother on the phone just to let her know he was on his way home. She was still slurring her words from the bourbon and ginger ale she drank every night.

"Hi, Mom. You okay?"

"Yes. This was our night to go see Al and Bev. As usual there was a big party and you know your mother. It wasn't wasted on me."

"I can tell. I didn't mean to surprise you. I'm on my way west. I was hoping you could make some clam chowder. I think I need to be home for a while."

"How wonderful. I'll make you some fried chicken, too, and I'll stock up on bourbon. You're father will be so relieved."

"Me, too, Mom. It's been a long trip."

"Someone called for you from Colorado. Steamboat? She didn't leave her name, but she was very nice. She didn't know about *Serendipity*. She cried when I told her about the reef."

Nate's heart stopped suddenly and the ringing came back in his ears. He wasn't sure what he heard his mother say.

"How long ago did she call?"

"I don't remember. Maybe a month and a half. Where have you been? I didn't know what to tell her."

"I don't know, Mom. I don't know where I've been. Drinking too much in Key West, for one thing. I had to leave."

"I'm glad you're coming home."

"I'll call before I get there. Thanks, Mom."

Nate hung up the phone and sat alone on the bed in the motel room in Beaumont with his heart pounding like the surf again in Josiah's Bay.

Nate got up the next morning and checked to see if Steamboat was covered on the map he had of the Southwest. There were a lot of gray side roads and blue highways and in another time he would have taken them all the way into Steamboat. Nate took the freeway west to Houston and then turned north for Dallas and then Lubbock and Amarillo beyond and after another marathon drive, he pulled into one more sleazy motel on the outskirts of Denver where he fell asleep for nearly ten hours. He awoke and showered and shaved and then left the motel for a coffee shop on the road into Denver. Nate took the map with him and looked at the options. He wasn't sure what he would find in Steamboat Springs.

Nate left the coffee half-finished and drove north until he found Interstate 70. Driving west again he was so nervous he missed the sign for the road into Steamboat. He backtracked and found the off-ramp and then slowed and looked around at the high hills sparkling in snow and at the rivers running cold and at the sky, blue and cloudless and forever. He drove slowly all the way up and over Rabbit Ears Pass where the roadside drifts were thick and dirty from the plows and then across the mountains where he began the descent into the valley. Steamboat spread out in front of him like a trainboard village in the window of F. A. O. Schwartz at Christmas.

Steamboat Springs might have been a ski town, but it also had ranchers and fishermen and hunters and backpackers. Nate drove down Lincoln Avenue and never got the feeling there were tourists around. Someone honked behind him and he turned right just to go around again and look at the Western town one more time. At the end of the street, he found the small park and the hot springs for which the town was named. Nate pulled into the parking lot to look around. One of the springs bubbled with sulphur dioxide. The steam rose high into the late winter air and smelled very much like Brady's volcano in St. Lucia. Nate backed away and took the worn wisp of paper out of his wallet again.

Britton – Steamboat – (209) 554-2271
I just need time
alligator food

Nate's hand was shaking when he dialed the number. He nearly hung up the phone, but he held the receiver to his ear and on the eighth ring someone answered.

"Hi...My name is Nate," he said. "I'm looking for a friend...I'm looking for someone I knew in the Caribbean."

"Oh, my. Is this Nathan? Rilee has told me everything. Are you here in town?"

"Yes, down across from the hot springs. Is Rilee there?"

"No, she and Andy went to the grocery store. They were going to walk up to see Fish Creek Falls if the snow isn't too deep. They won't be back for a bit."

Nate didn't know what to say. He held the phone to his ear trying to think. The voice on the other end came back.

"You know...If you drive up to the falls you might catch them. I know the road has been cleared. They always walk up to the lookout. They usually stay because Andy likes it there. Try that, and if they show up here, I'll send them back. It isn't very far."

"Thanks, I'll do that. Are you her mother?"

"Yes. Rilee hasn't been the same since she came back from her trip. She's not with her husband anymore. She's dying to see you, but she didn't know how to find you."

"I had a few problems along the way."

"You go find Rilee. I'll see you later."

There were clouds of steam from Nate's breath when he asked the gas station man how to get to Fish Creek Falls. He didn't want a speeding ticket and so he left the Pinto in first gear and drove east on Lincoln until he came to Third Street where he turned left. He followed the signs for Fish Creek Falls and drove to the right a mile or so up a narrow road lined with snow berms until he came to a parking lot where he could hear the roar of the falls in the canyon just beyond the road's end. There were only a few cars around. Nate wasn't sure which trail to take so he chose the higher one that followed the edge of the canyon on the north side.

The path was narrow and winding and his feet sank into the snow so deep he could hear the crunching over the roar of the falls. There were low shrubs on either side and trees that bent over the walkway and the air was quiet except for the thundering. At the end of the path there was a viewing point and a rock wall and a bench covered with snow. Nate stood looking out over the canyon and at the thick ribbon of water flanked in ice that cascaded into a pool far below. His breath was coming in short bursts it was so cold. All he had to wear was the yellow foul weather jacket he salvaged from *Serendipity*. Nate stood on the lookout shivering even though the air was still and the sun was high overhead. The snow all around looked blue and cold in the shadows and he kept thinking of the Caribbean and the warm wind from the east that never quit and the water clear as gin that cradled *Serendipity*.

Nate didn't know how long he stood on the lookout and he thought about leaving when someone came up from behind. He turned to see a little girl with a thick green parka and matching boots and a pie pan face, pink from the cold and smiling back at him through her hood. She looked at Nate and giggled and then ran back down the path with her arms flailing and her boots crunching the snow. Someone else stepped from the shadows beneath the trees into the sunlight. Andy and her moonface smiled at Nate again and then she hid behind her mom. Rilee came closer. Nate could see in her eyes the color of the water over the banks in the Bahamas, the same color as the water around Gorda Cay where he had to leave *Serendipity*. He could see a separate universe filled with tears.

Andy looked at Nate from the shadow of her mother. She was shy and grinning, hiding behind her mom. She peeked up at him again.

"Mommy wants to know where can we find some alligator food?" she asked, and then she laughed and wiggled and ducked behind Rilee once more.

Nate kept looking into Rilee's eyes. The Caribbean was there again with the white water streaming aft from the bow on *Sandpiper* and the stars over the beach on Peter Island, and he could see again in her eyes the way she looked at him that first time in the red glow of the nightlights. Nate smiled and took Rilee by the hand.

"The alligator food is right here, Andy" he said quietly, and he held Rilee's hand over his heart. "Right here."

ALLIGATOR FOOD

GLOSSARY

Aladdin – The brand name of a kerosene-fueled lamp that used a mantle instead of a wick. These lamps were common aboard many cruising boats and were used in lieu of electric lights to conserve battery power.

backstay – The aftermost rigging wire supporting the mast; extends from the masthead to the stern chainplate.

backstay bridle – A backstay is sometimes split into two wires just above the deck, forming an inverted "V", each leg of which is attached to a chainplate at the stern of the boat; one to port, one to starboard. *Serendipity* used a bridle to make room for a self-steering vane mounted on the centerline at the stern.

beam reach – A point of sail where the wind is at ninety degrees to the centerline of the boat, either from the port or from the starboard.

bight – A small bay, usually narrow.

bimini cover – An awning mounted on a stainless steel or aluminum frame used to shade the cockpit area of a boat.

Bimini bread – A soft white bread unique to the Bahamas, sliced thick and often served with conch chowder, a national delicacy.

binnacle – A cover over the ship's compass, usually at the helm.

broach – An accidental maneuver where the boat is forced sideways to the wind and/or a following sea.

broad reach – That point of sail between running directly downwind and having the wind on the port or starboard beam. Any point of sail where the wind comes from the aft quarter.

chainplate – A metal plate bolted, fiberglassed, or welded to the hull where a shroud or stay is attached.

ciguatera – Reef fish may ingest dinoflagellates that contain toxins. These fish are then eaten by larger species. The toxins move up the food chain and collect in the flesh of barracuda, grouper, or other predators. Ciguatera is the term given to the illness caused by eating the flesh of these predator species.

clevis pin – In this reference , a short stainless rod used to secure an anchor, usually in a channel on the bow that also contains a roller.

clew – The aftermost bottom point of a sail where the foot and leech come together.

close hauled – To sail as close as possible to the direction of the wind. The sails are sheeted home close to the boat's centerline.

close reach – That point of sail where the wind is forward of the beam but aft of the point where the boat is close hauled.

coaming – The raised border around a cockpit or hatch that keeps water from intruding.

CQR – The brand name for a popular anchor shaped like a farmer's plow.

cutter – A single-masted sailboat with an additional rigging wire set inside the forestay so that multiple jibs can be flown.

davits – Small cranes used to raise or lower small boats or dinghies, usually mounted at the stern.

forestay – The forward rigging wire supporting the mast; extends from the masthead to the bow of the boat. In a fractional rig, the forestay is attached several feet below the masthead.

genip – Trees found in the American tropics that produce green, leathery fruit the size of large table grapes.

genoa – A large headsail that overlaps the main and is attached to the forestay, generally used in lighter winds.

Grumman Goose – The local flying service, Antilles Air Boats, operated several of these amphibians in the British and U. S. Virgin Islands. The G-21A "Goose" was an eight-passenger aircraft fitted with a pair of Pratt and Whitney nine-cylinder Wasp radial engines. They were a common sight taxiing down the harbors of Charlotte Amalie, Road Town, and Christiansted.

gunwale – The upper edge of the side of a boat, sometimes covered by a decorative cap of teak or mahogany.

halyard – Line used to hoist sails.

hank – To attach the luff of a headsail to the forestay or jibstay using small, bronze clips called piston hanks.

head – The top corner of a sail; that part of the sail where the halyard is attached. Also, the common term used for a marine toilet.

jenny – Slang for "genoa", the large headsail.

jib – A triangular headsail that does not overlap the mainsail.

jibe – A maneuver where a sailboat changes the wind from one side to the other across the stern while running downwind. The boom crosses over the centerline, sometimes with excessive force unless controlled by the crew.

ketch – A sailing rig where a shorter mizzen mast is set aft of the taller main mast, but forward of the rudder post. This arrangement allows the sails to be broken into smaller units that can be easier to handle.

lazarette – A locker aft of the cockpit, forward of the transom.

leech – The trailing edge of a sail.

Lido 14 – A national class of sloop-rigged, fourteen-foot sail-boats manufactured by the W. D. Schock Company.

lines – There are no loose ropes on a sailboat. All "ropes" designed for specific uses are referred to as lines.

luff – The leading edge of a sail; also, to sail so close to the wind as to cause the sail to billow along the leading edge.

main – Mainsail, the primary sail extending aft from the main-mast.

marine head – The nautical term for a toilet aboard a boat.

nightlight – Aboard many cruising boats, red lights are used below decks after sunset to preserve the night vision of the helmsman and any of the crew that venture on deck.

painter – A line attached to the bow of a dinghy, used for towing or to secure the boat.

Perkins 4-108 – Fifty horsepower diesel engine manufactured in England. The "4" refers to the number of cylinders, and the "108" refers to the displacement of the engine in cubic inches.

piston hank – Bronze clips on the luff, or leading edge, of a jib, staysail, or genoa, used to attach the sail to the forestay or jib-stay.

plow – Generic term for any anchor, such as the CQR, shaped like a farmer's plow.

port – On the left side, or to the left.

primary winch – The largest line-handling winch.

quay – Wall of timber, stone, or concrete lining a harbor where boats are secured; pronounced "key".

roadstead – In this context, an exposed anchorage open to the sea located in the lee of an island.

rode – The line used to secure a boat to an anchor; can be all chain, all line, or a combination of the two as found aboard *Serendipity*.

round up – To be overpowered in a sailboat by carrying too much sail in windy conditions. The boat tends to round into the wind until the helmsman can steer the boat back on course.

running rigging – Lines used for raising, lowering, or controlling the sails.

sabot – From the Dutch language meaning "wooden shoe", a 7'11" sailing dinghy popular with youth programs at yacht clubs. Often used as a yacht tender.

schooner – Considered to be the most beautiful of all sailing yachts, the schooner is a fore-and-aft rigged vessel with two or more masts of identical height. More often, as on *Dame Foncé,* they are two masted sailboats with a tall main set aft and a shorter foremast set forward.

secondary winch – Smaller line-handling winches on a sailboat used to draw in jibs, staysails, and the like.

shackle – A U-shaped fitting with a removable pin used to attach sails at the head, tack, and clew to the halyards, lines, or sheets, and often used to attach the anchor to its rode.

sheer – The top edge of the gunwale, from stem to stern. Having a "pronounced sheer" means to have a sweeping curve at the sheer.

sheer stripe – A painted stripe on the hull, usually of an accent color, just below the sheer line.

sheets – Lines used to adjust or control sails or booms.

shrouds – Rigging wires that support the mast, extending from the mast to the deck amidships, port and starboard.

sole – The floor inside the cabin of a boat.

standing rigging – The shrouds and stays used to support the mast.

starboard – On the right side, or to the right.

stays – Wires fore and aft that support the mast.

staysail – A small triangular sail, like a small jib, set on a wire aft of the forestay and set from a deck fitting to a position part way up the mast.

stem – The foremost end of a boat; the vertical section of the bow.

stern – The back end of a boat.

SumLog – Brand name of a mechanical sailing speedometer consisting of a small propeller mounted below the waterline attached to a dial by way of a stainless wire cable.

tack – The lower, forward corner where a triangular sail is attached to the bow or deck fitting.

tacking – The act of steering a sailboat across the wind to change course, either while being close-hauled or running off before the wind. Lightweight boats like *Serendipity* tend to tack in the wind while at anchor.

transom – The flat portion of the hull at the stern.

trimaran – A light, extremely fast three-hulled sailing vessel developed first by the Polynesians. Trimarans carry no ballast, relying instead on the buoyancy of the leeward hull to keep the boat upright in the wind.

turnbuckle – A threaded, adjustable fitting used to tension shrouds, stays, and lifelines, etc.

VHF – Literally, Very High Frequency, this is the type of radio transceiver used for general communication between boats, usually with a range of about twenty-five miles.

Volvo MD2B – Twenty-five horsepower, two-cylinder diesel.

Watling's castle – The 17th Century pirate John Watling established his headquarters on the south end of the Bahamian Island of San Salvador. The remains of his "castle" are still standing.

wingdeck – On trimarans, this is the area of decking that extends outward from the main hull to the floats or "amas". This area is left open on trimarans meant for racing.

winch – A line-handling drum, sometimes with more than one gear ratio, that allows for considerable mechanical advantage when drawing in a sail toward the centerline of the boat, something sailors call "sheeting in".

windlass – A manual or electrical winch mounted at the bow used for retrieving an anchor. Most windlasses are set up for both line and chain.

WWV – The radio station in Ft. Collins, CO, that broadcasts time standards worldwide. The station also broadcasts notices of atmospheric disturbances at sea that might affect mariners.

LEW DECKER

Author of the critically acclaimed memoir FINGER-PRINTS…A Coffeehouse Reader, Lew Decker has also written for the sailing magazines "Cruising World" and "Latitudes & Attitudes", and for "CQ", a magazine devoted to the amateur radio community. He spent several years building the forty-foot Norman Cross-designed trimaran "Sun Flower" and then cruised from California through the Panama Canal and up to the Florida Keys. After working as a professional yacht delivery skipper on the East Coast, he became a charter captain in the Bahamas and in the Virgin Islands. Lew has crossed the Atlantic under sail and at various times in his sailing career has visited nearly every island in the Caribbean. He spent a year hanging around the bars of Key West and still considers the island town to be his spiritual home. A retired middle school teacher, Lew resides in San Diego with his wife Kathleen and an English Springer Spaniel named Riley Dog. ALLIGATOR FOOD is Lew's first novel.

Made in the USA
Lexington, KY
22 March 2011